TYGER BRIGHT

BAEN BOOKS
by T.C. McCARTHY

Tyger Burning
Tyger Bright

To purchase any of these titles in e-book form, please go to www.baen.com.

TYGER BRIGHT

T.C. McCARTHY

BAEN

TYGER BRIGHT

A Baen Books Original

Baen Publishing Enterprises
P.O. Box 1403
Riverdale, NY 10471
www.baen.com

ISBN: 978-1-9821-2517-2

Cover art by Adam Burn

First printing, February 2021

Distributed by Simon & Schuster
1230 Avenue of the Americas
New York, NY 10020

Library of Congress Cataloging-in-Publication Data

Names: McCarthy, T. C., author.
Title: Tyger bright / T.C. McCarthy.
Description: Riverdale, NY : Baen Books, [2021] | "A Baen books
    original"—Title page verso.
Identifiers: LCCN 2020050078 | ISBN 9781982125172 (trade paperback)
Subjects: GSAFD: Science fiction.
Classification: LCC PS3613.C3563 T93 2021 | DDC 813/.6—dc23
LC record available at https://lccn.loc.gov/2020050078

Printed in the United States of America

10 9 8 7 6 5 4 3 2 1

For Hannah Watters Wever;
your family and friends will never forget you.

BOOK ONE

CHAPTER ONE

Win gazed into the hologram, absorbing its emptiness. *Static.* He knew where they were going, and why, but preferred the lies because truth guaranteed a gruesome death by their enemy where lies promised victory—a chance that at least some of them would return from this excursion instead of being sliced open. There were slower ways to die and Win clung to another lie as if it were a buoy: If caught, he and the crew would die quickly by rifle fire, not by one of the slow methods, the ones reserved for cowards. There was nothing more offensive to the Sommen than gutlessness.

His captain, Markus, glared. Hatred splashed over Win's mind and he tuned it out, doing his best to ignore the acidity, a fluid kind of anger that threatened to soak the fabric of his thoughts and weaken them with distraction. What did the captain matter, or his name? *This man is corpulent.* It would be easy to spear the captain with one of the legs from Win's servo harness—one of the two things that made Win look different from the *Higgins*'s crew. The other was his head. *With the drugs come physiological changes; with the changes come sight and power—the power of Sommen thought, the greatness of war and corpses.* Elongated after so many treatments, the shape of Win's skull attracted looks wherever he went and even after months in space nothing had changed; his body's muscles had continued to wither and without the armored servo harness he'd be immobilized. The crew thought him disgusting; their thoughts washed over Win too, a sewage that wouldn't drain.

I am a weapon. Through the absorption of hatred and aversion I power my thought, and with thought I will cut my enemy's throat.

3

"Captain, we couldn't reconstitute the recording at all," an ensign said; the man "sat" next to Win, suspended in zero g. "Its base files are lost and we had to move on. But the metadata is there and there are E-M spectra consistent with Sommen patterns. My guess? They slaughtered our people."

The captain nodded. "How long ago?"

"Like Win said: just before we arrived at Childress transit."

The captain pinched the bridge of his nose and Win studied the signs; the man had taken off his suit helmet to reveal a bald head, its muscle tremors screaming that exhaustion made him less human, more zombie than anything else. The man feared war. Win imagined war was coming whether the captain wanted it or not and that conflict would be the life of their offspring, prayers a poor method for preventing destruction. Sommen invasion fleets were still decades away, but they *would* come.

I am a weapon and war is my promise.

"What's the damage to the signal buoy's shell?" the captain asked. "Can we get anything from that?"

"Outer shell vaporized, and the rest of it pretty much scorched. The only thing operational was the locator beacon but it lost power almost immediately. Standard missile damage, propellant and warhead consistent with Sommen weapons signatures."

"I want intel working on this around the clock," the captain ordered. "We make our transit into Childress in three hours, so get as much information as you can. Meeting's over, I need the conference room."

Win was about to release the straps keeping him in his seat when the captain waved.

"Stay put."

The others unhooked from the table and pushed themselves off, drifting toward a door. One at a time, they glided from the room.

"Zhelnikov," said the captain, "is safely aboard the station and we move into an area where we know the Sommen are now operating. I've got orders to do what you say. But I won't move this ship another meter unless you tell me about the mission. Now."

"I can tell you this, Captain: Zhelnikov wants us to pop into the Childress system, reconnoiter, and return to him with any remaining research data that the Sommen haven't destroyed."

"Data? Like what?"

Win cleared his throat. "I can't answer that." When he saw the captain begin to speak, he added, "Zhelnikov was clear. We pop from Childress wormhole and then make for the research station. Get in and get out. But what I'm to do at the station is classified and not for you. Not yet."

"I don't like it. Zhelnikov wants the *Higgins* for a high-risk mission; okay. I accept that. But to not give me the details as we enter what could be hostile territory where the enemy is active? *Un*acceptable."

"Understood, sir. I'll pass your thoughts on to Zhelnikov."

The captain's glare faded.

"That . . ." he stammered, "that's not necessary. Forget what I said. What's your full name, anyway?"

A sucking sound rang through Win's helmet when the suit's automatic systems began their periodic removal of saliva that had begun to run from his chin. "I'm Burmese. My father named me Win and nothing else. His last name was Kyarr. My mother died when I was little and I never knew her."

"How the hell did you get drafted into Zhelnikov's little show, and what the hell did he do to you? To your body?"

"I am a weapon. Zhelnikov put me in charge because he and I know how scared you are, and that you've no concept of what we face. But I do. I've seen it. You will hide under rocks and mountains on that day."

"Your father," the captain said, pointing first at Win's head and then gesturing at the rest of him. "He agreed to make you into *this*?"

Win held himself back, wanting to push off the wall and strangle the man, killing him in micro-increments to see the fear of death as his eyes' lights dimmed. It would have made everything right. A burst of memory blinded him, a picture of his father in the Charleston slums with the other Myanmarese playing backgammon in the street while they squatted and pulled on cigarettes. Many of them had no teeth. Some stumbled, drunk and with emaciated leg muscles that somehow held the men up. His father grinned at Win; then he held up the dice and threw them on the board.

"My father disappeared when I was young, Captain Markus. I chose to do this to myself."

"You're either insane, or the stupidest son of a—"

Win cut him off and unhooked from the table, pushing toward the hatchway. "Captain, I don't have time for this. You will hear from me when we get closer to the transit point."

I am a weapon. He moved through white corridors, making his way toward the ashram. Zhelnikov hid in the safety of a hollow rock; he would not be taking the risks that Win did in visiting the scene of a Sommen massacre. A distant ship's voice warned of imminent evasive maneuvers upon entering the wormhole and Win strapped into an emergency couch sunk into the ashram's floor. After turn upon turn, the gees dislodged deep memories and pushed Win into a twilight place where there was just enough light to see but not enough to chase the shadows. Soon they'd be locked into a fight; conflict was almost here and the instant the *Higgins* crossed over, they'd be outside the zone permitted to humans—an act of war.

The wormhole grew with every second and Win watched, fascinated, examining the silvery orb that hung in space as if someone had placed it there like an orphaned Christmas ornament. He squinted, zooming in, to try and see what kept the wormhole alive.

"Our guys salvaged a message." The captain's voice crackled in Win's helmet. "The buoy is from a Fleet drone carrier, the *Majestic*. Go ahead and play it over coms."

Win whispered at his faceplate so that when the message began, a spectral analyzer danced across his heads-up, forming a series of jagged green lines blurred with static.

"Contact at fourteen-thirty-three hours Earth time, Zulu. Patrol reports multiple unknowns coming from, we think, an uncharted wormhole in the direction of the Orion arm. I sent half our squadron of fighter drones to intercept and the rest are falling back to carrier patrol. Weapons research was successful and installation complete on one vessel. Doctor McCalister seems to have..."

The recording ended in a hiss.

"That's all we recovered, sir," someone said. "Nothing from the base itself and our semi-aware calculates an eighty-seven percent chance that all Fleet vessels, including the *Majestic,* were destroyed. Doctor McCalister was Childress's lead scientist and the head of the Childress mission."

"One of Zhelnikov's?"

Win broke in. "Yes."

"Thank you, *Win*. That's confirmation; it looks like Childress fell to hostile forces. Likely Sommen."

"Captain," Win said, "it *was* the Sommen. I have *seen* this. And you have no idea what they've done to your Fleet comrades."

Win's spectral analyzer continued to dance, its lines reacting to the soft sound of static but coming to life at occasional *pops* in the noise. When the captain spoke, the spectrum and his tone indicated he was furious.

"Battle stations. Have the computer plot an evasion course beyond the hole, post transit; we can't do high g because our passenger isn't engineered, so if we get hit, thank Win. Once we determine Childress space is safe, one of our shuttles will make for the research station. That is all."

Win shut the analyzer off. Soon the wormhole would fill his helmet's screen with white light and he closed his eyes before pressing a button on his forearm; inside his suit, a tiny needle jetted out and buried itself in his neck, just long enough to push green fluid into one of his veins. He suppressed a scream. The liquid burned, coursing its way towards his brain which it soon entered. He shed a tear at the agony as new neural masses grew, forcing connections and firing electric pulses. *This is the price of sight, the promise of victory,* he decided, just before passing out. Win came to in a few seconds, his eyes open but his vision focused elsewhere, beyond the wormhole and into Childress space; he may not have been engineered for high-g maneuvers, but Win *had* been engineered by Zhelnikov for this.

I am a weapon—not a timekeeper. I am not the clockmaker, or the keeper of dreams. There is one who sets the time, one who draws the pictures, and one who calls out the minutes and seconds. I ring the alarm of war. It is in war that my mind awakens. It is in war that the mind settles into its killing course where neurons spark and blood flows. It is in the death of enemies that I am reborn . . .

The ship melted away. An illusion of acceleration shifted his insides as he popped into the wormhole, the slide through mirrored space making him nauseous. As soon as he popped out the other side a blinding darkness surrounded him, filled with Sommen whispers; their tongues clicked and he heard the gurgling of their throats when the things got angry, spitting insults while Win did his best to penetrate but it was as if he had been immersed in an ocean of ink. *Nothing* worked. No matter how hard he concentrated, the mantras ran empty and useless, the darkness impenetrable. A few seconds later he woke; Win's arms and legs trembled and his undersuit stuck to his skin, soaked in sweat.

"System—this is Win," he said. "Get me the captain."

A second later the captain's voice responded from the wall panel. "What?"

"The Sommen hit Childress and are somehow blocking my readings. I've never seen this."

"High-g maneuvers in ten seconds. The Marines are staged in acceleration couches so that when we stop maneuvers they'll move to the docking airlock for station boarding. With you. Now would be a good time to tell me everything, Win."

The *Higgins* pitched and yawed, throwing Win into the couch and then against his straps in a random series of movements. His suit's servos whined. A warning light flashed red on his heads-up, alerting him to the fact that his harness's structural integrity was in danger of failing. It frustrated him that the captain could operate under these conditions while Win had to marshal his resources, scraping just enough breath to speak.

"You and your ship are to stay here near the wormhole transit point, Captain, and not approach the station. I and the Marines will dock with Childress using the shuttle, scanning for enemy along the way. If we see them, the shuttle turns runs back to the *Higgins* and then we drop passivated nuclear mines on this side of the hole and the other; passive mines are hard to detect. Then we wait. If the Sommen enter human space, we accelerate from transit to transit, rejoining with the main group—the *Jerusalem* and the *Bangkok*."

"And if we *don't* see any Sommen?"

"We head for the station, investigate, retrieve relevant information, and then fall back. The station computer contains plans for a weapon that will change everything. If possible, Zhelnikov wants the base nuked. Nothing is to remain."

"If the Sommen have already taken it, it's too late to retrieve a damn thing."

"The Sommen don't care about our tech. They came here to make a point: We broke the treaty. Zhelnikov was a fool to put this base here in the first place."

"Why the hell *is* there a base out here?"

"To avoid Fleet curiosity while Zhelnikov's people work, something that might help him retake control of Fleet and win the coming war. I can't give you the details but it's based on Sommen tech and we had to test it. Someone up there thought that a demonstration outside our territory—that we were already capable of matching their weaponry, and didn't give a damn about their rules— would also be a good idea. But we were betrayed. Zhelnikov's enemies contacted the Sommen and alerted them."

"Let me see what we have so far. We just punched through; the *Higgins* is now outside human territory." Win heard the click of someone else joining the conversation.

"Finished first scans, sir. There are still a few sweeps to go, but sensors are clear."

"They're out there," said Win. He didn't need the ashram to tell him that; every nerve in his body hummed. "The Sommen are watching."

"Stop evasive maneuvers," the captain ordered. "Take us back to the wormhole and hold on this side."

The ship stopped its violent movements and Win breathed a sigh of relief, taking a deep breath and almost missing the captain's next words. "Win, meet the Marines at the shuttle; take them in and let's finish this. Get your ass back here if there's trouble; if we detect any Sommen and they close on the *Higgins,* you're on your own."

Marines loaded onto the shuttle, the men ducking under a tight hatch just large enough for them to squeeze through in battle kit. They wore blaze orange suits. Each had multiple layers of polymer armor that shone under the ship's hover lights and their facemasks were similar to Win's: A curved plate filled the space where their face should be, its surface coated with banks of sensors sending pictures to an internal screen. Win wondered if the Marines ever got claustrophobic—sealed into an armored sarcophagus for hours on end. After the last one pushed in, he followed, strapping himself to an empty couch.

The shuttle launched with a bump. Win closed his eyes and willed himself to stay calm, meditating in an effort to fight the panic that rose from not being able to see anything except the bulkhead next to him, and not being able to hear anything except his own breathing. The pilot called out the distance. Win knew what had happened at Childress Station: Zhelnikov had sacrificed an entire scientific team so that he and his allies could start a civil war. His thoughts spun downward in a vortex of prediction, imagining what would happen at each step of Zhelnikov's plan, the moves and countermoves after the religious within Fleet discovered the plan. Win soon thought himself to sleep, his helmet clicking against his chest until an adjacent Marine elbowed him awake.

"We're here, sir."

Win punched out of his seat harness. He waited for the airlock to open then followed the group out the main hatch, filing through and onto Childress Station.

"Jesus," someone said. "Look at this place."

A cylindrical chamber stretched before them for almost a hundred meters, and papers and equipment spun in microgravity. Scratch marks covered the walls. Deep gouges punctuated smooth rock where Sommen warriors had dragged their knives against it, and Win noted the depth to which their blades had penetrated; whatever material comprised Sommen knives, Fleet hadn't yet duplicated it. And the strength it had taken—to bury their blades into hard rock . . .

"Set the nuke," Win said. "Time it for three hours and put it someplace hard to find. The rest of you on me. *Move.*"

Win led them through the cylinder's center and then turned into a side passage, a map of the station outlined in green on his suit's heads-up. *The project had worked,* he told himself again. Zhelnikov assured it. There was no reason for the Sommen to have any interest in the system, which was one reason it had been chosen. No resources, no gas giants, nothing. A worthless star orbited by a tremendous field of rock and ice that alone shouldn't have attracted Sommen attention.

Win reached the door to the science section and punched in the access codes, forcing it open.

"Stay here," he said. After his sensors adjusted to the sudden increase in brightness, Win surveyed the horrors his new surroundings contained: Men and women had been split almost in half so that over a hundred bodies hovered in midair, bloated from having been dead for some time, and Win sighed with relief that he couldn't smell the odor. The cuts fascinated him. Win grabbed the nearest body, brushing aside clouds of dried blood, and his servos hummed when he pushed his hand through, his fingers visible on the other side when they protruded from a dead man's back.

"What the hell are you *doing*?"

The Marine lieutenant had ignored Wilson's order, entering behind him where he locked to the deck and scanned for threats.

"They are perfect."

"What?"

"The Sommen. This is what they do: destruction perfected. These are Childress scientists and each knew that they were to avoid being captured; they died with honor. And I told you to wait outside."

"You're telling me they killed themselves, sir? Suicide?"

"Not at all. I'm telling you the Sommen gutted them from chin to groin and these men and women sacrificed themselves for a mission. If our scientists are this brave, maybe we'll win this war after all."

The lieutenant said something else but Win ignored it and moved further in, where he activated his harness's leg magnets so he could clamp onto the metal grate floor. He clanked his way toward an area with no handholds. Droplets of blood—dried into jagged brown shapes—rose from under the grate and crept upward as he walked. Win barely noticed it, instead centering on hundreds of computers ahead that ringed a huge spherical object, over a hundred meters in diameter, and which rested on a tripod in the middle of the compartment. It took a minute to reach. Win scanned the object and found its data ports, yanking out a series of tubes that he stuffed into a bag until the last one slid free.

"Contact," the captain said, his voice buzzing over Win's helmet speakers. "Vessel inbound, maybe more than one, a million klicks out. Sommen."

Win made sure the bag was sealed, shouted for the lieutenant to get moving, and then deactivated his magnetics to travel faster. He pushed off toward the door. His servo harness hadn't just been designed to support his withering frame, but had been altered to facilitate rapid movement in zero g, the controls wired to hookups in his skull so that Win just had to think and the suit reacted. Small jets of gas puffed. Within seconds he screamed through the air and out of the research lab, where the main group of Marines grabbed Win by the arms and began pulling him through the empty station using their suits' own gas jets.

"Come, sir!"

"The Sommen are close," said Win. "I can feel it. If we die, die with honor and they may forgive this second incursion outside human space."

"Sir?"

"War. Die bravely and we may avoid an early start to it."

"We're here, sir."

The Marine pushed him into the airlock where another one grabbed Win and ushered him into the waiting shuttle. By the time Win re-strapped himself in, he had already felt the gravity increasing as the craft accelerated out of Childress docking, and the communications net erupted with activity.

"They're trying to lock on us," the Marine pilot announced.

Win's mind raced. He glanced at the bag that he'd filled with data storage tubes, resting in a webbing harness at the shuttle rear.

"Arrival at *Higgins* in twenty minutes," the pilot continued. "Hard lock. They're going to launch."

"At least they aren't close enough to use that plasma," another Marine commented; a few others chuckled.

"Launch detected. Approximately three hundred targets inbound, probable enemy missiles. Impact in fifteen minutes."

Win burst out of his couch and a nearby Marine tried to grab him, screaming something about evasive maneuvers and that g forces would smear him across the bulkhead. Win slapped the Marine's hands away. He grabbed the bag, ripping it out of the webbing storage space, and then pushed off the wall toward the shuttle's engine bay where he opened a small hatch to expose the craft's emergency data buoy. He yanked a cable from his suit's chest compartment. After jacking the cable into the buoy, several panels sprung open; as fast as he could, Win began stuffing the Childress data tubes in. He sealed the missile-shaped object for flight, punching in Zhelnikov's coordinates so it would arrive at the right location on the safe side of the wormhole.

Win detected movement out of his peripheral vision. Two Marines jetted toward him, yelling to strap in, but he punched at his forearm keypad again, cursing. The buoy was too small to have enough fuel for the entire trip, but Win hoped it would go far enough that a Fleet ship would pick up its beacon.

He hit the launch button and then ripped his cable out. The interior panel slid shut at the same time the Marines grabbed him by the arms, and the pilot announced that an emergency buoy had been dropped to burn toward transit. Win sighed with relief; at least now there was a chance Zhelnikov would get what he needed.

The two Marines forced him into his seat and then strapped him down, cinching the harness as tight as it would go. A moment later they began evading. Win screamed at the g forces, which threw him from one side to the other and crushed him into the acceleration couch as if the pilot wanted to suffocate them all. Win blacked out several times, coming to in a stupor where, for just a second, he thought maybe they'd dodged the missiles.

"*Higgins* docking bay, five minutes," the pilot announced.

The computer clicked in. "*Missile impact thirty seconds.*" Twenty seconds later, Win closed his eyes and prayed.

I am a warrior; this is a fitting end. I go willingly for this is my purpose and this is my role. I am a warrior . . .

He hadn't imagined this would ever happen, not two months ago, and certainly not years ago when he had first been tapped for service. *Zhelnikov,* he thought. Win hated even the name and remembered the first time he saw the man, when he got his first look at the scarred face that now haunted him at death.

"New launch detected," the pilot said.

"Where from?" Win asked.

"The *Higgins*. She's continuing to launch, expending her entire missile store and sending them on an intercept trajectory. It's a good thing there's no atmosphere in space or we'd feel what's about to go down. This will be close; brace yourselves, in case a Sommen warhead gets through."

Win switched his view to the shuttle's optical sensors, just in time. Over a hundred missiles detonated a kilometer beyond the shuttle, expanding into clouds of metal and plastic that screamed in the direction of the incoming Sommen warheads, protecting the *Higgins*'s shuttle with a wall of debris. It worked. All the Sommen weapons detonated prematurely, and the Marines shouted with joy when their shuttle screamed into the hangar bay, slamming to a stop after its front end buried itself in a bulkhead. The maneuver crushed the pilot and copilot, but the rest of the men scrambled out of the hatch, and Win heard the *Higgins*'s alarm claxon scream; a voice over ship's speakers warned everyone to get into acceleration couches.

CHAPTER TWO

San Kyarr's knees trembled. *You are a force never before seen,* her mother had said, *and everyone recognizes that someday you'll have a chance to prove it. Your father, rest his soul, knew a Buddhist monk who saw it all, the future; something big is headed your way, and it's your job to prepare so you can defend what's good. Death is coming. It moves quickly, and travels astride powerful engines.*

She risked a glance at her fellow candidates, their eyes fixed ahead. They resembled San. All had shaved heads so that after she peeked down the line it reminded her of a row of cue balls resting on stubby torsos, each girl four and a half feet tall. Their bare heads glistened with sweat. Summer in Texas crept in through narrow windows, open on each side of the barracks, their metal frames gray with paint layered so thick that it gathered in drops, dried over the years into oval-shaped tears of color. Gray, the color of Fleet. Anything metal, wood, or plastic had been coated with it, a tradition that lingered from the days when mankind's primary navy had been one of metal and water, the paint meant to protect precious materials from the corrosion of salt.

She glanced at her skin, its light brown just enough to set her apart from the others. One girl glanced over, grimacing. San wished that Fleet could paint *her* gray, hiding San under thick layers from the acid looks of Earth-born candidates, Americans who somehow knew from her skin alone that her father had once been the enemy. *Myanmarese.*

The girl mouthed words, silently: *Go back to Mars.*

"I doubt any of you know this," the sergeant began, "because most of you are too stupid. But your bodies are perfection—all *Fleet*. Lovingly altered to absorb oxygen at a more efficient rate than unmodified personnel, and capable of producing excess glucose and improved hemoglobin for surviving combat g-forces. Your short stature and thick bones also help, but don't think your breeding gives you an automatic pass. Some of you will be going home, washed out."

San waited. On either side of them stood rows of bunk beds and despite being on Earth for the first time, her body handled the increased gravity with no problem. Sleep was another issue. The transit from Mars had taken forever and it was her first trip, so San hadn't rested much and now she fought to keep her eyes open. Exhaustion had accumulated in the corners of her thought, gaining mass with every minute until it gathered on the outside of her eyelids, tiny weights that pulled downward, her eyes on the verge of surrender. They were about to flutter shut when a woman in a black uniform entered.

"This is Sister Mirriam-Ann MacGuire; you will address her as Sister. She has something to say."

The girl who had thrown a dirty look whispered to one next to her, loud enough for San to hear. "First a freak from Mars. Now a freak from the Church."

Sister Mirriam-Ann walked on stubby legs, squat. She had white hair tucked under a nun's coif and dark circles around her eyes. Half her face had been torn apart and rebuilt. San imagined that whoever had reshaped her skin had done it using clay, sculpting it so it retained an inherent symphony of lumps. It reminded San of the lava flows on Mars, rock frozen by the cold atmosphere before it had a chance to run far, forming enormous globules of solid material that looked fascinatingly grotesque. Those were all black; basalt. Sister Mirriam-Ann's skin looked bone white, pale except for masses of pink scar tissue that punctuated her appearance to invoke revulsion from anyone who stopped to look. When she spoke, San expected her to sound as ugly as she appeared; instead the nun's voice was surprisingly soft.

"Good evening. In case you are wondering, yes, I have been to space to minister to the faithful assigned at forward operating outposts; I was there when the Sommen first invaded. *They* gave me this face." She pointed to her cheek. "I wasn't much older than you are now. Eighteen. My order visited Karin-Two and I don't remember much of the events except for waking up on a tanker ship converted into a hospital, headed back to Earth, where a field medic did his best to rebuild me—without the assistance of bots. Most of the hospital acceleration couches were empty except for me and a couple of sisters from my order; the Sommen didn't leave many alive. They *never* do."

The nun paused and leaned against one of the bunks. "My order is in a Fleet ancillary order that has many elements but, most importantly, we have . . . special skills. Ones that Fleet thinks should be fully integrated into their operations. That's why I'm here; this is your final, pre-Fleet test. I will determine your strengths and weaknesses so that we can better determine where you will best serve and weed out those who aren't suited before we invest in the final training courses for Fleet occupational specialties. Your personal wants and dreams have no place here. All of you, including the boys—who are getting this same lecture in their dormitory right now—have potential, but that is all. Potential means almost nothing. My order decides who becomes an officer and who winds up in latrine engineering. Sergeant," the Sister said. She turned toward a door at the back of the dorm, and headed through. San caught a glimpse of a small office beyond; its furnishings were sparse, with a large wooden crucifix attached to the rear wall.

Since when had the Catholics, or any religion, been part of Fleet? she wondered.

"*Line up,*" the sergeant barked. The girls jostled into position, some of them needing help from the woman's swagger stick. "You will be called one at a time and will enter Sister Mirriam-Ann's office when ordered. What you are about to experience is classified. You will not discuss the questions you are asked at any time. Not now, not tomorrow, not ever."

Part of San felt nervous—not scared, the kind of energy she always felt when something exciting was about to happen. *Classified? What did that even mean?* Lost in thought and tired, by the time it was her turn San stumbled into the office to stand at ease, almost missing it when the nun ordered her to sit on a metal chair.

"Have you ever heard claims that human beings only use ten to fifteen percent of their brains?" Sister Mirriam-Ann asked.

"No, sir. I mean, Sister."

"Well, people *have* made that claim and they continue to, even though it's ludicrous. There's no way our entire blood-pumping system is dedicated to support so much dormant tissue. What *is* true"—the nun stood and faced the wall, her back to San—"is that you can get some interesting effects by increasing the number of synapses and tinkering with other portions of the brain. Does this make sense?"

"No, Sister; I don't know why this is relevant."

"We face two great evils, child. They are on the horizon and you and your kind will have to face them before you're ready; one evil works from within Fleet and another works from without. But that discussion is for another time. It is only important that you remember these words, and understanding will come."

"Now, then." The Sister lowered herself back into her chair. "I'm going to ask you a series of questions, and I want you to answer them honestly and completely. Understood?"

San nodded.

"San Kyarr—San for short—daughter of Maung Kyarr and Nang Vongchanh. Second-generation Fleet. Your parents relocated to special duty on Mars where they entered you into the genetic breeding program soon after your mother's pregnancy, correct?"

"Yes, ma'am."

"Father, Buddhist. Mother, Roman Catholic. Do you believe in ghosts, San?"

The question surprised her and she laughed, stifling it almost immediately.

"Something funny? Am I entertaining?"

"No . . . no, Sister."

"No, you don't find me entertaining or no you don't believe in ghosts?"

"Yes, Sister, you are entertaining . . . I mean . . ." San's hands shook; she was blowing it, her mind too sleepy. For a second she wished that her parents hadn't placed her in the Fleet program in the first place, wondering about the normal Martian kids—tall and slender, elegant in gravity and so sure of everything. Even with her brown skin, *nobody* would guess she was Myanmarese if she had the bone structure of a Martian. Her mother's words surfaced in a dim memory.

There is goodness in the world; have faith. Lies are for cowards.
Sister Mirriam-Ann slapped her desk. "*Answer the question.*"

"Yes, I believe in ghosts."

San wished she could take back the words after they'd been uttered. Forget about the fact that the nun was trying to fluster her; the answer she'd just given was a wash-out response. Fleet discharged anyone showing signs of psychiatric disorders and now San waited for the nun to snap her fingers and tell her to pack her bags.

"I see." Sister Mirriam-Ann leaned forward. The woman stared and San waited but soon felt uncomfortable in the silence and looked away, glancing at the wall and trying to ignore the sensation that someone peeled through layers of her brain to find disappointing results. This woman was different—the whole thing *bizarre*. A nun? For Fleet? What the hell was going on and why would Fleet outsource its decisions to a religious order with no publicly advertised military connection whatsoever?

"Interesting. Let's try something different. A Fleet officer approaches and there's nobody around. He tells you about an impending disaster: A cargo ship named the *Minerva* will crash into Phobos Station in three weeks. Immediately afterward the man disappears into thin air. Do you, *A,* ignore the experience, thinking that you must be exhausted and it was just a random hallucination brought on by micro-g drug treatments, *B,* report it to Fleet Command, or *C,* turn yourself into the squadron therapist?"

No answers came and San felt sweat on her forehead at the same time a sensation of cold swept through, the chill of failure and its associated terror. *I have nothing to lose now,* San figured. *The Sister told us this was a test; a test for what?*

"I'd report it to command."

Sister Mirriam-Ann jotted something on a note pad.

"Next question. Do you ever get déjà vu? The feeling you've been somewhere or in some situation even though logically you know it's your first time?"

"Yes, ma'am."

"How often?"

"I don't know. Sometimes."

San began to sweat, her sense of failure mounting. After a few minutes it felt as if someone else answered the questions while she floated to the side, watching her body shake and her chances for making a Fleet assignment plummet. Years of training in Mars' orbit, her breath fast and shallow from the fear of emergency decompression drills where they punctured candidates' suits and handed them a roll of patching tape, did nothing to help. Reality was always slightly different from the tanks. In the tank, despite the fact that everything seemed so authentic, the mind knew; it *always* did. Tank training and drills were as close to the real thing as one could achieve, but underlying it all was the foundation of simulation, an odor of dishonesty that crept into one's mind no matter how rational the scenario. Her consciousness moved further away, a sensation of dislocation increasing by the second.

Sister Mirriam-Ann paused to read her notes and then tapped the pencil against her front teeth. "Tell me something, San. Are you having an out-of-body experience? Where it feels as if you're watching this from a third-person perspective and someone else is answering the questions?"

A chill passed through her. *How could the woman know?*

"Yes, ma'am."

"Does this happen a lot?"

"Sometimes when I fall asleep I see a light, as if someone is turning a lamp on and off in front of my face. Then my chest gets tight and I can't move. The next thing I know, I'm soaring. If I want to, I can fly through my house, into the street or anywhere. But it doesn't happen all the time, Sister."

"How was your home life?" the nun asked, changing the subject. "Was it bad? Abuse, sexual or physical?"

"No! I have a *good* family. Mars is different from Earth, and I lived on a base all my life. So if anything it was a little boring. My mother raised me as a Catholic—to sacrifice everything for Fleet."

Sister Mirriam-Ann nodded. "I'm sure that's true but irrelevant; last set of questions. I'm going to show you some Zener cards and I want you to tell me what's on the other side. I'll look at them, but you'll see only the blank side and have to guess or sense what I'm seeing. Ready?"

"Zener?"

"He was a researcher in the twentieth century with a fellow by the name of Rhine at Duke University; it doesn't matter. You just guess what's on the card. You have five choices: wavy lines, circles, squares, crosses and stars." The nun held one up. San saw nothing but the back of it, a pattern of red and black diamonds, but without warning a vision came and went so quickly that she almost failed to notice.

I'm crazy, she thought. "Wavy lines."

The nun repeated the process at least fifty more times; by the end of it San had a headache.

"Okay," Sister Mirriam-Ann said while jotting a final note. "Dismissed."

"Did I pass, ma'am?"

"We'll have everyone's results tomorrow. You'll find out then."

San walked from the office and shut the door; she couldn't shake the feeling that she'd failed the interview, and by the time she reached her bunk the girl wiped away tears before sobbing into her pillow.

San stood at attention, sweating in the morning heat. The sun hadn't yet risen but Texas's summer filled the air with moisture and she hadn't ever experienced humidity, so the saturated air made San gasp for breath, a cloying sensation that infused her gray uniform with sweat. One child fainted and a pair of medics dragged her away to a waiting medical transport. Minutes ticked by. When the sun peeked over the distant horizon it hit her face with more unwelcome warmth and San closed her eyes, praying for the ordeal to end.

"Are you from Earth?" a girl next to her whispered.

"I don't think we're supposed to talk," said San.

"It doesn't matter. If I don't talk, I'll pass out like that other girl. Are you?"

San had to stop herself from shaking her head. The movement would have been seen, getting her in trouble. "No. Mars."

"I thought so. You look different from the rest of us."

"Different?" San asked.

"A tiny bit shorter and stockier. Plus your skin is darker."

San struggled to hide her nervousness. The next set of questions was always the same. How many times had she seen her father throw out his chest when answering the same queries, his voice tinged with hatred at having to defend his heritage, his right to even exist? How many times would she have to do the same? These were supposed to be the best candidates and if the program on Earth was the same as on Mars, the girl had spent the better part of her years corked into semi-aware systems and getting her brain stuffed with facts and computations. There should have been a greater tinge of logic to their thought processes but, clearly, San thought, common sense wasn't part of the Earth-side program.

"I was modified while inside my mother's womb. It was the first time they tried it, and that's why I'm stockier than you. And my skin is darker because I'm half Myanmarese, half Laotian. Normal Martians are very tall and slender because of the reduced gravity."

"You mean you're Burmese?" the girl asked. "Same ones we fought in the Great Pacific War?"

"Myanmarese. Yes."

"I thought so. Some of the other girls noticed too. I didn't know any of you had the means to even *afford* genetic alterations. It's shocking they let Burmese into Fleet."

San felt sick. She urged her eyes to stay open in the heat and fought the combined sensations of incredulity and rage, suppressing an impulse to lunge at the girl. Another candidate dropped two rows in front but this time the medics did nothing, instead snapping to attention when someone approached the group from behind. San's knees threatened to buckle. She remembered a trick her father taught and bent her legs a bit before clenching her thigh and arm muscles, forcing blood back toward her torso and head. The dizziness passed and Sister Mirriam-Ann crept onto a podium at the head of the field, her cane shaking as she climbed the steps; the nun tapped a microphone to make sure it worked.

"When I call your name I want you to load up in the two transports at the edge of the parade field. Double time. Adams. Aders. Adleson."

The nun read from a list, her soft voice echoing over the parade ground. Wind dried sweat from San's forehead and provided relief from the agony of standing at attention while names rolled from the woman's mouth in an avalanche of identities. When she passed the *K* names without calling hers, San figured they must have her listed under *S*. But when the nun finished those and moved on to names beginning with *T*, San's eyes snapped open and the girl's stomach tightened.

Sister Mirriam-Ann snapped a portfolio closed and smiled. "At ease."

San's shoulders slumped and she moved her feet apart, glancing to either side. One other girl stood nearby. The two were the only ones left on the massive parade field and a breeze picked up, blowing dust across in waves. Sister Mirriam-Ann lowered herself from the podium before she motioned for the two to approach.

"That's it. You two washed out and may God help you both. What a waste, especially you, Kyarr. Sixteen years of corking into sims and genetic alterations and you still couldn't get it. You may think that 'it's only two of us so how come it's such a big deal?' but do the math. You two are Fleet products, not creatures of God. How much did the military spend on you at a time when power, food and materials are priceless?"

San's face went red with anger. She was about to say something when Sister Mirriam-Ann raised her hand. "Don't speak; it can only get you in any more trouble than you're already in, Kyarr."

"I tried, ma'am."

The other girl composed herself long enough to speak. "Me too."

"Trying isn't the point. Your test answers may be indicative of psychological or neural defects that went undetected. You know the regulations; there are strict rules governing psychiatric cases."

"Yes, ma'am," said San.

"Don't need to call me ma'am anymore, Kyarr. Fleet already out-processed you both administratively so we don't even need you to sign anything. For the first times in your lives, you're both private citizens."

The other girl began sobbing and San fought against doing the same. *Private citizen?* She'd been Fleet almost from birth and on turning eighteen had re-signed the paperwork making her their property for another ten years. And now, that quickly, she was out? It felt as though someone had stripped her of even a soul and she imagined she stood naked, unprotected and alone; if anything happened, Fleet services wouldn't—couldn't—be there to help from now on.

"Daughters," Sister Mirriam-Ann said. "Don't lose perspective; you are both Fleet trained and geniuses. There are plenty of private freight companies that will take you on as navigator, pilot—whatever. I'm sure you'll figure things out eventually."

An auto-transport whirred onto the parade field, its tracks spitting up dust and soil as it motored straight for the small group; the vehicle stopped a few feet away and the doors swung up on either side, reminding San of wings.

The nun pointed at it. "That's your ride."

"That's it?" the other girl asked, speaking between sobs. "We get an auto-transport—to where? How can you just turn us loose after all we sacrificed?"

Sister Mirriam-Ann was about to respond when a medbot disengaged from the side of the transport and unfolded legs that hummed with electricity. San shivered. She hated the way bots moved under full gravity, with clicking legs that reminded her of colossal insects as they shuffled from place to place, their blinking lights a testament to the soullessness of semi-aware machines.

"No, that's not it. There's one last Fleet regulation: We have to vaccinate you both."

"Vaccinate against what?" San asked. "We've already been poked and shot up with everything Fleet can think of."

"It's not for you. Over the last day here you've been exposed to Fleet personnel who have been in deep space recently, to the far outposts where all sorts of bugs grow. We have to make sure that nobody at home catches anything."

San rolled up her uniform sleeve. The bot moved toward her and she closed her eyes to avoid having to look, then winced at the needle prick. She gritted her teeth as the fluid burned. The bot finished with the other girl and the pair rolled their sleeves back down.

"Good," Sister Mirriam-Ann said. "And Fleet thanks you for your service. The transport will take you to the Houston airport, where you'll be given orders and tickets to get both of you home."

The nun hobbled away in the direction of the administration buildings while the medbot sauntered, clicking alongside its companion as the old woman talked to it. San couldn't make out the words until the breeze stopped, when she heard the sister ask *how long?*

"This isn't possible," the other girl said. "And whatever they just injected is burning the hell out of my arm."

"Mine too. What's your name?"

The girl looked at the auto-transport and wiped tears from her cheeks. "Stacy Kang. From San Francisco. You?"

"San. San Kyarr. Mars."

Both girls walked toward the transport and San looked in; a smell of air freshener hit and made her feel nauseous, an odor of pine penetrating her nose and into her brain.

"My dad is going to kill me," Stacy said.

"Mine's dead. But my mom won't be happy at all."

"At least you have to get to Mars before telling her. Plenty of time to work things out in your head."

"Time to think. That's *just* what I need."

"Sorry. I didn't mean it that way."

Something was bothering San, and she searched until it popped to the surface of her thoughts. "Did Sister Mirriam-Ann say anything to you about evil? An evil within Fleet?"

"No. No, she didn't. But what does it matter?"

"I always wanted to be involved, to be a part of the fight. With Fleet. I thought I could be one of the good guys. But that idea was stupid. Maybe we're just kids, after all, and maybe the idea of good fighting evil is outdated."

CHAPTER THREE

Beyond an ancient stone building came the sound of crashing storm waves, visible when lightning flashed. Win grabbed his head and screamed.

The old man, Zhelnikov, stood next to him and smiled while sucking at the end of a cigar. He blew smoke into the darkness and Zhelnikov's cloak flapped in the gale, its draped material shining under lightning at the same time its hood obscured the man's face. Sheets of rain pelted them both. Win stopped screaming and the old man straightened, stretching his back and pulling the hood off so water soaked his white hair. It ran into crevices crossing his face—a mixture of wrinkles and scar tissue.

He waved a holo-readout to life and watched the data scroll. "This is the beginning; your brain is already changing."

"I'm long past that," said Win.

Zhelnikov drew on his cigar again and exhaled. "Nonsense. I wish you could see what's in store for you. Your father, Maung, would be proud. *There* was a warrior."

Win opened his eyes. Rain threatened to blind him but he ignored it, blinking as if he wasn't there while the storm shouted meaningless threats in lightning and thunder. A thirty-foot wave crested on the beach below then boomed against a cliff, the ground under them vibrating when Win turned to look at the old man.

"My father means nothing. Meant nothing, even when alive. And I can see much, even now, while my biochemistry shifts so I can feel it, Zhelnikov. The headaches are a sign that brain-structure changes are taking hold and pressing against my skull. It has opened my eyes and once the changes progress past a certain point I will see everything. You have no idea what you've created."

"That . . . that's impossible," Zhelnikov stammered. "We've just started the treatments. Significant structural changes will take weeks, maybe months."

"You're scanning the data; see for yourself. The path is open to me now and I see the things you've done; your past is a roadmap unfolded."

Win's mind raced. Without warning, he drifted into a waking dream where Zhelnikov's plans took shape like a web, upon which he traced with a finger to expose lines of plots and schemes. Some he thought ingenious. Others ended in nothingness, stillborn elements drawn by an organism with no ability to see the future: a man. A sick man, with a mind sharpened and specialized for killing on a strategic level, so that part of Win admired Zhelnikov's skill and realized that among normal humans, he was a separate thing—a super genius in the death trade. At the center of his web lay their enemy.

The Sommen, Win thought. That way was still blocked, which meant that Zhelnikov was right that this was the beginning, and Win sensed it would take time for new neurons to arrange themselves in the proper pattern—one that would allow him to see *them.* Upon the web, the Sommen and their warships resembled one of the black thunderclouds now shooting lightning toward the sea. They were an opaque mass without form or definition. He peered for what felt like hours while diffuse clouds shifted into different shapes, all of which were meaningless and without sharp lines. Then the picture changed. Win glimpsed through the haze for a second and saw the concentrating faces of Sommen; they pointed at something: a seaport far to the east. The picture faded almost as soon as it had formed but before it disappeared, Win felt a pulsation of rage and urgency from the Sommen. They wanted him to act.

"I am decaying," Win said. "My mental abilities multiply and my muscles erode."

Zhelnikov nodded. "It's part of the treatment. A side effect that we knew would be a problem but there was no way around it; the Sommen formula and manuals are very clear on this, and we think muscular deterioration is even worse for *their* priests. We will have to put you in a full combat suit, with a neural-linked servo harness so you can walk."

"You will turn me into a freak. A mechanical thing, which our troops will fear and hate. Mostly flesh suspended in a robotic frame to move in fits and starts across your battlefields. You enjoy the thought; I can see it. You're afraid of what I'm becoming and making me a mechanical curiosity gives you hope—that you'll regain control."

"Are you reading my mind?" Zhelnikov asked.

Win glanced at the old man again. He picked up small muscle twitches, heard the change in Zhelnikov's breathing patterns, and watched the shifts in diameter of his pupils. Together it formed a pattern.

"No. I'm not a mind reader. Not yet. We must attack any remaining Chinese before it's too late. The Sommen are on the verge of coming back to Earth early if we do not."

"The Chinese left Earth years ago," Zhelnikov said. "What remains of their population and nation . . . it's a complete wasteland."

Win looked into the rain again. He put his arm across the old man's shoulder and together they hobbled toward a tiny oak door at the base of the closest stone wall.

"There are pockets of survivors that your systems couldn't detect. Flesh and metal hybrids. The Sommen see this, and are ready to strike."

"You communicate with the Sommen?"

The door slammed shut to muffle the sound of waves and thunder behind five inches of solid oak. Servos slid locks into place. Win felt safer in the structure, and he could almost feel the age of the molecules from which it had been constructed, their atomic bonds so old that almost all vibration had ceased, the lack of energy palpable and comforting. It made him feel a part of history. Hover lights flicked on overhead, following them as they shuffled, and humming as superconducting magnets followed along a tracking strip set into ceiling beams.

"Not the way you're thinking. They sent me a message. They can see me, but I can't see them."

"You're barely a man, Win. We can't possibly send you into combat now; you're not ready. First we have to fit you into a servo harness and construct a custom frame. And we have to operate. To relieve the pressure inside your skull."

"A ceramic expansion shell."

Zhelnikov nodded. "It's the only way. We can make more room and grow jack-skin over it so that it looks real. Normal."

"Normal." Win shook his head. "A bald man with an elongated jack-skinned head, suspended inside a modified combat suit and robotic harness with cables connected to my brain. Who will follow that freakish creature, Zhelnikov?"

"We will *make* them follow."

Win thought while stumbling forward, finding himself outside the medical station. Through thick glass he saw his empty bed. Surgical bots surrounded it, their long spidery arms waving in response to electrical stimuli that he felt against his skin even at this distance. Large vials of standard masker—a code name for the drug responsible for changing him—hung from a metal frame, the pale green fluid reminding him of drying grass, half dead.

"You must start now. Continue the standard masker doses and make me the servo harness and frame. Condition the troops however you can. I will take five minutes now to draw up the plans and will send them to you when finished."

"Five minutes?" Zhelnikov asked.

"You doubt me?"

The old man blew smoke against a stone wall, filling the corridor with an acrid smell. "I'll take a look at the plans when you finish, and then I will decide if this is worth doing. Where will we first land?"

"The Sommen pointed toward Hong Kong. We will slaughter what remains so there are no Chinese left. You are an accomplished killer, Zhelnikov. This should be second nature to you."

Zhelnikov closed his eyes. "Prepare yourself. I had anticipated the need for a servo harness and the armorer will need to perform a fitting. Altering your skull will be... painful, Win. We can't use sedatives for fear they will interact with the standard masker."

"Do it."

The glass door rumbled open. Win shuffled toward his bed and rolled into it, then waited while the surgical bots arranged themselves and Zhelnikov's footsteps faded. He winced at the touch of cold metal. A bot cradled him off the bed, rotating him to face downward through a gap in the mattress to give Win a clear view of the floor. Sandstone tiles, hundreds of years old, formed a pattern that reminded him of the desert and his eyes lost focus, their vision fixed on nothing when a picture took shape of the old man. *I cannot control this; it is like having one foot in this world, one stuck in a place of shadow.*

Win watched as Zhelnikov moved through the corridor. The man arrived at a steel door, where he waved his hand at a sensor to send the slab upward into the ceiling, revealing a labyrinth of tight passageways beyond. Zhelnikov passed one security door after another, weaving his way through an arched stone tunnel where in places he had to duck when the ceiling got low, until he arrived at a spot where the corridor widened into a large room. A small army of bots sprang to life. After scanning the old man, their mechanical arms removed his rain poncho and then the rest of his clothes; two of them began spraying him in a fine mist, forcing him to close his eyes while it coated his face. Zhelnikov then slipped into paper coveralls. He squeezed into a plastic suit, which the bots zipped to encase the man from head to toe in clear plastic, a hose dangling off his side.

Zhelnikov moved into an airlock, where another mist sprayed from jets that sprang from the walls and he held his arms up, rotating in place so that his suit coated evenly. When it was done, the other airlock door opened. Zhelnikov connected his hose to a jack that hung from the ceiling, his source of air travelling with him along a track while its guide wheels clicked.

Something filled the vast open area around Zhelnikov. At first Win couldn't make it out, but then hundreds of hover lights snapped on and lit a football-field-sized cavern, each square meter of it taken by hospital beds. Win studied their occupants: children. *Not children,* he corrected himself, *barely men, young warriors that hadn't reached twenty years of age.* Each had a cable socket at the top of his bald head, into which had been jacked a thick black cord, and Win watched as they squirmed in agony. Zhelnikov touched one on the shoulder. The young man moaned and wouldn't stop, only going quiet after a medbot scooted in and injected him with clear liquid.

Troops, thought Win. *A special army, not the ones normally trained by Fleet.* He recalled Zhelnikov's schemes, trying to fit the vision within the man's web of plans. *I am not whole,* he thought. *My vision has blind spots and gaps, traps within which I can destroy myself if not careful; this place is not in the schemes.*

Win's vision blanked; he winced when a surgical bot injected him with something, making him go stiff, and the whine of a microsaw erupted from nearby, filling his thoughts with the promise of pain. Even knowing what was about to happen, it didn't prepare him for the burning agony when a laser cut into his scalp, followed by the sensation of metal grinding through skull.

The last thing he had heard from Zhelnikov echoed, trailing Win into unconsciousness: "Slaughter and dispose of all subjects operating under ninety-five percent combat efficiency. I need them perfect."

Win felt water on his forehead and a blast of cold air, compelling his eyes to blink open; it took a moment to see Zhelnikov, who hunched over his bed and began a laser scan of Win's retinas.

"The operation went well. So far the bone is fusing with the ceramic carapace and the artificial lining is in place."

"Won't I have to be careful?"

"About what?" Zhelnikov asked.

"The empty space. There's nothing to support my brain matter toward the back of my skull unless it grows enough to fill the void."

Zhelnikov straightened and Win saw on his face a mixed look of pride and arrogance. "It's packed with a gelatin my staff developed. There is no empty space. As your brain tissue pushes out and expands, there's a tiny hole where the gel will escape, pressed out by your gray matter. You should see yourself. You look like those ancient Egyptian pharaohs—the ones with elongated heads. We are out of jack-skin but more is on the way and I can do that procedure on the way to Hong Kong. Enough skin is on hand for your spinal-insertion operation, to install the head servo and actuator rod. Are you ready for another procedure?"

Win tried to sit up. He lost balance and almost slipped from the bed but two bots sped in to keep him from falling. Win reached up to feel his new skull and traced it, an oblong protrusion that made his head jut backward at least twelve inches. No matter how hard he struggled, the weight was too great for his wasting muscles and he gave up trying to lift his head, panting from the effort.

"Your brain growth is proceeding as rapidly as your muscle

deterioration," said Zhelnikov. "Both faster than predicted. We'll have to equip you with an artificial heart because it won't be long; your smooth muscles are on the verge of failing. The mechanical, servo-driven actuator rod will hopefully take care of all your necessary head movements."

"I'm not human anymore."

"Win. You are something greater."

Win tried to see again, concentrating and closing his eyes to read Zhelnikov the way he had when they'd been outside during the storm, but this time nothing came. When he opened his eyes the old man was cutting the end off another cigar.

"Those visions of yours. You are going to be a priest," he said, "similar to the Sommen in many ways."

Win nodded. "I know."

"The Sommen gave us vast amounts of data on their ways of combat; it's a religion to them, Win. Their priests are the strategists. One priest per invasion. *Always.* They keep this priest in a bunker in the rear, as far from the action as possible so that it remains safe while the warriors exterminate. Then the priest surveys what's left, and orders the murder of the last remaining enemy. Total eradication."

Even without the visions, Win sensed that Zhelnikov held something back. "The purpose of religion is to worship a higher being or group of beings. How can their religion be just about combat?"

"It isn't. It's about a search. The Sommen believe there is a higher being who watches over the universe, and they have a prophecy—that their warriors will see God only after meeting a race they can't conquer. So they attack, they invade, and they haven't lost a war yet. Not one."

"With such a record, it's no wonder they continue with a singular strategy."

Zhelnikov chuckled. "That's not what's interesting. What's interesting is the irony: They *want* to lose."

Win listened to the medical bots hiss, their servos whining as they made minor movements to adjust monitors or wipe the sticky droplets off the back of his head. He tried to recall the early lessons Zhelnikov had given: The Sommen had conquered every planetary system they invaded, waiting for the proper time to expand further. The just-conquered system became home. Construction of cities and factories went into overdrive, the Sommen-subjugated alien races forming work crews and engineers while warriors garrisoned and prepared themselves for what came next: reproduction. Half the Sommen force would enter their nests, hibernating and multiplying like insects, forming the basis of a new invading force.

Earth had been off their path. The Sommen never would have come close to Earth but for a signal, their invasion coming just after Allied forces tested a prototype interstellar communications system decades ago...

"Why were they afraid of Fleet's communications experiment—at the beginning of it all?" he asked.

"It's complicated. They are afraid of a certain type of communications, anything that involves taking advantage of the multiple universes that surround us. I proved this technique with the first communicator and then perfected it using an alternate universe to send quantum particles at faster than light speed to distant spots in our space time."

"A wormhole," Win said.

"Kind of. An atom-sized doorway into a universe that's not ours. For a brief period of time I had access to the Sommen religious texts; they warn of something dark that can sense when these doorways are opened so upon detecting our test transmissions, the Sommen attacked us—partly because of their faith, but also to keep us from attracting attention. The attention of *what* they never explained. And their texts said nothing."

"Do you believe all the texts they left us?"

Zhelnikov nodded. "Yes, but I didn't get to read the religious texts, which cover what we're doing to you. Sommen technical manuals only partially reference it; they describe the transformation of a candidate and what is to be done at certain stages. When your brain reaches an advanced state, you will be able to access visions at will, and, maybe, the ability to communicate over interstellar distances; it's the only way that the Sommen could possibly coordinate their military operations. And, you will be given a new drug. Translated, I think it's called *Numbers from Clouds,* but the team that isolated the active ingredients calls it *the serum*. It's plant derived."

"How did you get one of their plants?"

"The Sommen left them behind at their ground stations. We found one in Charleston where your father first defeated a Sommen warrior so long ago. Our teams cloned them and are growing a small crop in an ammonia atmosphere."

Win closed his eyes when the bots grabbed hold of him again, flipping him to face the floor. *His father.* He dug into memories and his expanded brain mass picked them out, one by one, all the way to the day he was born. Win settled on an old image, when he'd lived in a tiny hut in Charleston's spaceport ghetto: the last time he'd seen his father, who had cried when he left.

"My father was a fool."

Zhelnikov said something but Win ignored him, instead getting ready for the pain. The bots lased his back. Win smelled burning flesh as they cut through the thin layer of skin over his spine and he was glad for the paralytic because the sound of a high-speed microdrill filled the room and made him want to run. The drill bit into each disc. One by one the bots bored hundreds of tiny holes, and then fished thin platinum wires through, bonding them with artificial nerve endings to the main portion of his spinal cord. They felt like tiny spears, each one adding a new layer of agony. With the pain came a sliver of his vision and he floated above everything, near the ceiling, where he looked down and saw a forest of metal porcupine quills that protruded from his back.

The bots then joined the wires to a narrow, plastic slab, one side consisting of jack-skin. They coated the underside of with bioadhesive to make it look shiny and salmon colored, pressing the assembly against his back so it encased the wires and his spine under a strip of black polymer and metal, to which they affixed a telescoping rod and universal joint. A bot grabbed hold of the rod with thin pincers. It extended it just enough to reach the base of Win's new ceramic skull where it squirted a droplet of adhesive, then held the rod against the ceramic and lit the area with ultraviolet light. When they finished, Win saw that a monopod—a black arm with servos that whined when he turned—now propped up his head.

"That was fast," said Zhelnikov.

Win couldn't respond. His back felt as though someone had taken a red-hot piece of metal and rested it along the center of his spine, invoking a level of pain that forced his breaths to come in ragged gasps.

"*The pain.*"

"Yes, I know; it must be excruciating to undergo these procedures without the aid of anesthesia."

"No. *The pain.* For now it's what makes me able to see things. Causes a change in brainwave patterns and conduction to create a favorable set of circumstances for having visions. Does the serum cause pain?"

Win couldn't see Zhelnikov; paralytic drugs took effect, immobilizing him so he remained facing downward; he heard the man's neck pop when he nodded.

"Yes. Incredible pain. They have a ritual to go with it but we aren't there yet, Win. You will become addicted to suffering but first there's a long road of learning. I'm sorry, son; if there was any other way to prepare for the Sommen, I'd take it, but we now have less than eighty years. When they return, it will be a war we've never seen."

"Stop," Win whispered. "I understand the logic. I don't require your apologies or sympathy."

"None of us really understand, Win. Not even you. Not yet. Do you know what the Sommen concentrated on during all those years they occupied Earth? Before they left and gave us a hundred years to prepare for war?"

Win tried to shake his head, soon realizing the attempt was futile. "No."

"The Catholic Church. Its history, its artifacts, everything. They took over the Vatican and razed Jerusalem entirely, scraping everything down to the dirt and rock from about A.D. 30."

"Why not Judaism or Islam, or any of the others? What's so special about Catholicism?"

Zhelnikov lit his cigar. The smell comforted Win, who had now spent so much time with the man that breathing smoke had become second nature, something that invoked a Pavlovian response equating the smell of burning tobacco with a sensation of security. He had never known his father. All Win had known was *Zhelnikov*.

"We don't know. They reviewed all of them, for sure, but their main examination revolved around the Catholic faith and some think it's because the Church's teachings and prophecies match the

Sommen's. Those bastards actually think *we* are the race to defeat them. In a way, I guess you could say the Sommen love the human race, a love affair that started when some random Ukrainian slave refused to become a Sommen merchant twenty-something years ago, and which their review of our religions only strengthened."

"For our sake," said Win, "I hope they're correct."

Zhelnikov stood, and the leather of his calf-high boots creaked. "Get some rest. Tomorrow we begin construction of your servo harness and frame, and you need to send me your plan for Hong Kong. If what you said is true then we need to move fast against the remaining Chinese."

Win recalled his visions and remembered the level of destruction that was about to come; *there would be so much killing,* he thought. *Killing and murder will become my new religion. I will be known as the butcher of children and all men will fear me, their terror forcing them to follow me into darkness and death.*

CHAPTER FOUR

Get to Ganymede...

Jupiter filled a quarter of the sky and San scrutinized the swirling gas. It shifted, the colors mixing in a hypnotic motion that she swore hissed and moaned, punctuated with sparks of bright light. War was coming. Across the jagged landscape of Ganymede's ice, a line of figures wandered, their armor-suited shapes obscured by phase shifters—cloaks that bent light to render wearers invisible. The figures hadn't secured them so the cloaks moved as if in a gentle breeze, swaying from side to side in Ganymede's low gravity, exposing parts of the soldiers to make them an army of dismembered legs and arms.

San was about to turn away when a bright glow erupted above Ganymede's surface and grew in less than a second into a massive fireball, a sphere of plasma that blinded her as it blossomed larger, the radiative heat so intense it vaporized the warriors and melted a wide swath of ice in an instant. Before the plasma reached her, its spherical shape broke into pieces and tendrils. Then the fireball disappeared to leave behind a shallow crater. Clouds of ice mist hovered, creeping back toward the surface. *War was coming,* San thought again. *Soon.*

Get to Ganymede...

She woke from the dream to find her arms and legs strapped to a table in sick bay, with thick straps across her waist and chest. *How?* San thought. *What happened and who put me here?*

Get to Ganymede... This time the voice wasn't in her dreams; it was an old woman, real, and inside her head.

"Shut up! Stop talking to me!"

The medbot spurted a jet of vapor and glided toward her, its mechanical-sounding voice making San's skin tingle with fear.

"Rest, Ms. Kyarr. You need to rest."

San couldn't tell if the bot was *thinking*. It had no idea: war. She imagined that the thing had sympathy, that if she told the bot to set her free, it would. San could make her way into deep space, well beyond the Neptune elliptical into everything cold and dead, where Fleet would burn past her without noticing the tiny hole she'd dug in one of the ice balls of the Kuiper belt—just her, alone. Without energy signatures nobody would notice; the sense of failure would form a coating, a blanket of shame to keep San warm from the absolute zero of space, and a bubble to maintain atmosphere under a dome of disappointment. It would be better than facing her friends as a washout. San dreaded the thought of explaining it over and over, followed by the expressions of sympathy and the—

A pair of arms unfolded from the bot's spherical core and one of them reached toward her as a needle snapped out. It plunged the needle into her arm. San struggled, trying to remember her train of thought and keep her focus on *expressions of sympathy,* but instead descended into darkness.

Get to Ganymede Orbital Station . . .

Voices mumbled nearby, but not the one telling her to run to Ganymede and San gritted her teeth at the thought of disembodied words returning with no warning. For now, it was silent. The ones she heard were soft, *real,* and San rolled in zero g, the weightlessness a welcome relief after having been in Earth's gravity for so long, her muscles able to stretch enough that she imagined she could gain a full inch of height if she stayed weightless long enough. Then the straps bit into her wrists. Without looking San knew she was still secured to the table, trapped in a loss of time-sense that made everything surreal, fuzzy when she risked peeking from one eye.

The ship's medical officer floated next to her, grasping the table's side and flanked by bots. He spoke with two men. Both visitors wore black pressure suits with thin armor plating covered by Fleet markings that San couldn't recognize, even after scouring her mind, sifting through all the data stuffed into it; if these were Fleet markings, she *should have recognized them.* The men's faceplates were down, tinted gold to hide their features, and it sounded as if electronic masking altered their voices.

"Dump the girl."

"Until she is transferred to family," the doctor said, "I can do nothing. The regulations are clear: Medical issues must be resolved prior to release, so that injuries sustained during Fleet duty can be documented. She was in a Fleet transport when San fell ill."

"You have *orders*," one of the men said.

"*Which conflict with regulations!* I'm not endangering my career just for you people."

"Release her, Doc, or we tell your wife everything."

"Everything what?"

The other man, the one who hadn't yet spoken, pulled his colleague to the side and gestured for him to head to the hatch. He turned prior to leaving.

"About the brothels. The drugs. The girlfriends. Then we cancel university allowances for your children. They'll never find a job other than dock maintenance in occupied Singapore. San Kyarr isn't Fleet responsibility anymore, and she sure as hell isn't worth the risk you're thinking of taking."

Once they'd gone, the doctor let go of San's table and curled into a ball, drifting toward the middle of the room where he cried. The sight unnerved San. The man was much older than her, well into his forties, and for some reason it felt as though he was too old to be afraid. Her father had never cried, not even at his end. She remembered only laughter and the occasional outburst of anger when his frustrations with Fleet regulations boiled over, but these were rare and her father was there—always—when she finished a tank session. San recalled how he'd help her dry off just before playfully snapping the towel and then scooping her into both arms.

But he never cried. He'd even grinned while whispering his last words: *"Never a reason to fear if you're on the right path."*

"I hear things," San said. They'd strapped her to a guidance gurney, which used tiny jets and magnetic-field generators to make sure she couldn't bump into walls or hatches while the doctor pushed her through narrow ship's corridors. Crew members watched as the two passed.

The doctor nodded. "I know."

"What's wrong with me? What happened? I don't remember anything after the space elevator in Charleston."

"We're at Phobos Station. Your mother is waiting to take you home."

"But what *happened*?"

The doctor grabbed a handle on the gurney and stopped their forward motion by using his other hand to press against the wall; the corridor was empty. He glanced around to make sure nobody listened and leaned close to San, whispering.

"You lost your mind and tried to steal an escape pod, almost killing two crewmen in the process. The whole time you were screaming about having to get to Ganymede Orbital Station. There is no orbital station on Ganymede. So I ran some tests and found something with your brain. It's ... changing."

Get to Ganymede ...

"There's a voice in my head, even right now. It's an old woman *telling* me I have to get to Ganymede. Why is my brain changing and what do you mean?"

The doctor started pushing her again, floating behind the gurney. "It's a kind of tumor, but one which is snaking itself throughout your neurons and tissue. Inoperable. We haven't had time to do a biopsy but the remote reading indicates it's a novel type, causing auditory hallucinations. The voice isn't real, San; try to remind yourself every time you hear it. New synapses are growing at a rate that's impossible and if we didn't have you dosed on pain killers, your head would feel as though it's splitting in two."

"Who were those men?" she asked. "The two men in black pressure suits who came to speak with you."

"The less you know, the better. I don't know who you are or why you're so interesting to them, and I don't *want* to know. I just want you off this ship."

At the airlock, two crewmen punched in a key code so the inner door cycled with a hiss and one of them pulled the circular hatch toward them. The doctor nudged her into the tiny room. Both San and he waited for the door to seal behind them, which triggered the outer door to hiss open, after which he glided through, yanking San's gurney. He didn't get far before a woman's voice cried out.

Her mother looked worse than when San had left. Even weightless, the woman's spine twisted so badly from infection that she stooped into a near C shape, her bone disintegrating and muscles tightening. San's father had looked the same before he died. She fought back tears at the sight before noticing something else had changed: Her mother, Nang, wore a black robe over her pressure suit and long hair had now been cropped close, almost bald. *Nobody told me,* San thought, *she had joined an order.* The robe was so dark that its shadows gave birth to shadows, drawing her focus so that the vision, combined with the drugs administered earlier, pulled her into a darkness which encased San's thoughts. *The Church,* she thought. It had risen from the death of obscurity and emerged from the catacombs of time, reasserting itself with at least enough vigor to have captured her mother in its grasp.

San began sobbing in the microgravity of Phobos Station; tears welled and detached, drifting toward air recirculation intakes along the corridor floor, one droplet larger than the others. *Maybe if I can concentrate hard enough, it will block the voice.* At first it worked; the water undulated in gentle air currents, back and forth, then settled into a perfect sphere that reflected the ambient lighting in a display of sparkling flashes.

Get to Ganymede Orbital Station . . .

San started screaming. She stopped when her mother grabbed her hand. "I'm here, San. You must be strong. This is not the end."

"I'm going insane."

"No. You are not. This is only part of your journey. Your father and I decided to take this course long ago, when you were still inside me and I do not regret a thing."

"You made me a short, fat *creature.* And now I've failed at what I've been designed to do. Where do I go now, especially now that I have a brain tumor?"

Her mother smiled again and used the sleeve of her habit to wipe the tears off San's cheek, then turned to the ship's doctor. Her voice became stern. The commanding tone made San feel safe—a child again—and she was almost certain her mother would fix this.

"I work in one of the research institutes planet-side. Why is my daughter strapped down like an animal?"

"Ms. Vongchanh, this is Fleet's decision. I don't have the authority—"

"Fleet," her mother said, "has abandoned my child. They have no say here. What happened? She was fine when she left."

Their voices disappeared. San saw the doctor's lips move but it was as if a throbbing hum swallowed all sound and before she knew it he had grabbed the gurney handle again and San flew through Phobos Station's tunnels. The voice again materialized in her head, intruding into her thoughts: *watch and remember.*

The odor of humans trapped inside a rock hit San, making her wince with the smell of recycled sweat and disinfectant, just enough chlorine spray to prevent mold from growing within pools of condensation. Phobos reminded her of a prison. Narrow cylinders had been carved into the moon's rock, with silver handrails that its occupants used to pull themselves along in microgravity. San tried to grab one, forgetting that she couldn't move, but her arm came free of the straps and both hands moved through the rail, which gave no resistance at all. *You're hallucinating again,* she thought. As if to confirm, San now floated off the gurney at the same moment a man emerged from another corridor and passed through her body, so that she began to wonder if she had died. *How else could this be possible? I am a thing made of air and consciousness, nothing else—a phantom soul.* The humming volume increased to a roar, drowning her thoughts, and the voice reminded her to watch so that San concentrated, following her mother's flowing black robe while they moved past another docking airlock. This one had been emblazoned with the warning symbols of a ship preparing for imminent departure. San stopped; she pressed her face closer to the screen, which danced in a series of red and green data markers, the shorthand of Fleet and indecipherable to anyone but those practiced in the vagaries of logistics and space port regulations.

She absorbed every detail, taking in every system status no matter how inconsequential: a scout ship, military—fueled and waiting for its pilot who was returning from Mars' surface in just a few hours.

Get to Ganymede Orbital Station . . .

A memory flooded her thoughts: Fleet had needed something.

Her father had been the key to one of their research programs but even now San sensed secrets behind secrets in her mother's face, tensed muscles causing her jaw to quiver with the stress of knowing a thing that *nobody* would want to know, and San had once asked why her father had been so important. She'd asked it on the day of the accident, via vid-coms; both her parents had been quarantined. The one thing her mother had admitted was that a bacterial vector had been used for something. *For what? Genetic alterations? What could have been so new and important that such an ancient and unreliable vector would have been risked?* Whatever the reason, her mother had mumbled that either the vector had mutated or that it hadn't been understood in the first place and she and three other scientists had exposed themselves before anyone knew there was a problem. Then, just as suddenly as they'd been quarantined, the infection vanished.

Within a week her mother and father had been released from medical lockdown and for a few weeks the fear vanished. The tests had been successful and her father had called, grinning from ear to ear to let her know that the experiments had been completed and Fleet no longer needed him—or the cybernetic portion of his brain— for poking and prodding. That's when San had first heard the name *Zhelnikov*. She'd never met the man. But the tone of her father's voice said everything she needed to know: Zhelnikov was evil. San's father *never* spoke with that quiet and even tone unless it was in reference to something despicable.

A few days later, her father started coughing. It soon grew into a hacking so bad that he'd gone to medical and one day they'd pulled San from the tanks, calling her to the Fleet training administrator who gave her the news. Both her mother and father were dying. Whatever had infected them had altered her parents' DNA and touched off a human self-destruct sequence that was working its way through their brain cells and spine, shutting everything down; the best doctors could do was slow the wasting. But with her father's brain makeup, where so much of his gray matter had been replaced, he had only lasted a few months.

Soon, I will also lose my mother—because of Fleet.

San yanked herself from thought and glanced around. The pair waited in a tiny sleeping cubicle where Mars' orbital station surrounded them with its hum and made it hard to talk, Phobos so small that the noise of supporting machinery echoed through the rock. The walls rang with metallic sounds and clanking.

"It's good to see you again, Daughter."

"I washed out."

The woman kissed San's forehead. "You don't see the future. There is a plan and you're part of it; don't give up even if you can't see the point."

"What's wrong with me?"

"Well..." Nang's voice cracked; her face looked worn with thin wrinkles that hadn't been there when San left, lines that made her ancient instead of middle-aged. "They say you may have an aggressive brain tumor. But I have never trusted in the wisdom of physicians; they rely on diagnostic equipment, algorithms, and bots that, if they can't identify an illness, conclude it must be deadly. You don't have a tumor; you have something *similar* to a tumor. The two are *not* the same."

San looked away. "You are a Proelian now. A nun? Why? There is no faith anymore; you raised me in the Church, and I don't feel any closer to it."

"I think I've always been a Proelian at heart. I just hid it from your father. He was very Buddhist and I didn't want to cause any arguments between us. The universe is changing, San; it's smaller than we thought. I have learned much about the Sommen during my time on Mars and you will too. They gave something to the Proelians: hope, and a way to grow. Now the Church rebounds. It has finally come out of hiding and in just a pair of decades our order has found its home throughout Fleet-occupied territories. You are on the side of good. But you have to have faith."

"Tell me now. What about the Sommen gave you faith?"

"It's not time. You still have to be tested and you're young. But when you learn, you will understand. There is evil within Fleet, and evil outside."

Those words. The drugs had begun to wear off, but still San's brain refused to function normally and she had to concentrate, finally recalling where she'd heard them before.

"Sister Mirriam-Ann said the same thing. When will I understand?" She looked down at the straps still binding her to the gurney and realized there was no way for her to break free; they were too secure, too tight.

"Soon. Someday. For now we return to Mars; the shuttle won't be here for a few hours but when it arrives we can board."

"No. I have to leave. I'm not losing it, Mom; I just need to find out what's going on at Ganymede. You told me how Dad had to run to escape from investigators in Charleston, when you first met him. I have to do the same thing. Something is happening to me and I don't get it."

"San." The woman wiped a tear from her cheek and shook her head. "Stop this."

"*I'm not crazy!*" San told her about her vision of a scout ship preparing to leave Phobos, including the name of its pilot, its manifest number, and ship numerical identifier. The memory was fresh, a photographic image stored in her mind. "I don't know why or how, but I know that I have to get on that ship and someone or something is guiding me."

Her mother gaped in disbelief. The woman then pushed off from the wall and the door hissed open. Before pulling herself outside into the corridor, she turned and shook her head.

"San, if this turns out to be wrong and you only imagined all those details from the ship's manifest, will you stop talking this way and agree you need help?"

"Okay."

"I wish your father were here; we need his abilities."

"For what?"

"Wait." Her mother unsecured the gurney and pulled it toward the cubicle door, looking both ways in the corridor outside. "Because he would be able to access the station's logic systems—to see if we're being monitored and surveilled. And he would be able to find that ship without having to venture outside."

"What difference would that make? I'm strapped in and can't go anywhere."

Her mother unsecured the straps, freeing both wrists and ankles. San stretched. Her muscles ached from being pinned to one position for so long and the webbing had chafed so that she had to rub them for a few moments, urging the pain to subside. She hugged her mother, who felt so frail that San imagined a strong embrace might crush her.

Eventually she pushed San away. "Go. Get to that shuttle. If it's there and you got the details right, then take it. Head to Ganymede while station security is too confused to react. If your vision was wrong or it's not there, come with me to Mars. Come home."

"What? You're not going to argue with me anymore and just let me go? What if Fleet finds out you're responsible for my escape?"

Her mother smiled and then hugged her again. "You're not a prisoner, San. And there's much you need to learn, but I can't tell you. If you feel so strongly about this that you're willing to risk everything, then what you're hearing... it might be real." Her mother then shrugged. "Besides. I will tell them I was asleep and have no *idea* how you freed yourself. Don't trust everyone in Fleet—only in God. He will watch over you. Whatever you do, do not trust Zhelnikov. He created something awful, which neither I nor your father wanted you to face."

"*What the hell is going on?*"

"You don't know yet what we're up against, what your father and I were working on for all these years. There are competing weapons research programs, empires and fortunes of power. When you learn more about why we're preparing for a war, one most don't even know is coming, you'll understand." She kissed San on the cheek and then pushed her away. "Go. Find the path you must take. I will be gone the next time you reach Mars so know this: I love you. Soon, I and your father will be watching while you make us proud."

San struggled to hold back tears and did her best to remember the smell and feel of her mother, not knowing what the future held. Tears blinded her. By the time she blinked them away, minutes had passed but the corridor ahead remained empty. She crept forward and gripped the guide rail to keep from spinning head over foot, stopping a few meters away at a computer terminal. After a few taps, a web of green lines and dots popped up. Her mind struggled to concentrate through the pain, and she dug into the data that Fleet had fed into her gray matter during all those years of instruction, cable connected into semi-awares and simulation tanks. Soon she'd accessed the scout ship's logs: specifications, navigation data, and Phobos Station docking details; they all matched what she had seen earlier. San pieced together the start of a plan, and then traced the lines on the terminal's map to the point where she found the maintenance shops. She headed deeper into the center of Mars' moon, where the clanking sounds got even louder and a roar of air handling enveloped her.

A group of men laughed. The sound echoed through the narrow shaft and recycled air carried with it a tinge of ozone mixed with oil, almost making San cough. Ahead of her a thick pressure hatch rested in the open position and bright blue light spilled into an access shaft, which otherwise was lit by dim LEDs placed to show handholds carved into the rock. San took a deep breath. Her heart pounded and threatened to shake her chest into pieces but she ignored the sensation and pulled her way to the hatch, slipping into the small compartment beyond.

"I need help. Do any of you have a set of torx drivers and needle-nose pliers I can borrow? Or a spare fix-all?"

The men said nothing. Then one of them pulled on an e-cig and puffed a cloud of vapor into the air, which drifted across and between them, eventually sucked into an air intake. Three maintenance personnel sat strapped onto makeshift chairs around an empty cable spool bolted to the rock to form a table, upon which they had been playing cards. The cards were magnetized. One of the men slapped his hand to rest on the metal table and stood, placing his other hand against the low ceiling to keep from bouncing upward.

"What they do to you, tiny?" he asked. He and the others were long and thin, crammed into the space—native Martians, the opposite of San in appearance.

"You mean why am I so short?"

"You aren't just short," another one said. "You remind me of a cube of that old stuff people used to eat. Spam. They took meat and poured it into a block-mold."

San's face went hot with embarrassment. "Yeah, funny. Look, do you have tools I can borrow or not?"

The first one nodded and grabbed a belt from a wall locker. "What you need fixed? I'll do it."

"My mother and I are waiting for the next transport and her oxygen generator is acting up. I know how to use a fix-all."

All three laughed, confusing San; she hadn't made a joke. She'd been gone for a month but already Mars was a foreign land, the men's accents out of place, and if this was no longer home where was it?

The man yanked a fix-all from his belt and pushed so the tool flew across to San.

"Thanks," she said.

"It's not right what they're doing."

"What do you mean?"

"You. The others they engineered. It's not natural and they've started re-assigning normal people—*real* humans—to crap jobs. We used to be flight officers. Navigators and weapons techs. Fleet has us fixing low grav toilets and soon you won't be able to enlist with Fleet unless you turn yourself into an ugly little brick of Spam. Give me my tool back in ten minutes or I'll come find you."

San reversed out of the room. The three men glared and the hair on the back of her neck stood up so that she didn't feel safe, even after she'd reached the access shaft outside.

The main panel indicator light blinked red, indicating that the airlock had been sealed and San entertained the idea of a software hack. The idea faded; it was always easier to hot wire security doors. But her hands shook as she brought the fix-all closer to the panel because as soon as she began unscrewing the main plate, an alarm would alert Phobos Station security of unauthorized access to station systems. At best she'd have five minutes—a few more if the guards weren't paying attention to their status terminals. Even then bots would alert if the guards failed to respond, giving her ten minutes at the most.

San grabbed a nearby handhold and brought the fix-all close to the panel before activating it. It hummed to life. The square black chunk of metal dangled via a thick wire attached to a handheld terminal, and she began punching one finger on the pad, entering commands. Almost immediately, the black metal transformed. Microbots released from the chunk and swarmed over the screws, which spun then flew away, until finally the panel drifted from the wall at the end of a tangle of multicolored wires and fiber optic cables. When San heard shouting in the distance, her hands trembled again.

"*Come on!*"

She continued punching at the keyboard, ignoring the fact that she floated in the corridor, her head bumping against the ceiling. The microbots swarmed again. Now they climbed over the panel's wires and began severing connections, then glowed as they fused new ones until the red panel light turned green. The airlock door clunked open. Its servos chugged as they swung the giant metal square away from San, who dove through the gap and into the airlock.

San hit the main panel on her side of the door and waited for it to inch closed. Someone shouted from outside. She urged the door to speed up and heard the scrape of boots and metal against rock as someone moved, headed straight for her. The airlock shut with a clang. San pounded on the locking button and then activated the fix-all again, keying in instructions for the microbots to seal the door permanently. She grinned and pushed off for the scout ship's door.

Get to Ganymede...

"I am getting to Ganymede!" San yelled.

A voice crackled over a speaker inside the airlock. "San Kyarr, you're under arrest; stop what you're doing and open the inner airlock door."

"I'm sorry. I'm normally not a thief. But you'll get your ship back."

The ship's outer door had no security activated so all San had to do was palm the open button, allowing a slab to disengage and disappear into a wide slot. She pulled her way in. There, she snaked herself through narrow shafts that ran between engine and fuel compartments, barely hearing it when the ship's airlock doors shut behind her and San focused on making her way to the pilot's compartment—a cramped space near the triangular nose of the ship. She strapped into the command couch. Controls swung from the wall and encapsulated her in a confined pod so that instrument readouts and switches surrounded on all sides, the ship encircling her in a protective embrace. *This* was her natural habitat; San's hands danced across the panels, forcing the docking locks to disengage with a clank, the noise invoking an overwhelming wave of relief.

"I'll get to Ganymede," San whispered. "I'll make you both proud."

Her mother's warning still rang through San's mind: *Do not trust Zhelnikov...*

CHAPTER FIVE

Win wriggled into his straps. The servo harness encased him from head to toe in a carapace of polymer and ceramic armor, shaped for a slim frame but with a head-piece large enough to accommodate his new skull. The suit hummed as he took careful steps, suspended six feet off the ground from the middle of a metallic power pod, off of which four spiderlike articulated legs extended. The legs moved with jerks, pounding on the transport's metal grate floor as he moved down the ramp. Win wished he could scratch his head; the new jack skin was taking hold, merging with his nerves, and the itching threatened to drive him insane.

Hong Kong resembled an ocean of destruction. No buildings remained and suit sensors pulsed data across Win's heads up display: the war had sent to the city multiple nuclear weapons followed by saturation with conventional munitions. Despite the years of peace, it was as if the blasts had occurred yesterday and in the distance a few spires remained in tattered form, like the bones of fingers reaching out of Earth. A mist formed around them, raised by wind. Almost instantly the computer identified it as the breakdown products of old Allied nerve agent, safe as long as the ocean breeze continued blowing at Win's back. The immediate area in front of the transport had been cleared down to bare concrete; there, thousands of troops stood, their green combat suits lending a kind of forest appearance. As soon as Zhelnikov and Win stepped off the ramp, they snapped to attention.

I disgust them, Win thought.

He zoomed on the closest one, the man's helmet clasped in the crook of his left arm; Win tracked his forehead muscle movements and the soldier's gaze darted toward him, gawking in combined expressions of horror and fascination. *This is what revulsion looks like. They can't see me, but whatever the servo harness contains, they know it isn't human.*

"So we have *re*-conquered Hong Kong," Zhelnikov said, chuckling at his own joke. "It wasn't easy to assemble the forces needed in such a short amount of time, but luckily a Marine Expeditionary Force was already running exercises with our Korean allies. It was just as you said: a small group, maybe ten thousand Chinese hold outs who were trying to rebuild. They're all dead."

Win shook his head. "Not all of them."

He gritted his teeth at a wave of pain that coursed up his spine and into his brain. It took all Win had to stifle a scream. When it had passed he reduced the flow of standard masker, stored in pods along the side of his carapace, necking it down to a drip, the pale green fluid travelling through a narrow tube that passed into a port affixed to Win's skull.

"What do you mean, 'not all'?" Zhelnikov asked. "General Scheuer assures me that Hong Kong has been secured. He lost five thousand dead and eight thousand wounded, Win."

The General stepped forward from behind them. His face looked polished and as if peeling layers of an onion, Win imagined the man's appearance after stripping layered pseudo-plastic jack skin treatments that cost a small fortune to keep him looking young. The General's hair had been combed into an immaculate coif.

"I assure you: my Marines got them all."

"*No.*"

"Son, what the hell are you talking about?"

Win spun to face the General, extending the spider-legs so that he looked down on the man. The General stepped back.

"You chase young men. Boys. I've seen this. There are thousands of children, still alive and being monitored and stored in a makeshift camp near the amphibious landing area. You plan on using them for pleasure and sale."

"I . . . I have no idea what you're talking about." The General's face went bright red and he pointed a finger at Zhelnikov. "If this is some kind of scheme, Zhelnikov, I swear to God I'll destroy you . . ."

"Not one of mine." When Zhelnikov glanced sideways, Win recognized the old man's expression of concern; Zhelnikov was signaling: this General had connections.

"I see truth and lies," said Win. He lowered himself and turned back to the troops. "Nobody here is scheming except you. You're visible to me—everything. On the way in I spent the time working with multiple semi-awares to scan for patterns in your behavior and purchasing, who you've bribed, identifying trusted brokers and cutouts for the human trafficking ring you've established. But I needn't have taken that route. Your voice and face tell the story." The General spun to walk away, but stopped when Win continued. "One more step and I report everything. You'll spend the rest of your days cleaning radioactive waste off the streets of Pyongyang. I'd hate to see all that jack skin go bad."

"What the hell is this, Zhelnikov?"

"He had nothing to do with this," said Win. "I don't need Zhelnikov. Not for seeing. You are so obvious that it amazes me someone hasn't killed you slowly."

"You son of a bitch," the General growled. "What do you want?"

"I want them dead. The children."

Zhelnikov shook his head. "Impossible. Those children were leftovers from their research programs. Rejects that are fully formed humans—not engineered for merging with machines. With care, they can be turned into relatively normal people, Win."

"Normal is not in our modern vocabulary. And it's not me that demands their death, it's the Sommen." Win extended one leg to point at the troops and then turned his head to look at the General. "Kill all the children. And I want to inspect the Chinese production nests. When I'm finished, we will lace the tunnels with nuclear warheads and make this island disappear. As long as you perform, there's no need for me to speak to anyone about your . . . proclivities. I don't give a damn what you do with your time off."

The General gazed at Win briefly, before spinning on a heel and striding off the ramp; the troop formation melted. Win's vision began to shift and he had trouble concentrating on the data feed so that the green troops morphed into a sea of algae, dispersing with the tide and currents to leave only concrete. *I am seeing again,* he thought. *And if I see I will hear; I will hear the children and their slaughter.*

"Win . . ." Zhelnikov started.

"I know what you're thinking. That we will hang for killing these children because it's against the rules of war. Against the laws of men."

"I'm thinking that *because it's true*. What's happening with you? You can't just make these decisions and then bark orders as if you're in charge. You're not; *I am*."

"Do you feel in charge?"

Zhelnikov shook his head. "Damn it, Win. I'm stopping this."

"No. If you do that, the Sommen will return and you will have doomed all of us to extinction. Why? *Because of children*. These children are already prepared to permanently merge with semi-awares and they must die to show the Sommen we understand. To fail in this would be an act of war, a violation of the treaty; tell your masters this and they will understand."

Win glared at Zhelnikov and for a moment his vision returned to normal, at least to the point where Zhelnikov's face and body were clear except at the edges, vibrating and shifting colors. The old man reached for a pocket. He lit a cigar and Win saw the stressors of decision force Zhelnikov to stoop just a bit lower. The creaking and popping of bones was almost audible. One more slaughter on the pile of Zhelnikov's already sizeable heap had added weight and Win wondered if he was too old for war.

"You're changing quickly, Win. This isn't what I anticipated."

"Relax, Zhelnikov; I'm not *yet* Sommen, and will likely be something different altogether. Come." Win moved, his metallic legs stuttering across the concrete in clicks. "I have to inspect the Chinese nest soon; those idiot Marines could destroy the very things I need to see."

"Wait. I have something."

The old man lifted his suit helmet and spoke into its mouthpiece before lowering it again, attaching it to hang from his belt. Win heard marching. From the other side of the transport a long line of soldiers emerged, each of them dressed in black battle dress, thin armored plates so matte they almost sucked light from the sky. *Safety never came from the minds and ideas of even the most genius of men. War is the way. Safety is a byproduct, a temporary condition resulting from the death of one's current enemies and the creation of fear in those who will emerge in the future. Earth's historic generals even had a name for it: deterrence.*

"These men are for you," said Zhelnikov.

"I recognize them. These boys."

"How? I had them made in secret, hidden even from you. These are the top candidates sourced from infants taken out of brothel orphanages, culled and sifted using over a thousand variables, all of which center on combat. On killing. These men are more deadly than any you've ever seen and they answer to you and me alone."

These men will disappear, Win thought. *I will not remain on Earth for long, and nothing will protect me from what is coming.* And Zhelnikov had done something to them; something to their faces . . .

"Why do you think I need boys encased in ceramic? And you've replaced their eyes with something I've never seen. Something new."

"They are your guard. And yes; so that they maintain adequate vision in all environments we swapped their biological eyes with combat models; it's classified tech developed on Mars. This way they can always see as if they wear helmets, whether they wear them or not."

And this way you can tap their visual feed to keep tabs on me, Win thought. *And you got this technology from vivisecting my father, slowly, over the course of years.*

"I will be in danger for all time," he said. "I have seen the future; it does not include these guards."

"Normal troops hate you, Win. Especially if you give orders to kill children. Yes; you're in danger and you need a personal guard. These boys are perfect. And their training included constant operation in your virtual presence, as you are now."

"So they won't even blink at the fact that when I take my helmet off I'm a monster—excreting fluid from my head and drooling because of the lack of some muscle control in my jaw. You've thought of everything."

Zhelnikov was about to respond but Win pushed past toward a distant gap in the rubble. He sped. Behind, the troop of guards jogged to keep up and Zhelnikov shouted *wait,* but Win was in a hurry and knew that the man could find a vehicle. First there was a thing to do. He had seen it in the vision provided by Sommen, a vault deep inside the Chinese nest far beneath Hong Kong and the path to access it. Win closed his eyes to avoid the data feed scrawling across his screen, instead putting his servos on auto-traverse, making sure the shaking framework maintained a low enough speed so the guards could keep up.

Zhelnikov will not have the strength to see the truth; his schemes are abortive. I do not yet see the way, but I smell the futility of a genius with no clear vision. Even without clear sight, the future had at least been traced in faint pencil: mankind as a whole would be enlisted in the war, with their children, creeping toward a genetic shift that blurred the lines between Sommen and humanity. *Their faith will be our faith. Children will live and breathe in the immersion tanks, fed combat training and mathematics, strategy and tactics, and their toys will be Maxwell carbines and worse. The hope of mankind will be rekindled in the fires of war, a fire that they would never let die and that their children's children would carry into the universe as the Sommen had done for millennia. I am alive and my role is already written: glory and, one day, galactic empire.*

Win stopped. It took a second for the guard troops to pull even but none of them looked out of breath and they stood at attention, waiting for his next move. He checked his vitals. Everything read normal, but Win knew the thoughts he'd had just a moment ago weren't something he'd have had even the previous day, and not prior to the standard masker. His fate felt locked to a track. There was no turning away now, and the locomotive of destiny pushed along a straight path toward an ocean of blood; Win was already drooling from the continued dosages, but the thought of killing made him salivate faster.

"The place we're looking for is just ahead. We'll wait there for Zhelnikov and then move underground into the Chinese nest."

"That zone is still showing chemical agent signatures," one of the guards said.

"So? Secure your helmets."

By the time they reached the entry tunnel, Zhelnikov pulled up in a tracked transport that spat dust as it whined through the rubble to release him out the rear hatch. The old man wore armor like the guards', jet black with a skull and crossbones on the shoulder pieces, but he also wore a phase-shifter cloak that he activated while walking toward them. In less than a second, most of him disappeared. Win's visible light sensors picked up a shimmer where the cloak mimicked Zhelnikov's surroundings, but nothing else.

This is how someone will get to me. When I can't see a face and read expressions, my enemy will spring the trap.

"I'm ready," said Zhelnikov. "This place is off-gassing nerve agent still; we need to be careful."

Win pointed at the guards. "Which one of them is in charge of the others?"

"None. All of them will die to protect us."

"There are over a hundred men here. How many did you kill? The ones that didn't meet specifications."

"I stopped counting, Win; that isn't something worthy of remembrance."

Win's legs squealed, their joints becoming rough with an intrusion of dust and concrete particles, but they carried him toward the tunnel entrance where the group plunged into darkness; he switched to infrared. His helmet spotlight scanned the way ahead and illuminated the tunnel to reveal the wreckage of Chinese weaponry, dead soldiers peppering the corridor as it spiraled downward. *They are the same; these men are as me.* Each soldier was a mixture of metal and mechanical legs, spiderlike, in the middle of which rested a carapace containing a form—the remains of genetically engineered occupants consisting of a head and torso hard-wired into the shell's battle computer. Just enough brain matter to make a deadly weapon. The guards paused at each one, plunging knives into the corpses to make sure all of them were deceased.

"They haven't changed their design since my father fought them," Win said.

Zhelnikov nodded. "These ones weren't interested in research and development."

"It was always a poor choice, and its future variations always will be. The Chinese put too much faith in automation and semi-awares. Had they succeeded in destroying us they would have eventually been taken over by their own research and mankind would have been lost forever. The Sommen are right to want them all dead."

"It worries me—the speed with which you adopt their philosophies."

"I thought that *was* your plan."

"Never mind the plan; do you even know where we're going?"

Win reviewed his vision. The corridor would bring them hundreds of meters beneath the city in a coiled snake of a passageway and then open into a complex labyrinth of chambers and tubes, the ant farms of Hong Kong. He tracked the group's progress, overlaying in his thoughts their location from his vision. There had been something else; Win recalled the memory of what he'd seen of Zhelnikov's master plan for fighting the Sommen and while they walked he traced each line from memory, pausing to consider the implications, fighting to reconstruct the portions that he'd already begun to forget. A new pattern emerged. Win glanced at Zhelnikov, unable to see him except for where his boots kicked rubble or scraped through piles of dust, and a scrap of respect for the man began to take shape; he'd almost succeeded in hiding one of his objectives.

"My father had another child," said Win.

Zhelnikov stopped and pulled the hood from his helmet; Win paused too, and the guards took up defensive positions.

"How did you know?"

"I only just realized. When I read you, back in England on the cliffs, I saw some of your plans. You don't understand, Zhelnikov; I see things I don't even want to. They're forced on me as if my mind is a bottomless garbage bag, into which the universe can stuff as much as it wants. It comes and goes."

"And so you had a vision of her."

"Her? So I have a sister. No, that's not what I said. Your plans gave her and others away. I'm one of two different experimental programs, aren't I? There is another one—one funded via Fleet Acquisition and Logistics, one you want eliminated."

Zhelnikov remained silent. Dripping water sounded in the distance and an occasional chunk of concrete fell, cracking on the floor like an echo of gun fire. Win marveled at the strangeness of it all. With a flick of concentration he viewed the universe as if he'd been the one to create it and its network of matter, a kind of nervous system that consisted of energy and dust punctuated by wormholes and warfare, with a Sommen trail of destruction cutting across everything. He was part of its fabric. There in the tunnels they all played a role, minor but connected via a thin trail of quantum particles, their interaction tangled and related, joining into a greater web, one that wrapped itself around everything and everyone—so real that Win wondered why this was the first time he'd seen it, and why he couldn't *feel* its suffocation.

I will become too dangerous and they will erase me. Unlike the soldiers who didn't perform to expectations in simulations, I will be taken out by those who fear my perfection and my power. My sister will help destroy me, although she won't even realize what she does.

"It doesn't matter," Win said, continuing onward. "You don't have to answer. We must finish before the Marines arrive."

"Why the rush? We can delay the nuclear weapons detonations as long as we need."

"You don't want anyone else to see what I'm going to show you, Zhelnikov. The Chinese didn't just run; they are committing suicide. And they want us to come along."

Win increased the power of his infrared light, playing it back and forth across a long empty room where a single Chinese soldier now writhed, gurgling from its blown open carapace. He drove one of the servo harness's legs through the thing, ending its agony. Beyond the dead soldier stood gigantic columns of equipment and machinery that reached upward into darkness. *It is a forest of metal,* thought Win. *These are the only kinds of trees I'll ever see in real life, now that I'm engaged in war; destruction will precede me. I'm here to review the hells I create.*

"This is almost identical to our original design," Zhelnikov said. "They stole our technology."

"Not yet operational, however."

"What was their plan? Activate the communications device, punch a hole through an alternate universe, and send messages out into space? To their brethren—to whatever system the rest of the Chinese forces ran years ago?"

"That was exactly their plan. But the Chinese have no idea that this communications system could bring unwanted attention—and not just from the Sommen."

Zhelnikov spat against the closest column of equipment. "Then the Chinese Fleet, out there, also has the plans. They are probably building one too and could activate it. Soon."

"Yes. This is also likely."

"You're calm," Zhelnikov began with a mutter, but his voice rose to a shout. "For someone who knows better than anyone *that the Sommen themselves are terrified about what's out there, Win!*"

Win froze. Another bolus of standard masker merged with his bloodstream and coursed through his brain, seeping into the neurons and forcing growth of cells, extending old ones to twist into a sea of looping brain tissue. He screamed with the pain. It wormed its way through his nervous system in a river of needles and acid, forcing Win's breathing into a tattered series of short gasps, only ending when he'd reached the verge of unconsciousness. In its wake a new image appeared: a single Sommen. This wasn't a warrior, he realized. The Sommen's body looked emaciated and frail, suspended in a tank of pale fluid, almost clear, with an oversized and grotesque head covered with nodules as if the thing had become diseased with age. Win knew nothing of their biology, but this one's physiology and bearing had marked it as a Sommen that mattered.

"You are becoming one of us," it whispered. The sound materialized within Win's head, out of nowhere.

"Who are you?"

"You. We are you."

The Sommen repeated the phrase several times and a hologram appeared. It showed the Earth, spinning, with a single red dot that blinked and shifted in intensity.

"There," the Sommen said, its hologram fading. "You must begin to see the truth: that you are a mistake."

"Win!" Zhelnikov shouted.

The guards had gathered around them both, and Zhelnikov pounded on Win's carapace, reaching to pop the access cover for the life support system. Win stepped back before the man could finish.

"I'm fine."

"We've been trying to talk with you for over ten minutes. What happened?"

"We need to go, Zhelnikov. Have the Marines nuke all of this. We need to leave now."

"What the hell are you talking about? Where do we need to go?"

"Portugal. There is something in Portugal and we have to get there. Fast."

CHAPTER SIX

Ganymede's broken surface sped past, the monotonous grays and whites punctuated with craters and ice fissures that, San guessed, would have dwarfed the canyons on her home planet of Mars. It was her fiftieth orbit. The ship's fuel gauge blinked a warning that meant she had a few more passes, after which San would have to land and deploy melting mats. *That* process was difficult even with a team. In this case San would have to land the ship and then drag out the massive network of cables before erecting the tent and collection system, which would route sublimated steam into collection tanks for conversion to oxygen and hydrogen. She didn't want to visit Ganymede alone. The planet looked dead, and San recalled something her father had said: *if you die in space your soul could be lost forever; die where your ancestors can find you.*

She laughed at herself. *This is what I was bred for,* San reasoned, *to travel in space, and I'm too scared to do it?* For the hundredth time she ran through the ship's sensor diagnostics system, making sure she hadn't missed something.

"Ganymede orbital, do you copy?" San had set the radio's power to its lowest limit, hoping Jupiter's magnetic fields would prevent the signal from going too far. Out here, she thought, anyone could listen.

"Ganymede orbital, this is an uncharted scout ship requesting emergency docking; do you copy?"

Still no response came. San reached for the console, about to shut off her radio to conserve power for water collection when a woman's voice broke through the static.

"Transmit docking code."

San's hands shook; she increased radio power to make sure her response got through. "I don't have any codes; I told you I'm unchartered."

"Transmit docking code," the voice repeated.

"Are you receiving? I do *not have* a code."

"Transmit docking code."

"This is an unchartered ship. I have no codes. I'm low on fuel and request permission to dock. Where is your location, Ganymede orbital? I have no fix on your position and all sensors are blank."

"Transmit docking code..."

The voice repeated itself and faded into static when San's ship transited around the moon, moving further from the signal's source. She slapped the console in frustration. San muttered into her mouthpiece, ordering her semi-aware computer to calculate the most likely location for the transmission based on her positional changes while receiving. It took less than a second. The answer blinked in a holo that rested in the air and San reached out to touch it, her mouth open in disbelief. There was no orbital station, or, at least, the transmission hadn't come from one; it came from a point at the bottom of an enormous canyon a few kilometers below a flat plain of ice that surrounded it. She never would have received the signal if her ship hadn't traversed an area directly above it.

San plotted a new course. The computer's voice, its suggestions and warnings of low fuel weaving into her calculations, faded with concentration. She started the burn but a feeling in her gut—that she would have only just enough fuel to land as long as everything went perfectly—made her palms sweat.

The white and gray on her screens transformed into a vision of blue and light blue, with a wisp of an atmosphere that sent a shiver through her craft when it entered, spiraling in a wide corkscrew toward the surface and bleeding as much velocity as it could against what little gas existed above the moon. The computer counted down. When it reach zero, San closed her eyes against the g-forces of the ship's retros, which threw her against seat restraints. She grunted for breath, wondering how much worse it would be for someone *not* genetically engineered for these forces. They wouldn't have made it, San figured. With the deceleration she'd used, anyone with the wrong physiology would have suffered retinal detachment, suffocation, and blackout. At the very least, they'd need a hospital after landing.

"*Landing beacon detected,*" her computer announced.

"Location?"

"Immediately adjacent to the radio transmissions, which have stopped. Two-point-three kilometers below the ice plane we currently traverse, two hundred kilometers ahead."

"Make for it and land."

"This ship cannot land; we have not received clearance."

San worried that maybe her hack hadn't been thorough enough or that the stolen scout ship's semi-aware had detected it and began to unravel the codes, pushing its way back toward realizing that San wasn't an authorized pilot. That would be a disaster. With no fuel left, if the thing's security program ordered it to launch in the direction of the closest Fleet post, she could find herself flung into space again to coast for God knew how long. Her fingers tapped on the consoles, only stopping when she was sure her code was fine.

"I said land. Override normal landing procedures."

"*Landing now.*"

"And let me out of the bridge confinement; I need to put on an environment suit so notify me when we're about to set down."

"*Understood, miss.*"

It took San a few minutes to find the ship's suit locker, and Ganymede's weak gravity tugged at her, pulling her to the floor so that she stumbled twice. Despite zero-g drugs and her engineering, San still had to reacclimatize. By the time she buckled on the massive globe of a Scout's helmet, the computer finished counting down when the ship scraped against ice, and she squeezed her way toward the air lock. Its inner door slid shut behind her. Air cycled out of the narrow room and while the pumps chugged San's forehead dampened; she ignored a sense of growing nervousness, slamming her fist against a large button to lower the loading ramp, which opened onto canyon shadows, her suit lights flickering on to illuminate the way down.

San looked up. Jupiter filled the opening far above and the sight made San dizzy so that she stumbled in the light gravity, having to skip sideways to maintain balance. Her boots crunched in a thick layer of coarse ice crystals as she moved closer to the canyon wall.

San imagined the weight of the universe as it crushed down on her, the distance to her mother so infinite that she guessed the woman dead already and that Nang's soul had merged with Jupiter's gaseous maelstrom, which refused to release anything from its red grip. Tears formed, blurring her vision.

"Show me the location ellipse for the signal, damn it," San radioed.

Green lines of a topo-map popped onto the glass of her helmet, showing her as a red arrow that now moved toward a blinking red ellipse. It distracted her from the sadness. A breeze consisting of almost nothing blew overhead, outside the canyon, and San looked up to see a faint shower of silver flakes cascading off the canyon lip so they settled into shadow, whispering a reminder to stay in the present and forget—for now—what couldn't be changed.

"There's nothing there. It's just more ice."

"That is the beacon location," the ship insisted.

"Recalculate and make..."

San stopped talking when movement caught her attention. Part of the canyon ice in front of her gave way and sent a shower of shards onto the shelf, the faint Ganymede atmosphere transmitting the noise to her audio pickups as a soft thud, almost inaudible. Warm yellow light spilled from the opening, out of which a small figure shuffled, a person wearing a black environment suit whose thick armor plating had been emblazoned with white crosses. The figure wore a phase shifter. Its cloak rose in another light breeze, the moon's gravity so weak that San imagined it would continue to billow upward, carrying its wearer aloft on a pale kite.

"I've seen you," she whispered, forgetting that her radio was active.

"Of course you've seen me, child. If you couldn't see us, you never would have found your way." The voice was that of an old woman. It cracked but San sensed a tone of command, carrying threats that never had to be enunciated; they just *were*.

"Come." The woman motioned for San to move toward the opening. "You're the last one to arrive, San Kyarr, and we'll have to get rid of that damn scout ship you stole."

"There's a voice. I hear things."

"Have you had a serious head injury or are you simple and dim-witted from birth? Of course you heard a voice. We sent that message. And I know what you're wondering: no there is no orbital station on Ganymede. We couldn't very well send our exact coordinates because if one of you got captured and was forced to talk, you'd give it away."

"But I had to *steal* a ship. To get here."

The woman sighed. "Yes. And every one of your classmates stole a civilian ship. But not you. You stole a military vessel, a Fleet fast scout equipped with semi-aware logic controllers and, with them, a closet full of tracking devices."

The woman turned and shuffled back toward the opening in the canyon wall, returning to the yellow light. "I won't repeat myself. Get inside or die out here on the shelf. It's the last choice you'll get to make for some time."

San bounced after the woman, moving side to side to minimize her upward arc. She bounded through an outer airlock door, just as it slid shut to cut her off from the outside, from Ganymede, and the two removed their helmets.

The old woman wore the head covering of a nun and a small line of stubble at the top of her forehead suggested she'd shaved her head bald. "You're a Proelian," San said.

"Of course I'm a *Proelian*. What did you think? That *Fleet* would send you a message and convince you to steal one of their ships?"

"No … I mean … I don't understand. Why is your order out here, in space? How did you get here?"

"There is so much for you to learn, child. The lucky thing is that you've *already* learned it. All we have to do is unlock your mind."

The inner door opened and San stopped, placing a gloved hand against one wall and squinting in the yellow light cast by illum-bots— spherical things that kept aloft in the low gravity by squirting invisible jets of gas—whose lower sections shone with a string of old incandescent lights. *The walls,* she marveled. San removed one of her suit gloves to touch wood, *real wood beams,* that stretched upward to form curves that met at a sharp point overhead, reminding her of the pictures she'd seen of old churches and cathedrals on Earth. San had never been in one. But the wood felt and even smelled real, giving an odor that screamed of ancient Earth and history, as if the material had recorded memories in its cellulose, recollections stretching back centuries.

"It's from Rome," the woman said. "The wood is original. Come. You're already late and we have to open that brain of yours to let all the junk out."

"Rome? On Earth?"

"What other Rome is there, child?"

"But how did you get it all here? It must have cost a fortune. Where did you get the resources to pay for it?"

"If I tell you, will you please hurry and follow me?"

San nodded.

"The Sommen. They recovered as much old structural material that they could from our churches and cathedrals, and gave us this place; it only took them a month to build. It was the one way we could have survived the wars on Earth. Since then, Fleet has added to it."

"The Sommen? But how . . ."

The old woman cut her off. "No more questions. *Move.*"

The pair bounced down to the corridor's end where it opened into an arched antechamber, artificial candles humming to life. Against one wall was a row of cubicles. The old woman gestured to one, moving into her own cubicle at the other end.

"Get in and take off your environment suit. There will be a pair of coveralls and a cloak for warmth. We minimize temperature controls to conserve power."

"But what . . ."

"Get dressed and meet me by the double doors. The time for questions will come, child."

San closed the door and shivered. Cold air already made its way into her suit at the neck and once she pulled off her second gauntlet, the air pushed its way through her undersuit. Her teeth chattered. The coveralls were plain green ones, a thick wool material backed with a layer of cotton on the inside, over which she draped a cream-colored woolen cloak that clipped across her neck, finishing with soft boots slipped onto her feet. By the time she exited the old woman already waited outside, frowning while she grasped the frame of large, wooden double doors.

"You are slow."

San struggled to keep the cloak from waving around her face. "Why these clothes? Why not a jacket that won't constantly get in the way and why wool? There are better fabrics, synthetic ones."

"Discomfort is a tool. It stimulates nerve endings to help break down mental resistance, a little at a time. When the mind's edges fray, the rest of it opens to experience. Stress and agony will be your closest companions for quite some time."

"Why would you *want* that—for anyone's mind to 'fray'?"

"There are many things we want, but only some we need. And all of them carry grave risks. You showed promise, child. Now show us that you can survive. You are about to face your next test, the one that determines if you can be a member of Fleet after all."

The woman pushed a button so the doors swung open and San's jaw dropped at the size of the chapel beyond, as if an entire medieval cathedral had been constructed under Ganymede's surface. It had tall pointed arches identical to the ones in the corridor outside. Countless stained glass windows, dark in the absence of sunlight, lined the walls and at the far end a huge one filled the space over the altar—a square dais, atop which was a deep-gray stone block. It looked as though it had been carved from a local source. Into the rock had been embedded banks of electronics and thick black cables so that, at least from a distance, San wondered if instead of an altar it was something else. She was squinting at it when the woman grabbed her arm.

"*Do not move into the nave!*" she hissed. "You have not earned the right. This way."

The woman guided them around to a side aisle and as they moved forward in light gravity, San noticed that the pews near the altar were occupied. A group of five people stood watching, all of them dressed in the same manner. Their cloak hoods had been pulled low to mask their faces in shadow but next to them stood four Proelian nuns in black robes, the women's heads bare and hairless, shining under artificial light. They watched as the old woman pushed San forward and onto the dais, where she turned her attention from her audience to the altar.

"There is blood on it," she whispered.

"Yes, child. But it dried long ago. Climb up and lie on your back, with your head resting on the padded section closest to you."

"Why?"

"We are preparing for the nocturn."

"I'm not getting up there. Tell me what's going on. What's the nocturn?"

San stepped back, trying to put part of the altar between herself and the nun. She had barely moved when the old woman's left hand flicked out from beneath her robes and grabbed San's wrist in a bony grip, hurting as it squeezed tighter. The right hand held a metal device. It wrapped around the woman's fingers, the palm side covered with hair-thin needles. The old nun slammed the device against San's back, sending its points through both cloak and coveralls so they pierced her skin.

Her back ignited with fire. San screamed and imagined that the woman had turned her spinal cord into the wick of a candle and without realizing it she'd obeyed the old woman's orders—climbing onto the altar and lying still as one of the other nuns stepped forward. She began strapping San down. When it was finished, the old woman withdrew her hand, allowing San to breathe.

"What was that?" she asked.

"A means to control. A device that sends electrical impulses through your spine to render your somatic nervous system more susceptible to suggestion and orders."

"What are you doing to me?"

"The nocturn; it's the next step in your development. I slice open your scalp to reaccess your old cranial data port. Then we reconnect you to one of our training semi-awares to help you access the old lessons. You don't remember, but I was there, child. When you were born. Your mother knew what was best and during your time in Fleet data tanks, our order added an additional training regimen to the standard programs."

"I don't remember anything related to the Proelians."

"I already told you that you wouldn't remember; we designed the plan that way. Your lessons have been stored deep inside a part of your brain that can only be activated with the procedure I'm about to begin. Until I finish, there is no way for you to recall what was pushed into your mind."

San noticed the flash of metal from the corner of her eye: a scalpel.

"*No!*"

"Child, we appreciate the old ways for some things. Be still."

"I do not give permission!"

"You will learn to hate me. Permission is a matter of perspective."

San struggled against the straps. They cut into her wrists and ankles, and the one across her forehead cinched itself tighter each time she pulled against it. She gave up, crying. A moment later San heard the buzz of an electric razor, which skimmed her scalp just above where her head rested. Then there was silence. Soon, a murmured prayer began from the group watching from the pews, and San felt a pressure against her scalp. A searing pain tore through when the blade cut down to her skull.

"Shush, child. No screaming. Almost there."

"I want to go home."

"I'm about to reconnect you with our semi-aware. You must know certain things. First, do not struggle. Let the memories and lessons flow around and through your thoughts. They will be a tidal wave; if you fight, you will drown and your nervous system will shut down. Second, do not try to understand. What I am about to release into your consciousness are memories, not experiences, and if you try to understand all at once you will go mad. Then we will have to send you to the institution, where you'll live out the rest of your life, insane and useless."

"Do most survive the nocturn?" San whispered.

"Of the five you saw in the pews, there were originally fifteen. So, no. They do not."

The old woman slammed a cable into the rear of San's head and her vision erupted with sparks and glowing orbs, coalescing into a single brightness that overpowered everything. San stopped struggling. The first memories came in a trickle, a gentle wash of sensory input so real that she was now an infant, suspended in a tank of gel and the warmth of safety. Without warning the next set of memories hit. San writhed on the table, straps cutting into her skin so that blood dripped off her forehead and wrists, while lessons in combat, history, and the Church broke free from where they'd been waiting; they invaded her brain, elbowing past anything that got in the way and making their presence known with a scream. *How could they have done this to me,* San thought. *To infants...* While the assault continued, she heard a new voice muttering to the old nun.

"Her heart rate and brain wave patterns, Your Reverence."

"I see them."

"The others never saw this much pain; will you let this continue or end it for her?"

"We will let it play out. I will not prematurely stop what could be exactly what we need to counteract Zhelnikov's atrocities. That thing he created will end us if we don't take some risks. Zhelnikov's monster may not be the beast, but he is almost certainly the beast's prophet, and to do good we must be guilty of a slight evil."

San grunted with the torture, trying her best to ignore the women, the additional sensory input almost too much for her to handle when the flood of memories peaked into a crushing flow of input. Pain made her clench and unclench both fists, opening wounds where her fingernails split both palms.

"Perhaps at least an analgesic, Your Reverence."

"Step back," the old woman said. "Step back. You are not welcome here, Sister. *I* will manage this. There will be no sedatives."

Suddenly it ended. San inhaled when the last memory flowed out of storage, snapping into place the final part of a toy model, the ones she had built with her father so long ago. New information weighed on her thoughts. She imagined that her brain had just been saddled with an overstuffed pack, one that made autonomic functions struggle under the weight of new requirements and tears ran from both eyes.

"I need food," San whispered. Her eyes fluttered open to see the old nun grinning. "*Salty* food."

"You did it, child. I must say I'm pleased with your performance."

"I need something salty."

"I should say you do. We will hook you up to a saline drip immediately; the test and unpacking forces the brain to use a lot of sodium during signal processing. All electrolytes get dangerously depleted. How do you feel, child?"

"Squeezed. Empty."

The old nun patted San's hand and shook her head. "Nonsense. You, child, are a weapon now loaded. Full. And maybe our most formidable weapon yet."

CHAPTER SEVEN

Win sensed that part of him, an old segment of his brain not yet transformed, recognized the scenery as something familiar and it urged him to turn back—to revert to the way he was, *a human*. He stepped down the ramp in a jerky series of movements. Rolling hills surrounded him and the transport, their tops a deep green with trees that swayed in a strong breeze, and his display shifted temperature readings every few seconds but the numbers stayed within a range of sixty-two to sixty-four degrees Fahrenheit; it would have felt pleasant against bare skin, Win thought.

His legs clicked down the ramp. Although the distant hills were green, the area where they'd landed was a sea of black, where no grass would ever grow because the soil itself had been fused into a dirty kind of glass, melted to the point where Win tested its depth out of curiosity. He slammed one spiked leg down. Nothing happened. It took several tries to break through, smashing a section of the earth to show that the glass was at least three inches thick.

"The Sommen," Zhelnikov said.

"Of course, the Sommen. Who else?"

"They hit here soon after their arrival. It has always been a mystery. Nobody came to visit this place, it had no military presence, and only a few crazy old nuns and monks occupied it."

"What do you mean, *mystery*?"

"This used to be an important religious site. A shrine, hundreds of years old. There were many buildings, most of which eventually crumbled into ruin of disuse. The Sommen sent an entire force here

73

and then to Rome. They destroyed everything, and left nothing but glass in their wake. We never figured out why."

"That is because you have no eyes to see. I figured it out in Hong Kong. All these years and you, the smartest man in Fleet, couldn't see what was right in front of you all along. Rome is empty. But here they left something behind."

"Win, I assure you; there is *nothing* here."

"Come."

Win ticked forward, the suit rubbing blisters on his shoulders and forcing him to wince with each misstep; he had learned to control the servos to an extent but his neural changes made the interface, which had been designed for human brains, less forgiving of any differences in thought pattern or electrical current. He gritted his teeth in frustration. Instead of exploring a vast expanse of possible futures that stretched like a flat landscape within his mind, Win had to concentrate on moving each leg to make sure he walked in the right direction. One of his guards moved too close. Win smiled and ignored the screams around him to stop. He slammed one of his spikes through the top of the man's helmet, then watched as it sprang from the center of his chest, trailing a streamer of blood that slid down the metal leg. He breathed with the satisfaction of having killed something and barked into his radio for everyone to keep moving. Listening briefly to Zhelnikov's angry protests, Win eventually hissed that *it was an accident* before switching his radio off.

He led the group across the glass, cresting a small rise where they pushed through tall grass and weeds, an ocean of green and yellow punctuated with white flowers that reminded Win of stars. He forgot that his brain had become something new; Win remembered his first moments in America, so long ago when his father had taken them to the mountains of South Carolina where they'd hiked and camped for days. It was one of the few occasions Win recalled that his father hadn't been forced to spend all his free time looking for a job, anything that would pay even just a little for rice. He was so deep in thought that Win almost missed the shrine; his left front leg crashed through it, sending a statue of the Virgin Mary to roll through the grass.

"This is it," Win said, turning on his radio.

"What is?"

Win stabbed a front spike into the grass near Zhelnikov, almost impaling the man's foot. "This. Under here. Have your men scan this area for an entrance to an underground site."

The armored men assembled in a circle, setting up a perimeter around Zhelnikov and Win, while several broke down their packs to remove folding shovels. They went to work at the dirt near Win's feet. Within fifteen minutes they had dug a narrow trench in the shape of a square, where sharp-cornered concrete lay exposed.

"We located it," one of them said over his speakers. "A large hatch or door."

"What next?" Zhelnikov asked.

"We knock."

Win slammed his left front spike into the hatch with a thud, sending shards of concrete in every direction. He did it again. He was about to do it a third time when a loud grinding noise filtered up through the grass around them, and the group moved back to watch the square section of earth and concrete inch to the side. A low hum came from the dark shaft now open before them. Win peered over the edge and adjusted his sensors to maximum range, doing his best to see into the depths, which looked black and empty. He watched until a platform took shape, rising upward toward the surface.

A single nun stood on the platform and smiled, then glanced around to look at the guards who pointed weapons in her direction. She bowed to Win and Zhelnikov. Win noticed how young she looked. He scanned her features and compared the data to biometrics that now streamed into his system via an antennae, but nothing matched, and Win guessed she couldn't be more than thirty years old; a part of him recognized beauty.

"I've been waiting here for some time," she said.

"For what?" Zhelnikov asked.

"For you and your pet. The monster we all knew you'd create."

Win noticed the cloak she wore—a phase shifter, not activated so its folds combined a drab mixture of pale greens and reds. "You're a Proelian."

"Of course she's a Proelian bitch," Zhelnikov spat. "Only they would live in a hole all these years, then come out pretending that they'd been waiting the whole time for us. It's all a trick, everything an act with them."

"Silence," Win said.

The woman smiled again. "Your pet knows, Zhelnikov. Even though he's more animal than human, he knows the truth of everything standing here now—including the truth that sometimes it's important to keep one's mouth closed."

"Truth?" Zhelnikov stepped forward and drew his pistol. "I'll show you and your order the truth."

Win swung a leg to the side, hitting the man in his midsection and driving the wind from him; Zhelnikov flew backward to land in the grass. The old man struggled to get up and eventually stood, gasping for air and holstering his weapon.

"I said silence," Win said. "This is not why I'm here."

"Why are you here?" she asked.

"My name is Win."

"We don't acknowledge anything so inhuman by giving it a name. Surely you knew that."

"But if you know the truth," said Win, "then you know why I'm here."

"I know only that some truth eludes you. No matter how much of that chemical cocktail you consume, there are some futures you cannot see because they are not *for* you. For those things, you need the papers. The written words. And you need humanity."

"But why?" Win asked. He wanted to step closer and drive a spike through her head, the anger unexpected. He took a moment to trace its origin to a sense of fear that rooted itself in a deep terror at the base of new neurons: He was afraid she was right. Some things were obscured from him—always would be—and such blindness horrified him more than anything else.

"Because you are of lies. Anything born out of lies will never see the truth."

"I want the papers," said Win.

"They are gone and *you* will never find them."

Win stepped forward. "What did the writings say?"

"What will you do? Kill me?" The nun laughed and threw the cloak's hood up to cover her face in shadow. "That would not give you the outcome you want."

Win stabbed. He meant to spear her shoulder but was unable to control it and the metal rammed through her gut and out the back where it pierced the phase-shifter fabric. The woman grunted with the blow. Then she looked toward the sky and whispered something, but Win's sensors couldn't pick up the words. She grinned at him, her teeth blood stained.

"Just as I knew you'd do. A monster."

"Win," Zhelnikov started. "What are you—"

"Not now. We need to get down in the shaft and find out if she was lying about the papers. The Sommen wanted them too, but it's possible they left them in the care of the Proelians; it's not clear how these nuns won the Sommen's confidence—why they were spared."

"But *what* papers? *This is madness.*"

Win was about to explain when a guard started screaming. Then another shouted, dropping to the ground and rolling. Soon all the ones closest to the hatch had dropped their weapons to tear at their armor in a frantic effort to disrobe, and Win stepped back in confusion.

"Microbots," said Zhelnikov. "From underground. She laid a trap. Those men are being eaten alive."

The rest of them ran. Win bounded over the grass, tripping twice after they reached the glassy area where he managed to right himself after rolling to a stop. Zhelnikov kept pace. By the time they reached the transport and looked back, a trail of guards had strung out from their craft to the dead nun, most of them still except for a few who still struggled with the tiny robots that now attacked them from within, burrowing into their flesh and consuming heart tissue. The door shut and the transport lifted with a jerk.

"So much for your Praetorian Guard, old man."

"What papers?" Zhelnikov asked again.

"A prophecy. The Sommen wanted it because it meant something to them and they knew it was here. One from ancient Earth, centuries ago. There was a visitation at this location, a woman who gave a prophecy to three shepherd children."

"That nonsense? Why is it so important? Can't we find that in history books?"

"We can find the lies in history books. The actual words given to the children were transcribed and brought to Rome. They returned here, just prior to the Sommen arrival and just after the rise of the Proelian order."

"But what was it supposed to say?"

Win sighed. "It told how the world would end. And how the universe would collapse soon after, taking all of us either into perpetual darkness, or into a new age of peace."

CHAPTER EIGHT

"Mathematics is truth and therefore the language of God. All solid foundations rest on mathematics." San spoke the mantra with the rest of her small class, while they bounced in low gravity on a stone floor, their feet hooked into straps to prevent them from shifting too far from their assigned spot. "To give consciousness to a computer is a sin. To trust in them for computation a weakness. We are weapons because of mathematics, instruments of fact thanks to the clear sight it lends. We see lies because, open to the truth, the mind sees untruth as the calculus of those bent on evil. I will never again put my faith in computational systems granted awareness. I will never rely on computations from outside my mind. I am an instrument of truth. I am a computational certainty."

Sister Frances—San had learned that was the name of the nun who had welcomed her on Ganymede—clapped her hands. "Enough." She rose from behind a massive wood desk, and slid open a drawer. One by one she pulled daggers out and flipped them toward the group, the metal shining in the light with each rotation.

San grabbed hers from the air and examined it. The steel was bright except for spots that had pitted with age, and its edges had been ground almost to those of a razor. She tested the point and winced.

"Yes, child, they are sharp."

"What are they for?" a boy asked.

"Access a deep memory section, combat, calculus of the European arts."

San closed her eyes. Her breathing slowed and she relaxed the major muscle groups one by one, then concentrated on the section Sister Frances had referenced. Her memories unfolded; as if she watched a movie, San soared through thoughts as a younger version of her sparred with an armored adversary twice her height, with black chainmail that dangled to the man's knees. He swung a large broadsword and San almost shouted when the man's weapon whistled through the air toward her head. The younger San dodged; she rolled closer so his sword would be useless, and then thrust the dagger upward into his groin, careful to swing it up and under the chainmail armor so the man collapsed, almost crushing her under his weight.

In an instant she recalled everything and San was about to open her eyes when something else drifted by, nudging her mind with the gentle sensation of kindness. She sensed them all—the other candidates in the room. San grinned at the impression of rolling in waves of innocence as the others leaked thoughts and memories, dousing her with their names and histories mixed with the nervousness of not knowing what lay ahead. *They are like me,* she realized. *All of them good, all of them frightened.*

By the time San opened her eyes, everyone stared at her.

"Something wrong that it took you so long, child?" Sister Frances asked.

"I was so little," she lied. "And I couldn't find the memory at first."

"For some it takes time to access early memories—the ones where you first succeeded after strings of failure. Experiences in the tank are built one on another, layered; if you want to access the earliest ones, plan on meditating for hours. *Now,* concentrate, children."

Sister Frances clapped her hands again. A round hatch spun open in the floor and from it rose a humanoid figure, a robot, the metallic frame of which had been covered with pink rubbery skin. "Line up one at a time. Let's begin putting actual muscle memory into the mix and see how well the lessons took. Wilson. *You first.*"

Wilson, the boy who had asked what the daggers were for, was the one closest to San and she recalled his leaked memories, of his joy upon finally being part of something after his failure in Fleet selection. She examined him closely. All of them had been bred for the Fleet program and so had the stocky appearance of ones meant to live in high g, and San barely saw Wilson's neck; it was as though his head went straight into his shoulders. When Wilson glanced at her she looked away and felt her face redden with embarrassment.

"Flirting later," Sister Frances said. "Fighting now."

"What is this?" Wilson asked.

"Combat trainer. We designed it in our labs here on Ganymede and produced it on our factory floor."

"But isn't it semi-aware? I thought you taught us that the Proelians never used semi-awares."

The nun slid from behind her desk and reached for the robot's head. With a few taps and then a twist of a knob, she opened the thing's clamshell skull. There was almost nothing inside. Wires ran from the eye sockets, which had been designed to function as human eyes, and terminated in a small gray box that had been wrapped in a kind of metal coil.

"There is no computer. This is brain-wave controlled, remotely. You will be fighting our masters in various martial arts, perfecting the forms. One Sister Jessica is controlling it from somewhere above us, and her brain signals are beamed into this receiver. The receiver translates her commands at the same speed as your nervous system, controlling the musculature and movements. It is pure, Mister Wilson."

Wilson stood, waiting for the nun to close the robot's head and move behind her desk. The rest of the group made a space around them.

"Mr. Wilson. Whenever you're ready."

"I was thinking . . ."

"This is not about thinking!" Sister Frances slammed her hand on the desk, launching herself upward a foot.

The bot sprang. In Ganymede's low gravity it pushed off and travelled the distance between it and the boy in less than a second, all while airborne. A bright rod-shaped object dropped from its wrist, extending outward. Before Wilson could dodge, the bot slammed the thing into the boy's chest to send radial sparks of electricity, which induced a writhing kind of fit in him that only ended when the bot stepped back. Wilson slumped to the floor, unconscious.

"You," said Sister Frances. "San; get up. You're next."

San rose. She felt the blade's grip, its synthetic leather slippery with sweat, then relaxed her mind and willed it to access the tank memories, to mainline them to her muscles. Time slowed. Her eyelids drooped into a squint and San dropped to a shallow crouch, just before the bot pounced.

San waited for its feet to leave the ground before she slipped to the floor, wincing at the sensation of electricity when the bots "dagger" passed just overhead. Without looking she slammed her fist upward. The bot contorted to evade so that the dagger tip nicked the thing's shin, and then landed both feet against the far wall, its torso parallel to the floor; less than a second later the mannequin figure pushed off in a downward dive, straight at her.

San leaped. Her feet left the floor and she somersaulted upside down, grabbed the robot's head below her, and slammed the dagger into its neck. The bot's hand smashed into her thigh sending San's body rigid with spasms.

"A wonderful display of acrobatics, child. But you died. The goal is to kill the enemy, not enter the afterlife along with him. Or her. *Next!*"

The next morning San's muscles ached from the uncontrolled spasms induced by combat training. She rubbed her arms and winced. A nun, a new one who was younger than Sister Frances and who wore a shiny set of coveralls and safety glasses, pointed at the laboratory equipment around them.

"I am Sister Joan. The abbess, who you know as Sister Frances, established this laboratory decades ago, long before any of you were born, but in a way this is the place where all of you were conceived."

The woman began tapping on buttons and soon a holographic display rotated in front of her, a diagram of a human head—see through, so that San saw the skull, brain and spine. A cloud of microbots appeared. They entered through the skull's nasal passageways, a fog creeping into the image and then working its way through membranes and into the brain cavity where it formed a dark line between brain and bone.

"This was the first step. Your parents knew the dangers this solar system faces and decided to offer up their greatest love: you. All for an idea."

"You're talking about what you did to our brains?" Wilson asked, interrupting. "Was it your idea or the Sommen's?"

"Do not interrupt, Mr. Wilson. But it's a fair question. Fleet placed most of its faith in their chief scientist, Vladimir Zhelnikov. Truly a brilliant man, but as far from God as an ant from the sun. And Fleet weren't idiots. They wanted a backup plan, a separate pathway to research that could take over in the event Zhelnikov failed. Plus, the admiral at the time was Filipino and a devout Proelian."

Sister Joan paused to sneeze before continuing. "The Sommen gave us all the data they have—everything stored since the beginning of their written and spoken language. This included their brain structure. But one thing was absent: interstellar communications. Zhelnikov was furious. He gave up for a bit and concentrated on their plasma weapons technology, but a mouse of a nun, Sister Alfonsa, had been concentrating on Sommen religion. This is where the breakthrough came: Sommen interstellar communications is not in their technical manuals. It's in their Bible, if I can make that analogy—a pillar of their faith. Zhelnikov took credit for the discovery, but Fleet knew. That's when they funded this program and helped the Proelians keep Ganymede Station hidden. We think that not even Zhelnikov knows this place exists."

San was transfixed. She felt as if everything had turned surreal as mysteries of the Sommen unfolded—after so many years of wondering about them and hearing whispered warnings from her parents. Her father had encountered one of their warriors. He had used his illegal wetware systems to become a super-aware, a hyperintelligent cybernetic Dream Warrior, and had infiltrated Sommen armor systems to kill it via asphyxiation. Had he not been able to do that, San would have never been born.

"We will go to war with the Sommen in about seventy years. They have promised to return, but as part of their faith they must give an adversary time to learn their ways and technology so that it will be a fair fight. That's where you come in."

War, thought San. She had sensed it in visions when first navigating to Ganymede, but now that Sister Joan put it into words the reality of it hit. She fought back tears. Seventy years was a long time, and San might even be dead by the time war started, but what if she had children? Why bother with anything if the Sommen were going to return in seventy years and wipe out the human race? San fought a growing sense of fear and did her best to remain composed as she raised a hand.

"Yes, San."

"Did you inject microbots when we were kicked out of Fleet training?"

"Yes. You never washed out; *you succeeded*. And now you children are going to help us prepare for the coming war and will be the first generation of your kind." Sister Joan pointed to the holo-display. "Although this shows the microbots entering via your nasal passages, we actually injected them and they crossed into your cranial cavity where they began eating a layer of bone matter. You all were genetically engineered to have thick skulls and extra matter for cushioning the brain—to withstand high g-forces. We needed some room. These microbots gave us an extra millimeter, and if you've been having headaches, that's why."

"You needed room for what?"

"For *today*, since you asked. San, come forward."

Sister Joan pulled an autoinjector from her desk, its needle glistening under yellow lights. San hesitated. For some reason the sight terrified her and she stopped, both legs paralyzed with uncertainty. Uncertainty transformed into paralysis; San felt the other candidates around her, their trepidation ripping across her own thoughts and causing sympathetic tremors of fear. She shook her head.

"No."

Sister Joan shrugged. "Fine. We'll do it another way."

Before San could react, the nun bounced over her desk and toward the small group. She slammed the autoinjector into San's shoulder, then hooked one arm around her, telling the others to grab the girl's legs and hold tight. San shouted for them to stop, just before her head erupted in pain.

"What San is experiencing," said Sister Joan, "is a lot like trying to push lava through your veins. It hurts. But she's the lucky one; San gets to go first and will not have to suffer the fate of watching and knowing before receiving the treatment. Wilson, *you* will go last."

San screamed. She convulsed in the nun's arms, and her back arched at the same time her legs and feet kicked, at one point threatening to break free of the other students' grasp.

"Don't let go!" Sister Joan shouted. "I've injected two serums. G6 is to grow an additional network of synapses within the space our microbots created. This process takes only a minute with their help. The second, G7, is a mixture of compounds that both stimulate the production of neurotransmitters, and block natural enzymes whose job it is to break down these neurotransmitters to stop the signals. Miss Kyarr is, in effect, dying of nerve-agent exposure. Her neurons are firing out of control right now; all except a few associated with critical autonomic functions."

San opened her eyes. The room had filled with a bright fog that lit at random, as if behind the mist flashed lightning and explosions. She could breathe, but everything else constricted into vicious cramps and her sight alternated between normal and a kind of pinpoint tunnel vision that made everything at the periphery black. Deep inside her consciousness a sense of embarrassment formed. San knew that mucous had begun to flow from her nostrils and there was nothing she could do to stop it.

"Help me," she said.

One of the other girls started to let go of San's leg and Sister Joan jerked a dagger from under her coveralls. "Do not let go, Miss Benin," she said. "All of you will have to go through this. But all of you have the ability to control body functions. With the added brain tissue and nerve connections grown as a result of these treatments, you have the power to control which enzymes are blocked, which synapses release their transmitters. *You* control whether you live or die, not us."

"How do we control our biochemistry?"

"Ah, Mister Wilson. An intelligent question. And here is my intelligent answer: I don't know. Figure that one out on your own. Everyone's physiology is unique on the biochemical level, a fingerprint. The only advice I can give is *feel* your way through."

San stopped screaming. She had heard everything and her consciousness flew somewhere above the group, later sinking into her body with a snap. San marveled at the clarity of vision and began to try to control the motion and focus of her senses, willing herself to move further inward, deep inside her own flesh and through her ribcage. There, San saw the heart; it beat a constant rhythm and she reached out to touch it, not seeing any kind of hand, but sensing that she had some semblance of physical form. Her heart raced; the muscles thumped and she started laughing at the control, willing it to slow, then forcing her receptors and enzymes to rid themselves of the chemicals that had been introduced.

Sister Joan nodded at the others. The group let go, and San lifted herself so she sat on the floor.

"Good work, Miss Kyarr," Sister Joan said, pulling the autoinjector out again. "Miss Benin; it's your turn."

San's hand shot up. "Wait. Something else is happening. I can see things. It's like I can see all of you and simultaneously look at something else—Ganymede's surface."

Sister Joan leaned forward and whispered in her ear. "Then let's really test this. Let go. Find a Fleet battle group and tell me what you see."

A flash of light blinded San and she accelerated from the moon so rapidly she almost passed out. Ganymede faded. Planet after planet whipped by and after five minutes of travel she stopped, well outside the solar system and in deep space, where San found herself surrounded by stars and blackness.

"I'm here," she whispered.

"Tell us what you see," Sister Joan said. Her voice came in a whisper, from light-years away.

A huge ship appeared, its surface coated with pitch-black tiles, and San watched as four-thousand-meter-high red letters snuck silently by: UFS *STALINGRAD*. Beyond it drifted an ocean of ships. There were so many that San gave up trying to count the craft, instead filled with a sense of dread upon realizing that the only reason Fleet would send so many vessels was for war; this was no exercise.

"The *Stalingrad*," San said. "It's hideous. I've never considered how ugly warships are. It's an entire Fleet led by the *Stalingrad*."

The others laughed and Sister Joan shushed them quiet. "Describe it to us, child."

"It's a fighter carrier, *Wonsan* class. No aerodynamic features. It's passing beneath me and judging from the size of its antennae and defensive batteries, it's a twenty kilometer long shoebox, with thousands of smaller boxes and black domes sticking out."

"Get closer, child. Give me details on its defenses."

San sped toward the ship; she had begun to concentrate on missile launch ports, hangar decks, and plasma cannons when illumination from behind her, so bright it cast a glare across the entire hull, made her flinch.

"Wait." San turned, trying to locate the source of the flash. "It's under attack."

Thousands of fiery streaks appeared out of nowhere and sped toward the *Stalingrad,* twisting as they adjusted course. Most of them impacted against the outer shell but two struck aft, near what San knew were the power plants and the gargantuan vessel started to list. Then a second and third wave of missiles struck the ship's interior shells in spots, and San watched as vapor puffed from the craft, with tiny dots—human bodies—jetting into the vacuum of space upon plumes of frozen, glittering water crystals.

"They are dead," San said. "The dead of war."

"But who, child? *Who* is killing them? Look and *see.*"

San concentrated, trying to divine the direction from where the missiles had come but she couldn't see anything. Then something moved. A substantial and dark object skulked toward her, blocking distant stars and yet the lack of light prevented her from making out any details. From behind, a volley of missiles streaked from the *Stalingrad;* they snaked their way around her and in the direction of the enemy ship, but before they could hit and cast light with their explosions San returned to her body. She inhaled sharply, gasping for breath.

"So many dead," San said. "They never knew—icy in a vacuum."

Sister Joan grabbed her by the shoulders. "San, you have no idea what this means."

"What?" Wilson asked. "What does it mean?"

"The serum and the treatment. She actually saw something. Come, child. *Now!* The rest of you stay here, and meditate."

Sister Joan grabbed San by the wrist and bounded from the room, pulling her through the door; it sealed behind them. The nun sped, an illum-bot struggling to keep pace as it weaved through the tight corridor trailing streamers of gas. San bounced too high. She almost slammed her head against the ceiling but managed to throw up her arm and absorb the shock. The images of what she'd seen still haunted her, fresh and vivid as if she'd been there, between two warships in deep space until Sister Joan pulled her into the abbess's bedroom, yanking her back to reality.

The space was tight. San marveled at the mahogany panels and rich upholstered chair that rested on Ganymede rock, and beyond it stood an enormous desk in dark wood with a red leather top. Sister Frances struggled to get out of bed; she pulled on a heavy woolen robe and glared at both of them.

"What is this?"

Sister Joan bowed. "Abbess. We administered the serum to San. She had a vision almost immediately after new matter grew into place. It works."

"I'll be the judge of *that*." Sister Frances rose to her feet and stepped toward San, leaning forward so their faces were inches apart. "What did you see?"

"She saw the . . ."

The abbess held up a hand, silencing the other nun. "Calm yourself. I want to hear it from the girl."

San looked at the floor. "I felt cold. The cold of space. I've never seen anything so vast as deep space, away from the solar system and in the middle of nothing—absolute emptiness."

"I didn't ask how it felt, child. I asked what you saw."

"I saw a ship. The *Stalingrad*. It took multiple volleys of missiles from another ship, a vessel in the darkness."

"Did you see the *Stalingrad*'s fate, child? Was it destroyed?"

San shook her head. "I didn't see the end. I returned to my body before anything else, except . . ."

"Except what?"

"The *Stalingrad* fired back. It wasn't destroyed by the first three attacks."

"Of course it wasn't." Sister Frances bounced to her desk and moved her hand over the surface in a pattern that San couldn't follow. Soon a humming came from overhead. A massive bank of computers and electronics descended from the ceiling in front of the nun and her hands flickered over the controls while the woman whispered into the air.

"What is that?" San asked.

Sister Joan whispered. "We have different equipment than Fleet. The Sommen religious texts provided insight on alternate modes of computation and communication. Not even Zhelnikov has seen this kind of device."

"Is it a radio?"

"In a way. It works on the principle of quantum entanglement but only for short-range communications—nothing outside the solar system; this is how we sent the message to you, to get to Ganymede. We have an entire production floor for ships and equipment based on Sommen technology like this."

Sister Frances finished and sent the bank of electronics back into the ceiling. She stood and turned, straightening her robes.

"Fleet will try to raise the *Stalingrad,* but it will take forever for a fast scout to reach her. The fools at Fleet sent a task force, along with the *Stalingrad,* to look for the new Chinese base of operations."

"It's too soon."

"Of course it's too soon. Even if those Chinese lunatics are trying to construct a super-aware communications device, we still have time. But there's something else."

San watched a tear slide down the abbess's cheek, the speck of moisture triggering something that rocketed her from the room, back to Earth where she saw a dead nun in the grass—her corpse half-eaten by microbots and a dark stain on her robes where she'd been stabbed.

"She's dead," San whispered. "I think her name was Sister Patrice. She was so young."

"Yes child," Sister Frances said. "She was. And Sister Joan was correct: *You can see.*"

CHAPTER NINE

"We lost the *Stalingrad* along with its entire task force. All hands gone." The admiral sat and motioned for Zhelnikov to sit in one of the chairs before glaring at Win. "I assume *you* can somehow make *yourself* comfortable."

Win moved to Zhelnikov's side. A long conference table stretched out, lined on both sides by staff officers with holo-terminals streaming data; the soft glow gave the entire room a greenish tint. Win imagined that the tint was a reflection of their rot, its color an indicator of corruption that had long ago taken hold of all those who occupied the space, officers who pretended to care about their streams and associated archaic symbols representing Fleet movements. Tactical bots whined in and out, striking Win as being more busy and authentic than the personnel they served.

"Where are we on the Sommen plasma weapons?" the admiral asked.

Zhelnikov tapped at the screen in front of him. "We have their schematics but the material synthesis is far more complex than we can handle for now. Researchers at Lunar Station are working around the clock. Once we crack materials production, the rest should be easy."

"How did you lose the *Stalingrad*?" Win asked.

Zhelnikov glared at him and whispered. "*Silence!* We are on trial."

"It's all right, Zhelnikov. So this is the one who bravely slaughtered that nun in Portugal. Your little experiment." The admiral stood and walked toward Win, stopping a few feet away to examine the servo harness. "All that metal. We've put a lot of money into making you possible. The Proelians got the Sommen religious texts and we hear all sorts of stories about the weird tech they've developed. It's hard to believe that we thought you, a psychopath, would be the future." The admiral turned to look at Zhelnikov. "Does he have the kinds of visions you told me about?"

"Yes. His brain matter is still in development but we've seen evidence for Sommen mental abilities already."

Win tried to control himself, willing his voice to remain steady. "I am not psychopathic. I am the weapon that will win this war, along with those who come behind me."

"Those are interesting words," the admiral said.

Zhelnikov rested his head in his hands. "Win, *please*. Be quiet!"

Win slowed his breathing. He concentrated on the admiral, shifting all his sensors into the visible spectrum and zooming in to get a clear view of his face. Win's eyes rolled back and his mind swung between consciousness and sleep.

"Admiral Vincent Posobiec. Half Polish, half American, you grew up in a world of privilege. Wealthy parents in Connecticut, you first thought you wanted to be a priest but the Church had all but disappeared and so you chose the next best thing: the Academy. That way your father could buy your success . . ."

"*Zhelnikov*," the admiral said.

"But you're scared," Win continued. "The Sommen reverse-engineering program is colossal and dispersed. Your and your staff's planning was almost sound but the key areas—the ones involving the most powerful Sommen weaponry—are still a problem. At the current rate you're going, you won't be ready for their return. Unless . . ."

"*Zhelnikov!*"

"The Proelians. There is a parallel program. I can't see it but I can sense the gap, a dark void in the middle of your spidery network of contacts and influence. From the flavor of your thought patterns, it's clear that Fleet has placed its faith in them—not Zhelnikov. You sometimes openly insult the Proelians; but deep down, you are one."

The room went silent except for the hum of bots. Win sensed rage emanate from the admiral in waves, which crashed into his mind, making it ache. The staff around the table waited and looked toward the admiral, who stayed silent for what seemed like hours as time downshifted into a creeping low, a powerful gear that was pregnant with horrors of a coming war.

"Is this true?" Zhelnikov asked, breaking the silence.

"Is what true?"

"That you sympathize with them, as did your predecessor. And that you've established a parallel R-and-D program with those religious maniacs?"

The admiral cleared his throat. "Clear the room. Secure mode."

They waited for the admiral's staff to exit. After the holo-displays powered down, a red glow from illum-bots lit the area, giving everything a sinister appearance. The main door sealed shut.

"Yes, it's true. You already knew that we used them for the serum program. Your people and the Proelians both got a chance."

"My program worked. Win is developing the same capabilities as Sommen priests."

The admiral laughed. He paused to slide a cigarette from his pocket, lighting it with a snap and filling the room with smoke that wormed its way through Win's suit vents.

"You created an abomination. Look at this thing." He pointed at Win. "Nobody wants *that* on our ships. And I've heard the reports, Zhelnikov. Win has stopped being human; did you think we wouldn't hear about him spearing our own troops? We can forgive the Chinese atrocities. In fact, I applaud his Hong Kong decisions. But a nun?"

"I act according to the logic of war," Win said. He felt fear in his chest, a panic from not having seen ahead of time that he and Zhelnikov might be in serious trouble. "I sense the importance of what the Proelians are hiding from us. From you. It is critical for the coming war and they treat ancient documents as though nobody but adherents to a dead faith can see them."

"He's right," Zhelnikov said.

The admiral blew a thick cloud of smoke toward the ceiling. "No. He's wrong. You have no idea what progress they've made—the technology shift. Going back and forward in time simultaneously. We're developing ships with no vulnerability to Chinese cyber infiltration. Communications are being revolutionized. Interstellar. Without having to build gigantic accelerators."

"That's impossible," Win said. "I was to be the means of interstellar communication."

"That's correct: you *were* to be the means, son," the admiral said. "But I've read Zhelnikov's reports. You have become something different than we anticipated, in many ways powerful and with great promise. But the consensus among my staff is that as your abilities grow, your brain matter shifts further away from humanity and closer to that of our adversary. And you murdered a Proelian nun, boy. I had to fight to keep you from being executed as soon as you got here, and then I had to fight to keep you out of confinement. If Zhelnikov and his people hadn't vouched for you, you'd be dead."

Zhelnikov pounded his fist on the table. "Damn it, Admiral, Win is only the first! I'm ready to start on the next generation of telesthetics; we have hundreds of candidates identified and can start now. Within a year, each Fleet vessel will have one onboard—able to reach and see what's out there. Able to communicate with each other in real time, no matter where they are in the universe."

Telesthetics, Win thought. *That's what I am to them: a radio of sorts, and nothing more.* It was the first time he'd heard Zhelnikov refer to him that way and he had to dig in his memories to find the definition, soon realizing that *telesthesia* described but one facet of his capabilities. Win saw futures—potential ones, yes, but ones representing the most probable outcomes based on a subset of decisions and actions. He could read people. Even now he scanned Zhelnikov and felt the man's fear as if it projected outward in an energy field that pierced Win's servo harness and crackled against his skin. He dug more to find a Sommen mantra, not sure where he'd picked it up, and began to whisper it.

"*War is the cleansing. War clears the mind through fire and the sharp edge. War creates the iron core, necessary for what comes at the end, the iron demanded by the Great Creator who will return at the appointed time.*"

"What the hell is he whispering?" asked the admiral.

"It isn't important. Admiral, please. I have over a hundred programs, all of them showing progress. Are you talking about shutting them down?"

"No, Zhelnikov. Not shutting them down. Just putting them under new leadership. They will continue for the time being and we may cancel those that have obviously reached dead ends. But we're reassigning you and Win."

"What? What about the other telesthetic candidates?"

The admiral shook his head. "Cancelled. Any who started the treatment have been euthanized. The others have already been shuffled off to standard Fleet slots. Win will be the only one created using your methods, the first and last. We just can't risk that much of a deviation from the human form; it generates uncertainties."

Zhelnikov slumped in his chair, placing both hands over his face with a loud sigh. "Where? Where have I and Win been assigned?"

"We have a critical mission. There's been a breakthrough in our understanding of Sommen expansion patterns and we need you to join an excursion. I also need you to get on the team—to behave in accordance with Fleet regulations; the next time a Portugal event happens, I'll have you both court-martialed and executed."

Win closed his eyes and relaxed. In less than a second he saw the threads in the admiral's thought, and traced it to the source. "The Proelians. They had a breakthrough."

"That's correct. Their teams mapped out Sommen historical movements and traced them to their home world."

"So we can attack it," said Zhelnikov, "once the war begins. You want us to go and scout it?"

"Negative. The Sommen maintain garrisons and establish colonies on conquered worlds that are suitable to their biochemistry. Always. But we've detected an anomaly. There are a series of planetary systems with ammonia atmospheres, including their home world, which they've abandoned. Not only are they abandoned, but there is a network of outposts circling the region."

"They want to keep intruders out," Win said.

"No. We think they're trying to keep something in. Something that even scares the Sommen.

"You two are going to take a closer look so we can figure out what the hell is going on; the Sommen decision to evacuate conquered territory isn't explained in their technical or religious documents. And our models suggest knowing *why* could give us a better understanding of how to scare the hell out of them. Or even beat them."

"When are we supposed to do this?" asked Zhelnikov.

"You leave now. We have two ships docked in orbit, the *Jerusalem* and the *Higgins*. You've been assigned to the *Higgins* and will burn to Jupiter to link up with another Fleet vessel, the *Bangkok*."

"The *Jerusalem* and *Bangkok* are both brand-new ship builds," said Zhelnikov. "Yet you're sending us outside of the exclusion area, into Sommen territory—an act that can kick off the war early—in the *Higgins*. It's a standard, old-design destroyer."

"It's a destroyer, yes, but one that's been overhauled; you'll be surprised. Besides, we need the majority of our new ships to find and destroy those Chinese bastards who took out the *Stalingrad*. I could only spare two; they've been assigned Proelian crews. And you *will* get along with them. That's an order."

It took them a full day to reach an orbital station and then board a shuttle intended to dock with the *Higgins,* which had been altered in its recent upgrade so that it no longer had docking locks consistent with the much older station. Zhelnikov and Win watched during approach. Win had been fitted with a small servo harness, one designed for use in microgravity and to navigate the confines of a warship. He pictured himself as an illum-bot. The long spidery legs had been replaced with much shorter ones, attached to an exoskeleton that ran the length of his arms and legs, and which amplified his neural signals to provide extra strength and stability. Thin rods supported and enabled head movements. A massive helmet encased Win's head, but during the change he had asked for a mirror, able to look at himself for the first time in months.

Win had gone still—frozen by what he saw. His hair had disappeared to be replaced by an egg-shaped skull, mottled in pink and gray because of the synthetic jack-skin, which would become normal over time. *But my face,* thought Win. Slack muscles made his skin droop so that cheeks resembled some kind of mask, a caricature of a human with loose flesh draped over an empty skull. Streamers of drool had fallen then, forcing Win to look away.

"We shall be within viewing range of the *Jerusalem* soon, on our way to the *Higgins*." Zhelnikov's voice brought Win into the present. "I've heard some of the shuttle crew whispering how strange it looks; this should be fascinating."

"I saw myself in the mirror, Zhelnikov."

"So?"

"I am no longer a person. Only part of me even remembers how I was as a human—to have a father. I see my face and know that normal people would be horrified, but I can't comprehend what disgusts a human being or what you think is beautiful. I am new. And so I doubt the *Jerusalem* will hold surprises."

"Win," said Zhelnikov. "You *are* new. This is a good thing because you are what the Fleet needs. They might not understand it yet, but you and I will show them."

"I miscalculated. In Hong Kong, and in Portugal. Doctor *Zhelnikov*, head of Fleet R & D, and I his latest invention. How could I have been so foolish to think that you had limitless influence? This will not happen again. I acted hastily in dispatching so many."

"What are you talking about?"

Win shifted his weight so that he could get a better view of Zhelnikov, strapped into a chair next to him. "You. The meeting with the admiral. Look around. I no longer have my guard, and you no longer have your research programs. My killing scared them. I did not see any of this, which means I have limitations—weaknesses—and so do you."

"I am *still* the head of Fleet R & D."

"You are delusional. They took your programs and left you with a title; Fleet would never send the real head of R & D on a risky mission such as this. They intend for us to be destroyed and didn't have the will to just execute us on the spot."

"Sometimes I hate you, Win."

"Don't misunderstand me. I have no hatred for you, or love. I think I hate my father but even that is fading with the remaining scraps of my human past. Right now we have no power but I will make an effort to incorporate these lessons into my plans going forward. I will not make the same mistake twice."

"It's because you're still a child," Zhelnikov said.

One of the pilots announced they were within visual range of the *Jerusalem*, but Win ignored it, fascinated instead by what Zhelnikov had said. He reached out and grabbed the man's wrist.

"Watch it!" Zhelnikov yanked his arm away to rub it. "Your amplification servos are pretty strong; you could break someone's arm."

"What did you mean—that I'm still a child?"

"Not a child, a young adult in your twenties. And so your brain was still forming experiential connections when we gave you the first treatments. We assessed early on that this could cause complications while adapting to your new neuronal makeup."

"Explain."

Zhelnikov studied a display that the pilots had flicked on, showing the shuttle's route past the *Jerusalem*. Win ignored it. He leaned forward, closer to Zhelnikov's ear.

"What do you mean, complications?" he asked.

"Complications. Experience plays an important role in information storage and relationship construction within human brain tissue, and so we postulated that the same would apply to your new Sommen-like makeup. But your experiences would still be human. So the question we had was: What effect would this have? How would your hybrid brain deal with the problem of adapting human experiences with novel tissues? The answer is that it doesn't deal with it well; and so you've become a murderer."

Win sat back. He went over the new information and closed his eyes, doing his best to remain calm and tamp a sensation of vulnerability. The thought that he could overpower and kill everyone on the shuttle almost became a singular thought, one he latched onto to overcome his fear, but Win had begun to realize the danger with such impulses: They weren't *his*. *No*, he corrected himself, *they are mine, but they aren't normal human ones, and as long as I'm surrounded by them I have to constantly shift those thoughts into something else. Those are Sommen instincts—not my thoughts in the strict sense.* Win marveled at the fact that he'd missed something so simple. His own mind, as powerful as it was, was a sort of enemy— its aggression sabotaging his standing among Fleet.

"What the hell is *that*?" Zhelnikov hissed; he leaned forward against the acceleration couch's straps, pointing toward the pilots' main window.

One of them chuckled. "That's the *Jerusalem*. Crazy, right?"

Win looked forward at the view screen against the shuttle's bulkhead. The *Jerusalem* had its running lights on, giant spotlights spaced at regular intervals to cast a bluish glow across its hull, which, to Win, almost looked like it had been assembled at random. The screen and picture went in and out of focus, making it hard to discern, but the ship had no right angles and he couldn't suppress a sensation that the *Jerusalem* looked familiar.

"That isn't a cruiser," said Zhelnikov. "It's too big."

"It's a cruiser all right, sir. It's big, but from what we hear, its weight, power, and weapons capabilities are all within cruiser specs."

"What weapons does she have to make it so big?"

The pilot shrugged. "That's all we know. The details are classified, but you're in luck. The *Higgins* isn't ready to receive you and I've been asked to divert to the *Jerusalem*. This should be exciting; I've never even docked there."

Win cleared his throat, and a suction line opened in his helmet, clearing saliva from his chin. "I think the design is Sommen."

"How?" asked Zhelnikov. "I've seen the specs for their battleships, and their fighter and troop carriers. This is nothing else even resembling it."

"It's theirs," Win said. "We've adopted human materials to achieve Sommen-like effects."

The shuttle docked with a bump and both men unstrapped. When the door swung open they moved into a small airlock, its surface a mottled tan and green with control panels that looked twice as big as necessary and with bubble-like lights that blinked green or red. The pilots transferred their bags and then closed both the shuttle and outer airlock doors.

Win waited. The hiss of jets from his servo harness kept him in one spot, and he noted that the neural interface seemed more efficient than had been the case in his previous harness. He willed himself to move an inch left, satisfied with the controls' sensitivity.

"What are they waiting for?" Zhelnikov asked. "Maybe the door is broken."

"Why would it be broken?"

"Look at that entry pad. That's technology from the late twenty-first century and you can only see examples of it in the space museum outside Washington; I don't know what we've gotten ourselves into."

The inner door opened. Win noticed that a crewman worked it manually, cranking a handle up and down to actuate hydraulic pistons that turned the main mechanism. It took almost a minute for the gap to open wide enough that he and Zhelnikov could push through, dragging their floating bags behind them.

"Welcome to the *Jerusalem,* Doctor Zhelnikov," the captain

greeted; he ushered for an aide to take their bags and glanced at Win. "You must be the telesthetic, Win. I'm Captain Jerome."

Win examined the man's environment suit and noticed the marking on his shoulder.

"What is that patch?"

"We're a new part of Fleet, based on some developments that have come from the Proelians. That's a crusader's cross, from ancient times."

Zhelnikov snorted. "So Fleet is now *openly* religious."

"Not exactly." The man shook his head and laughed. "At least, not in the sense that you mean. There's a classified shipyard and training facility, based on breakthroughs that the Order has achieved with their Sommen texts. The *Jerusalem* and most of her crew, including me, just arrived from there. It's a long way from Earth."

"Where?" Zhelnikov asked.

"Sorry, Dr. Zhelnikov. I'm not at liberty to give the location."

"I have flag-level clearances, Captain. I'm quite certain I have the right *and need* to know." Zhelnikov gestured to the aide, who now led the way as they drifted through the tight ship's corridor. "Is your aide the problem?"

"No, Doctor. You don't have *these* tickets, and there's nothing I can do to permit access. My apologies, sir."

Win fixed his gaze on the captain. While part of him concentrated on following through the passageway, pulling himself along railings attached to the wall, another part of Win's mind relaxed—willing itself to absorb the man's thoughts. At first there was nothing. Then he caught a sensation of excitement, which came with an image of the captain in monks' robes, his head shaved clean and someone swinging a censer that smoked with thick incense. Win was about to dive deeper when the captain glanced at him.

You can't read my mind, son.

Win stumbled, missing his next handhold and somersaulting in midair so that the aide had to pause and grab Win's shoulder to stop the rotation. He grabbed hold of the railing again and breathed.

"You're Proelian too," Win said.

"Yes. And I can permit you to see one thing; the thing that makes this ship special."

The captain told his aide to continue onward with the bags. He pulled Win and Zhelnikov into a side passage—one even tighter than the one they'd left—where Win felt the judgment of the ship's crew press in from all sides. The corridor constricted with activity, forcing personnel to squeeze by as they floated in the opposite direction, and, like he did with the captain, Win sensed emotions but nothing detailed or of substance. He disgusted the crew. It wasn't his appearance; they all *knew* who he was and looked at him with a combination of recognition and horror and Win realized that by killing the nun he had done more than make a mistake: He'd started a war with an enemy that he hadn't understood. *All* of them knew what he'd done. And now it appeared that the Proelian reach was greater than Zhelnikov's, an understanding that came too late. Win would never get close to any of these personnel without raising suspicion.

While the captain pulled himself through the shaft, Win concentrated on every muscle twitch no matter how minor; there was deep training. The man wasted no movements. His reach incorporated the precise and fluid motions of an organism native to this environment, a species that spent its entire existence in space, the vacuum and radiation responsible for influencing genetics and evolution into a perfect being; the captain—like the rest of the crew—was short and stocky, reminding Win of an oak stump.

"How long have you been on ships, Captain?" Win asked.

"This is my first."

"What?" Zhelnikov almost stopped in the corridor. "How can you be a captain already if you've never been on cruisers?"

"Because," Win said, "they are all tank trained. Corked and stuffed. Look at them, Zhelnikov; the crew are all the same age, the products of Fleet."

"Roughly," said the captain. "Fleet incorporated Proelian screening methods years ago, the same time we began to grasp Sommen space-travel methods and tech." He paused at a hatch and grinned. "We're here. This might make it all less confusing."

The captain hammered a stubby finger at one of the ancient-looking control pads, and then spun a hatch wheel, bracing one foot against the access way so he wouldn't spin in the opposite direction. The hatch popped open. One by one, they pulled themselves through the opening, on the other side of which Win grabbed a handhold, fighting a sensation of vertigo at the vast emptiness that now confronted them.

"This is the ship's computer," the captain said. "We use it to calculate vectors, navigation, and to plot solutions for homing missiles. Anything and everything we need."

Win had never seen anything comparable. They hovered in a cage at the top of an immense cylindrical space where, below them, bank after bank of indecipherable mechanisms stretched in either direction, disappearing through gargantuan bulkheads. A clicking sound filled the air. Win recalled an ancient machine, the typewriter, and wondered if the ship had been filled with them, wired to each other for the sole purpose of making noise.

"That's a mechanical computer," said Zhelnikov. "I've never seen such a monument to stupidity."

The captain shook his head. "It's a *carbon* computer, with moving parts at the scale of nanotubes. Yes—mechanical at its base, but far more advanced than you think. And absolutely bulletproof against hacking."

"I'm sure that once the Sommen board us, they will be duly impressed."

Win analyzed Zhelnikov's voice patterns, recognizing that his sarcasm was an attempt to get the captain talking—in the hope that he'd divulge information.

"That's the point, Zhelnikov. The *Jerusalem* and *Bangkok* are undetectable. The ships only have electronic computational and communications systems as backup. Engine control is handled via mechanical systems, intercom is all fiber, and the outer hull is shielded to prevent any stray emissions that might result from minor electrical systems—our keypads, whatever."

"What about navigation?" Zhelnikov asked.

"For now, that's classified too. We're moving out in twenty-four hours to Jupiter's ecliptic, where we'll rendezvous with the *Bangkok* and take on our navigator. You'll find out then. When the *Higgins* is ready to receive you, I'll send you on your way."

Win broke his silence. "Captain. The admiral told us where we're headed, into Sommen space, but where exactly is that?"

The man's expression became grim. He was so much shorter than

Win and Zhelnikov that it almost looked funny, and the captain ran a hand over his bald head.

"Far away. The Sommen home world is in the Perseus arm, centered around the I-quad border."

"*Nobody has ever travelled half that distance,*" Zhelnikov hissed. "Once we transit the first two wormholes, that's it; we cross into uncharted territories and now we have to find wormholes without the benefit of advanced scouting systems. And at any moment the Sommen could stumble on us."

"Maybe, maybe not." The captain moved back out the hatch and waited for Zhelnikov and Win to follow. "Come. I just received word; the *Higgins* is ready for you now and there's no time to spare."

CHAPTER TEN

The war, San thought, *is my entire reason for existing.*

The abbess lit a pipe, filling the classroom with the odor of raisins and San closed her eyes with a smile, inhaling through her nose. Smoke curled around the nun's head. It climbed upward into the dark wooden rafters and one of the illum-bots shifted to avoid the plume, a tiny red light blinking on its side. San waited for the fire alarm to go off but the nun waved her hand and whispered something, after which the red light blinked out.

"You have all mastered the basics," she announced. When San raised her hand, the woman coughed and pointed. "San."

"We've trained with just bladed weapons. And most of us have only used our vision once—twice at most."

"Do you have a question, girl?"

"What do you mean, 'mastered'?"

"Follow me."

The abbess moved out the door, her long robe and phase shifter swishing as she passed, the fabric flowing in the gentle breeze that blew from a nearby vent. San followed, inhaling thick smoke as she went.

Sister Frances accessed a small hatch at the end of a narrow stone corridor and the group followed, winding up a spiral staircase. The illum-bot did its best to light the way. San blinked at the shadows, realizing that to keep from tripping she had to stare at the nun's back or the shadows would trick her eyes, creating a slip-dance of black and gray. The climb took forever. By the time the abbess reached a

105

hatch at the top, San's wool clothes had soaked with sweat and she panted at the effort of lifting her short legs to mount the final steps, even in low gravity. The nun opened the hatch and ushered them through. Once beyond it, San emerged into a small dome somewhere on the face of Ganymede, tucked between massive boulders of ice that rose on three sides. The overhead view had caught San's attention and she strained to lean her head back to get a better angle.

"It's so beautiful," she whispered.

Jupiter's surface was so close that San imagined she could touch its edges, which curved away in swirling stripes of red, orange, and tan. She struggled with a mixture of feelings. Being in space, with a Fleet mission, had always been her dream and the view underscored a sense that she was almost there—that her adventure would soon begin. But as it had when she first landed on Ganymede, the sight emphasized her solitude, the remnant of an Asian family at a vast distance from Mars and everything she'd ever known. San fought a thought, one which emerged out of nothing and grew into a thunderclap: She'd never see her mother again.

"Do you see?" the abbess asked.

San shook her head with the others. "No."

"Then watch and learn."

The abbess gestured to a gap between the boulders in front of them where a section of flat ice stretched to the horizon, and she muttered into her wrist band, "*Launch the vessel.*" San felt a tremor. A crack had formed in the ice plain and now widened by the second until it stopped, creating a rectangular cavity the size of a small sea, perfectly straight on each side. San and the others moved closer to the glass walls. Something crept upward and the group waited as a huge spacecraft lifted itself with jets of gas, blowing ice off the surface and into a cloud that drifted toward them. It sprinkled the dome with glittering crystals and San squinted at the ship, pressing both hands against the glass to lean forward.

"I've never seen such a thing."

Sister Frances nodded, blowing smoke into the air. "The order has a shipyard here."

"I still don't get it," said Wilson. "What does the Sommen religion have to do with building ships?"

The nun glared and San felt tension; she watched the woman's face, recognizing signs the abbess was hiding something important, a weight almost visible in her humped back.

"Not all is for you to know, Mister Wilson. Not yet. When the Sommen first attacked our ships couldn't detect them, let alone lock weapons. We got their data stores and Zhelnikov thought the answers would be in technical documents. They weren't." The abbess pointed at the ship, which had begun a slow turn to climb higher over the ice. "The Sommen ships had a minimal amount of electronics and an advanced thermal-dispersion system. Almost nothing to give them away. We have been tasked by Fleet with the production of ships based on what we learned from their religious texts; space travel, Mister Wilson, is part of their religion—not their technology."

"But how would they navigate?" one of the other students asked.

"And communicate?" San added.

"Sit, children." When the students had arranged themselves, the nun continued. "They navigate and communicate similarly to the way we are about to—with priests. *You* are navigators and communicators. Truth is mathematics and mathematics keeps us on the path. Trust your intuitions; because of your time in the tank as infants, your hunches and guesses will always be steeped in fact, even if you don't recall the memory from which they originate. Fleet has approved the plan and each of you will ship out in the coming weeks. In the meantime, we shall train nonstop."

A cold fear crept into San's spine and she pulled her robe tighter, fighting the urge to shiver. She *wanted* her first mission. But now that it was on the verge of arriving, San wondered if she'd been hasty; the thought of leaving the group to be stationed on a huge vessel made her hands tremble. She would still be alone, but this time sailing through nothing, surrounded only by the cold vacuum of space-time.

"Do not be afraid. All of you succeeded in demonstrating sight. With the help of serum injections, you can reach across space and communicate with each other and, with time, you will perfect this skill and adapt—capable of sensing fluctuations in quantum states and spin, the particles in *you* entangled with those surrounding me here, on Ganymede. These fluctuations will form the basis of messages. That is how the Sommen communicate: on a quantum level. You will do it too."

"Quantum fluctuations?" San asked.

"A mental nudge at first. As your tank memories continue to surface and you hone your skills with experience, the messages will become a noticeable tapping in your mind. Then it will be a conversation in real time. Children, *this* is the most important lesson we can teach you: On your first day here, we broke the seal on your memories. As soon as you began to train, this uncapped information began seeping into your consciousness, some within your control, some outside of it. *Let* it happen; get out of your own way and stop thinking. The deeper memories will come later, with contemplation.

"And as far as navigation, our new ships have complex micromechanical computation systems to assist. Practice your mantras and remain submerged in mathematics. It is through this practice that you will reach out and see the course to provide basic input for the ship and its normal human occupants. All of this you can do now, children; you just don't realize it. We will spend the next week practicing basic navigation so that once you deploy it won't be a shock."

Sister Frances looked at her pipe, which had extinguished, and San noticed that the woman had started crying. "I am sorry that it has come so soon. But we received a message a few hours ago and two of you must be ready to leave in a matter of days. Fleet is sending a mission into Sommen space."

"Who?" Wilson asked. "Which two of us?"

"You, son. And San." The abbess gestured to the others. "Leave us, children. Report to Sister Joan for navigation training. What I say next is for San and Wilson. Alone."

San watched the other students rise and bounce toward the hatch where they disappeared into the staircase. The last closed the hatch with a soft thud and its seals hissed.

Mathematics is truth, San recited. *The truth is a path through the stars, traversing the curvature of space and time.*

San flinched at the words, which had come out of nowhere along with the memory of a Proelian monk whose phase-shifter hood had been pulled over his face, masking the features. She sat among the stars. San corrected herself: not just among the stars, but atop one of the new ships and inside a small glass dome. Two other ships burned engines to pull alongside. One was identical to the ship that she'd just watched burn from Ganymede, the other a standard Fleet vessel that, she recalled, would carry a full battalion of Marines.

"San!" Sister Frances shouted. "Where do you go in these moments—ones that require your full attention?"

"I am to be stationed on a ship that is part of a three-ship mission."

The abbess smiled, wiping a tear from her cheek. "Yes. You will be on the *Bangkok*. Wilson on the *Jerusalem*. This is the most important assignment anyone has faced in the history of Fleet, children. I'm sorry to place it on your shoulders, when your bones are still so young."

"Why are you scared?" Wilson asked.

"Why do you think I'm scared, child?"

"You are crying. But it's more than that. I can see it in your muscles and hear it in the frequencies of your voice, your tone."

The abbess smiled again. "Already you grow faster than we could ever teach. I am proud of you both." Sister Frances looked at San. "You have heard me speak of Zhelnikov. What do you gather in that case, from my tone and words?"

"That's easy, Mother Abbess: You hate him. You think Zhelnikov is evil at worst, misguided at best. He has made mistakes that jeopardize us and humanity."

War is coming, San thought again, *and all I can do is pick a long path, for all of them lead to death.*

"I am sending you into a trap," the abbess said. Her face went hard and the woman no longer cried. "And you must be brave. Find the way through this trap and you will come out stronger, a tool of warfare capable of making Zhelnikov meet a fool's end. Although he is both brilliant and focused, he is also blind."

"What is the mission?" asked Wilson.

"You are both to board your respective ships. From there, your group will travel outside the human zone, where you and San will navigate through uncharted space. The destination is a region near the Sommen home world. The Sommen have migrated away from their home and nearby conquered systems, running from something in contradiction of their faith. This is an enigma; they do not retreat, ever. So you are to travel there, find the reason for their retreat, and bring that information back. It could be critical for the war."

"My God," San whispered. "You aren't just sending us outside human-permitted space, but to the Sommen home worlds. If it's a trap, why not avoid it?"

"Because, child. Sometimes one must gamble—a calculated risk—to overcome and gain more than you would by taking the path of safety. Zhelnikov will be on a third ship, the *Higgins,* but he won't be alone. He tried to create a cadre with sight, as we did with you two, but refused to limit his work to human biochemistry. Instead he fused Sommen and human biologies. He had to; Zhelnikov didn't have the religious texts and didn't know the horrors associated with the path he chose: the creation of a human-Sommen hybrid. Zhelnikov thought that by taking this route, the Sommen teachings would emerge organically. He was right—to an extent."

"You or other Proelians didn't warn him about the danger?" Wilson asked.

"We did, child. And we warned Fleet. But Zhelnikov is a powerful man with powerful allies in the military and the government. And so he was permitted to create his monsters. Thank Our Lord that now only one monster remains instead of hundreds; we convinced Fleet to stop his program but not before Zhelnikov and his creation murdered one of our sisters at a secured site in Portugal. Zhelnikov's monster is a killer and a liar."

The abbess reached out and took San's hand. "Child. I need you to be strong, because this mission will fall on your shoulders more than on Wilson's. You *know* the monster Zhelnikov created. He was a boy from the capital, orphaned when his father abandoned him at a young age, whom Zhelnikov used as a test subject for Sommen chemical treatments that transformed his brain matter into a mass of Sommen neurons."

"I *don't* know him," San insisted.

"You've never met him, but you know him. And you will recall the memory among the thousands that will surface. Zhelnikov's pet used to be your brother. Your *half* brother, Win, son of Maung Kyarr—your father."

San couldn't breathe. Blood pounded in her head, making the room blurry and half real, a mirror of the confusion that took over her mind. She tried to remember. Vague recollections of something about a half brother surfaced but nothing she could grasp, so she studied Sister Frances's face instead, which had transformed into a road map of concern and fear—the same face her mother had when San had first left Mars for Fleet.

They are sending us into Sommen space, to our deaths.

"I don't remember him. I know you're telling the truth but I don't recall ever having a brother."

"That's good, child. Because he is no longer your brother; he stopped being human months ago, so do not make the mistake of thinking about him in those terms. I need you to do something for the Order, San."

"What?"

"Kill them both. Destroy Zhelnikov and his creation at the first opportunity, and do it in a way that will not trace back to the Order. Zhelnikov *must* be stopped. The war has already begun, children, and in order to be ready for the Sommen we first eradicate enemies within. God cannot help those whose core has rotted through."

"What have we done?" San asked.

Wilson stopped in the corridor and the illum-bot hovered overhead, spraying them both with a cold jet of nitrogen. "We haven't done anything," he said. "Not yet."

"That's not what I mean. I always thought that being with Fleet would be adventurous. Burning through the galaxy, moving from wormhole to wormhole and exploring things unknown. I didn't count on war with the Sommen, or being told that my first job is to infiltrate their territory in an effort to assassinate one of the most valued members of Fleet: my brother."

A half brother. The realization hit San again, washing her in a sense of bewilderment that she should *care* about this person she'd never met because he was family, but that in reality there were no feelings. Nothing. The name Win was a blank slate to her and why should it be otherwise? For whatever reason her parents had kept his existence a secret and how could she be expected to care about him when this person had only just sprung into existence?

She slammed her palm against the stone wall. "I haven't killed anything, Wilson. Nothing. And now the abbess wants me to not just kill, but to do it professionally so it won't get traced to us. *We will die on this mission.*"

"Come with me," Wilson said.

"Where?"

"Sister Frances didn't say when we had to report to Sister Joan. So I say let's take a detour and find the shipyard. I want to see more. And besides, you need a break."

"What if we get caught?"

"Then we explain that because we are about to be deployed we felt that we should get to know these ships as much as possible. Up close."

Wilson grabbed her hand. At first San followed, too stunned to make sense of anything, but then she felt the excitement of holding hands with a boy and realized that this was the first time she ever had. San felt her face run hot with embarrassment and she pulled her hand away, following Wilson as he bounced and moved through the narrow corridors, making turns that San didn't recognize and leading them deeper into Ganymede. She sensed the weight of rock and ice overhead. The impression intensified with each narrow staircase they navigated downward. San guessed they headed in the general direction of where the ice field had cracked open, but the corridors soon became a maze and before long she lost track of the turns.

"We're lost," she whispered.

"No, I have a photographic memory. I know the direction we're heading and how to get back."

"Why haven't we run into anyone? If this place has a shipyard there have to be more than just nuns. Engineers. Technicians. Security."

"So?" Wilson asked.

"Where are they?"

Wilson shrugged; he moved into the left corridor after getting his bearings. "I don't know. But this has to be the way."

The corridor ended in a bare stone wall, solid and gray with white streaks of quartz veins that ran vertically. Wilson put a hand against it. He motioned for San to do the same, and at first she felt nothing, but soon her fingertips tingled with the vibration of machinery and San placed an ear to the wall, hearing a high-pitched hum that reminded her of a dental bot's drill.

"Fine. So we headed in the right direction, but there's no way to get there. Not from here."

Wilson ran his fingers along the corners. "There has to be a secret door or something. Why would they create a corridor only to have it dead-end? It makes no sense."

San lowered herself to the floor and crossed her legs. While Wilson kept searching, she slowed her breathing. San became aware that Wilson had stopped and now watched her, but she ignored his insistence that visions wouldn't come without serum. She repeated a mantra that welled up from deep memory so that within a minute the words took hold and began opening the back of her mind, forcing everything to slip by in a vibrating haze that had both no mass and infinite weight simultaneously; her body melted away as if it consisted of hot gelatin. When San's eyes snapped open, she floated in the corridor above where the illum-bot hummed through her head.

San sped through the wall. The other side opened into an immense rock cavity that extended so far it appeared to go on forever, disappearing in clouds of smoke and dust. Steel girders wrapped their way upward toward the ceiling, hundreds of feet overhead and marked by bright white lights that cast a strong glow throughout the space. Beneath her worked teams of men. She failed to spot a single robot on the work floor, and half of the welders smoked cigarettes, sending gray streamers to well upward and around the girders where they formed a layer of haze. The sound of drilling and arc-welding nearly deafened San. She hurried forward, above where a warship had begun to take shape, its outer bulkhead secured in massive steel cradles. San was about to return to Wilson when a group in Proelian robes caught her attention.

The abbess and two other nuns moved through an opening in the ship's half-assembled bulkhead, bouncing over sharp metal sections and heading toward the partially assembled bridge. San sped toward them. By the time she caught up, the nuns bowed their heads. In front of them stood a man who wore similar robes, but white, blackened in spots where they'd contacted ships parts or machinery. The man pulled the welding mask from his head to reveal a face wrinkled with concern.

"Your Excellency," Sister Frances said.

"What is it?"

"Everything is on track. The two students are preparing for their mission aboard the *Bangkok* and *Jerusalem*."

"Do they understand what's needed?"

"Zhelnikov and Win will die, Your Excellency."

At first the man said nothing. He glanced upward and San wondered if he could see her, and he held the pose for so long that she almost moved behind a girder to hide.

"When the Sommen first came to us at Fatima," he continued, "we did not know. We thought they'd come from hell itself."

"I was not there," Sister Frances said. "I was still in Africa, in hiding."

"The Sommen dragged all of us into the field where their ship had landed, and one of their priests emerged from his ship."

"Your Excellency," one of the other nuns hissed. "You've *seen* a priest?"

"Silence!" Sister Frances said. "This is the bishop."

"It's all right, Abbess. These are dangerous times and I don't mind the question. Besides, I'm too old to weld all day." He nodded at the other nun. "Yes. And I've spoken with one. As close as one can get to speaking, at least. This was before the Sommen had given us their translation tech or language documents."

"What did he want?"

"*It*. The Sommen have no sex, no gender; they are partheno-genetic, reproducing asexually. It wanted to know all about the three secrets and the miracle, the ancient messages from the early twentieth century that everyone except us had forgotten. We had already heard reports of Sommen atrocities regarding other remnants of faiths on Earth and so were sure that at some point they would finish us off. It was a sight I'll never forget. Their priests cannot support their own body weight under gravity, did you know that? Four of their warriors, huge creatures, held this monstrosity on their shoulders and it hissed at me, urging me to repeat myself if it didn't understand my words or if it wanted more detail. I told the story slowly, because I wanted to stay alive as long as possible. When it was over, the thing just stared—with those black globes they call eyes. Sommen eyes look empty and soulless, filled with malice, and it never blinked. Not once. It was all I could do not to suffocate from the ammonia that escaped from its face mask."

A horn sounded, startling San. One by one the welding lights blinked out. The men and women shuffled off the floor, some of them laughing and talking to each other as another group filtered in from a distant portal. She moved closer to hear the bishop continue.

"At the end, it entered my mind," he said.

The abbess shook her head. "That would have been difficult, Your Excellency."

"It was not. It was magical. I saw their faith—not just what we read in the texts, I saw it, experienced it through the eyes of Sommen from the start of their civilization and then all the way to the present. It is *real*, Abbess. These things in their text: they actually happened. Imagine if we didn't just have the testaments, but also the literal memories of their contents, downloaded into our brains from one generation to the next; we could *see* what Moses saw, and hear it. That is their faith, and it is why they die for it, always. God has spoken to them, and commanded them to war. I just hope it is *our* God."

"What does this all mean, Your Excellency?"

The bishop lit a cigarette and stretched. San noticed that the man's face was gaunt; the backs of his hands looked lean and striped with veins. These were strong hands that had worked all their life and she knew enough about the faith to know how unusual it was. He had to have been the first bishop-welder in the Church's history.

"It means we must continue. We are on the right path, no matter how difficult it seems, even when it involves murder. The Sommen spared the Church for one reason: Our teachings and our miracles, *everything* matches their prophecies regarding the final days of the universe. They believe our Armageddon is their Armageddon. I'm afraid that's all I can tell you. Some details of what I witnessed must remain hidden; they are not in the Sommen texts but I've shared them with those who need to know."

He paused to take a drag from his cigarette. "Send the children to Sommen space. If Zhelnikov's allies get technologies that forced the Sommen to abandon their home system, they could use them to destroy us. Already he and his pet, Win, plot to take over this little excursion and we've intercepted transmissions from him to his associates. They expect him to divert to a research station just across the border in unauthorized space. We don't know exactly where it is or why he needs to get there."

"A research station outside the human zone?" the abbess asked. "Is he mad? Who built it?"

"Zhelnikov, using private funds to keep it secret. We already sent an emissary to the Sommen, notifying them of the breach in treaty and assuring them that the station was beyond Fleet's control—unauthorized. Even if your students fail at their mission, we hope the Sommen may succeed; I hate that we must send these young people."

"Then *why* send them, Your Excellency?"

"The treaty must hold. And because if the Sommen find this research station, there is no guarantee Zhelnikov and his abomination will be there. Lastly, we need intelligence. Maybe your agents will succeed in their mission—travel into Sommen space and discover why so many of their conquered worlds have been abandoned. I have only a guess at what our enemy fears, Abbess. Even if we can learn a tiny bit firsthand it could help in ways you can't grasp."

San began moving away. She fought, trying to drift back toward the group to hear more, but soon she flew through the air as if yanked by gravity, a force pulling her back into her body where she snapped her eyes open and gasped. Wilson shook her back to reality.

"San!"

"What?"

"Sister Joan sent someone looking; I can hear them shouting for us."

"Wilson, I'm scared."

"Why? Do you realize that you just practiced the vision *without* serum? What did you see?"

"We're walking into a *Sommen* trap. They'll be waiting for us. The Order doesn't just want me to kill a brother I've never met, they know there's a good chance we will all die during the process. Show me the way back; we should return."

San moved through the hall, her cloak billowing as she struggled to keep up with Wilson, who wound his way through the corridors and made one turn after another. When she finally recognized their surroundings, San stopped him.

"What?" he asked.

"I've been thinking."

"Have you found a way for us to get out of this?"

San laughed, grateful for the humor and its effect on her fear. "Yes. We go through it. I didn't tell you all that I learned; I saw the bishop himself. For whatever reason, Fleet and the future of Earth depends on us to get into Sommen space and learn what we can. This is a risk we have to take, and even if we found a way to get out of it they'd just send someone else."

"So?"

"So, what if they send others, who die in our place? I can't live with that on my conscience, knowing that I was too frightened to be a member of Fleet after all." San pulled at Wilson's cloak, leading him forward. "We must do this."

Before long they arrived at Sister Joan's laboratory, its hatchway sealed. San heard voices on the other side. She did her best to key in the entry code but her hand trembled and it took three tries to get it right before the hatch cycled open. *Such will be the wormholes,* she thought. Doorways into unknown worlds, passages like those twisting their way beneath Ganymede's ice, but which led to an unknown destination—one she knew held her fate.

"Well there you are," Sister Joan said. "Our two missing. Care to explain what were you doing, San?"

"I was looking for something, Sister."

"And did you find it?"

San nodded, her hands ceasing to tremble. "Yes."

BOOK TWO

CHAPTER ELEVEN

Win moved through the *Higgins* in shock. His servo harness snagged every so often on angular pieces of equipment that jutted out from the tight passageways and more than once he tumbled head over foot in zero g. Men and women passed, crew members in loose orange environment suits, and every one of them squeezed themselves against the wall, doing their best to get out of his way and not stare. A sense of embarrassment grew in Win's chest. At first the attention worried him, forcing him to move faster to get to his destination, but soon he became enraged. The crews' minds were impenetrable, like the captain's. Still, expressions of horror flickered across their faces as reflections of what he'd become: a tall skeletal figure with an inhuman head, barely a caricature of human form. On the one hand he understood; on the other, how could such people—pale reflections of humanity themselves—look at *him* with disgust? Even knowing ahead of time that Fleet officers had all been genetically altered for optimal performance in a warship, he still felt ill at the sight, all of them the same: compact masses of flesh and muscle that were as wide as they were tall, and whose heads loomed large because of extra bone matter. *I am as human as they are.*

A female voice crackled over a loudspeaker nearby. "Five hours to burn time."

"You." Win stopped a passing crewman. "Which way to the ashram?"

"Stay on this passage, through the next three intersections. On the fourth go up. Keep going to the end and the ashram passageway is somewhere up there."

"You can't upload the path into my suit?"

The crewman laughed. "No. Even though the *Higgins* has the standard semi-aware outfitting and electronic coms packages, our mission parameters state that we can only use them for critical functions. Minimization of electronic signatures."

"You *people*. Insane."

Win continued down the passageway. This was a standard Fleet destroyer, whose corridors had been polished clean to a brilliant reflective white, the electronics and piping concealed behind resin bulkheads. Win compared it to the *Jerusalem*. In contrast, the Proelian ship's passages had been simple gaps amid open pipe galleries and sieved fiber optic conduits so that Win imagined what would happen in those new ships if a coolant pipe burst, releasing superheated water in a jet that could cut steel. At least the *Higgins*'s resin would prevent such catastrophe; he'd already become lost in its maze of passages. Each intersection consisted of at least eight other access ways that led in every direction—up, down, and sideways. At what he guessed was the fourth intersection, he flew upward, squeezing past a pair of crew doing last-minute pipe welds through an access panel.

"Hey!" one of them shouted. "That section is off limits."

When Win ignored him, the man shouted again. "*Stop!*"

The pipes sped by his view screen as Win yanked hard on handholds to go as fast as he felt was safe in zero g, and soon his muscles ached from not being strong enough to sustain the movement. The passageway eventually ended, sooner than he expected. Win tumbled into a T-shaped intersection and slammed into a bulkhead on the far side so that he saw stars. The lights in this section had been dimmed, replaced by red emergency ones formed by plastic half-spheres that hummed and flickered, not even providing enough illumination to see. Win whispered *light amplification,* replacing his view screen's image with one painted in shades of green.

Now he was *hopelessly* lost. Win sensed the welder moving behind him up the shaft he'd just exited and he guessed the direction of the ashram, pulling himself toward the ship's bow. Win closed his eyes. At first nothing came; this section of the ship had been shielded, wrapping Win in a cocoon of resin, metal, and ceramic, the combination of which blocked all his efforts to reach out, to see. Maybe, he thought, there was a material combination that could protect not just stray electrical signals from emanating into space, but mental ones as well.

Out of nowhere, another crewman appeared, blocking Win's way. The man carried a stun rod; he held it out, the tip glowing blue and sending out tendrils of electricity, and Win saw the man's environmental suit was a deep blue, a security patch on its right shoulder.

"You. This area is restricted."

"I'm trying to find the ashram."

By this time the welder arrived from behind, panting. "This guy blew past me. I told him he couldn't come up here."

The security crewman gaped in confusion. "The ashram?"

"The dome. At the top of the ship. All vessels are supposed to have been retrofitted with them, usually near the front and just behind the bridge."

"You mean the coms center. Natural silica glass dome."

"Yes," said Win, wondering why he called it the coms center but not wanting to discuss it. "That's what I mean."

"You're Zhelnikov's guy."

"I am."

"Follow me."

The welder slapped a hand against the wall. "That's it? Shouldn't you put him in the brig?"

"He's authorized," the other one called out over his shoulder, leading Win further in the direction he'd already been moving. "Don't over think this, Chief, and go back to what you were doing."

As they travelled, Win noticed a hissing from his helmet speakers. "Is there a ship's communication frequency?" he asked. "All I'm getting is static."

"No radio coms whatsoever, except in emergencies. That includes no external suit transmissions of any kind. But you can jack in with cables."

"What about ship's announcements?"

The security crewman laughed. "You'll hear a message over the ship's speakers. And"—the man pointed at a small box as they passed—"these are the ports where you can jack in or use a handset.

They just finished installing them all over the ship, at fifty-meter intervals. It's all fiber coms—like being back in the twenty-first century."

The crewman arrived at a short passage that broke off above them, where he disappeared and punched at an entry keypad. A thick hatch opened. Then the crewman backed out, making way for Win to pass.

"It's kind of ancient stuff, but the *Higgins* is still a killer. Don't let the old tech fool you. The layout, materials, and new weapons installations make this one of the Fleet's finest. She's got a few surprises and one day, she'll be a Sommen killer."

"I'll believe that when I see it."

"You'll have to wait about seventy years," the man said, laughing again. "God willing."

Win swung his way through the hatch. He soared upward past the floor as the hatch closed behind him, until he bumped against the dome where he pushed himself downward. Win hooked his feet into loops, attaching himself to the deck.

At first all he saw was a solid green field dotted with spots, but Win switched off the light amplification and blinked in amazement. Stars surrounded him. As the ship spun, the Earth crept into view and filled the visible area above, clouds swirling in thick white masses over a deep blue ocean. For a second the colors woke something and Win smiled at the sensation, a reminder of summers in Charleston where the bay's waters glistened deep blues and greens under a clear sky; they had not all been bad times. His mind wandering in such memories, Win forgot what he had come for, instead transfixed by his recollections.

An intercom crackled and beeped nearby; it took Win a second to work the access panel and pull out the handset, an ancient design that involved putting one end to a helmet receiver so the other end rested near his suit's external speaker.

"You made it," Zhelnikov said.

"Barely. The ship's layout is a puzzle. I have no idea how to get back and they refer to the ashram as a coms center."

"That's because once we're on mission, you will be our only means of sending messages. You need to contact your special friends, now. Handset coms may be monitored so I can't say too much but we also need to know if you can communicate like the Proelian candidates."

"I will," said Win. "I am sure this will work."

"You've contacted them before?"

"I don't know if I contacted them as much as they found my signature and then reached out to me. But yes."

"Do it again. And report back when you finish. Just ask the crew for directions to my quarters, you'll find your way."

Win replaced the handset. He pulled on the loose ends of his foot straps, cinching himself toward the floor, then closed his eyes. *I am the next iteration of death. The future. The mind is a weapon, my sight the way to aim it, and I will destroy the world.*

The glass overhead shattered as Win rocketed outward, both expanding and accelerating through space. He moved for an eternity. The motion then slowed and Win hovered, motionless in the midst of blackness, the stars so far away that they barely looked visible in tiny pinpoints of light. He concentrated. Win sent thoughts in every direction and willed them to travel as fast and as far as possible, trying to recreate the conditions he'd experienced the first time he'd contacted a Sommen priest.

Nothing happened. Win felt the pricking of cold on his skin, the absolute zero of deep space doing its best to attack his consciousness and remind him that there were things old and powerful in the universe. Time itself shifted so that Win *knew* every minute was a year on Earth; soon his bones and skin would disappear into dust, the *Higgins* an empty husk of metal and plastic on a decaying orbit back to Earth.

You are nothing, a voice said. *Dust is where you belong. A fitting end.*

Win's consciousness buzzed; the space around him remained a vacuum, the voice in his thoughts. *You are Sommen?*

We have seen you, but now we know. We see you in the light and not in the dark, and we see your plans. We know the flaws. You have no faith.

I don't know what you mean.

Win felt a blast of heat. It was as if something transformed the words into an understandable sensation—an emotion, disgust, converted into kinetic energy.

You know of the document, the prophecy and its words, but even if you found it you would be too stupid to recognize its meaning. Human priests, your priests, are the faithful. They know the way and are on the path. We too warred amongst ourselves, long ago, but not like you; you and your allies have no honor.

Win focused, sending a wave of anger. *I do not understand. You said I was like you. Why are you now displeased?*

The priests, especially the female priests. They are true to your kind and understand the way. They created navigators out of human flesh. You are an abomination. And we now know of your base, the one outside the human authorized zone, and it is only because the female priests spoke of it that we still honor the treaty. You and your master are marked. When we find this base I will have my warriors dismember you, personally.

Win broke contact. His consciousness returned to his body where he woke, still "sitting" in zero g, bouncing against the straps. He disconnected and moved toward the hatch, not able to spin the wheel with his weak arms, instead pounding on it with the metal of his servo harness.

As soon as the security crewman opened it, Win pushed through, knocking him against a conduit so the man cursed. He pulled into the tight corridor. Passageways enveloped him in their intersecting paths and Win soon lost his bearings, moving first in one direction and then another until he reached a dead end and slammed his fist against the wall. A crewmember then showed him the way, escorting him through the tunnels until he stopped, opening Zhelnikov's hatch with stubby arms.

Win burst into Zhelnikov's room and tried to seal the hatch behind him.

"They know."

"What do they know? Slow down, boy."

"I am not a boy and the Sommen know something. They know *what* I am and they know about you; they talked about a human base, one located outside our authorized territories."

"That's not possible. How could they know?"

"Proelian whores. They must have sent an emissary to the Sommen—risked a journey into their space. What base is this, Zhelnikov? The Sommen haven't yet found it, but they search."

"We will head there. I've arranged for a diversion, one that will excuse us temporarily from the mission so we can detour—to Childress. That's where the base is."

Win sunk into his mind where images flashed one after another of Zhelnikov and Fleet flag officers in a distant planning room. Each of them wore bulky environment suits. One of the officers, a woman, glared at a stream of data that flickered in midair, a holo-image of troop strengths, budgets and research status—an endless river of information that went blurry any time Win tried to grasp it. The last image was of Win's brain, which only remained in midair for an instant, replaced by a weapon. Along the spine of a heavy battleship ran a semicylindrical piece of equipment, hundreds of meters long and punctuated by rectangular protrusions.

"You have a weapon," said Win.

"Yes. We have a weapon. The Proelian influence is unacceptable to a segment of Fleet flag officers, and this weapon will rid us of their influence."

"All this intrigue and yet Fleet worries about me."

Zhelnikov nodded. "Win, you have changed. We did not generate adequate predictions of the direction your cellular evolution would progress."

"I cannot keep having this conversation, Zhelnikov. You're incapable of grasping what I see and how far my vision reaches."

"*You* agreed to this program, Win—before we began the treatment. You are a Fleet officer, subject to the chain of command and your behavior has my superiors greatly concerned. We are out *here,* in this piece of crap ship, because of your actions. I lost most of my R & D programs *because of your actions.*"

"I am not the same. Not the way I was before signing up."

"Well." Zhelnikov sighed, shaking his head. "It doesn't matter that you've changed, Win. I think that's the point. You are a Fleet asset whether you're human or not, and because of that we needed to regain control."

Win felt a chill. Zhelnikov's face had hardened and where there had been muscle twitches and a refusal to look at Win because of fear, now there was nothing. The man stared at Win's faceplate and its cluster of vision globes.

"What have you done, old man?"

"We introduced a poison in your last treatment. We couldn't risk altering your brain chemistry or physiology so this is targeted; it permanently binds to receptors on your few remaining organs and will interfere with their operation, sending you to a slow death. It will hurt. And it's the only thing that makes having to live on the *Higgins* bearable: the thought that I can kill you now if you step out of line."

Win latched onto a handhold, the loop of fabric attached to the wall via thick metal studs. "You don't see the bigger picture, old man. I . . ."

"Silence. Right now, as long as I administer the antidote with your treatments, you live. I am in charge here, Win. Not you."

Win struggled for a response. Zhelnikov's quarters were larger than most, fitting for a flag officer, and had been appointed with faux wood panels that resembled dark mahogany, stained almost black. His zero-gravity chair resembled leather, with padded straps to keep him in place. Even his illum-bot looked expensive. The tiny robot hovered overhead in zero g, glittering in its own light that reflected off brass coverings that had been affixed to every sharp corner. There was history here, thought Win. Not the room itself, which was new, but in the sense of naval traditions stretching backward centuries and in a flash he recognized that in all his calculations he'd failed to account for human weaknesses. First among them: jealousy. It had been an error for Win to assume that Zhelnikov and the others would see the logic in his decisions because they didn't yet see the connections and relevance. They were minor beings with power who believed Win had overstepped his authority. There was no more heinous a transgression than acting without permission, he realized, in the minds of talentless bureaucrats.

"Zhelnikov. You don't understand what's happening. Out there."

"It doesn't matter, boy. Here we are."

"The Proelians have the Sommen texts."

"Yes. So?"

"The Sommen have prophecies. I don't know what they are but in my visions I saw it: faith without doubt and steeped in views of the future that led them to a path of nonstop war. War without end."

"Win, please."

"Stop. I'm trying to communicate something, for which there are no words. The Sommen eradicated all faiths on Earth because they didn't match up with their prophecies of war and destruction. None of them."

"Except for the Proelians," Zhelnikov said.

"Except for the Proelians."

"Why didn't you tell me this earlier?"

"It is so obvious. I see these things as pictures and visions so that they immediately snap into an overall framework, one that forms a strategic vision. Complex but clear. The question I ask myself now is this: Why didn't *you* see it?"

"And so those documents you wanted in Portugal. They were about a Proelian prophecy?"

"It isn't about *a* prophecy." Win moved his hands to draw a circle in the air. "It's *the* prophecy, the one that closes the loop with Sommen faith. And the Church lied to the public. It happened in ancient days, early twentieth century, and afterward one of the children to whom the visions appeared wrote them down. Three secrets."

"And you don't know them."

"The first two, yes. But nobody knows the third. I can't see it. It's like having a splinter that you can't extract, Zhelnikov, except this splinter is in my consciousness."

"But why would the Church lie?"

"Because whatever the third secret's text stated, it was so frightening that the Church thought it better to hide the truth."

"Once the microbot threat is extinguished in Portugal, my allies in Fleet will send in a search party. We'll find the secret."

Win felt a tiredness descend, making his eyes close and his speech slow. "And your men will find nothing; it's not there anymore. I saw it on the nun's face as I killed her. If I knew what the text said, I could start attacking the Sommen belief that the Proelians are their best allies, and the ones against whom they should war."

"I will never understand it," said Zhelnikov. "How the Sommen can see a race of people as allies while planning to eradicate us."

"War is the great cleansing. War clears the mind through fire and the sharp edge. War creates the iron core, necessary for what comes at the end, the iron demanded by the Great Creator who will return at the appointed time."

"You whispered that when we were with the Admiral. You're saying that the Sommen faith is the explanation."

"I'm saying," Win said, "that the Sommen honor us by their intent to eradicate humanity. You will never understand because you can't; it's in their DNA, but not yours. Tell me about this weapon you have, Zhelnikov. I saw it in my mind: a gigantic thing, down the spine of a heavy battleship. What's in Childress?"

Zhelnikov coughed, his body shaking with the effort and at first Win thought the man might pass out. When the fit stopped, Win waited. The old man's environmental suit draped over his thin frame, almost swallowing him in a sea of gray fabric, the color of Fleet senior officers. Zhelnikov ignited an electronic cigarette and inhaled as much as he could, exhaling a cloud of mist that dissipated long before reaching Win; at the same time a distant hum rang through Zhelnikov's quarters.

"The engines have started," Zhelnikov said, "and soon we will enter the long sleep. My scientists tell me that your biochemistry will handle it well, but we must be careful. I will need you and your abilities after we transit the first wormhole."

"But the weapon. Childress."

"Plans, Win. Strategies. The fewer who know, the better, so what I'm about to tell you can go no further." Zhelnikov paused, blowing another cloud of mist. "The weapon is a plasma cannon—more advanced than any we've created in the past and the first step in reverse engineering the Sommen handheld plasma weapons. No fusion reactor is needed. This weapon taps a star, requiring a fraction of the energy you'd think, and creates a beam so powerful it makes standard Fleet cannons irrelevant. Impotent."

Win's mind went into action. He ran through the physics and math, numbers and formulae shifting and spinning through his thoughts.

"It's interdimensional."

"Interuniverse," Zhelnikov corrected him. "At its core is a group of Sommen-designed microaccelerators that open a gateway into a parallel universe, but in a way that is acceptable to the Sommen faith. Not the same mechanism used by our old communications device, the one that attracted their attention and brought them in the first place. This device opens a portal inside a star. The star is in an alternate universe, and we tap its plasma, venting it via a massive barrel that tunes the beam via magnetic fields."

Win imagined the destruction. His mind reeled at the thought of directing the energy contained in a star's corona and he almost lost his grip of the strap as he grappled with the implications.

"You could sweep a planet with such a destructive source—render it sterile."

"Yes." Zhelnikov nodded. "But that's not our intent. Not yet."

"You will arm your ships with it," said Win.

"And once that is done we will take back Fleet. By force. But the base outside Childress must not fall. Not yet. It's where the research has been done and the first tests were successful beyond our hopes. Already two battleships and a drone carrier are on their way there, for outfitting with the weapon. Then my associates and I will oust Admiral Posobiec, who is sympathetic to the Proelians. We will take back control."

"It is a sound plan. I will help."

Win was about to say more when a voice came from the room's speaker, announcing that the ship would begin its burn out of the solar system in an hour. It crackled with static. The sound echoed in Win's mind, reminding him of the hiss of deep space, which wasn't really empty but filled with particles and waves, mindless energy that had its own frequency to broadcast a single message: futility. Entropy would win in the end.

"I had better get into my acceleration couch," he said.

"Win, wait. There's one more thing. I'm happy that you will help us, but you need to understand: I don't control your antidote. I don't know who does. No matter how often you try to read me or figure out where the antidote is or how it gets into your treatment, it won't work. There are allies on this ship who have been trained by the Proelians but whose loyalty is mine. One of them leaves the antidote for me and only controls a small supply at any one time."

"For now, old man, you have no need to fear."

Zhelnikov handed Win a box. "Go to your quarters and strap in. Then inject yourself with this. You and I aren't engineered for Fleet operations and will need it to handle the g-forces of high acceleration and deceleration. Pray that we don't have to fight."

"Why?"

"Because. If the crew has to take evasive maneuvers, nothing they can give us will work; the gees will compress our internal organs into jelly. One last thing: I need you in the ashram the moment we come out of cryo. The *Higgins* won't be going where the admiral thinks, so remember: into the ashram when you wake up. Now, go."

Win finally managed to spin the hatch open and moved into the corridor, almost colliding with crewmembers that sped through the passage on their way to complete last-minute tasks. He pulled himself a short distance. Inside his compartment, he strapped in and closed his eyes, opening the box and removing an autoinjector by feel. He pressed it against a small membrane sunken into his suit arm and pulled the trigger, slipping everything into a webbed overhead pouch after finishing.

Win screamed in agony. Whatever Zhelnikov had given him made if feel as though his internal tissue had begun to harden into concrete, and he worked through his mantras, hoping that the concentration would distract him and lessen the pain.

War is the great cleansing. War clears the mind through fire and the sharp edge. War creates the iron core, necessary for what comes at the end, the iron demanded by the Great Creator who will return at the appointed time.

"It is only in war that I am reborn. War is the crucible that prepares a warrior for final presentation to the Creator."

CHAPTER TWELVE

San ran star charts through her head, doing her best to ignore the tightness of *the tomb*, its space so confined that it seemed about to collapse around her, compressing her into breathless dust. She lay on her back. The *Bangkok*'s captain had named it the tomb because San had to crawl into the space between two immense banks of steel and electronics, which had been machined and designed to fit her frame with precision, after which the two blocks closed in a clamshell to sandwich her in place with both arms outstretched. Thousands of needles then plunged into her skin. The thin steel connected with nerve cells, inducing an itching in her scalp—so intense that at one point San screamed. The needles ran to banks of relays that would translate her thoughts into mechanical actions and allow control of the ship, but they would also make the ship an extension of her mind. Signals travelled in each direction; San felt the tingling coldness of space on her skin, and her vision was that of forward optical sensors so she marveled at the view of stars, invoking a sense of awe that forced her to start over with breathing exercises. Once calmed, she compared the tiny points of light to those on her memory of charts.

Mathematics is truth. It is the foundation of navigation and I must let go; by controlling my faculties and organs I open the road, allowing memories to emerge. All things must be considered, the gravity well a curve in the road of space-time. Mathematics is truth . . .

The *Bangkok* gently turned. One thousand meters in length, the ship was nowhere near as large as Fleet drone carriers and heavy battleships, but still managed to cram ten thousand men and women into five living areas; in the event of a hit, at least some crew had a chance of surviving. Each crew compartment contained cryo beds in addition to banks of emergency ones near the ship's center, pressed between gargantuan fuel tanks and the central mechanical computing core. San pointed the ship in the direction of the first leg toward their destination. *A wormhole,* she thought. A tunnel in space whose creation Fleet still couldn't fathom, or who had created them, but now so common that people didn't bother discussing the mystery. They just *were.*

Two ships flanked her: The *Jerusalem,* the ship where Wilson now navigated, and the *Higgins* with her brother, Win. San winced at the *Higgins.* A destroyer, the ship was an older design and even with orders to run silent, waves of radio signals and electromagnetic noise leaked from its hull but San recalled *that* was partly the point: the *Higgins* would play a dangerous role; Fleet had decided that in order for the mission to succeed, the group would need a ship to burn ahead through transits and test for hidden Chinese sensors and detection cells on the other side. The *Higgins* had been loaded—packed to its limits—with extra passive and active electronic sensors and emitters that even now broadcast its data to the *Jerusalem,* where it flowed into San's calculations. *Its crew will never make it back,* San thought. *I could do nothing, and my brother would die anyway; and if not the Chinese but the Sommen detect our incursion outside the human zone: war. And we* all *die.*

You're leaking, Wilson sent.

San laughed out loud, and had to pause her mapping. *We are underway; I was just about to de-tomb and take a break while I can. The computer estimates a year just to reach the first wormhole.*

Yeah but don't look at the time it will take for the whole journey, round trip.

Why not?

Depending on the route we take, we'll be gone ten to twenty years, San. Mostly in cryo. My parents are going to be old; everything will be different when we get back and we'll be the same age we are now.

My mother, San thought. Why hadn't she realized the implications? Even with the most advanced propulsion systems, cryo had been an integral part of space travel as long as San had known;

it had been one of the first technologies born from Fleet's work on Sommen technology. But now that she faced the reality of spending years asleep, San felt as though her chest was about to break open and a tear ran down one cheek; if she wasn't dead already, her mother would be when San returned.

I have to go, Wilson, she sent.

Wait. I have one more thing for you. I used the vision. I saw your brother on the Higgins.

Not now, Wilson. I have to go.

He's bad, San. Really bad. And half the Higgins's *crew is totally freaked out; the other half . . . I don't know. They've already been trained to be comfortable with him, or something.*

San shut him out. She whispered *disengage* and waited for the needles to retract before starting to cry, and at first didn't hit the tomb's opening mechanism; San didn't want anyone to see her tears. The sound of her sobbing would never make it through the banks of steel and minutes passed until San regained control. She used her tongue to activate the fiber-optic headset.

"Captain? This is navigation."

The captain's voice crackled in her ear. "Go."

"We are on course for leg one. Primary burn in one hour, three gees."

"That's a lot of sustained gees; you're going to make our nonengineered guests on the *Higgins* very uncomfortable."

"They can take it, sir. I'm going to get something to eat before cryo."

"Negative. I need you on the bridge; get your escort to take you, they know the way. Then you can eat."

San waited for the clamshell to open. Four Marines flanked her, two on each side of the tomb and fixed to the steel floor by magnetic boots; they faced outward, looking away while San floated to don her undersuit and environmental suit. When she'd finished, she tapped one on the shoulder.

"Okay, Marine. The captain wants me on the bridge."

The abbess had been strict about the need for Marine guards and made it clear that San was to be grateful for their presence; these men were Proelian—selected based on a sincere willingness to die to keep her and Wilson safe. But San saw the unspoken truth that Sister

Frances tried to hide: The men would kill her if ever it became clear that she could be taken. The abbess had also given her and Wilson a pill. It hung in a tiny plastic pouch, tucked inside her black environment suit near the neck ring where she could reach it. *But what if I was wearing a helmet?* Somewhere, someone hadn't bothered to think it all the way through and San knew one thing: In the event of capture, she was expected to take the pill and never fall into enemy hands—Chinese or Sommen.

The main navigation hatch opened and one of the Marines, a lieutenant and leader of the group, nudged her.

"Helmet on at all times, ma'am. We can't lose you in the event of emergency evacuation. If you go, we'll have a hell of a time getting anywhere, including home."

"That's not smart planning."

The Marine grinned. "Someday we'll carry two navigators, one as a backup in cryo full time. But my understanding is that right now there aren't enough of you to go around."

San locked her helmet in place, after which her team escorted her into a small passageway that enveloped them with pipe galleries. It made her feel claustrophobic again. Despite having been conditioned to serve on deep-space vessels, the *Bangkok* was a different animal than anything she'd trained for and San couldn't put her finger on it. *Why* did this ship feel so different?

"Because it's big," the lieutenant said over his shoulder. He led them down the passage, turning at intersection after intersection and pulling them further into the ship's interior.

"How did you know I was thinking that?" San asked.

"I thought it too. All of us did. The size of this girl makes it feel as though you're surrounded by a mass so dense that it could collapse inward on itself to form a black hole. Also, these passages are smaller than normal ship designs; the engineers and designers needed more room for the computation core. But what the hell, right? I mean, we're engineered for tight spaces, high gees, and the pure boredom of space travel."

The other Marines laughed and San shook her head. "Maybe *you* are prepared. I was too smart to qualify for Marine."

"I don't know, ma'am; there's still time. You might qualify for honorary Marine someday." He stopped at the end of a long corridor, punched a code into the lock pad, and began spinning the hatch wheel. "This is the bridge. We'll wait here."

San squeezed past. The bridge consisted of multiple control stations packed into a tight compartment, into which she wormed her way. Her environment suit barely fit in the crawlspace as she navigated, peeking into each crew compartment, just large enough for one genetically engineered person; although not directly like San had done in the tomb, the bridge crew partially merged with the ship itself by stuffing themselves into narrow pods. When she reached the captain's station, San had begun to sweat with the effort of squeezing through its constricted passages.

The man popped his helmet release and pulled it free. "San, we just received a tight-beam transmission, from Ganymede. Take your helmet off and deactivate your suit pickups." When she had, he leaned out of his tiny station and whispered into San's ear. "Fleet sent additional ships after the *Stalingrad*. One of you, a new navigator, scanned the region and there's no sign of a Chinese home world. Nothing. So now Fleet intelligence thinks there's an even greater chance the Chinese are sending ships to ambush any Fleet vessels that approach wormholes—at least the ones closer to Earth. That's where the *Stalingrad* got hit."

"Did the navigator see that?"

"No. This is just a best guess from Fleet intelligence. So once the computer locks in the full navigation solutions, we'll go into cryo. But we're coming out early."

"For what?"

"I may need you to look ahead, San. To find any Chinese vessels that might be waiting for us; even with the *Higgins* as a decoy I'll need every advantage I can get. Go eat and then I need you back in the tomb to finish setting courses for all the transit legs."

San left the mess hall with her head tingling as she struggled to pull her helmet back on; she sensed Wilson's reach. Instead of concentrating on his message San brushed it aside and sent a quick *not now*, motioning for the Marines to follow. She pulled herself through the corridors. Thoughts of nervousness and apprehension about the coming cryo sleep leaked from the minds around her, filtering into her brain in the form of unwanted messages that San tried her best to reject but couldn't. By the time she reached her quarters she'd started crying again.

"Are you all right?" asked the lieutenant.

"I'm fine; I just wanted to change into a new undersuit before the burn. But..."

"But what?"

"Lieutenant, did you know that almost all this crew grew up as orphaned children? I can't read their thoughts, but sometimes thoughts leak."

"Yes, ma'am. I did know. We're orphans too. Fleet prefers us now because of how much time it takes to transit to and beyond wormholes. We don't have much to miss back on Earth."

San shut the door and spun the wheel. She popped her helmet and curled into a ball, rotating in midair so that the tears spun off her face and hung to form small crystal globes as they drifted toward the air intake; in a universe where Fleet used orphans and the Proelians altered children to suit their needs and goals, who was good and who was evil? In the moment, everything became a problem set so overwhelming that San felt herself begin to hyperventilate, control of her physiology slipping away in an instant of panic that crashed through her mind.

She had just started to sob when movement caught her attention. A small panel opened above her cryo couch; the motion triggered a deep memory, which now filled her mind with the low voice of an old man. *Death surrounds the faithful. One must always consider weapons of choice among our enemies. Chief of these is assassination— a profession as old as prostitution, and as common as oxygen. The assassin moves in darkness. The assassin relies on his victim's complacency.* San's heart raced with fear and she held her breath, staring at the opening only a few feet away.

A finger-sized device emerged from the opening that had formed; San grabbed a nearby strap to halt the spin, doing her best to freeze when she identified it: *butcher bot.* A tool of Chinese killers, it was one of the most feared among politicians and Fleet flag officers, and so San wondered why she, a relative nobody, would have been targeted. *There was no time;* as soon as it detected her heat signature it would act. And the small plastic sphere on its back indicated the thing would kill with poison instead of explosives or projectile, making her want to scream for help from the Marines. But her guard would never spin open the door fast enough to stop what was about to happen; *there was no time!*

The suit helmet, San realized. It spun nearby but still out of reach and she would have to push off the wall to get closer. Fear had turned her legs to lead. Even if San grabbed it, could she seal the locking ring in time? Without a perfect seal the agent would enter the tight confines of her suit, and San knew she'd only be able to hold her breath for a short time. Besides; the agent was probably a skin penetrator. Less than a drop would do the job whether she held her breath or not. San broke the chain of thought, angry at herself for having wasted even a second; *there was no time.*

San kicked. She pushed off the wall and sped toward the helmet, fumbling with it when her back impacted against the door. The bot screamed forward. Time slowed with adrenaline and she almost laughed at how it took her several tries to get the helmet on and then several more to work the neck-ring seal, cutting herself off from the room's atmosphere.

The bot clinked against her faceplate. Its sphere burst to release a small cloud of mist—forming droplets on her helmet—after which it deactivated and bounced toward a corner.

Someone pounded on the door.

"Ma'am, are you all right?" the lieutenant asked, his voice muffled by thick steel.

San grabbed the wheel to stop it, engaging the lock. "Don't come in! There was a Chinese butcher bot, with poison gas. Tell maintenance to shut off air handling in this section and send a decontamination crew." She paused to grab the end of a cable within a recessed wall mount, and pulled, jacking it into the side of her helmet. "I'm plugging into coms now."

The channels filled with activity and San listened to Marine security teams, who closed the system to all traffic except theirs. Everything blurred. *They tried to kill me.* San began crying again, almost forgetting to switch on her oxygen supply, which, she thought, would have been ironic given the amount of trouble someone had gone to poison her. Hypoxia or poison—either would have made her just as dead.

They tried to kill me.

The lieutenant clicked onto her speakers. "Ma'am, Marine security and decon teams are on their way. Are you okay?"

"I was able to get my helmet on before it detonated but I'm covered with some kind of agent."

"How much oxygen do you have left?"

San checked her suit computer, then opened a pouch on her side. "Enough. I have an extra cartridge. Hours."

"Captain," the lieutenant said. San had to recall her rank—to remember that navigators all made captain upon deployment, bypassing lower officer ranks, and that the Marine was still speaking to her. "Who would want you dead? I need you to think. Who would go through all this trouble to go after you?"

And who would have had the access needed to install such a device, San thought. *Who would have been able to make sure she would be assigned this room? It couldn't have been Chinese agents.*

"I don't know. My first guess is that it was planned a long time ago, when the ship was under construction. The bot was concealed within a secret compartment near my cryo bed and the easiest time to install such a thing would have been during a time when lots of people had access to the area and could easily make changes. Then someone else would have had to make sure I got assigned here."

"But why chemical? Whoever did it had to know that you'd be in an environment suit. You're lucky they didn't add a suit penetrator."

They didn't have time for proper planning. San shook her head, doing her best not to start crying again. "It activated after I broke seal. I think it was programmed to go into action when the sound of helmet removal was detected."

"Yeah, but wouldn't an explosive been more sure? Wouldn't . . ."

"*I don't know!*" San interrupted, shouting.

"Sorry, ma'am. The decon team is here and we're coming in."

San unlocked the hatch, its wheel spinning as she moved away, creating enough room for two men in white environment suits to enter; the corridor outside had been sealed with dense foam. The men ran a scanner over San's helmet and the handheld device spoke, listing the names of several chemicals that San didn't recognize.

"Three agents," one of the men said. "Two nerve, and one blood. Whoever wanted you dead, wanted to be sure."

One began spraying a white liquid, which foamed and turned blue on contacting live agent, while the other sucked it up with a backpack unit. They released a cloud of microbots. After a few minutes one checked his scanner again and gave the thumbs-up, removing his helmet to breathe what little air remained in the room. He laughed when he looked at San.

"It's okay, ma'am; we know what we're doing. Your suit is now decon'd too." He pulled a cable jack from the wall and plugged it into his helmet, holding the mic close to his mouth. "Air is safe now. Security teams can enter and activate normal air handling."

The lieutenant burst in. He grabbed San by the arm and pulled her through the hatch, after which two of his team led the way, shouting at crewman to get out of the way as they barreled through a foam wall and upward, heading toward the tomb.

Something bothered San and it took her a second to figure out. "Why the tomb? Wouldn't that also be a logical area to place an assassination device?"

"Yes," the Marine said, "but far more difficult. The security measures put in place by the Proelians made it so only certain people could work either on *the tomb* mechanisms or on this part of the ship. It's the safest place."

The group punched through the hatch and into the tomb chamber, where San watched. Marines scanned everything. The room cramped with activity as the men ran deep-penetrating search electronics over every surface, comparing the images with schematics from the original ship's blueprints to make sure nothing was out of place. San had begun to cry again by the time they finished.

"It's okay, ma'am," the lieutenant said. "They won't fool us twice."

"What if they try again? Maybe my cryo tube is sabotaged, or one of *the tomb* needles coated in slow-acting poison. How can I live this way?"

"The needles are clean, their mechanisms sound. And right now our teams are scanning your cryo compartment."

She was about to respond when Wilson broke into her thoughts, stopping her.

They put one in my cryo chamber. We heard about the incident on the Bangkok *and our security teams checked. They found one set to activate as soon as my sleep began.*

Who did this? San sent. *The Chinese?*

We think it was made to look *Chinese. But I'll give you two guesses. Zhelnikov and my brother.*

Wilson's response contained a sense of rage. *Not literally, but yeah: their kind. I started scanning the* Higgins's *crew when I got the chance and most of them are resistant to penetration. All of them Proelian trained to hide thoughts. A few aren't very good, but none of them were involved.*

Ganymede infiltrators, San sent. *The abbess underestimated Zhelnikov's reach and the abilities of his faction. She thought that her station was still a secret to non-Proelians.*

I reached out to notify her already, through the other students. I suspect the Proelians are turning Ganymede upside down as we speak. Could it get any worse? We have three enemies: Chinese, the Sommen, and Fleet traitors. At least the Sommen threat is far off—for most people anyway, if not for us.

This is why we are here, Wilson; the abbess knew we'd be in danger and they won't be surprised if we die. This is why she wants us to kill my brother. The war, in a way, has already started.

We have to get into cryo, San.

She almost started crying again. *Thank you, Wilson. I'll see you at the wormhole; I just want to run one more calc.*

San hooked a foot on a floor strap and unlatched her helmet, then began undoing suit seals. The Marines looked away. The chamber felt cold, its steel deck freezing against bare feet. San heard the lieutenant say something but she ignored the man, instead pushing off the wall and diving toward the tomb's entrance. Once she lay on her back, the two halves sealed with a thud. A moment later the needles sprang from their holes with a *snick* sound, their penetration somehow calming her in the face of everything that had happened.

I am the answer to war. I will see all and by calculation and design will know the future, will navigate my brothers and sisters through the jaws of our enemy.

"Navigation linkage off," she whispered. "Administer serum, one dose."

San shifted in a microsecond, now hovering over Zhelnikov who looped one arm through a wall strap so he could face the other occupant in his quarters: her brother. She fought a sense of disgust.

The feeling threatened to break her concentration with its distraction of emotion, yanking her from the river of quantum particles that flowed around her in a cold current of electricity. She struggled. Soon the emotion had left and San resubmerged into the flow, wallowing in the energy of its promise.

"The Proelians are phantoms."

Win shook his head. "This was stupid, Zhelnikov. Your brothers are too eager, take too many chances."

"I didn't know of this plan. They never should have made such a blatant attempt. Now the abbess is scouring her ranks for traitors and she will find them. It will put us back."

"And we were here, Zhelnikov. Right here in the middle of Proelian crews, in a ship immediately adjacent to one where an assassination attempt just failed. I look forward to the questioning. Tell your people they are morons."

San drifted closer. She lowered herself to face Win, inches away from his matte resin faceplate, curved and faceted with clusters of sensors that made him even more of an insect, the folded arms of his servo harness its legs. *Where is the web?* A spider always had a web and Zhelnikov appeared as though he'd been stuck to its strands for decades, pinned against sticky silk that would never let him free even if he *wanted* to flee. For Zhelnikov, the web would have been a comfortably familiar home.

Come, young thing.

As if an invisible fist grabbed her by the ribs, a force ripped San from the *Higgins* and dragged her outside, into space, where Jupiter passed, then Pluto, the acceleration constant and marked by stars that smeared into bolts of light. Part of her wanted to slow. The stars drew her attention, their energy palpable at a distance but even more intense when her consciousness moved through the furnaces themselves, a sea of fusion-charged gas and brilliance. San stopped fighting. Resistance was pointless, this was a Sommen grip. They had found her and pulled her consciousness to wherever they wanted.

Days seemed to pass. San stopped, landing in a dark space lit by pale blue lights that hovered in midair to reveal black and green arches joining far overhead. Alcoves at regular intervals held statues. The figures depicted Sommen warriors in poses of violence, their black trunks naked and striped with thick and cabled muscles, and with faces contorted to reveal row after row of needle teeth. *And those eyes.* Even though lifeless statues, the black orbs called to her, almost making her miss the fact that a live Sommen floated in the middle of the vault, encapsulated within a long, transparent container filled with fluid. It gestured to her with thin arms. *A priest.*

Yes. A priest. And a killer.

I have never killed, said San.

You will. And at first you will enjoy it. Then you will learn to ignore the attraction of death and its power, and you will emphasize calculations and their meaning.

Mathematics is the way.

Because mathematics is the way through space and time, the solution to life, and the path toward the glory of destruction. It is good that you know. Let me look at you.

San felt herself dragged closer, just outside the liquid tank. The Sommen slammed its head against it and its movement startled her, almost jolting her out of her trance with the realization that a leader among the most violent threat mankind had ever faced was now mere inches away; it didn't matter that it wasn't in real life. *Reality was always relative.*

You are human, the thing said.

What else would I be?

There was another. At first we admired your progress, but then saw that once more you had strayed. It was not human. No species should change its essence and stray far from what they are. If they do, they lose what was meant to be.

I don't understand. Another?

You know him. I see him in you, but you are different. Un-defiled.

My half brother. I only found out about him recently.

The Sommen made a gurgling noise and San sensed gentle waves of joy. *It was laughing.*

Your thoughts leak, it continued. *You need more practice. I see your brother's death and you as the killer. I see that this has been ordered by your elders. It is wise for your old priestess to order this destruction and it is a thing of art to give you the task. This is a moment, in which you will learn much about war, about death, and about what it will take to become strong. We approve of what we see in this plan.*

Why did you bring me here? she asked.

To see and talk. You aren't the enemy. Humans are the way, the doorway to life eternal.

I don't understand that either.

Now San sensed joy again, this time directed at her. *So young. You've never seen the shadows of dead civilizations, or any of the things older than my species and that are long gone now. Forgotten, but still deadly. How could the maker have gifted your kind with so much? It is another piece that, when put in place, tells us that you have been chosen. All this is in the books.*

The religious texts? I have them, in my mind, but I can't access them yet; they have to emerge on their own.

They will. Tell your masters that we approve. Go.

San woke in the tomb, her forehead damp with sweat at the same time she shook, part of her mind still trying to absorb what had just happened, another trying to rid itself of any remaining serum. She heard a crackling nearby and ordered the clamshell to open a bit, just enough room so she could free one arm and drag the headset into place.

"San!" the captain yelled in her ear.

"Here, Captain."

"The *Jerusalem* has finished its calculations and is already starting its burn, and the *Higgins* will be ready after that; we've approved of a minor course change for the *Higgins* so we don't all arrive at the same spot simultaneously, but will approach from multiple directions. We need you to run the last-minute calculations."

"I'll get on it now, Captain."

"And when you're done, get your ass into cryo; we're not wasting any time once the new route is locked in."

CHAPTER THIRTEEN

Win vomited into a vacuum line. The hose had popped from the ceiling and he pressed the mask against his face while suppressing a scream; all his muscles had cramped. Cryo sleep hadn't agreed with his biochemistry and both hands erupted in pain when he moved them, forcing the fingers to disconnect the chem-tubes one at a time, their ends glinting in the cabin's light and reminding him of malaysian susuks—charm needles. He threw up twice more during the process and then hit the button to open the chamber, allowing him to spill out and into his quarters. Soon the compound he'd been given to handle sustained high-g acceleration wore off, leaving him with a sensation that he'd been converted into a deflated balloon.

Win knew their route would have taken them in a line that passed through the hydrogen-rich atmosphere of countless gas giants, a delicate mathematical operation that had to ensure more fuel was taken on than was lost in such a massive gravity well. And maybe there had been one or two water runs. Something tugged at Win's mind; he was supposed to do something when cryo ended.

Get to the ashram . . .

Win struggled into his undersuit. In this weakened state he would never have been able to do it on Earth; weightlessness was a gift. By the time he'd wrestled the armored servo harness out of its locker and squeezed into it, he had a chance to look at the chronometer and froze. He double-checked and hit the button telling it to resync with the ship's clock, but the answer didn't change.

Almost a full two years. Gone. Anything could have happened on

Earth during such a long period, and Win wondered how much he'd missed during transit. The exit into the corridor outside raised even more questions; Win emerged to see a group of crewmen shackled together, some of them unconscious with head wounds that trailed beads of dark blood and smears of red now covered the previously pristine walls. Three Marines guided the prisoners. Each of them held Maxwell carbines and one saluted to Win, the maneuver tricky in zero g.

"Morning, sir."

"What happened?"

"We had orders to round up these ones after cryo. Some of them resisted."

The confusion threatened to make Win nauseous again and he sped in the opposite direction, trying to recall the way to the ashram. His memory resisted. Win saw his recollections as if they'd been dipped in fog that he wiped off before calming his nerve endings, willing his head to stop pounding. By the time he reached the ashram, the communication station was already buzzing and Win paused to look through the glass dome. Wherever they were, the *Higgins* was alone in empty space, with only distant stars as companions and no sign of the other ships. He grabbed the handset.

"We were out for two years, Zhelnikov. When I woke up, Marines had detained a bunch of the crew."

"*You* were out for two years, Win. I came out of cryo a couple of times to oversee things and make sure we came out on top."

"What are you talking about?"

"We transited two wormholes while you slept. Even with the reports of potential Chinese ambushes we had to take the chance and go for transit without having you scan ahead; the Proelians on board had rigged the cryo-tank monitoring system so that if we had thawed you, half would have automatically awoken. I needed them all asleep."

Win closed his eyes. Part of him shot out but then stopped, close enough to Zhelnikov's quarters that he felt the man's brainwaves leak through the bulkhead, juxtaposed with the handset's sensation of cold plastic. The awareness of being two places at once made Win feel sick again and he opened his eyes.

"You left the group. You took a different route than the other ships, and now the *Jerusalem* and the *Bangkok* have no idea where you are."

Zhelnikov nodded. "We're making for Childress Station—my research facility. One more transit and we're outside the human authorized zone. I and my organization planned for the detour prior to boarding this vessel on Earth and we were able to staff the *Higgins* with a large number of loyal crew and Marines."

"But not all the crew."

"No. Not all."

"What will happen to the Proelians? You can't keep them in the brig during acceleration; there are no couches. Even with their engineering if we get into a combat situation they'll be slammed against bulkheads and broken open like watermelons."

"We don't need them. And we couldn't risk sabotaging their cryo chambers; it could have been detected. You and the Marines will jettison them from the shuttle airlock after finishing your scan and we will say they were killed in a Chinese ambush. Right now I need you to recon through the last wormhole transit—Zebra-Two-Five—and survey Childress Station; it's outside the human-permitted zone. I want to know if anyone is around, Sommen or Chinese."

The thought of killing so many Proelians excited a part of Win, who grinned as he spoke into the handset and ignored the suction sounds of his suit drawing saliva from his chin. He willed himself to be calm.

"I see the wisdom."

"Win, one last thing." Zhelnikov paused, interrupted by a coughing fit that sent scratches of static through the line. "If the Sommen are there, I want to know everything. How many ships, how many warriors—*everything.*"

"I understand, Zhelnikov." He replaced the handset and, without waiting, injected a bolus of serum.

This time it was effortless. Win's consciousness disengaged from his body as it hovered, a shell of material with arms that looked lifeless while it remained in trance. He sensed the ship's engines, dormant as they coasted. Soon an instinct emerged from what he assumed was the Sommen part of his neural structure and Win urged his presence to expand, forcing him to imagine that his soul transformed into a diffuse cloud of dust—one that filled a vast portion of space on his side of the wormhole—an invisible nebula. Anything that travelled within range of his expanded presence would collide with a part of his soul, sending a tremor along its network and leading him back to the source.

I am a messenger of death. Garrisons live by my message, warriors fight on my word alone, and merchants cannot supply without my knowledge. The words were Sommen. He almost stopped concentrating on the task of scanning to instead take a closer look at how the passages had infiltrated his thoughts, but Win stopped, reminding himself to stay alert. *Without my sight, the empire collapses into disconnected settlements, doomed to a slow death with the passing of time. A death without war, without combat, and without meaning. I give meaning to empire and glory.*

Something entered his network. At first he didn't feel it but after the thing moved for some time it became clear that the object was tiny, tumbling end over end through space and in the direction of the *Higgins* but still far enough away that the ship's sensors would never have picked it up even if they'd been switched on. The thing gave no emissions of its own. Whatever it was, Win decided, it wasn't supposed to be there but lacked power, suggesting that its arrival was unusual. Curious, he focused, collapsing his consciousness back to a point where he could view the object close up.

A signal buoy.

Win recognized the black scarring on the buoy's metallic surface and realized that something had shot at it, missing or else the buoy would have disintegrated, but close enough to damage the thing's propulsion unit and power supply. Now it coasted, dead. After noting speed and position, he lined up its trajectory and flew alongside it, backtracking in the direction from which the thing had come, tracing a path to a small white star. Not a star, Win corrected himself: the wormhole. The buoy had transited the wormhole from Childress Station.

He broke trance for long enough to grab the handset and message Zhelnikov.

"I'm sending you the coordinates of a signal buoy. Its propulsion unit is destroyed and the thing looks like it may have come from Childress; it's a human buoy for sure, Fleet design. Have the ship move to intercept."

"Win," said Zhelnikov. "When you start scanning the other side of the wormhole, be careful. If the Sommen are operating there, they will have a priest with them."

"Is it safe to use another dose of treatment?"

"Yes."

"Then do not fear, old man."

Win whispered a command into his helmet mic and then gritted his teeth when a needle inserted at the top of his spine and between the vertebrae. He hissed. His heart raced, picking up so much speed that it felt as though all four limbs vibrated with the pulsation and Win fought the urge to vomit, willing the sensations to pass.

Without warning, a searing heat erupted within Win's skull and he screamed inside his suit, loud enough to deafen his own ears. He laughed at the irony: *Nobody else can hear me.*

As if pulled by a magnet, Win's consciousness flew again from the ashram; he watched as the *Higgins* shrunk and then disappeared in darkness. Then Win turned, the wormhole now close-by and enormous, growing as he sped forward. He imagined it was a mirrored marble the size of the sun, which emitted a cold light of its own that brightened as he closed in, its bluish-white rays blinding in their intensity. In a blink he was through.

Backlit by the wormhole's light, Win moved into the darkness on Childress's side and mentally ran through the coordinates Zhelnikov had given him. His mind overlaid a map. He oriented as quickly as he could, ignoring the hiss of space and streamers of particles that jetted from the wormhole. By the time he moved out, Win had started his mantras.

The way is always toward the inevitable, toward death. There can be no glory without war, no war without planning and no planning without control. My mind is a vessel. With this vessel I contain my thoughts, and by containing my thoughts I control them. Thoughts are a transmission. Thoughts can run astray, can be intercepted. An intercepted thought can bring defeat.

A burst of light caught Win's attention. Then another. He moved in faster, the view of battle taking shape where a Fleet vessel already burned—a carrier. It had been cut into three pieces that now moved together in a straight trajectory, the sections tumbling out of control and spewing gases along with personnel. Win closed his mind to their mental screams. It was a distraction, a threat to his concentration, and if this was a Sommen attack he needed to remain undetected. There was no room for error.

A Sommen ship moved past. It emerged from the darkness of space and a section of its side began to glow a bright orange where three jets of plasma rocketed from it, heading toward one of two remaining vessels, both battleships. The ship began to turn, attempting to evade. Before it could dodge the plasma beams, one of them slashed into the vessel along its spine, cutting through the hull in a fraction of a second and almost slicing it in two down the ship's length. The other two Sommen plasma beams missed, dissipating in the distant blackness of space.

The last battleship turned, its bow now facing Win and the Sommen ship. Win prayed for it to fire. At first he had trouble picking out the vessel's details because it was so far away, but as it closed Win saw the tip of it start glowing in preparation for attack. Both vessels fired. Blue plasma streaked from the Fleet ship and passed over the top of Win's head. A miss. Even missing, the beam had come close enough that Win saw a portion of the Sommen ship melt and then disintegrate, spewing white gas into the vacuum.

The Fleet battleship flew into hundreds of small pieces. Sommen plasma intersected with the ship's bow, cutting through the center and deep into the core where, Win guessed, it had hit the magazine. His heart sank. Win didn't care about the crews; this would be bad news for Zhelnikov and his group, who had been counting on these vessels and their new weaponry for use against the Proelians.

Your thoughts have leaked. They're refuse, tumbling through space-time to be picked up by anyone who looks.

Win felt a twinge of panic. He was about to retreat when the voice stopped him.

Don't run. We want you to see. To witness. You are the abomination; we grieve because now we know your body is not here to dismantle slowly.

I'm difficult to find, Win sent. *Even harder to kill.*

It is better this way. You watch the destruction of your fleet and will spread fear among those who broke the treaty.

I am like you; I do not fear.

You are a poor imitation. It fooled us. Your masters know they break the treaty by abandoning your race. Your priests and priestesses have saved you from an early invasion; we will honor the treaty because of them, and because of your sister.

She is nothing.

Win sensed amusement in the priest, a kind of laughter infused into his response. *That is an erroneous conclusion. Come. Watch. Get closer to your station and see what we do to those who break treaties.*

Win followed the Sommen vessel as it burned toward the area that had been occupied by the Fleet ships. Another warship emerged out of darkness: a squat, oblong box, constructed in the usual Sommen green material—translucent, resinlike plates that overlapped in leaves. A troop carrier, Win thought. The ship crept closer to an asteroid so large that it resembled a small planet, with a rocky surface gouged by long black trenches where Sommen plasma had already destroyed whatever Fleet missile defenses had been present. As soon as the Sommen ship docked, Win flew; he moved through the rock until popping into a corridor, its walls bored smooth.

Armored Sommen warriors poured through the station's airlock, not bothering to use rifles and instead opting for long knives. None of the station's defenders had weapons that would work against Sommen personnel armor anyway, Win figured. Within seconds, thirty Marines lay dead, sliced open from neck to groin.

This is our faith, the Sommen sent. *Those are brave men. My warriors honor them by refusing to use rifles. They wanted to remove their armor and use only breathing gear, but I forbade it.*

Why?

Because we are not here to fight for honor. We are here to teach a lesson and punish. There is no point in seeking glory when spanking a child.

We will destroy you.

Again the Sommen laughed. *That is what we hope. But there are things darker and older than my species; what will you do with them?*

In a blink, Win returned to his body on the *Higgins*. He twisted in midair, using a gas jet to push toward the hatch and then out into the corridors. Blood floated in every intersection. Win sensed that Zhelnikov wanted to see him, but he ignored the thought and instead moved in the direction of the main airlock where he found a group of Marines, their magnetic boots grounded to the deck while prisoners hovered nearby.

"Are these *all* the Proelians?"

A Marine nodded. "All the ones that lived. I'm sure you've seen the corridors; we've spilled a lot of Proelian blood."

"Get your men out of the airlock."

Win backed up with the Marines so they all stood inside the ship, watching as the huge inner bulkhead door slid shut. It closed with a thud. He looked through the window, expecting the prisoners to cry or scream, begging for mercy. Instead they had all joined hands.

"What the hell are they doing?" Win asked.

"Praying, sir."

Win slammed his hand on the airlock controls, punching in his security code and then pulling the outer door handle. At first the Proelians were there, then they weren't. It ended in a puff of gas and Win imagined that the group now sped through space, a cluster of dead bodies holding hands and frozen in prayer. He grabbed the Marine's shoulder and pointed at a nearby communication port.

"Jack in. Tell Zhelnikov I'm on my way to his quarters."

His sister. Nothing in Win's Sommen physiology had prepared him for the rage he felt at realizing the Sommen had accepted her but rejected him, and as he moved through the red-streaked corridors he began to wish that he'd been awake—to help with the slaughter of Proelians. He imagined the satisfaction of stabbing her. A memory of his father, from long ago, bubbled out from underneath his mantras to remind Win of their hovel in Charleston; the image stirred his thoughts, generating a stream of bitterness. *My father abandoned me to start another family, with a Proelian whore.*

He burst through Zhelnikov's hatch and shut it behind him. "I want to know everything about her. Now."

"Who, Win?"

"Don't pretend to be confused!"

Zhelnikov shook his head. "Her name is San. She is a Proelian. For now you need worry only about the mission, Win—not reliving past slights or the fact that you grew up without a father. None of that matters. She is a Proelian theurgist and you don't have to deal with her. Not yet."

"It matters, old man, and I *do* have to deal with her. I saw the

Sommen. Spoke with their priest. Not only do they want me dead because my creation broke the treaty, I saw in his thoughts: My sister has been assigned the task of killing me."

"Damn it, boy!" Zhelnikov shouted. "Look around you. We just took over a Fleet vessel and are one transit from leaving human space; when we eventually relink with the main group, we'll be well *inside* Sommen space. *I need you focused on the mission.* What did you see?"

"The Sommen have Childress Station. Everyone is dead, and your three ships destroyed."

As Win told the story, the hair on his neck stood with a feeling that things had changed. The ship had begun accelerating. Win's feet touched the room's deck and his servos hummed as suit joints accepted weight and picked up the gentle vibration of ship's engines. When he'd finished his report, Win leaned against a bulkhead.

"We are underway?"

"We have two bases—one on either side of the wormhole. You said that the Sommen priest warned you about things out there that are old and dark?" When Win nodded, Zhelnikov continued. "Then you need to see something. We'll be at the human-side base in under an hour, near Childress transit."

In deep space there was no visible light to illuminate the object Win's shuttle now approached, and his view screen showed only a field of stars with a circular section that had been blocked by a moon or asteroid—a perfect circle so empty that Win imagined their shuttle headed into the throat of a black hole. He altered his sensor settings in an attempt to gain perspective. Without any markers or shadows, the one thing lending a sense of distance to the object was radar data that cascaded through his heads-up.

"It's artificial," Zhelnikov said.

"I thought it was an asteroid."

"Everyone does when they first see this. I did. Its mineral composition absorbs and blocks all emissions and the only way you'd know it was here is if you kept a close eye for gravity anomalies or swept with radar. We found it when one of our destroyers slammed into its surface, the entire crew lost."

Win had been searching his memories for any indication of

Fleet having built artificial asteroids, when Zhelnikov's words registered.

"You mean Fleet *didn't* build this?"

"It's artificial." Zhelnikov pointed at a rectangle of light that had just appeared in front of them, where a landing-bay door crept upward to allow the shuttle to enter. "And it's hollow. And yes: Fleet did not build it. As far as we can tell, the Sommen didn't build it either."

Win wanted to say something and opened his mouth to talk, but nothing emerged. The shuttle entered and his screens lit up on all sides to show the cavity, which consisted of glittering rock lit by human activity within a cavernous expanse—large enough to hold several battleships or towns. Holes and openings littered the walls. Win asked Zhelnikov to zoom in on one of them, and he saw a series of walkways, staircases, and ladders that connected each hole to another, forming a network of sorts that resembled an ancient settlement he'd seen back on Earth.

"I've seen this, in an old documentary about Earth."

Zhelnikov nodded. "The Puye Indians, North America—or one of any hundreds of cliff-dwelling civilizations. But whoever lived here wasn't human. The distance between steps suggests they're huge. Giants. Bipedal for sure, with three toes on each foot, three fingers on each hand. Clawed."

"What did they do here?"

"They travelled. Nothing remains except the spaces where they once lived and had equipment and machinery, but we can tell that this was a spacecraft. They hollowed out an asteroid and voila: a massive ship."

"Nothing is left?"

"*Almost* nothing." The shuttle bumped on a rock surface and metallic claws swung up to grab its landing gear, securing it to the rock. Zhelnikov grabbed his helmet and waited for the pilot to pop the airlock doors. "I need to show you something."

"What about vacuum? Aren't you going to wear your helmet?"

"We transited through an airlock, it's pressurized. And there are growing stations for oxygen generation and O-two generators to compensate if something goes wrong. Plenty of fusion power."

Win followed Zhelnikov out the door, drifting down toward the rock; his servo legs kicked up dust. Both men navigated through a maze of shuttles and small destroyers, winding their way through Fleet personnel that scurried toward the shuttle in bouncing motions. Win stretched, relieved to be outside the confines of a ship. The gravity, although almost unnoticeable, was enough to make him feel better, banishing the constant disorientation of navigating in zero g.

They weaved their way toward the closest wall. When Zhelnikov started to climb one of the staircases, Win noticed how awkward it would be—the wide gaps between them requiring the use of both arms and legs to move upward.

"Don't fall. Even in slight gravity, once we get high enough, the fall can kill you. We lost three people the first time we explored."

By the time they made it to one of the lower holes, Win's systems had started to warn of his elevated heart rate and rapid breathing, and he felt the sweat slide off his forehead, making its way toward his undersuit. The hole was too big. Win's servos whined as he extended both arms, which couldn't touch either side, and he looked up to see that the top of the opening was at least six feet overhead. *Zhelnikov hadn't exaggerated,* he thought. *Giants.*

Zhelnikov motioned for Win to approach. He stood in front of a wall that stretched upward, so high it reminded Win of one side of a skyscraper. Floodlights clanked on to illuminate it with a cold blue light, the glare of which made crystals in the rock glint.

"They knew us," said Zhelnikov. "And they knew the Sommen."

"This is . . ." Win started, unable to finish the thought.

"Unusual?"

"*Impossible.*"

A series of carved frescoes covered the wall from top to bottom, the upper ones so far above that Win had to adjust his zoom. The sight made him take a step back. Win stumbled, catching his balance in time to prevent from falling and then scanned the images into his system for future reference.

"That's Earth, Precambrian. But there are far more life forms than we've ever been able to catalog. I don't recognize many of them. Then you have the Cambrian explosion. Those organisms are consistent with the ones we've documented." Win cycled through the frescoes, naming each geologic epoch. When he approached the bottom-most line of frescoes he stopped.

"That *cannot* be."

Zhelnikov shook his head. "I assure you it's real. Nobody could have come out here and carved this rock as a hoax. Only Fleet assets can travel here and we would have no need for this kind of deception."

"Then the Sommen made this place—to scare or influence us in some way."

"Win, we scanned every centimeter for traces of their material. Sweat. Nitrogenous waste. Bits of DNA. We found nothing. The few traces of carbon-bearing materials we did find we were scraps of some kind of fabric we were unable to identify."

"Did you date it?"

"We did but it was far too old for carbon dating. Instead we found a perfectly square section of the rock that these things had melted somehow, either to form part of an engine room or they had a power source in here that went haywire, malfunctioned, and liquefied everything around it. New zirconium crystals formed. They yielded uranium-lead dates at just over one million years."

"That's impossible."

"Repeating that won't make it true, Win. This place was created at least a million years ago by an unknown race that knew about Earth, and knew about the Sommen. Then they abandoned it. And we've never seen a trace of them since."

Win pointed at the lower row of frescoes. "Those are frescoes of things that haven't happened yet, Zhelnikov. Those are of us and the Sommen, *at war.*"

"Partly correct. The first few are humans and Sommen at war. The next ones show us fighting on the same side, against an unseen enemy. And the last one, the last section has been prepared for carving but they never completed it."

Win studied the pictures, moving forward but taking care not to bounce too high in low gravity. Zhelnikov was right. Sommen warriors—double the height of the humans beside them—fired plasma weapons, their frames encased in battle armor and faces obscured by their faceplates. The humans wore something altogether different. Win had never seen the kind of suits depicted in the frescos, skin tight and with helmets similar to an ancient crusader's, and he gave up trying to identify them, instead running his gloved hand over the blank section to test its smoothness.

"This is why we need the Proelian prophecy texts," said Win. "And the Sommen religious texts. Whatever is happening here, the Sommen have the answers and the Proelians have had a glimpse."

"No, Win. Right now I need you back on the *Higgins*. We had a modular factory shipped here years ago and installed, as a backup to Childress. But this facility is—*was*," Zhelnikov corrected himself, "subject to Fleet inspections. So we didn't want to risk storing the plasma weapon plans and equipment here. The plans were all on Childress; we need you to retrieve them. And on your way, pick up the damaged signal buoy."

"Why is this facility no longer subject to inspection?"

Zhelnikov hung his head, staring at the ground. "When you return from your mission on Childress we will take over this installation, eradicate the Proelian presence, and retrofit the *Higgins* with plasma weapons. There is more killing that needs to be done."

"Don't let it upset you, Zhelnikov." Win felt the Sommen part of him grow in a burst of pain, followed by the elation of having a mission and purpose: going to Childress after a Sommen assault would be dangerous. "The ability to ambush and kill unwitting Fleet personnel has always been your greatest gift."

CHAPTER FOURTEEN

San tried to shake the sleep from her head, coughing up mouthful after mouthful of oxygenated fluid at the same time a medic scraped cryo gel from her skin and then toweled her off. Two crewmen pulled her from the tube. She hovered in her quarters, squinting as her eyes adjusted to the light and shivering while a female crewmember helped her into an undersuit and environment suit; warm fluid circulated once her power flicked on, thawing her from the outside in.

"Gently," someone whispered. "Coming out of cryo for the first time is the hardest."

"Where are we?" San asked.

"About to go through transit one. You were supposed to be woken after passing through but the captain called an alert."

"An alert?"

"We sent a stealth probe through. Chinese ships are waiting for us on the other side."

"I thought I was supposed to do the scouting."

"You are. Normally. But Captain wants you to try communicating with Ganymede Station. We're going through to test the stealth features of these vessels and will engage the Chinese while you report the contact to the abbess."

The woman finished connecting San's suit and clapped her helmet on, sealing it with a click. They exited into the passageway. San did her best to move muscles that hadn't been used in ages and her vision filled with stars so that she had to blink to maintain clarity.

"How long were we asleep?"

"Just over a year. We had to stop for an engine issue, so you slept a little longer than intended."

"How long were *you* asleep?" San asked. "You look wide awake; there's no way you just got out of cryo."

"I'm part of the flight crew. We have three crews that rotate, so I've been awake for months. Here we are."

One year gone. San's attention shifted to Mars the moment she entered a tight conference room, a holographic star map rotating over the table. *My mother is dead.* She flew over the red and black landscape of the research station that had been her childhood and into the graveyard where her father had been buried, her mother now next to him. A basalt headstone had been carved with *Nang Vongchanh.* Mars' rotation generated a gentle wind from between crevices and dunes, and it howled in a moan that died in Mars' thin atmosphere as quickly as it had been born.

My mother is dead.

The captain entered and everyone in the room hooked their feet into floor straps while he positioned himself at the head.

"Miss Kyarr," he started. "I'm afraid I have some bad news."

"My mother is dead."

"Yes. A fast scout caught up with us months ago, carrying orders; the notice was with them. I am sorry for your loss. I can't give you the time you need since we're about to go into combat, but when it's over, do whatever you have to." The captain pointed at the hologram and started his briefing, assigning roles and responsibilities. San's thoughts and attention focused elsewhere.

When would she ever see home again? The sadness of having been rejected by Fleet—so long ago on Earth—seemed ridiculous, a reflection of past naiveté that now only embarrassed. *What had she been thinking?* Life in Fleet meant that nobody had a *life* at all; ships' needs dictated how every minute and hour would be spent, and had already mandated that the time would add up to years of life spent in hibernation, asleep without dreams while the universal clock ticked its way toward loss and inevitability.

My mother is dead.

"San!" The captain's shout pulled her from her trance.

"Yes, sir."

"I asked if you think you can communicate with Ganymede while we transit. It's my understanding that your and Mister Wilson's training was cut short before you could test long-range coms."

"It was. And to be blunt, I don't know. But I'll try."

The captain nodded. "Your Marine detachment is being woken now. They will accompany you to the ashram and the lieutenant will relay messages between you and the bridge, Miss Kyarr." He looked at everyone around the table and nodded again. "That's it. We transit with the *Jerusalem* in one hour. Everyone to your posts."

San couldn't move. The room emptied and she barely noticed when a Marine in a battle suit entered, taking her by one arm and pulling her toward the door where the rest of her guards gathered to form a circle, each man placing a hand on her shoulder and gripping. A song crackled from the men's helmet speakers as they sung. By the end of it she had started crying and the group carried her through the passageways, guiding her weightless form around corners and through forward hatches where they arrived at the ashram. The lieutenant shut the last hatch, ordering the rest to stand outside.

"She's gone," the lieutenant said. "It's okay to be sad. But . . ."

"But what?" asked San.

"But we're about to go into combat, ma'am, and I just found out that the *Higgins* is gone; Fleet approved another route for them and now we have to transit without our decoy. This is *our* reality, our *right now*. Your mother died while we slept and I'm sure that it's painful. But this ship needs you ready to fight in under an hour."

"When did you find out about the *Higgins*? *I don't want to be on this ship.*"

"Weren't you at the briefing?" When San shrugged he continued. "Look, forget the *Higgins*. Everyone goes through this—doubt. A sense that going to space was a mistake. Everyone. Fleet knows it, even expects it. But not during combat. If you can't do what's asked of you, then I need to tell the captain."

San submerged into thought again, looking up through the glass at a foreign starscape. The ship had moved closer to an inner portion of Orion's arm and had been oriented so the ashram faced the galactic core where billions of stars filled her view. In areas, they seemed close enough to each other to have fused into one giant pool of liquid light, reds and blues punctuated by bright white. She hated them. The existence of stars had robbed her of an alternate life; they had slipped into the ship and ripped the year away while she slept, solidified in frozen gel. Stars had become the enemy—selfish things that cared only about their burning and brightness, luring men from Earth with a promise of greatness that rotted into a reality of boredom and death.

"I will do it. Maybe killing will take my mind off the stars."

"That's the spirit." The lieutenant took up his position near the coms port, and lifted the handset. "We're burning toward the wormhole now. Face the bow and you can see it. Transit in thirty minutes."

"Have you ever killed anyone, Lieutenant?"

"Yes."

"Who?"

The man answered in a soft voice. "More Chinese than I can remember. You get used to it. They're not people anymore, miss—not after all the alterations to their form, all the cloning."

"I've never seen one. Not in real life."

"Then prepare yourself. The Chinese have almost no human left in them, but enough to make you realize how monstrous men can be. Tell yourself this if it helps: You're putting them out of their misery and it's a mercy to kill them. That is one hundred percent true."

San looked away from the stars, focusing on the lieutenant. "Once we start shooting, our enemy will detect targeting signatures. The *Bangkok*'s radars will give our position when it shows us theirs."

"No, ma'am. It won't because our stealth targeting drones are already on the other side of the wormhole. Once we pass through and are in position they will paint the enemy and transmit the coordinates of Chinese vessels to our gunners and missile batteries. Thousands of drones. We won't emit anything because our gunners, not computers, calculate targeting solutions and then the missiles guide themselves."

"Men are targeting our weapons? Manually?"

"I've seen the training, ma'am. On Ganymede. We have nothing those monsters can infiltrate—not a single targeting computer and the captain will cut engines so we coast out of the wormhole, invisible. It will be a slaughter."

As if the final piece of a puzzle had locked in place, the Marine's words closed a circuit that sent a pulse of electricity through San's mind. In a flash she saw the abbess and the bishop. They stood over Ganymede shipyard in the stance of watching angels, glowing with white light that spread from their outstretched arms and penetrated everything, including the minds of the countless Fleet personnel assembled below them. The Chinese would be an offering at Fleet's Proelian altar.

"So my sight is not needed for this fight."

"You are needed for something greater, miss; this is a sideshow. The *real* prize is in Sommen territory, where we're headed next."

San sensed something in his words. They represented the still water on top of an ocean calm, under which strong currents gouged the seafloor to send storms of sand and rock toward shore. *The lieutenant was terrified.*

"You know what we will find there," she said. "In the abandoned region of space around the Sommen home world."

"I know what I have been briefed. Nothing more. And much of that I can't speak of, not even to you."

"What *can* you tell me?"

"I can tell you that we'll need your sight. The Sommen are an ancient race but there was another that predated them. One that has gone extinct, destroyed by something that the Proelian nuns, their bishop, and the admiral's finest Fleet researchers haven't disclosed to us. The Sommen are terrified; can you believe that? They aren't supposed to be scared of anything, but whatever ended this ancient race has them shaking."

A wave of memories flooded San's mind without warning, washing across her consciousness so the lieutenant and the ashram disappeared when she submerged into a great cathedral. Sunlight streamed through stained glass windows. The colors splashed against her white dress, forming orange and green patches so intense that San almost believed it was real and incense smoke floated everywhere, penetrating even skin. The smell of spice made her sneeze, a nearby nun glancing with disapproval.

Out of the pit the Chinese forces came, locusts upon the backs of locusts that spread across Earth in a blanket of rot and filth. Men and women choked on their waste. All of East and Southeast Asia hid from their forces but there was no place to hide, no way to evade humans that had changed themselves into living sensors that could see through

walls and that had no humanity except for patches of flesh and pockets
of DNA. They had the faces of men, but were not men.

"San," the lieutenant said. "Are you with me?"

San returned to the present, blinking, and for the first time since
coming out of cryo, felt calm. "A monster has been released."

"What?"

"A monster. He's loose, but not on Earth."

The lieutenant replaced the handset and pushed off the wall,
drifting toward her. "Are you okay?"

"It's nothing. Something they put in my head a long time ago
when I was a toddler. But the Proelians believe it. They think we're
headed for some final battle."

"And maybe we are." The lieutenant moved back to the wall and
pulled the handset out again. "Turn around and get ready. We're
entering the wormhole. It won't be long now. I'll relay your messages
to the captain."

San shifted her weight and spun just in time to catch it: the
wormhole. It swallowed the front of the ship in a mirrored surface,
gobbling up the *Bangkok*'s bow before the ashram entered, the pool
of light so bright that it blinded her. They were through in a blink. As
quickly as it had appeared the wormhole was gone, behind San, who
marveled at how the star field had changed, replacing the thick
galactic arm with an endless expanse of darkness.

"Whatever you do to connect with Ganymede, do it now," the
lieutenant said. "The fighting will start in five minutes."

San slipped a dose of serum from a belt pouch and screwed it into
a socket at the point where the suit's arm connected with its shoulder
armor. "Where are the Chinese?"

"Out there. You can't see them but you will when we go weapons
free."

"When is that?"

"Four minutes, now, miss."

San hit the button. The shoulder mechanism snapped open a
valve and a needle jabbed deep into her muscles, pushing a bolus of
serum into her bloodstream. It burned going in. Her view of the
ashram wavered and resembled a screen with static where the
lieutenant came in and out of the picture, everything else fading into
darkness striped by luminous purple fog.

Something nudged the edge of her mind and San concentrated on the sensation, forcing the purple to shift into a swirling, black and gray vortex. A warm shadow enveloped her. At first there was a tapping sensation that San tried to interpret, the code obvious after her filter of mathematics snapped in place, but then it shifted again. Now, a voice whispered from the darkness.

This is Ganymede Station...

I am here, San sent. *I can hear.*

"Open your eyes, San." The lieutenant's voice broke through the shadows, muffled, as if the man had been buried under a mile of cotton balls and in a universe San couldn't reach. "You can't see the battle unless you open your eyes. It's starting."

Send us the data, San. The abbess orders it.

San opened her eyes. Chinese ships had opened fire on empty space, spitting missiles into emptiness so at this distance they resembled children's toys, bottle rockets that spun and twisted toward nothingness. Then they started detonating. One after another the warheads blew to send hot clouds of molten metal that impacted against objects so tiny that San hadn't noticed them: mindless things that, she guessed, were the targeting drones the lieutenant had mentioned.

The battle has started. I count two Chinese ships.

What kind?

How would I know that?

It is in your memories. Relax and dig.

"They're heavy cruisers," the lieutenant interrupted. "You're whispering and I can hear you."

San willed her mind to open further; she turned, aiming for her earliest memories, which surfaced easily—the survivors of a shipwreck, merging with her consciousness.

Heavy cruisers, both of them. Crew about a thousand. Automated systems and advanced electronic-warfare capabilities.

This should be easy, Ganymede sent. San sensed laugher in the message. *The Chinese have no idea what's about to hit them.*

Space itself lit with a blazing eruption of fire, followed by a rumbling noise that shook the ashram as columns of flame erupted from the *Bangkok*'s sides. Then the *Jerusalem* lit up. Exhaust fires leapt from the ship and stabbed outward in the direction of the

Chinese Fleet and at first San wondered if this was some new plasma weapon until she saw the corkscrewing motion of the flames, the motion of missiles. *But these were huge.* San judged from the rocket motors that the things were the size of a heavy-transport vehicle.

Missiles launched, she sent.

Understood. Relay to the Bangkok's *captain that he is to recover drones and burn immediately after victory. You are to exit that area in case there are other Chinese groups, close enough to reinforce.*

Speaking out loud while also maintaining the connection with Ganymede confused her. A splitting pain seared San's head. She imagined trying to dream and be awake, simultaneously, but once she'd finished the lieutenant relayed the message into his handset then turned back to face her.

"Watch this, miss; you don't want to miss it."

Explosions blossomed in the distance. The Fleet missiles struck Chinese vessels, their payload of molten metal penetrating and venting white gas plumes into space. Some of them targeted hydrogen storage, sending secondary explosions to rip through both ships and fragment them into chunks that spun into darkness. A wave of terror blew over her; San recoiled at the thoughts of dying Chinese soldiers, their sense of confusion and fear threatening to break her connection with Ganymede.

Both vessels destroyed, she sent. *My connection is weakening.*

Abbess says you've done a good job. She also says to tell you something important: This is the first time we've communicated instantaneously over such a great distance.

Who's 'we'?

Anyone. Everyone. Ganymede out.

San felt the lieutenant's hands on her shoulders; he shook her out of the trance and then pulled her feet from the floor loops, guiding her toward the hatch.

"What's wrong?" she asked.

"We burn in two minutes, to put some distance between us and the wormhole."

"But I haven't done the navigation; the captain won't know where we're going."

"That's not important, San; you can get us on course later. Right now we need to get the hell out of here. The remaining targeting drones are all back onboard."

San felt a tear form; it left her eye, hovering in midair as they opened the hatch.

"I heard their screams."

The lieutenant grabbed her shoulders again, this time with force. "*Never* be sad about that. I told you: These are animals. You've never fought the Chinese. I could tell you stories about them that would make your hair stand on end."

"My father fought them," she whispered, then realized it had been part lie. *My father fought for the Chinese, so long ago.* The two passed into the corridor, and the group began moving in the direction of their quarters.

"Lieutenant. Back in the ashram you were scared. I sensed something when you mentioned that the *Higgins* was on a new course."

The lieutenant glanced at her; San saw in the tenseness of his face that she'd angered him. "Fleet is at war with itself. On the one side you have Proelians, who gained favor years ago when it became clear that the Sommen war will be just as much about faith as it will be about killing."

"And on the other side?"

"Zhelnikov's patrons. Old Fleet. Power is a major influencer of decisions and that old man got corrupted by it a long time ago; he won't give up ruling status willingly. We doubt that he put that bot in your quarters himself, but I guarantee you one of his pals did."

"And so the course change for the *Higgins*—you think it was for nefarious purposes."

"They will rendezvous with us in Sommen space. I'm sure we'll find out then, ma'am." He opened the hatch to her quarters. "One minute to burn. We'll meet you out here when it's over because the captain wants you in the tomb again."

Soon after strapping in, San felt the jolt of acceleration push her into the couch, pressing air from her lungs as she struggled to inflate them. Even with her engineered body, the pressure was almost unbearable. The *Bangkok* groaned under high gees. Overhead pipes popped and creaked and San heard the roar of water flow through one as the fluid coursed rearward toward the reactors. She knew:

This was coolant. Another loop of piping would carry superheated water away from the fusion reactors so that if the pipe broke she'd be fried in an instant, her flesh melted and burned off, bones converted to ash. Instantaneous death.

Mathematics is truth. Mathematics is the framework and foundation, within which we judge truth versus lie, victory versus defeat. God gave us mathematics. It is with mathematics that we face our adversaries and carry out His will. It is a vehicle. There is no greater truth than the ones found in the exquisite problem sets.

Wilson's voice entered her mind, breaking San's concentration. *Did you see the dead?* he asked.

Yes.

I saw them too. Up close. I willed myself to watch from a point near one of the Chinese ships. When our missiles hit and the ship detonated, it cracked open the way you'd crack a lobster. Hundreds of them spilled out into space, screaming. I can't do this, San.

Yes, you can, Wilson. You have to.

Have you talked to anyone about the wormholes? he asked. *How they were created, who keeps them open?*

I know there was someone before the Sommen.

Exactly. If you view the edges of wormholes you'll see it, San. Machinery. Thin rings of it that resemble the lines on a basketball, which we pass between. I viewed it on the way through.

What's your point?

What are we even doing out here? We know nothing about the history of the universe and those who do know aren't telling us anything. We're guinea pigs. Fleet and Ganymede use us for coms and navigation, and for our little assassination mission, but we don't know the big picture. I'm scared of what's out there, and I don't mean the Sommen.

I am too, Wilson.

CHAPTER FIFTEEN

Win hovered in the ashram, staring at the wormhole they'd just fled. At five kilometers away the mirrorlike sphere threatened to swallow the ship and he sensed the waves of excitement in the crew below. The *Higgins*'s weapons aimed at the transit and her gunners concentrated so hard at their screens that men and women dropped mental barriers, their thoughts running through Win's mind in streams of words and images. Information, combined with pulses of emotion, became so intense that he had to block everything, shutting off the section of his mind that he needed most: the portion scanning for Sommen signatures. Instead he watched. And over his helmet speakers, he heard the captain announce Zhelnikov's on-ship arrival, followed by an announcement that there had still been no sign of Sommen incursion from Childress.

They should follow us; now they know I am here, and they want me—an abomination—destroyed.

The *Higgins*'s reactors thrummed with electrical energy that ran throughout the ship and made everything pulse with a slight vibration; it waxed and waned according to demand cycles of ship's systems. *I am a weapon.* Win's mind spiraled into thought as he squinted at the wormhole, convincing himself that he could see the alien structure—thin, spidery lines that wound around the sphere and, through magic, kept the hole open. This was technology beyond anything he'd seen in the Sommen manuals. Who were those who'd hollowed the asteroid that Fleet had converted into a secret base? Why had they created networks of wormholes throughout the galaxy, only to then disappear?

And how could they foretell the future?

The ashram hatch opened, breaking Win's trance and, startled, his servo harness shot a jet of gas, spinning him in midair at the same time his spiked legs rose to attack. Zhelnikov pulled himself through and shut the hatch behind him.

"Relax, Win. I'm glad you don't have a coil gun, or I'd be calling for a medic right now."

"They haven't come yet, Zhelnikov. Where are they?"

"I don't know. The captain thinks the Sommen are toying with us, waiting so that it maximizes our terror. Doubtless their priests have scanned and already sense our presence and location."

"I have not felt them. Nothing. I hear the thoughts of the crew, but nothing of the Sommen."

"The crew were all secretly admitted into the Proelian training program; you should not be able to read *anything*."

Win grunted. "Terror has a way of breaking the mind, even minds trained in the ways of Proelian trash."

"Come." Zhelnikov had taken off his environment suit's helmet, and now reseated it with a snap. "If the Sommen chase, we will be destroyed. You did good work; we recovered the plans out of your signal buoy and engineers are now working around the clock to construct a weapon for retrofit installation on the *Higgins*. In the meantime, you and I have something to do."

"What?"

Zhelnikov opened the hatch and exited into the corridor. "You'll see when we get there."

Win followed, by now with an understanding of where the passageways headed, and they moved in the direction of the shuttle hangar. His skin went cold. The thought of being in a lightly armored shuttle when the Sommen popped through the transit made him wonder what Zhelnikov could be thinking.

I am a weapon. Nerves and brain tissue weave themselves into an alien pattern, waking me into Sommen consciousness and turning my fabric into that of a warrior priest. Only I can see. Only I know the way. The sign is the withering of my body, the sign is the growth of my mind.

Zhelnikov waved for Win to continue following him into an old and battered lifeboat—not a shuttle after all—with a pilot and two couches, so small that Win almost couldn't fit. He strapped himself in and waited. The ship's engine roared to life, lifting them off the *Higgins*'s hangar bay floor and then pushing them forward into the blackness of space.

"Where are we going?" he asked.

"To the wormhole."

Win started to remove his straps. "Are you mad? *Turn this ship around!*"

"Calm yourself!" Zhelnikov barked. Win felt a wave of anger from the man and he sat back into his couch.

"We aren't going *through* the wormhole," Zhelnikov continued. "We are going *to* the wormhole. To examine the structure that keeps it open."

"I see." But Win struggled to understand; the news generated a sensation that combined fear with excitement, and a feeling that he had foreseen this in a vision he couldn't recall.

"No, you don't see. My teams have been there before. There is clearly an entryway to the structure but there's no mechanism to open it. No keypad of any kind. Nothing."

"What's inside?" Win asked.

"That's what I'm telling you: We've never *been* inside. We've never opened the wormhole structure's entry portal." Zhelnikov leaned over and grabbed a hose from the bulkhead, snapping its end into a receiver at the side of Win's servo harness. "You'll need a full tank of maneuvering gas. The lifeboat's docking structures aren't able to make a seal where we're headed so you and I will be going extravehicular."

"Into space?"

"There's nothing to fear. If we get into trouble, the pilot will be there."

"Zhelnikov." Win kept his voice even, doing his best to hide the fact that he was terrified. "I've had no training in this. What is it you hope to gain, even if we can open the door to an alien structure? This thing is so advanced that it may as well be magic."

"Not *we*. *You*. If there are no control surfaces to lower the barrier, then it must be actuated in another way."

"Me?"

"You will use your mind. It's the only thing we haven't tried. We haven't been *able* to try because my group never dared to ask the

Proelian theurgists to use their assets for such a mission. But now *you* are here."

"You didn't want the Proelians to get a first look," said Win. "Because you don't want them to gain an advantage."

"*They already have the advantage!* Use your mind, Win. You should be able to see all of this. The Proelians have the admiral's attention and the Sommen religious texts. They control Fleet. We are decidedly *disadvantaged.*"

"The Proelians could examine one of these structures any time they wished, regardless of you or your group's prodding. Why haven't they?"

"They are singularly occupied with the Sommen and war. For now, I don't think it's even occurred to them that they could—and should—be interested. The abbess and her bishop know of the old race. But it's a secondary concern to them; something they can ignore, only to be brought up *after* we defeat the Sommen."

Win concentrated on Zhelnikov's words, analyzing them while reaching out to sense the man's thoughts. *A common thread to tie the fabric of space inside a wrapping of time and quantum particles. The tendons of the universe demand conflict and we will provide it. The goal is the end. It is written in stone by our ancestors and the first warriors: only endless battle will bring forth the truth. And there is no greater goal. War is everything.* Win opened his eyes, surprised. *Zhelnikov believes that he can learn the unlearnable. The man didn't understand: Unlike the Sommen, whoever built these structures never left any manuals.*

"We may lose this war, Zhelnikov; the Proelians may be correct in a singular focus on an enemy. Your drive is split—the Proelians, the Sommen, and the mysteries of whoever built these structures. This is a path to failure. Without a framework of dedication you've been blinded to the reality of our situation, despite all your research and efforts to decode Sommen technology."

Zhelnikov chuckled, the sound echoing in Win's helmet. "I'm not doing this for my own benefit, boy. And I've seen the aftermath of what one Sommen, alone, can do to our forces—at the Charleston spaceport, when your father was the only one able to stop the slaughter."

Win lifted a spiked arm and placed it against the fabric of

Zhelnikov's suit. Before the sharp tip could penetrate, he stopped, the pressure hard enough that he knew Zhelnikov felt the threat. "Do not speak of my father. I am *not* his son."

"If I die, boy, so do you. Recall the poison. And who do you think will protect you once I'm dead? Nobody wants you here but me."

"I am not for you to tame."

The pilot interrupted, breaking through on Win's helmet speakers at the same time the ship decelerated, forcing him against the restraints. "Sirs, we're there. I've maneuvered to within twenty meters of the structure."

The door slid open and Win pulled his spike away, following Zhelnikov into the airlock. His heart quickened with excitement; it sent a wash of blood around his neural pathways, feeding them with oxygen and nutrients so that clusters of neurons sparked and filled the air with illusions of light. Despite his calculations that this was a waste of time, the excitement of what they were about to do was inescapable: *Nobody* had ever been inside.

The outer door opened, greeting them with the darkness of space. Win followed Zhelnikov through. His control jets pushed him out, forcing on him the disorientation of space, and Win directed all attention to the structure rising over them. It dwarfed the pair, a single arm of dark material that curved upward. Win lost sight of it in the glittering sphere of Childress transit, its light forcing suit optics to filter with a warning of excessive ultraviolet radiation. Win concentrated on Zhelnikov's boots. The pair of them drifted forward, and soon the sound of his own rapid breathing hypnotized Win, calming and dampening anticipation.

Zhelnikov stopped, grabbing hold of a portion of the structure, its surface as smooth as glass where Win grabbed hold. They hovered in what looked like a rectangular portal. Its sharp edges had handholds, shaped just inside the portal's frame.

"The doorway is five meters, side to side and top to bottom," Zhelnikov radioed.

"We already know these things were tall and wide; but how do we know this wasn't an entry designed for small ships or shuttles of some kind?"

"We don't. Switch to ultraviolet."

Win punched at his forearms, forcing the colors on his screen to shift, the structure glowing in light blue. He squinted. A meter above them, on what he guessed was the enormous hatchway, a series of markings had appeared in pink. Win recognized they were characters; it was as if a series of snake-shaped squiggles and angular gashes had been thrown together and then spread across the hatch's face.

"What have you learned of this?"

"It's clearly a language. We've had linguists feed the characters into supercomputers—even tried the Sommen translator tech. Nothing. We can't figure it out."

"There aren't any controls. Nothing to mark the surface at all except these handholds."

"Precisely. And when we bring our ships within fifty meters of the structure itself, it scrambles quantum computing. Fries computations as if this thing swaps particles randomly with our systems."

"Quantum interference," said Win. "That's why you think I can use my mind to open the doorway."

"I think you and others like you may *be* the doorway."

"What do you want me to do, Zhelnikov? *Think* my way in?"

"If this thing scrambled our quantum computers, even now it's working on our quantum states. Both my team and the Proelians believe that the key to Sommen interstellar communication is through quantum entanglement. So . . . yes."

"You want me to talk to a door."

Zhelnikov sighed. "We've tried everything else. Even our most advanced weapons can't mark this material."

Win pulled a line from a utility belt on his servo harness suit and clipped into the handhold so he wouldn't bounce off and away. He closed his eyes. His breathing slowed and his heart rate became a creeping thing, pumping at half speed so that the heating elements inside his suit had to increase power.

Win's mind tingled, a buzzing which grew so intense it felt as though he needed to crack open his skull to itch the insides, a maddening sensation that—had it lasted any longer—would have driven him crazy. Then it stopped. A new sensation replaced it, this one a regular sequence of what his mind translated into sounds, a pattern repeated over and over.

"Numbers."

Zhelnikov grabbed a hold of Win's suit, forcing his eyes to snap open. "*What*, Win?"

"Numbers. I heard numbers. Whatever controls this thing, it scanned my thoughts and then stopped—I think because it sensed that it was damaging my mind, maybe because I'm not whatever race created the transits. So it went basic: a series of tones, repeated in sequence, over and over. Then I broke contact."

"Numbers," said Zhelnikov.

"One through ten. One tone then a pause. Two then a pause. Zhelnikov, I think this structure houses some kind of super-aware, but one that is far more powerful than any we've ever created."

"Why did you break off? We'll have to return to the shuttle soon for new oxygen generators but let's see if you can reconnect. You have to learn a new language, which could take a while and there's no time to waste."

"It will be rapid," said Win. "I'm not learning *its* language. The thing is gathering data from me, starting with basic counting; it's learning *ours*."

"Do it. Now."

While they'd been speaking, the structure had been reaching for him, sending pulses of energy to attempt flipping subatomic particles in Win's mind and making his brain matter crawl. Even now it scanned. He concentrated on his thoughts, urging his mind to solidify into an immovable mass that nothing could change but the effort made him grunt with agony when the structure overpowered him, forcing its way in and over any defense he erected. Win gave up. A moment later he heard himself screaming in his helmet and felt Zhelnikov grabbing at his servo harness in an effort to shake him awake and back into control—a useless gesture.

Impure . . . Something spoke to Win, a voice in monotone that came in bursts, only some words intelligible.

Win managed to organize a thought. *Who are you?*

If the thing heard the question, it gave no indication; instead it continued pawing through his thoughts, ripping them apart in a kind of dissection. All the while, it continued to send information.

This is a dead pathway, an error. There are others on the correct route into ascension and maturity. Its race will be easy to erase.

Without warning, it ended. Win tried to catch his breath and gasped, starting a mantra to distract himself from the lingering agony as if he'd just removed his head from a microwave to find his neural tissue bubbling and cooked. Zhelnikov yelled his name.

"I'm fine," said Win. "Give me time."

"Can you get it to open the door?"

"I can't get it to do anything. By now it knows we want the door open but it completely ignored the request. It only concerned itself with an update."

"An update on what?"

"On humanity."

"Jesus!" said Zhelnikov.

"That's not surprising; if the structure contains a super-aware, one from a race whose proclivities included predicting Sommen and human futures, it makes sense that the thing would want an update."

"That's not what I'm surprised by." Zhelnikov pointed at the doorway. "*You succeeded.*"

Win had missed it. The smooth panel cracked down the middle and separated into two, sending a puff of dust to patter against his suit and then shoot into empty space. The area beyond blinked from darkness into light; artificial illumination washed an empty room with ultraviolet light at the same time it overwhelmed his UV sensors. The pair jetted inside. After they crossed beyond the outer doors, the two slabs reversed course and shut behind them, soon filling the area with a roar as atmosphere filled the chamber. Win's chemical sensors flickered to life; they analyzed molecules that now flowed into the space from a vent he couldn't see, but which soon pressurized the room.

"Some oxygen," said Zhelnikov. "Mostly carbon dioxide and nitrogen."

"Whoever they were, this is what they breathed. We'll go hypoxic if we try to inhale this. And they must see in a combination of the visible spectrum and the ultraviolet."

"The pressure has stabilized. Why isn't the inner door opening?"

"How should I know?" asked Win. "I never . . ."

A second set of slabs opened, cutting him off and making a long crack in the wall opposite the doorway they'd just entered. It stopped after forming a one-meter gap. The structure's lights blinked on and off, and Win's suit pickups sent an audible warbling noise across his helmet speakers.

"Malfunction?" he asked.

Zhelnikov kicked off the closest wall, speeding toward the opening. "We can make it through. Come on."

"How will we get out? Even if we make it back here, now that there's a problem with their airlock mechanism we could be trapped."

"Then we may as well get a look around our new prison. We only have about twenty minutes left on these oxygen generators. Record everything, Win: sound, video, sensor readings—*everything.*"

The corridor beyond the airlock dwarfed Win with its dim lighting, illuminating a structure that reminded him of a ribbed cylinder carved from black rock, glistening and wet. The dark throat of a demon, he thought. Where the exterior structure had been smooth and spotless, this was the exact opposite, a textured material alternating in shades of gray and black, with pitted areas that made it look as if it had been sandblasted or drilled to form holes at random. But they weren't random...

"Those are handholds," said Win. "Or whatever these things used instead of hands. They come in groups of three, suggesting your guess of three digits per hand was correct."

"How these things had only three digits for manipulation of items and material, and became so advanced..."

"What the hell is this place??" Win asked. "Aren't there any other rooms? Where is the machinery and power plants to support and sustain a fold in space for, what? Centuries? Millennia?"

Zhelnikov didn't respond. Win sensed the man's heart rate spike, his pulse so rapid that he wondered if Zhelnikov would have a heart attack, but he understood. His own pulse felt as though it would burst every vein. Win imagined that from a distance they resembled small dots of black, floating like dust amidst a corridor impossibly large, just a bit smaller in diameter than the dimensions Win had taken of the arm's external features. There was no room left for anything. If each arm of the station making up the wormhole was identical to this, he realized, the web was empty shell—a thin crust of alien rock or ceramic that separated them from the vacuum of deep space.

Win's suit alarm flared. In less than a second, his primary power source sparked out in a burst of red and white, forcing him to convert to his backup.

"We passed through a magnetic field," said Zhelnikov. "Backup power online."

"How strong would it have to be to fry shielded primaries?"

"Strong. This must be the secret."

"What secret?" Win asked.

"To how this station functions. There is no machinery or additional structure needed. Not like in the hollowed-out asteroid that we've converted."

"I don't follow."

"The form is the function. The material itself is somehow arranged to channel energy from wherever it's generated and focuses that power to sustain Childress transit."

"Speak *English,* old man."

Zhelnikov chuckled. "I told you about how Sommen plasma weapons work and you've seen the dimensional data too; there's no room in this structure for energy generation, at least not in a form we understand. Use that brain of yours."

Win's mind reeled. The vastness of the corridor threatened to overpower his senses, making it difficult to concentrate. "This entire structure is an antenna. It's channeling energy produced somewhere else and converting it into whatever is needed to fold space on itself, joining to otherwise distant points in three dimensions."

"That is my guess as well. With no visible machinery or mechanisms I would imagine that the function is achieved at a quantum level—the same way that this place communicated with you. There are no moving parts. This entire thing is built using a combination of materials, the organization of which is what gives it an ability to channel energy. And with no moving parts . . ."

Win finished Zhelnikov's sentence with a whisper. "It would last as long as its energy source, wherever that is. Maybe forever."

"Nothing is forever. But for our purposes, yeah. Basically forever." Zhelnikov punched at his forearm, then reached out to attach a line to Win's belt. "I'm out of maneuvering gas. Take us back to the airlock. We've gone far enough this trip and it's time to get back."

"Zhelnikov. Something comes."

From ahead, in the direction they'd been moving, Win had

detected motion. The corridor's gentle curve made it possible to see a long distance but the lighting and his sensor limitations prevented him from pulling focus. His screen rendered everything in a cloud of static, within which something approached in a fishlike swimming motion and now the sound hit them: a combination of screeching metal and tones, reminding Win of mechanisms unused for years and left to rust. He turned and punched at his maneuvering jets, sending them back toward the airlock.

"Move it," said Zhelnikov.

"I am."

"Not fast enough."

The inner doorway loomed ahead but Win's lack of perspective prevented him from judging the distance and he shot a laser, realizing that they still had some way to go. He pulsed his thrusters again, holding them open for seconds.

"I hope we can stop," he said.

"Just aim for the opening and get us through. We can risk slamming against a wall or two. I'm getting a good look at this thing, Win. We don't want it to catch us out here."

"Send me the image; if I look back it might screw up our course."

A small section of Win's screen lit up with Zhelnikov's transmission. He squinted. Whatever approached made him think of a combination of giant spider crab and octopus, with four sets of tentacles that jutted from an articulated, tubular abdomen. It had folded ten legs back along its sides, accelerating not with gasses, but, Win guessed, with energy that created a flickering aura, sparking in arc flashes against the section closest to the structure's wall. Win became so transfixed that he misjudged the distance to the airlock doors.

His gas jets fired in a last second attempt to slow, but it was too late; the pair sped through the narrow opening then slammed into the side of the airlock, spinning and impacting a second time, this time against the outer door. Win shook his head to clear it. Red lights blinked on his screen and a quiet hissing sound filled his suit while his computer calmly repeated the warning: *suit breach, suit breach, suit breach . . .* Zhelnikov appeared beside him and grabbed his helmet.

"Stay still! You're mixing gases with this atmosphere; major crack at your helmet rear."

"Seal it!" Win shouted.

"What do you think I'm doing?"

"I've lost too much oxygen, Zhelnikov; we have to get back..."

Win's voice froze. The hissing had stopped and his suit oxygen-mix indicator crept back toward normal but he ignored the sensors, his vision dedicated to the barely open inner airlock door.

"Zhelnikov," he said.

"I see it. Can't you send a thought and tell this damn thing to open the outer airlock door?"

"I'm trying. It's not working."

"Look at that *creature*."

Two thin articulated arms pushed through the crack, their ends tipped with tentacle digits the size of human arms, which touched the inside of the door—probing for something. Eventually they stopped. The tips began pulsing with light as they pressed and Win watched, hypnotized by the rhythm until he glanced through the crack. The thing's "face" consisted of an array of lights and angular protrusions, reminding him of a lobster. There was no color. Not silver, or white, he realized, something different, as if the thing had been drained of every pigment to be left with a dead gray somewhere on its way to turning black.

He probed it with his mind, recoiling with a sensation of something both intelligent and dead, concurrently.

"It's not alive," he said.

"What do you mean?"

"This is what controls the station. It's not alive. It's some kind of automaton, left behind to tend to the wormhole."

"Does it know we're here?"

"Yes."

"Why isn't it taking a look at us? Or attacking?"

Win's voice dropped to a whisper. "It doesn't care, Zhelnikov. We are nothing. It's something between us and a god."

Without warning, the tentacles retracted and a beam of blue light shot from the thing's face to first illuminate Zhelnikov. When it shone on Win he gritted his teeth in pain; a message came through, overpowering him with a kind of mental feedback: *Do not return.*

The inner doors closed, shutting the creature out. Win heard the airlock cycle to vacuum before the outer doors opened again, spilling the two into space where he sent spurts of gas to propel them in the direction of the lifeboat. By the time they reentered the small craft, sweat filled Win's suit and he fought the urge to vomit from the aftereffects of breathing so much nitrogen, his head still dizzy from mild hypoxia.

"Get us back to the station," Zhelnikov ordered the pilot. He turned to Win. "We need to rejoin the group soon; regroup with them in Sommen space."

"What about the weapon installation on the *Higgins*?"

"We'll accelerate at lower gees. They have to do low-g acceleration anyway because of you and me. Engineering teams will finish the work in transit."

"What did we just experience?"

Zhelnikov thought before answering. "I don't really know."

CHAPTER SIXTEEN

In the middle of nothing, San thought. *The unknown. Deep space, uncharted.*

She submerged into a pool of thought, its surface shimmering with reflected starlight that disappeared when she concentrated. Her subconscious had been packed with data streams. Some shone with the pledge of excitement while others buzzed with importance, the promise of information foundational to war and strategy. But one caught her eye: The flow looked plain and slower than the rest, and San examined it, wondering if it had been *meant* to go unnoticed, its banality a coating that almost camouflaged but which now demanded inspection.

"We need a navigation solution to the next transit, San," the captain said. The Marine lieutenant had stretched the handset from the wall and held it against her helmet. She opened her eyes; the stars shone through ashram glass, which made them look wavy and uncertain.

"I will return to the tomb soon, Captain. One thing to do in the ashram first."

"Fine. Make it quick, San."

The lieutenant replaced the handset. "What's so important, miss?"

"What is your name?"

"Richards, ma'am."

"Your first name, Lieutenant."

The Marine paused for a second and she sensed embarrassment when he answered. "Eugene."

"Eugene, please be quiet; I need to concentrate."

San closed her eyes again. She sunk into her thoughts and passed through them, submerging beneath the conscious information and then back to where the subconscious lived, moving toward the slow stream before she pulled away, startled by something. San's eyes snapped open. Alarms blared through her helmet speakers and the lieutenant grabbed her by the belt, dragging her toward the hatch. He banged his fist on the controls until it opened and then pushed her through and into the arms of a Marine who waited outside.

"*What's going on?*" San yelled.

Wilson broke through, his thoughts frenzied. *The Sommen are here—in our space. They've hailed both the captains, of the* Jerusalem *and* Bangkok.

For what?

For us—the "human priests." We're to shuttle to the Sommen ship immediately.

San froze, letting the Marines drag her while she began to hyperventilate. *This was it.* The one reason the Sommen would demand to see her and Wilson was to kill them both. Somewhere they'd been involved with a treaty violation while the Sommen had stuck to the agreement for decades, never once breaking its terms; their forces would only enter human space for violations of the treaty *by* humans. Even then, a Sommen incursion would be invoked for two additional purposes: to start the war, or to impose another penalty decided by their priests. The penalties listed in the Sommen texts were all death. The means of dispatch varied with the degree of dishonor for those involved in treaty violations, ranging anywhere from slow disembowelment to decapitation.

They're going to kill us, San sent. *What did we do? How could you or I have violated the treaty?*

We didn't. This has to be something else.

One of the Marines pushed his way through a maintenance crew, slamming a woman into a pipe gallery. He barked something at San, but she had long since been soaked with her own terror and that of the surrounding crew, the intensity of which rendered any sounds almost mute. She felt the man's fear; his thoughts drifted over her and San caught a picture of her ship, split into pieces by the fiery plasma of Sommen warships.

My God, Wilson. I can feel the uncertainty of everyone on this ship; it's overloading my mind. Their Proelian training has been forgotten.

Nobody knows what's going on, San.

Did your captain tell you anything?

The Sommen came out of nowhere. One medium ship, Hastatus *class, and three smaller vessels—*Sagittarii *class. We're being taken to the* Hastatus-*class vessel.*

San searched for the memories. Fleet had converted the Sommen names for their vessel classes into words taken from Earth's ancient history, from military terms used in ancient Rome. *Hastatus.* It would be similar to a heavy cruiser in Fleet terms, the staple of any battle group and produced in vast numbers. In Sommen terms, just one *Hastatus*-class ship could rip their two Fleet vessels apart.

Her escort pushed San into an oversized shuttle, one converted to carry troops, and two Marine platoons in full battle kit scrambled through the hatch after her. They strapped themselves in. The lieutenant shouted orders while two of his men strapped her to an acceleration couch and connected the secure coms cable to her helmet. As soon as the inner airlock hatch shut, a bump of acceleration followed and the shuttle lifted from the hangar, space soon wrapping them in its empty blanket.

"Ten kilometers out," the pilot announced. "It's hard to get a good reading; targeting drones can't fix properly."

It's the Sommen material and their ship design. It's why we built the Bangkok *and* Jerusalem *the way we did.*

"Did you say something?" the lieutenant asked.

"No, Eugene," San whispered. "I was thinking out loud."

She glanced out the nearest viewport. A tiny speck of light caught her eye and she zoomed in, her suit computer outlining the shape of an object and gauging the temperature of a hotspot near its rear as it screamed through space: Wilson's shuttle.

I can see you, she sent. *We are so small out here. Surrounded on all sides by a vacuum and absolute cold where mankind was never intended to live. Space is filled with death; if death could be mined like gold, we'd all be rich.*

Are you okay, San? She felt the concern, his question wrapped in a layer of worry.

Mathematics is truth, Wilson. But what they didn't teach us is that mathematics is murder and war and assassination. I saw this when we took out the Chinese vessels. And it keeps emerging from my calculations in the tomb. Mathematics is sterile. The Proelians understood this when they filled our infant minds with history, a history designed to influence our calculations; mathematics soaked in one-sided history isn't truth. It's a vast conspiracy.

This is war, San. The Sommen will attack in a matter of decades and the entire human race is at stake. If you really think this is all wrong, maybe the abbess will let you do something else when we return.

Before the Marines grabbed me to put me in the shuttle, San sent, *I was about to enter a data stream. One that is almost hidden. When I got close to it, I sensed that it contained powerful information that could influence us and all our calculations. Everything. It has to be something that could give us actual freedom in what we do. We aren't just navigators. We're communicators, but most importantly: We are intelligence collectors. Facilitators of death and destruction. We guide the Proelian and Fleet decisions but only inside the narrow confines of what we are allowed to do and how we are allowed to decide. With complete freedom of thought, we could finally do what's in everyone's best interest, not just the Proelians.*

Why would the nuns put that in our subconscious? Wouldn't it undermine their plans?

San did her best to hide the frustration; she could almost *see* his mind spinning at a rate much slower than hers and it reminded her of walking with a toddler, one that asked San to slow down.

Because, Wilson. It's all about faith. Even the Proelians can't escape the importance of objective truth; it's the underpinning of their and the Sommen religions. I think the stream I was about to examine involves a prophecy, maybe one that explains everything, even the Sommen. If the Proelians hadn't placed that data stream in our minds, they knew they'd be subverting something—a series of events placed into motion long ago, but one which demands we have free will. It's a paradox: They want us to act in one way, but they cannot trust in a course's authenticity unless we have complete freedom to decide.

Explain it again to me later; we're about to dock.

Wilson didn't see it, San realized, the most logical reason for the Sommen to have intercepted them in human space: they knew the *Bangkok* and *Jerusalem* were headed on a course to break the treaty and enter Sommen territory.

San looked out the nearest viewport, the form of the Sommen

cruiser filling the glass through which she stared. The usual material used for Sommen ship construction had shifted from green to a deep black, almost indistinguishable from the fabric of space. It was black within black. Then the Sommen hangar door opened, spilling red light into the area around them; it illuminated the shuttle nose and filled the troop area with its glow, reminding San of the fires of hell. The analogy was valid. In less than a minute they'd be docked on an enemy vessel and although grateful for the Marines' presence, it was doubtful they'd be able to save her or themselves in the event of conflict. Their small craft had just entered the belly of a fiend.

San punched at her forearm, switching the view on her heads-up by linking it to the shuttle's forward cameras, after which she paused in amazement. The cruiser's hangar enveloped them in its vastness— a space the size of several football fields in every direction. Racks of small Sommen craft filled most of one side, the ships reminding her of wasps. They had multiple segments and their bodies blistered with sensor packages and missile hard points, filmy insect wings the only things missing. Wilson's shuttle cruised before them, leading the way to a blinking set of lights on a platform where its landing pads extracted with a buzz. A moment later they engaged magnetic locks, and San heard the pilot breathe a sigh of relief.

"I didn't know if this thing had any metal we could lock onto," he muttered.

The lieutenant appeared at San's side, his hands moving over her shoulder sensors and back-mounted gear in a last minute check. "Everything is operational. Your Sommen translator working?"

"Yes. But I doubt the Sommen will be speaking much if they're taking us to a priest."

"We won't be met by the Sommen. One of their subjugated races will meet us at the platform and escort us from there to wherever we're headed."

The subjugated races. These were the alien worlds conquered by the Sommen, their sentient species scooped up to serve lesser roles in a military machine: ships maintenance, supply, anything not involved with the priesthood or with combat. They were slaves, forced to engage in work that the Sommen judged too cowardly. *Too safe.* San went numb with a mixture of fear and excitement; it would be her first time seeing an alien race, face to face, which almost made her forget that the meeting could end in her execution.

San glided into the elongated troop airlock, Marines crammed around her. When the outer door opened, they guided her through to join with Wilson's group, and she noted the atmosphere's composition—the ammonia-rich mixture of the Sommen. The Marines' magnetic boots locked onto a metallic floor. It was a black surface in an otherwise ocean of greens, where Sommen armor materials locked together in patterns that reminded San of a twisted jungle. She grabbed onto the Marine in front so she wouldn't lose the group.

"Look at them," Wilson hissed. He waved at the hangar surrounding them, over the lip of a small platform that held the two Marine shuttles.

Alien forms raced in every direction, jetting gasses from maneuvering packs. San couldn't gather words for a response. Some of them wore environment suits that concealed their forms in bulky material while others appeared able to handle more of the Sommen atmosphere, their insectile faces covered with a kind of fabric that San guessed must filter and allow them to breathe. She almost let go of the Marine while staring, trying to absorb and catalog everything until her group stopped moving.

A multilegged creature towered over them, blocking what San guessed was the platform's exit portal. It wore a full environment suit but its helmet faceplate was wide, filled with a clear pane that revealed a praying mantis–like face, its sharp mandibles clamping and unclamping to make an audible clicking noise.

San's translator sprang into action. "It is good that you came when ordered. It is good you did not resist."

"Where are the Sommen?" the lieutenant asked.

"You were not invited and will stay with your craft. Where are your priests?" San raised her hand along with Wilson. "You both will now follow."

The lieutenant stepped forward. He had to lean back to look up at the creature's face. "We are their guards—their escort. They go nowhere without us."

"There was concern about this." It lifted an articulated leg and slammed it on the platform; others of its kind streamed from the massive doorway behind it and arranged themselves in a wall, front legs lifted as if ready to attack. "We can kill. It has been permitted and means nothing to the masters. They care only for the priests."

"*Jesus...*" the lieutenant started.

"It's okay," said San, grabbing Wilson's arm. "We'll be okay. Wilson and I have full charges of maneuvering gas and new oxygen generators. We can go and be away for up to an hour."

"Miss, this is an enemy vessel. My orders are to stay with you at all times."

"I'm giving you a different order, Eugene: stay with the ships. If we come back we'll want to get out of here as quickly as possible."

It took everything she had to get the words out. San did her best to block the waves of fear from cascading, not wanting to let Wilson know that she was on the verge of breaking down. Her thoughts refused to stop a repetitive cycling of fear that forced San to bite her cheek, hoping the pain would bring relief. She didn't have to wait long; the lead creature turned and exited. Then the others formed a gap in their line to allow the pair through, and San reminded herself that it was not a dream, that it was happening when she and Wilson shot a burst of gas, following the thing off the platform.

San tried to record everything as they floated after their escort but when she and Wilson entered a giant Sommen corridor, her suit electronics malfunctioned. San punched at her forearm controls. Nothing worked except for her helmet lamp, which flashed awake to illuminate their way and cast emerald glints with its beam, turning their environment suits an odd shade of green.

"Many electronics will not function within," the creature said over its shoulder. "It is how this is done. My master has asked for me to tell you that it is one thing to learn from the Sommen texts. That is allowed. It is another thing to gain access to functioning Sommen systems and technology: to steal information by spying. You will not be allowed to leave here with data except that which you carry in your minds."

"So we are not to be executed?" San asked. Her translator converted the speech into clicks and whistles, a symphony of nonsense that she never would have been able to learn even after a lifetime of study.

"I am told that you are to be given a message and an examination. That is all."

"What kind of examination?"

"I cannot say. My master is a priest like you and your race is in a special category—neither enemy nor slave. Your race is somewhere else, and I am not to know the details." It held up a leg, the other five clunking on a metal floor so that she realized its appendages ended in magnetic caps. "Do not say anything about your race or why you have special status. I have been warned: If you tell me, I and my entire species will be erased from existence. Whatever you things are, my master and his warriors value your kind above all else—even war. They were on their way to battle and postponed it, merely to meet with you. I have never seen such a thing. To the Sommen, battle is more important than eating." The creature paused outside a circular hatch, dark green and almost four meters across. San did her best to keep from backing away, horrified to see its insectoid facial features up close.

"We are here." It waved its front arms, reminding San of a spider spinning webs. "Show no fear. It is allowed for me to show fear, but not you. Your status demands that you look the warriors and my master in the eye, and do not bow or show any sign of deference. Sometimes a warrior will challenge, to test you. Do not back down. If one charges and you try to run, it will make things worse; the warrior will continue the attack, acting on instinct. It is a small victory for them and the goal of these test aggressions: to make their adversaries run."

"Counting coup," said Wilson.

"I do not understand this reference; is there something wrong with your translator?"

Wilson shook his head. "We have an ancient race on our world. In combat they would sometimes charge an enemy just so they could touch him with a stick. The point wasn't to kill; it was to show that the warrior was brave and he would wear an eagle feather to show it."

"Yes. This is similar, but some of those words do not translate. Here, look at this." It lifted one of its center legs on the left side, the thing's suit fabric stretching taught so that San noticed a long strip of material sealed over it; it was a different color and age. A patch, San realized.

"This was where a warrior gouged me with its claws, when I first arrived for service. I backed away when charged. It is a lesson one never forgets. Are you two prepared to meet my master and his guards?"

"Who are you?" San asked.

"I am..." the thing started to answer, but its name failed to translate, the computerized voice replacing it instead with the phrase *unidentified words detected.*

"No. I meant, who are your people?"

"There is no time. Already I have exceeded my allowance for getting you here. I wish I could tell you all about my kind, but that is not the purpose. Perhaps someday we will meet again. Your kind resembles an animal we hunt on my home world; it is very soft and slow, but dangerous when cornered."

The thing slapped one of its front arms against a panel and the doorway slipped open, a sphincter valve mechanism hypnotizing San with its interlocking blades that spun apart. The creature waved San through, then Wilson. San's headlamp showed the floor ahead of them but nothing else, and she sensed that they'd stepped into an empty expanse so large that the walls and ceiling were beyond her lamp's range; she felt lost, having to examine the floor to make sure she didn't drift upward and lose all sense of orientation. San turned, waiting for their escort; the creature stood outside where it leaned down, peering through the open doorway.

"What is wrong?" it asked. "Why do you not move forward?"

"We can't see," said Wilson.

"What do you mean you can't see? Is this why your suits emit in a narrow frequency range—to illuminate your way?"

"Yes," San answered.

"I'm sure my master knows this but it was overlooked. Hold please."

Their escort pushed through the doorway and ran past, moving so fast on all six legs that San had only a second to dodge, her gas burst sending her into a gentle spin. By the time she recovered, the creature had disappeared in the darkness. A few minutes later, it returned, limping and with a fresh patch applied to its chest, the surrounding suit fabric stained black.

Their escort's voice sounded faint. "Go. You are late and my master is displeased." San then sensed that it collapsed, but in zero g all she saw was its body begin to sway, locked to the deck with magnets.

"I think it's hurt," she said. "Maybe even dead."

"We still can't see. Have you noticed how differently things sound here, San? In the ammonia?"

"I don't like this, Wilson. I think we should..."

Lights flickered to life, faint at first but then increasing in intensity to cast a glow throughout the chamber enabling her to see. San held her breath. She'd been there before: a long hall with sharp arches fashioned from a different material than the rest of the ship. It was an alabaster-like material, glistening where ammonia condensed on its surface, and pale blue light glowed from objects that hovered far overhead, weightless and rotating so the light shifted and cast shadows along the walls. She recognized the statues on either side of the vaulted room; they were the same ones from her previous mental visit with the Sommen so long ago, and the shadows made them seem as though they were living things—about to charge from either side.

She saw them at the far end. From this distance and in the dim illumination, San couldn't make out details, but she and Wilson jetted forward, soon approaching a dais. Atop it were two warriors. Each of them carried long, sword-shaped weapons, with clawed hands wrapped around the grips, their points embedded in the floor. The pair wore woven fabric tunics, a plain black that blended with their blistered skin, and, she guessed, black magnetic boots to lock them in place.

Between the warriors rested a tank—a horizontal and rectangular structure comprised of clear sides, which contained a liquid tinted blue and capped by a solid black slab. A Sommen swam inside. San squinted and recognized the priest, drifting motionless in the center with its black eyes pointed in their direction but nothing in its eye structure gave evidence that it knew her; San just sensed it.

"This may have been a bad idea," Wilson whispered.

"As if we had a choice."

When they got within a few meters of the dais, the warriors raised their swords and dropped one foot back so they now stood in a crouch, ready to leap.

"You should come no closer," the Sommen priest said. San noticed that it wore a kind of facemask, from which a green hose extended and disappeared, somewhere in the tank floor near the front. Its voice came from a speaker that San couldn't locate.

"Why are we here?" she asked. "We have not broken treaty."

"Perhaps you have not, but can you say the same for the rest of your people? Even now I receive reports of a human excursion outside your allotted space, not far from here."

"Who?" asked Wilson.

"By your abomination. I can sense in the female, in her thoughts and in her patterns. She knows this one, the one who broke our treaty. He is her brother. She and I have spoken before."

San's skin went cold. Their escort had assured them that they wouldn't be killed but now she doubted that assurance. The Sommen knew about her brother and wherever he was, Win had left human space. *What if he had been captured and revealed the entire purpose of the* Bangkok's *and* Jerusalem's *mission?*

"I know who he is, but I have never met him," she said. "I'm sure that if you captured him, he told you as much."

"We do not hold this one captive, nor do we take prisoners. We choose to ignore the breach in agreement. But we cannot ignore your race's transgressions for much longer, and this is the first reason why you are here: I have a message for you and your kind—the priests."

"We aren't . . ." Wilson started but San waved him quiet.

"Do not speak," the priest said. "Listen. When we are finished here, you are to return to your vessels and send a message to the females—the ones that trained you. Tell them this: The ones who fled your home world must be wiped out. They must be eradicated from the universe, for there is no place in our teachings or the prophecies for the impurity of flesh and machine fusion."

"The Chinese?" asked Win.

"That is what you call them. Yes."

"Our people," said San, "are already tracking the Chinese down. We will take care of them."

"You are taking too long. Here." The priest reached with a spindly arm, so thin it almost looked like the thing's bones had withered into twigs, and touched something on the tank floor. San's suit system woke; a light indicated that it was receiving data. "Those are the coordinates and system, in which these machines have hidden. We know you destroyed their vessels recently. This is good. We have also scanned your ships and commend you on their design. Our systems detect almost nothing—an indication of promise and hope for what will come."

"We will deliver the message," San said.

Wilson cleared his throat. "Do you have a name?"

As soon as their translators had transformed the question into Sommen, one of the warriors bared his teeth and then roared, spinning toward Wilson before it strode from the dais, careful to make sure each foot locked to the floor. It lifted its blade and was about to strike when the priest's voice rang from the tank.

"Stop!"

San caught her breath. It had all happened so fast that she hadn't had time to move, and, she guessed, neither had Wilson, who stood facing the warrior. She recognized his expression of terror.

"What did I say?" Wilson's voice shook with fear.

"Do you not have our texts?" the priest asked. "You should know that names are only given to warriors. Our priests are pure; a name would be an insult."

"We have not had time to review all the texts," San explained. "They sent us to space before our training could be completed."

"That is interesting." It stared at San again and she clenched her jaw at the sensation that the thing was examining her, looking for any stray thoughts or feelings. "What is so important that they would send you forth, your training incomplete?"

San thought, settling on something that was true; there was no telling whether or not the priest could detect her lies. "I have been sent to kill my brother—the one who left human space. My superiors decided it must be done quickly, and cut our training short."

At first the priest said nothing. San was about to repeat herself when it spoke. "I can see truth and its absence. I see you do not lie. This is good. I also see that this is not all the truth that answers my question. That is also good. One must never offer everything to one's adversary. I will give you a lesson." The priest, suspended stomach down, waved its arms in the fluid. "This tank is pure liquid ammonia under pressure, combined with our vision drug, *unidentified words detected*. It is this drug that gives us sight. It is this drug that I now must take to stay alive, and which withers my body so that I have a fraction of the lifespan of a normal Sommen warrior. I am pure. I am a mind, and little else. We live in these tanks so that we can see everything, everywhere, and plan our invasions through communications with other Sommen battle groups scattered throughout the galaxy. To give me a name would reduce me and other priests to something lesser. This is the Sommen way.

"You have not yet found *your* way," the priest continued. "Earth is a fascinating adversary. You require two genetically distinct organisms to procreate; we multiply on our own, during the birth season or during our death if there is sufficient time. And your race was just getting started on farming when we had completed our first interstellar campaign, thousands of years ago, after our priests found the first wormholes. Their existence confirmed what the creator had taught us: the way of war. Finally, we could spread out and act on the visions we had been given and even now I see them clearly in my memory, the recollections handed down to me from the first priest, down through the centuries, one after another so the thoughts merge with mine. I am not a single Sommen. I am a collective, one of many linked through time and space."

San asked, "Who created the transits? Were they there when you first expanded?"

The Sommen closed its eyes. San had never seen their eyelids, and blinked at the leathery orange-toned skin, rippled and bumped as if that of a lizard. "I see this question in an ocean of your intentions. Your people, even now, your brother included, are consumed by this race—the ones who built the wormholes. It is a waste of your time."

"But there is nothing of them in the texts. Did they create you and us?"

"No. And this is another insult." The priest waved to the warrior who stood near Wilson, forcing the Sommen back onto the dais. "Do not test my warriors, young priestess. Our creator, and yours, created them as well. We call them the machinists. All we know is that the creator made them first, and gave them the curse of machinery. As with your Chinese, this race fused themselves with synthetic materials and used intelligent machines to seed the galaxy with wormholes. The creator gave them the plans—showed them where to build their network. And when it was done, the machinists disappeared."

"How? What happened to them?"

"Their synthetic beings turned. Some of our most difficult battles have been against what remains of the machinists, scattered from system to system. It is a warning to all races: impurities destroy. Impurities eradicate entire species." The thing snapped its eyes open again. "Earth is fortunate that we caught you in time; had you encountered the machinists on your own, or had you continued down the path of hybridization, you too would be gone. What the machinists created to connect, their false offspring now use against the Sommen. But then, it was always written this way, was it not?"

San shook her head. "I don't understand."

"It was preordained by the Creator: that the Sommen would encounter your kind—a race with three secrets, prophecies."

The words slammed into her thought stream, stirring her mind into a frenzy of confusion so that San glanced at Wilson to see if he shared her opinion; he nodded back, his face going pale when he mouthed *this is real*. San closed her eyes. *Mathematics is truth; evaluate reality against the backdrop of its immobility.* Everything had been a myth. Fables. The Proelian teachings, the material stuffed into her mind when a toddler, she had doubted all of it and the realization that it might all be true—or even partially true—made her dizzy with implications.

The priest waited at first and then shifted its head to look at Wilson.

"I sense the confusion. I see its origin but cannot understand it."

"I didn't believe the Sommen religious texts," said San, "or the human ones—not really. Not until now, anyway. We can't see our predecessors' memories, not in the Sommen way; most on Earth don't believe because we have no evidence. Our texts can often instill faith, but not always belief. Faith is different."

"And now you have evidence."

San nodded. "Mathematics is truth. I compared your stories to what I know from our texts and it fits. I don't believe. Not yet. But you gave us more: information that is consistent with what the Proelians taught about the connection between Sommen faith and ours. The story of the machinists was never in your texts. Nor ours. But it fits."

"That is not why I brought you both here; why we entered human space in violation of the treaty. There is one more thing to accomplish before I let you go."

The priest reached with both arms toward the top of his tank, manipulating something out of sight; the stone lid began to slide. A hiss from escaping ammonia filled the room and the lid opened all the way, the tank boiling with the release of its pressure.

Both warriors rested their blades against it and then arranged themselves so that one stood on either side. They reached in. The priest emerged from the fluid, splattering the deck with droplets, and the group shuffled down the dais stairs to stand in front of San.

"Do you have material to seal your suit in case of breach?" the priest asked.

"Yes. But why would..."

The priest slammed its thin arm forward, extending his fingers so that sharp narrow claws penetrated San's suit fabric and plunged into her arm. She screamed. It lasted a second, until the priest yanked its hand away and pressed the claws against its forehead, smearing traces of San's blood against its flesh. While San floated, rotating while spraying foam sealant over her suit, she coughed at the influx of ammonia and did her best to hold her breath. The priest then did the same thing to Wilson. By the time it was over, both of them coughed in their suits, and San watched the warriors place their priest back in his tank, sealing the lid while fresh fluid bubbled up from below.

"Why?" San asked.

"It was needed. Your kind has breached the treaty, but not in a way that requires a full response. By creating an abomination, your brother, we needed to test you and the other human priests to make sure of your purity. It is good."

"Now what?"

"Leave my ship and go with a warning: I sense in you a desire to enter Sommen space. Do not. If Earth ships are caught one more time in our domain, it will mean war. Tell your priesthood this."

"We will," San said.

"And find the prophecies of your people, especially the third— the one granted in a place called Portugal. I sense that you do not know them."

San was about to ask for more information when the tank's glass turned opaque, blocking her view of the priest. The warriors lifted their blades. One pointed toward the hall's rear, and San and Wilson turned, venting gas to move from the dais. On the way out they passed the body of their original escort, the insectile creature. It was dead, San decided.

"Wilson, do you remember the way out?"

"I think so. But we've got to change our plans; there's no way we can go into Sommen space after this."

"You're wrong. After what we learned of the machinists and their fight against the Sommen, we have to complete this mission more than ever—including getting rid of my brother and exploring the space near the Sommen home world. The abbess will see it that way, too. She must hear all of this. Who else but the machinists could have forced the Sommen from their home world?"

"San..."

"It's always been about the machinists, Wilson; I see that now. The abbess wants their technology."

BOOK THREE

CHAPTER SEVENTEEN

"They are overdue," said Zhelnikov.

Win nodded. "They will arrive." He glanced out the ashram at alien star patterns, jealous that the Proelian telesthetics could make sense of it all and use Sommen balls of fire to chart a course. Even the empty space threatened the *Higgins* and its crew; since the transit into enemy territory, they'd been running at minimal electronics and two years of hibernation sleep hadn't reduced Win's fear that they'd be detected. He scanned the stars again, reaching out with his thoughts to probe the dark places where his vision failed.

"Relax, Win. We are adrift with only life support and gas maneuvering active. The weapon capacitors are charged. We cannot be detected by the Sommen."

"No, but my sister can find us. Your crew's thoughts create ripples that travel far, and which she can detect. And have you tested the weapon?"

"Our men worked the whole time we slept. They tested while we were still outside Sommen space, and now we are close enough to the wormhole that its emissions should scramble at least some of our crew's leakage. Even if it doesn't, our enemies first have to transit. We will get the first shot."

"You assume they haven't already come through."

"How?" Zhelnikov slammed his helmet on, locking the neck ring in place so that his voice now rang through speakers. "Why would they deviate from their course and transit schedule? We arrived well before the earliest possible time the group could have gotten here.

To get here any faster, both their ships would have had to undergo minimum gas and water collection—a low-fuel risk that they wouldn't take. Not when they were about to enter Sommen territory. They will come from the transit; you can stop scanning."

Win ignored the suggestion. This wormhole had been placed at the edge of a star system, a cold red giant so distant that its light barely reached them, but just enough that its glow filled the ashram with a faint orange tint. The light reminded Win of fireplaces on Earth, in wintertime, where wealthy Fleet officers could afford the magnificent older homes and the cost associated with burning cellulose. What a waste. But at least fire would provide warmth and a feeling of quiet exhaustion; light from the red giant was just strange enough that it increased Win's anxiety, making his skin crawl with the sensation that something was out there, getting ready to attack the *Higgins*. Once more he reached out, this time in the direction of the star.

Waves of weak energy, magnetic currents and particle winds, drifted around his consciousness and billowed the fabric of his mind. They clouded his vision. He saw the system as if it hid behind a thin veil and Win puzzled at the phenomenon; this was new. He'd never had trouble seeing into systems and there had never been this kind of interference except when in the presence of Sommen priests, so he traced the currents—imagining himself a kind of sniffer, moving along a gradient in the direction of increasing perturbations. The source appeared to be a tremendous planet, a gas giant so large that it must, he thought, have come close to collapsing into a star when it first formed. Its surface swirled in green and light blue, reminding him of a jade marble. Win moved in. By now the interference was so intense that he felt his body break into sweat with the effort. His vision cleared and he went still, transfixed by the sight of a pair of ships hidden in the gas giant's upper atmosphere.

Win snapped back into his body. "*Bangkok* and *Jerusalem* spotted."

"What?" asked Zhelnikov. "I don't see them."

"*In the damn gas giant!* They've been here the whole time, interfering with my sight."

Zhelnikov flew toward the ashram's hatch, spinning its wheel and then calling over his shoulder. "Stay here. I'm headed to the combat center. Report everything noteworthy."

"They detected me, old man. They're headed out of orbit now, coming this way."

"Then they miscalculated." Zhelnikov's voice came via radio, structural interference making it crackle. "That gas giant's gravity well must be impressive and even if they've been scooping gas this whole time, they'll burn a lot getting distance from the planet. We'll make them burn it all."

The *Jerusalem* and *Bangkok* were too far to see, even if he tied into the ship's sensor network, and they were still outside the *Higgins*'s active sensors—if Zhelnikov had been willing to risk activating them. Active wouldn't work anyway, Win reminded himself. The very construction of Proelian ships rendered radar and other electronic detection means unreliable at best; as if reading his mind, the *Higgins*'s captain ordered the launching of targeting drones. Win watched their engines burn. The flames formed tiny dots of light that rocketed away into the blackness until one by one they winked out, the small vessels coasting their way in a spread pattern toward the oncoming ships.

A burst of light caught his attention. Win spun his head just in time to see the fires of a ship's engine off the starboard side of the *Higgins,* and he watched, hypnotized while trying to figure out what it was. He clicked into the ship's network.

"Captain, unidentified vessel off our rear starboard quarter; it's on a collision course with us."

Win had been strapped to the ashram deck so he wouldn't bounce away, but he hadn't secured himself into its acceleration couch. The captain fired ship's engines. At the same time the *Higgins* vented maneuvering gas, sending Win downward against the deck so he couldn't breathe, and his vision narrowed with every second until he blacked out. When he came to, the acceleration had stopped. Win crawled into the acceleration couch and strapped in, only then glancing at the rear of the ship where he thought the enemy vessel had targeted for its suicide run.

At first, the *Higgins*'s aft section looked normal and Win wondered if the captain had successfully evaded. Then a wisp of vapor jetted outward. The wisp grew into a torrent of gas mixed with debris and white flickers of detonations, extinguished by vacuum where white-hot flame met space. A series of rumbling thuds shook the deck underneath the acceleration couch and Win reminded himself to stay calm, willing his heart rate to slow despite the communications traffic that erupted in his helmet. He gave up trying to follow the identities; instead, Win closed his eyes and let the words roll past.

"One main engine disabled. Engineering section two venting."

"Emergency bulkheads now shut."

"Thirty crew dead, fifteen unaccounted."

Win recognized Zhelnikov's voice. "Main weapon status?"

"Functional."

"Active detection; thirty-seven of our targeting drones are painting the *Jerusalem* and *Bangkok*. Coordinates entered into computer."

"These aren't clean readings. They're almost useless. Whatever those things are made of, it's absorbing all energy."

"*Captain.*" The ship's semi-aware computer sounded flat; it unnerved Win—to not read any emotion in combination with the words. "*Sensors indicate that these are Fleet ships targeting and attacking us. Why are we being attacked by Fleet? I recommend . . .*"

"Who the hell activated our semi-aware? Someone shut it down; keep it shut down."

"Main weapon in range . . . five minutes."

They're after me, Win realized. *Not the* Higgins; *me.*

As soon as his thumb hit his forearm control, the needle jabbed into his neck, sending Win into immediate convulsions with such a large dose. He broke free. Win moved from the *Higgins* in a streak of light to land in a corridor of the *Jerusalem,* its cramped space empty while the ship slammed back and forth during evasive maneuvers. The movement would have turned his bones into jelly had his body been there. Red emergency lights filled the ship's vacant spaces and before long Win gave up on searching, his mind filled with anger at having failed to find her—the one person who could answer his question.

I am here, she said.

I cannot see you, San.

I am so happy you finally came.

Win felt her hatred and basked in it, the sensation like a radiative heat that threatened to bake his intellect, but which made him smile at its purity. She, whom he had never met. What stories had this girl, his sister, been told in order to conjure an anger such that Win saw her eagerness for murder in a gleaming jewel—a beacon at the foreground of a dream? Who had told her these stories in such a fashion that she believed them, despite that they'd never met? Win had looked forward to this day. But now that it had come, he felt overwhelming disappointment at its lack of importance, her blind hatred so basic and devoid of calculus that Win almost pitied all of them, even his sister.

You, Win sent, *are only a servant.*

And yet the Higgins *burns.*

You think you win, San? You knew that the sisters sent you into a trap, and now you believe you've mastered it but soon you will burn too—so brightly.

Our targeting drones have your position. In a few minutes we launch. The Higgins's *drones have a guess at our position, but nothing more; and what will you use? Missiles? At best we lose an engine. You are finished. Nobody wants you alive, brother, least of all me.*

Win laughed at her words, the blindness in them—a total failure to understand her situation and that of her ships—but his laughter soon faded, leaving behind a sensation of emptiness. San and the Proelians weren't the adversaries he'd imagined. Confidence had inebriated them. They did not know of the new weapon and would be unprepared when it fired, the Sommen portion of his brain repulsed by a sensation that this fight would be without honor, his targets little more than village idiots who had completely let their guard down, sure in their victory. Win detected no mental interference and the clarity of his vision rendered everything so crisply he could read the smallest ship's markings from a distance; it gave him an idea.

Win sped through the ship.

Where are you going, Win?

I'm afraid, San, he lied. *I don't want to die. Spare us.*

They made you in vacuum, without a context. It twisted you. Neither human nor Sommen, you soar through the horror of daily life, existing for no purpose that you know of except to murder. It is our show of mercy: ending your and Zhelnikov's lives. Today.

You would have made an excellent nun. Perhaps there's still time.

The bridge looked different from the *Higgins*'s; Win felt claustrophobic within its confines and he stared at the flesh of its crew members, whose faces flattened under intense g-forces of acceleration. Their stations cocooned them within banks of mechanical and hydraulic actuators; *dials,* he thought. The ship had actual analog dials that flickered back and forth and the things so entranced him that Win almost forgot why he'd gone there. He sped to the navigator's station and surveyed the array of digits that clicked up and down, rows of white squares with tiny black numbers that danced to the tune of ship's maneuvers and referenced the ship's position against the red dwarf and its planets. After he'd watched for a while, he left. Win ignored his sister's laugher as it faded behind him, disappearing once he'd re-merged with the *Higgins.*

He clicked onto ship's coms. "Zhelnikov. I have readings from the *Bangkok.* They've engaged in evasive maneuvers but I have a general heading and I'm sending it to the targeting computers now."

"How?" Zhelnikov asked. "Where did you get this?"

"The Proelians failed to keep their interference up. They grow too confident. So I visited their bridge."

"One minute to firing range," someone announced.

She will die today, not me. I am a weapon, perfected in the fire of Sommen vision drugs, my body's withering a map of the cost of sight. This is the way of warfare. This is how I will conquer everything and everyone, with the tissue of a dedicated machine, tuned and optimized for death and its accompaniment. I deserve a better enemy than this . . .

"One of their drones," someone announced. "Incoming."

"Missile detected. Launch, launch, launch."

Win was so lost in meditation that he almost missed it. A Proelian drone had been adrift, invisible against the backdrop of space and the red giant, but now that it had fired he tracked the blue spark, watching as the weapon rocketed in a spiral path, locking onto the *Higgins.* He froze. The missile's rocket flame intensified as it approached and once it stopped maneuvering the thing flared with a last burst of acceleration, sending its warhead straight toward the ashram. No maneuvering could change things now, he realized; the warhead was too close. *Perhaps she was a worthy adversary after all.*

Someone whispered over coms. "Impact will be midship, top side."

"Affirmative. Ashram impact, three seconds."

"Lead ship is now within range of main weapon, Captain. Our best guess at its coordinates are locked."

"Begin the firing sequence; power main weapon."

Win's jaw slammed shut with the force of the missile's impact, making him see stars. He hyperventilated. His suit systems lit with yellow warning lights but none of the damage appeared catastrophic and his servo harness's combat carapace remained pressurized, its motors whining as he tested arms and legs. This was impossible; his mind swirled with the comprehension that he'd just survived a direct missile hit, and with no damage to himself or his suit.

A piece of debris appeared nearby; the ship fragment spun, its edges going from a bright red glow of molten metal to a dull orange and then black when it cooled. Win noticed a cloud of it. Cooling debris surrounded him on all sides along with flickering ice crystals, glinting in orange light so that he imagined being put in the middle of an exploding firework, trapped within a blossom of ship's wreckage and frozen water vapor that kept pace with him at a similar velocity; eventually, Win knew, the cloud would dissipate into nothing and his heart raced with the fear of realizing what had happened: The blast had thrown him into space.

"*Higgins*, do you copy?" he radioed.

Win glanced around, panicked. It took time for the *Higgins* to take shape in the star's dim orange light, the outline diminishing in size as the distance grew. Where the ashram had been there was now a gaping hole venting atmosphere, and sparks from electrical systems sent white dots in every direction. Win hit his forearm controls. Gas jetted from his backpack unit and the deceleration was more violent than he'd anticipated, almost forcing him to collide head-on with a massive hull section that had been trailing him. He dodged around it. The gauge on his heads-up showed the diminishing fuel supply but still Win hadn't reversed course by the time he had exhausted three-quarters of his maneuvering fuel in navigating the debris. He used almost all the rest to start closing distance with the *Higgins* until only a small fraction remained.

"*Higgins*," he repeated, "do you copy?"

Before he could ask again, Win's faceplate sensors sparked, almost all of them failing simultaneously and sending him into darkness.

He couldn't see his forearm controls. Win's heart threatened to pound from his chest and he heard the sound of his own heavy breathing while trying to figure out what had happened to his systems and what to do next. Win reached up. He fumbled at a tiny protrusion near the top of his helmet, snapping something open so that a projection appeared on his screen, his last chance to see and navigate through these surroundings. Suit helmets were equipped with backup optical periscopes, manually activated, but the red giant's light was so dim the thing projected bare and ghostly images, almost unrecognizable. Finally he spotted the *Higgins* again; her new weapon, arrayed in a series of mammoth cylinders on its port side, now glowed at the tip as if it had just been cast in the furnace of hell.

They fired, Win thought. *That's what overloaded my sensors. My god, what a weapon.*

"Zhelnikov," he said, hoping the suit's backup radio system still functioned. "Do you read me?"

"Win? Where are you and what's your status?"

"I'm outside the ship, trying to maneuver my way back. I'm uninjured but my suit is almost out of gas. All my sensors failed when the *Higgins* fired so I'm working off periscope with no way to get range. Thank god the suit radio still works, along with life-support systems. If you maneuver away, I'm gone."

At first Zhelnikov didn't respond; when he returned his voice sounded reassuring. "We're launching a shuttle. Keep radioing so the pilot can get a fix."

Win waited. Every so often he would say something, until a small shuttle flew into view while the *Higgins* peeled off, entering another series of evasive maneuvers. By the time he'd made it into the shuttle airlock he'd seen enough to realize they were making for the wormhole, in retreat.

Win strapped himself into a couch, still blind except for the periscope. "Is the *Higgins* running?" he asked the pilot. "She's about to get destroyed."

"Yes," the pilot said. "It lost an engine so we should be able to keep pace."

"Did the weapon work? What's the status of the *Bangkok*?"

Someone took Win's arm and he heard a snapping sound when

the person jacked a cable into the suit's forearm control unit. A second later he had access to the shuttle's sensors and coms.

"We missed. Minimal damage to only one Proelian vessel but I don't know which one. Both are now within missile range."

Win flipped through the sensors, settling on a combination of the *Higgins's* tactical feed and its wide-angle optics. He zoomed into a Proelian ship. The vessel spewed gas and debris along one side, from multiple gaping holes in its sheathing material but its engines burned as brightly as its sister's. Swarms of rockets lit from its front section, then from the other ship's. Win shook his head at the sight. He counted more than thirty missiles as they streaked toward the *Higgins,* and already the tactical readout had identified them as a combination of kinetic and nuclear warheads.

"The theurgists are done at playing school," he said. "Now we see their true faces. I was wrong about them."

"My god," said the pilot.

"That is not your god. That is your death—and ours with the destruction of our destination: the *Higgins.*"

The copilot pointed at Win, his voice filled with anger. "We should have left him out there. The *Higgins* has some neutron and gamma shielding; enough so that some will survive. This shuttle is a coffin. We died to save Zhelnikov's monster?"

"Those missiles aren't targeting us," the pilot said. His hands sped over the shuttle's control panel, a navigation holo popping into existence as he plotted a new course. "We'll burn for a few more seconds, then use maneuvering gas to send the ship in a wide arc, around where the tactical predicts the nuclear tips will detonate. We might make it."

"Might?" the copilot asked.

"We can't arc too far or we miss the transit. We'll definitely take some radiation."

Win absorbed their fear like a light rain that fell on his face, misting his thoughts with its vibrations and tremors. He mapped it. Every tick of the copilot's thoughts induced a new current of terror that provided insight and Win soon saw his opportunity.

"There will be enough radiation to disrupt your DNA," he said. "You'll escape immediate death, but from the distances shown on your course projection you'll still absorb a lethal dose. Not enough to cook you immediately, but enough so that within hours you'll become sick. Your tissues will behave as though they've been broiled from the inside out. And over the next few weeks you'll begin the exquisite road to organ failure and a painful death. If you can become comfortable with the thought of vomiting up blood, it might not be so bad."

Now the copilot's thought patterns came in intermittent bursts, the random firings of a person both panicked and never stable to begin with, and he saw the copilot's anger build. *He blames me.* Win watched the man clench and unclench his fists, his breathing shallow and ragged as the pilot locked in a new shuttle course. Its engines cut off. A sudden absence of acceleration sent their compartment again into weightlessness, punctuated by moments of inertia as the maneuvering jets spurted off and on to keep them on course. Win began to unbuckle his couch straps. The copilot spun in his chair to face forward, chuckling.

"You forgot one thing: You're in here too. With us."

"Yes," said Win, releasing the final catch that kept him in place. "But my servo harness has adequate shielding because Zhelnikov designed it for maximum survivability. I'll get a bad sunburn. Nothing more. *You,* on the other hand? When they bury you in space, it will be as though they loaded the coffin with a raw oyster."

The copilot hit a button on his armrest, releasing him from the acceleration chair. A maneuvering jet fired. Win had anticipated it, shooting the last of his servo harness fuel to compensate for the shuttle's acceleration while the copilot, hanging in midair and unable to change direction with the craft, flew headlong into a bulkhead. His suit helmet cracked open; a fraction of a second later, a sharp metal corner slammed into his skull, splitting it and filling the compartment with a spray of blood. Win disconnected from the coms cable, barely able to see through the helmet periscope while he scrambled for the man's seat where he finished strapping in before the shuttle jets fired again.

"Your copilot looks dead, but have no fear; he won't fly around. Your course will keep pushing him into the bulkhead."

"*Jesus!*"

"I need to adjust navigation."

"Any wider and we run out of maneuvering fuel. Closer, and I fry for sure."

"Please, forgive me. I can't afford to take the route you plotted; it keeps us in Sommen space for too long, and gives them a chance to fire at us."

Win slammed a spiked servo harness leg through the pilot's helmet, cutting him off. Killing *filled* Win with a burst of energy. He'd kept the urge under control for so long that Win imagined the sensation was the same as it would be if he rid himself of the servo harness, allowing cool air to flow over his wasting frame, drying the drool from his chin instead of sucking it off the skin. *I am meant to destroy—anything and everything. It is as I choose, the deity of meaningless expirations.*

He pulled the spike out, then concentrated on trying to find a spot on the control panel to jack into.

"I do not recognize you," the shuttle computer said.

"It's okay. I'm on the *Higgins's* roster; check your records for Win. Shuttle pilot and copilot are now deceased and I need control."

"Authorized. How unfortunate. Do you need medical attention?"

"Time to missile detonation?"

"Two minutes."

"Change course. Fastest burn to the transit."

"Such a route will put you within range of several nuclear-tipped warhead detonations, immediately post detonation."

"I know," Win said.

"You cannot survive."

"Do it."

"Your records indicate a lack of engineering for combat g-forces. I will keep them within standard range."

Win shut his eyes. If kinetic warheads destroyed the *Higgins* he would die, but if some of the ship's systems survived, even with a dead crew he had a chance to enter a navigation route and hibernate. How long would it take to reach Earth—from here, at the edge of Sommen space—if he chose not to use wormholes? What if the missiles took out navigation and all he could do was point the ship at Earth? *Thousands of years asleep.* The concept almost tempted him; Win could start over, arrive after the Sommen war to see who won and who lost, and, perhaps, reestablish himself as the leader of conflict and annihilation. Then again he'd have a constant need of fuel and would have to pray there were no reactor problems; the power systems required maintenance and overhaul every fifty years. Win chuckled out loud, prompting the shuttle semi-aware to ask, "*Is there something funny? Detonation in five seconds.*"

"Yes. If I am the only one left on the *Higgins,* and its navigation system is destroyed, I can't make it home. I'll die in hibernation, but live longer than you."

A blinding flash backlit Win's eyelids, the shuttle's sensors activating filters in the light of several new suns. A few seconds later, he opened them. Jets of molten metal streaked toward the *Higgins.* A glowing halo of energy surrounded the ship, expanding so fast that it enveloped the shuttle in x-rays, gamma radiation, and charged particles, forcing Win's control panel to spark and catch fire, the systems switching over to backups at the same time emergency vents opened the compartment to vacuum. Ten kinetic missiles had found their target. In the aftermath of the radiation bath the Proelian ships had just given her, the *Higgins* bucked at this new insult when glowing, orange streaks pierced its hull in multiple spots and then ejected out the far side in clouds of debris. The *Higgins's* engines cut off. Win had to blink when he realized gamma radiation had made it through his beryllium-doped polymer sheathing, leaving streaks of light across his vision as if fireworks had gone off inside his helmet. He squinted, willing the phenomenon to stop so he could see. By the time he regained his vision, the *Higgins* had begun a slow tumble, disappearing backward into the wormhole. Then came the shuttle's turn. A sudden feeling of exhaustion overtook Win, a portion of his mind warning that this was radiation exposure, and he shut his eyes again after struggling to keep them open while the mirrored wormhole surface expanded across his view screen.

"Wake up. Wake up. Wake ..."

"What?" Win asked.

"*You've been unconscious for thirty minutes,*" the semi-aware said. "*I was able to access your suit's medical unit and administer one dose of radiation mitigator, but your oxygen generator is almost empty. There are spares in the storage compartment between the pilot's and copilot's stations.*"

"Where are we?" Win asked. He fished a cartridge from out of the compartment and replaced his old one, dousing the suit's low-oxygen warning light.

"*I have successfully docked with the Higgins. We now drift outside Sommen space, three thousand kilometers from the transit point.*"

Win ripped the seat harness loose and pushed off, slamming his hand on the airlock controls. It took a moment to cycle through. Once in the *Higgins*'s airlock he saw the blinking lights on the other side of the door, through a small porthole: the ship's interior was in vacuum. Had there been an atmosphere Win would have heard the alarm klaxons while the ship's semi-aware listed damaged and destroyed systems over ship's speakers. The inner door cycled open and three corpses tumbled into the tight space, dead crew members who had bloated—as if someone had both burned and inflated them.

Win jetted through the maze of corridors, crashing through the dead, most of whom had ruptured suits from where large chunks of debris had punched through the fabric and then their bodies. He tried to remember. The *Higgins*'s combat bridge had been radiation hardened so the command crew would have the maximum chance for survival but it took almost an hour to find it amid the labyrinth of wreckage. He worked the door controls the best he could, cursing at a loss of backup power and the illumination of his small helmet lamp; the beam flickered, its boundaries defined by suspended dust and blood.

Suddenly, the hatch cracked open. It crept open further to allow a burst of atmosphere to escape from the cramped space, the crack widening enough that Win saw Zhelnikov's face through the glass of his helmet's faceplate.

"Win; you're alive."

"What happened?"

"We missed. The shot was close enough that it melted portions of a Proelian ship but not enough to disable it. When the missiles hit us, the ship automatically shut off reactors and our one good engine. She's dead unless we conduct some repairs."

"And the weapon?" Win asked.

"Salvageable." When there was enough space, Zhelnikov and several other crew pushed out of the combat bridge. "Come. There's no time. We have to get basic systems online before we travel too far, and before the Proelians come to finish the job."

"The Proelian *scum*," said Win. "My sister. They think I'm dead and will not come for us; they are in Sommen space and will continue on mission. But when she finds out I'm alive, she will try for me again. She will never stop."

"Well, then it's good that I laid a trap for her—back there, after we fired the weapon. Now: move, boy; there's work to do."

CHAPTER EIGHTEEN

We have lost both captains, San sent, her message part of a mammoth game of tin-can telephone where quantum particles in the tomb linked with ones thousands of light-years away, deep beneath the surface of Ganymede. *One died on the* Jerusalem, *when the* Higgins *fired its new plasma weapon. The other died on his shuttle, in transit. He was on the* Jerusalem *when the* Higgins *entered our space, and the captain tried to make his way back to my ship, midbattle. The plasma beam scored a direct hit, vaporizing both him and his craft.*

The response: *I have relayed this to the abbess. She says that the surviving executive officers are now the captains of the* Bangkok *and* Jerusalem; *both ships are to continue on mission, which you will direct, advise. What happened to your primary targets: Win and Zhelnikov?*

Presumed dead. One of our missiles scored a direct hit on his ashram while it was occupied.

The abbess congratulates you and the Bangkok's *crew. The same message is being relayed to the* Jerusalem *right now. Continue on mission.*

A sense of panicked fear threatened to choke San as it rose in her chest, settling in her throat; before long they'd all be in deep inside the territory of an overpowering adversary.

What about the Higgins? *She escaped through the wormhole and we must pursue, in case of survivors.*

The abbess says that it is critical to learn about the Sommen abandoned zone; to gather any data you can on the machinists. After your last report, she and Fleet have conferred and models are in agreement that Zhelnikov and Win could not have survived your attacks; do not pursue.

Her brother was dead. San let the concept seep into her thoughts and work its way downward to her chest where it blossomed into a picture of reality: She had killed, and not Chinese hybrids this time. This had been an entire Fleet vessel crewed by people like her, young men and women who'd joined so they could see space and operate in the service of humanity, to protect Earth the same way she'd always dreamed of doing. Her connection with Ganymede wavered with San's effort to fight back tears, a battle weakened by a growing sense of disconnection from reality that wedged itself between her thoughts and gray matter. Why should she mourn her brother? The *Higgins* had been manned by traitors and deserved the end they received, so why should she care at all about their lives or loss? San searched for something, anything, to distract herself from the questions, which she suspected had no answers.

Our landing craft, she sent, reestablishing connection, *are preparing for water collection operations. The battle and maneuvering in a gas giant's gravity well depleted our reserves. After refueling, we will continue.*

The abbess says to move out immediately after refueling, to put as much distance between you and the engagement area in case Sommen detected the battle. And, San?

What?

The coordinates given by the Sommen priest were valid. Fleet and the Proelians have wiped out the new Chinese home world, and are hunting for stragglers posted in wormhole ambush sites. She said to tell you "well done" and "thanks to your and Wilson's bravery, the erasure of Chinese errors will soon be complete." End communications.

San felt tears in the corners of her eyes. The tomb slabs opened and she wiped them on the bare skin of her forearm, sliding back into her undersuit before breaking into open sobs. The weight of death and killing settled upon her with the mass of a boulder and although she couldn't read their minds, the fear and uncertainty of the entire crew buzzed through her mind; it hummed, a thin wire tensioned to the breaking point. Once San announced Fleet's decision to the crew, it wouldn't take long for word to make its way throughout the entire ship that they were headed deep into Sommen space after all; many had thought because of the battle they'd be recalled. Disappointment would be a cancer.

Already she felt the blame from some of them, ones who had lost friends when the *Higgins* fired its weapons, because it had been San's plan—her idea to hide in the gas giant to ambush. *Why does this bother me?* San wondered. Because the crew would be right to focus their anger on her and Wilson; what experience had either of them except training on Ganymede and the one Fleet assignment—this one? Her knowledge of ship's systems and combat maneuvers came from what had been crammed into her mind as a child, in a tank, and for ships entirely different from the one she currently occupied so that she and Wilson had overestimated its capabilities. If the plasma weapon had been aimed one degree over, the *Jerusalem* would have been lost entirely; the captains may have led their ships, but it had been her plan that got so many killed. San collected herself, and climbed back into her environment suit.

"Are you okay, miss?" the lieutenant asked.

"No, Eugene. We are to continue on mission. Pass word to the executive officers on both ships that the abbess orders them to assume command and that the *Jerusalem*'s repairs will be conducted while underway." The lieutenant pointed at one of his men, who made for the hatch. When he turned back, San had started crying again. "I nearly got us all killed."

"Nonsense, miss. This is war, and that's what happens in battle. And we didn't lose everyone; most lived because of you."

"Who am I to make suggestions for ship-to-ship combat, for Fleet strategy? Why would anyone listen to my suggestions in the first place? I've never actually *been* in combat. These deaths? They're on me."

"San Kyarr," the lieutenant said. The word rang in her ears and she recognized the Marine's tone sounded grim. "Fleet is Fleet. The crew, and the ships' captains, are going to listen to you and Wilson because none of us has been in combat and you have special skills that none of us share. And you will continue offering battle plans because that's why you're here; it's your job."

"I don't want it anymore."

The lieutenant helped San into her helmet, locking it in place; San's eyes widened with a start when he grabbed both her shoulders, hard enough that it hurt. "Forgive me, miss, but I need your attention. Listen and don't forget: What you want isn't at issue here. There are greater things at stake than you or your remorse—the future of humanity, for one. *Pull it together.* The crew needs you the same way they need a captain." The lieutenant released her shoulders and took hold of her wrist, escorting San to the hatch.

"Where are we going?" she asked.

"While you had your helmet off, an order came from the new captain. Both navigators, along with a Marine detachment, are to take all the landing craft down to the surface of SX-1777 for water collection. Now that we've entered Sommen space you're to go on every planet-side landing, with us, in case we find something that requires your skills. Artifacts, machinists, whatever we discover."

San and a group of Marines sped to the hangar in silence, her gliding movements through the pipe galleries somber as if heading to an execution. She struggled to keep from crying again. The emotions of some crew members, still mourning the loss of their captain, leaked through her skull and seeped into her mind, making it so San began to have trouble distinguishing between her own feelings and those of the crew. With every second that brought her closer to the hangar San felt more excited about leaving the ship. It would distance herself from so much sadness. She boarded the closest landing craft and strapped into a couch, waiting for the other vessels to prepare.

"San," the lieutenant said. "You're in command of the refueling operation; the pilot is waiting for you to give the word."

San lifted a handset to communicate with all the ships, pressing it against her helmet speakers. "Take off when every ship is ready. No radio communications until we reach the surface. I want melt mats and collection tents up as quickly as possible."

After replacing the handset, she closed her eyes. *Wilson, take off as soon as your ships are ready; we'll meet you on the surface.*

San, I don't like this.

We're almost out of hydrogen. So are you.

I know; I'm not saying we shouldn't do this, I'm just saying we haven't had time to launch any drones and get sensor readings of the surface. There could be anything down there.

That's why we're bringing so many Marines, San sent. *The moment we sense any trouble, we'll take off with the water we collected.*

San's ship lifted off the deck and accelerated into space, the relief immediate. With every second, the mass of feelings that threatened to suffocate her on the *Bangkok* became more diffuse until they evaporated altogether, replaced only by the uncertainty of a few refueling crewmembers—a pervasive anxiety, arising from an imminent landing on an alien planet with no survey data. San considered launching a drone. At least it would be able to do one pass over the ice fields and although there wouldn't be time for a full survey, it would have a chance of detecting any Sommen or dangerous native life. Closer to Earth, the water-ice moons of Jupiter and Saturn had already been surveyed, their undersea organisms known and catalogued as harmless things to those on the icy surfaces, albeit some life-threatening if one ventured into their pressurized worlds.

San decided against it. Instead she watched as the gas giant's moon loomed larger in the ship's forward sensors, gravimetric readings showing that they'd have an easy time on the surface; it was half the mass of Earth, with almost no atmospheric pressure, which would make the business of sublimating ice into water gas even easier. By the time the ship touched down, she felt better. San waited for the compartment to evacuate then opened both airlock doors to step off, drifting down to the planet's surface in a puff of ice. The other ships came in, one after another. She grinned at the sight of them, their silent engines fiery against the backdrop of space just as their braking engines kicked up storms of crystals that pattered against her helmet and faceplate. The sound made her cold. By the time the last craft from the *Jerusalem* landed, San had begun to shiver and cranked up her suit heat to send warmth through undersuit capillaries.

Her crews extended hoses and melting mats. San sighed with relief; soon the tents would be ready, trapping and pumping water into the ships' tanks, filling them with not just a hydrogen source, but also oxygen and water—everything they'd need to survive and power the two ships now in orbit. Wilson gave the order to begin heating the moment equipment had been emplaced.

I actually love this process, he sent. *Look at it. Out here, water and ice are the most precious commodities of all, more than any precious metal or gem.*

Someday, maybe when I'm too old to prepare for war, I want to visit a sapphire planet.

Never heard of them.

There are several known ones but nobody has ever found a transit close enough to visit.

What are they? Super-rich with gems?

Sapphires rain from the sky. The planetary masses are at least five times that of Earth and the atmospheres have so much calcium and aluminum that gems form in the clouds themselves.

Wilson didn't respond. The pair waited and San watched for close to an hour as water vapor escaped through imperfections in the tents, wafting upward so that a white cloud assembled overhead. Her ship's tank was almost full when the lieutenant broke in via radio.

"Miss, movement. Near the perimeter."

"What kind of movement?" San asked.

"Point source. Deep. Sensor network places it about three hundred meters from me in the direction of the closest pole, still about a kilometer under the ice but moving upward."

San slapped her forearm controls, scraping the ice off and punching at the keypad. All the mats shut off. The crew began tearing down hoses and tents but, San knew, this was the slowest part of the process; nobody could touch the delicate webbing of the mats for at least a few minutes until they cooled off or the things would be ruined, their permeability destroyed. She relayed a status report into orbit, then bounced across the ice toward the lieutenant's men, telling Wilson to join her.

"It's out there," the lieutenant said when she arrived, pointing first at a holo map that spun in the air, and then at the ice field. "It's moving upward fast. Now five hundred meters down, shifting in this direction."

"We should have done a drone scan," said Wilson.

"There wasn't time. Even if we had detected something, then what? We need the fuel and would've landed anyway. How long before its arrival?"

"Two minutes."

San broke into the radio. "Water operations; how long until you finish break down and can take off?"

"Five minutes, ma'am."

San froze. The Marines checked weapons and she felt alarm emanate from them, the mental nudges of fear almost bringing with them an odor, the pungent rot of bog and mud. A blinking blue dot marked the thing's progress through the ice. San closed her eyes and reached out, placing a hand on Wilson's shoulder so she wouldn't fall while thinking of the ice, willing her mind and thoughts to brush up against whatever came toward them. Her eyes snapped open.

"What is it?" Wilson asked.

"*That thing!*"

"What thing?"

"It's a monster, under the ice. Nothing but rage and hunger, and it thinks we're a competitor. Apparently there are other creatures that live under and on the ice, only coming up to reproduce; they are its primary food source, and it thinks we're one."

"Tell it to go away!" the lieutenant suggested.

"It's an animal. All emotions and intensions. I can't communicate with it."

Wilson backed up. The Marines noticed and San sensed their disdain.

"What do we do?" he asked.

San glanced at the display again. The creature was on the verge of breaching the ice in front of them, and crystals jumped from the ground near her feet, breaking loose with vibrations.

"Miss!" the lieutenant insisted, grabbing her elbow.

"When that thing breaks through," San said, "kill it. At all costs, you are to prevent that thing from getting to our landing craft. If you don't, we all die after the *Jerusalem*'s and *Bangkok*'s reserves go dry; we can't get all our fuel from a gas giant, we need this water. As soon as our ships launch, run. One will stay behind for you and your men."

"Yes, ma'am."

"And lieutenant." San paused, unable to look at him. "I'm sorry."

"Don't be. This is the kind of crap that Marines live for."

San was about to turn when the ice erupted. She flew backward in a cloud of white chunks that slammed against her chest, knocking the wind out with a gasp and sending her to slide several meters. Wilson landed next to her, rolling over and over and slamming to a stop against hard-packed snow.

Whatever had erupted from the ice, it yanked a memory from

deep within San's subconscious: *Some scientists from ancient Earth once speculated that the octopus was never native to the planet, but had been transported there—an invasive species.* This wasn't an octopus, but it was similar. The thing had chewed its way through the ice with a sharp beak at the top of its head, which even now clamped shut and open as if unaware that it had broken through. It had no eyes. San guessed that the heat had attracted it, because it used more than thirty long, barbed tentacles to pull itself toward the ships, the thing scuttling past Marines too stunned to fire.

"Shoot it!" San screamed into her radio.

As if broken from a trance, the Marines opened up, but the vacuum and cold must have caused tracer fléchettes to malfunction because they wouldn't ignite; a silent ballet played on the ice as bursts of flesh tore from the creature with every hit the Marines' scored, and the monster began thrashing. Chunks of ice flew in every direction. At first it swung blindly. Then, one of the thing's tentacles swept out and knocked the lieutenant's legs from underneath him, sending the man spinning upward, head over foot, after which its spikes buried themselves in the next Marine's head. The man's voice rang through San's helmet; he managed to gurgle a cry for help before another tentacle wrapped around his neck, ripping the man in two. When it had finished, the creature searched, its mass of tentacles feeling its way from Marine to Marine, each one ripped apart as soon as it grabbed them.

"We're ready, ma'am," someone radioed.

San had forgotten about the water collection operation; the announcement voice gave her a burst of hope.

"Take off! Get back to the ship. Leave my vessel here; we're making for it now." San waved her arms at the Marines and shouted over the radio. "Eugene, run! Get back to my ship now!"

San took off, scrambling through snow and ice with Wilson close at her heels. The lieutenant had landed just behind them after tumbling overhead, and San grabbed him by the backpack unit, dragging the man to his feet. It didn't matter that San couldn't see behind her; she felt the frenzied vibrations in the ice underfoot, a rhythmic pounding that resulted from each impact of the creature's spikes as it pulled itself after the launching ships and fleeing Marines. Her pilot gestured from the airlock. San and Wilson launched themselves at the opening and soared forward to impact simultaneously against the man, sending him backward into the craft's passenger spaces, after which San turned. The lieutenant leapt through the opening, followed by several more Marines, but the number was far fewer than what they had brought with them. She saw the remains of the others, strewn across the ice in bright red streaks, the one color visible on an otherwise barren moonscape.

"Take off," she said.

"The airlock door is open."

"Launch. *Now!*"

The monster was ten meters away when the craft's engines ignited, thrusters under the hull sending blue flame in every direction and charring the first set of tentacles that came too close to the ship. It was the first indication that the thing could be hurt. San's body pressed downward from the force of acceleration, the weight so great she was barely able to reach the door control. She looked out. While the ship banked away, the thing continued on its rampage throughout the ice, looking for some remnant of what had attracted it in the first place, the warmth that had now disappeared in a terrorized flight to the *Jerusalem* and *Bangkok*. She lost sight when the outer door inched shut.

"How many Marines did we lose?" she asked.

"Twenty. I wasn't expecting anything like that, miss; I'm sorry."

"And how much water did we get?"

Wilson clicked in. "With radio silence we can't know right now. But I think every ship got away with almost a full load. Including this one. Plenty to get us to the next transit. We'll know for sure upon our return."

"Captain," the lieutenant started, but San held up her hand.

"I don't want to talk right now. When we get back, take me to the tomb. And Wilson..."

"Yeah?"

"Don't forget to give your new captain a full report on volume of water collected."

San crawled under high-g forces, making it to her acceleration couch where she strapped in. Images of Marines appeared behind her closed eyes, replaying the fight on the ice where that thing had ripped them apart, its nervous system failing to register coil-gun fire. It had been invincible. Would this be what war with the Sommen held? If any of their ships had been within range, the enemy could have detected the battle with the *Higgins* and the thought that every death was her fault still whispered. San blinked, trying to erase the visions of dying men. Instead tears flowed from both eyes, forcing her helmet to engage moisture recirculation so it could ingest the floating droplets, preventing them from fouling electronics.

Visions of death swirled, so real that San never remembered arriving at the *Bangkok*. She concentrated. Memories welled up from her subconscious, fusing with the Proelian mantras so that San barely knew they'd been added but sensed they came from a deep place, from wars long ago fought and ended. *Mathematics is truth, death the only absolute. Through death we find our worth, and in threats we gauge our potential for they are the mirror of our courage. Decisions create results. Actions cause reactions. Through mathematics we build the foundations of our strategies and let the dead accumulate. Mourning is only for the end, when all has been decided. Feelings have no place for those seeking the perfection of victory in His name; His, not ours, is the role of Secretary for the Exchequer of Fates.*

It took San longer than normal to reach out, making the connection with Ganymede.

Both ships refueled. We lost twenty Marines on the moon's surface. Local fauna, undetected in our rush to stock water.

The response took forever. San was about to send again when it arrived. *Abbess didn't expect to hear from you so soon. She wants to know if you are under way yet, if you have found another transit to bring you closer to their home world.*

No. I am about to start the search now. In the meantime, we will burn out of our current system to put distance between us and the site of our battle.

I am supposed to let you know something: Fleet found a hidden station near Childress transit. They raided it. Zhelnikov's allies had perfected ship-mounted plasma weaponry in secret; they hid the discovery from the Admiral and Fleet.

I know of this weapon, sent San. *They damaged one of our ships with it.*

It is Christmas, Captain Kyarr. The abbess says to remember all that is holy. Now that we have this weapon, all future Proelian vessels are being fitted with it. End communications.

San refused to disengage. She latched onto the person on the other end and, for a split second, saw through a boy's eyes, a candidate she didn't recognize—but then again years had passed since she'd been on Ganymede. The boy turned from his station. It was the abbess's room and in the corner a tree had been erected, shining with bright colored lights and ornaments that glittered against the dark stone walls. The abbess was there. She said something but the words failed to take shape and San disengaged, returning to the *Bangkok* in an instant with the memory of an abbess aged beyond her years, hunched over in a chair and connected to a medical bot. Her face had creased with deep lines and both hands trembled with palsy.

She switched onto the command net, linking with the bridge.

"Captain, Ganymede orders to start a burn out of this system, in case the Sommen come to investigate."

"Where to, Captain Kyarr?"

"Your choice. Just get us away from here. I'll start my scans for the next transit."

"What about the *Jerusalem*? Shall I radio them?"

"No. I'll contact their navigator and will let them know to follow. If our luck holds, I'll have a new course to a Sommen wormhole within a few hours."

San switched off. She closed her eyes and reached out to Wilson, sending him the orders. After finishing she added, *Did you know it's Christmas on Earth and Ganymede?*

No.

Neither did I; I'd never even seen a Christmas tree until just now. And, Wilson?

Yeah?

Our abbess is dying.

CHAPTER NINETEEN

"Adrift in Sommen space," said Win. "And I can find no Proelians to kill."

Zhelnikov chuckled. "We will be fortunate if, when we transit, the Proelian theurgists are gone; in our shape, a fast scout could take us out just from the vibration of docking. And the sleep was short, Win—two months; there were minor injuries to your neural structure and we couldn't address them with you awake."

"Do you ever ponder on time, old man?"

"In what way?"

"It has no meaning. We travel and sleep, and years pass without touching us. What will your Earth look like when you get back, Zhelnikov? Have you thought that maybe the war will start without you if we stay out here long enough? For all we know, it already has."

"Then we are the last of our kind. The last humans in the universe, in the last place the Sommen would look for us: on our way to their home world."

"I," Win said, "am not human."

"Come." Zhelnikov secured his helmet in place, and opened the hatch from his quarters. "We are nearing the transit and with just fifteen to crew the *Higgins,* we will be needed in the combat bridge. It's blind luck the Proelian missiles missed our one good engine and reactor section; the chief was able to save three quarters of our water."

"Why not just return home? This is hopeless."

"We repaired the weapon. And the mission is to salvage any tech we can find within the Sommen abandoned zone. By now, my little surprise for your sister has wormed its way onto her ship and with luck, she will be dead soon."

"You are too pleased given our lack of accomplishment, Zhelnikov."

Win picked his way through the ship's corridors, their spaces now filled with cables and piping, the jerry-rigged fixes of a craft on its last legs with just enough functioning infrastructure to keep a single engine running. He dodged the sparks. The sense of a destiny soaked in combat had left Win, who now wondered how long it would take for someone to catch up with them and finish the job his sister started—either the Proelians or Sommen. He laughed at the irony: With so few crew and functioning systems, the *Higgins* ran truly silent, the possibility of detection due to leakage no longer a concern. They crammed their way into the combat bridge.

"Don't bother strapping in," someone said. "We can't evasive maneuver in this thing anymore; it'll fall to pieces."

"How long to the transit?" Win asked.

"We're moving through now. We'll be out in a few seconds but if you recall, this one is a bit longer than the others. The navigation solutions indicate we'll be coming out in five seconds."

"Zhelnikov," the captain started. His face contorted with pain and a nearby medbot sprang to life, injecting him with something to take the edge off his broken shoulder and arm. "Has your boy been able to look ahead and see what's waiting for us?"

"No, Captain. There wasn't time."

"We should turn back," Win reiterated. "Go home. The *Higgins* is barely operational; what can you possibly expect to accomplish in this heap?"

Zhelnikov slammed his fist against the wall. "*Enough,* Win. What about the Proelian religious texts? There was a time when you had a sense of mission. This isn't about us, the *Higgins,* or you; this is about whose vision will carry us to victory over the Sommen war. The Proelians cannot be allowed to maintain control or we will lose."

"And yet," said Win, "it is a Proelian who almost destroyed us. *They* who have developed undetectable ships and a viable means for interstellar communication and navigation that does not go against Sommen thought—not to mention the treaty." Win paused. He hadn't been able to place his finger on it in Zhelnikov's quarters, after being awoken from hibernation, but now that the drugs wore off, they or his injuries had left him with an overwhelming sense that something was missing. "I am tired, Zhelnikov. I still see the plans, the pattern laid out in my sight, even now, a web of what has been ordained and what is still left to chance. Some of the blanks have been filled in so that I see more clearly. You created an amputee; there is a part of me that should be here, and I feel it like a phantom limb, but you never bothered to create it in the first place."

"Create what?"

"Faith. I will kill; it is what I know, what I do. But you and this mission were never going to succeed. I don't need the religious texts now; they are useless. The information they contained is now in sight, in my dreams and in the present. The Sommen and human races linked, racing toward the end of the universe and the discovery we've all been searching for."

"What discovery?"

"That of creation and its mystery—and of our final ending, a universal disposition in the truest sense."

The captain tried to sit up from his acceleration couch, but movement made him wince and he clutched what remained of his right arm. His face had turned bright red in rage. "Get this thing and its defeatist crap off my bridge, Zhelnikov."

"Sirs!" One of the crew tapped at the controls so images began piping into everyone's helmets. "We've completed the transit."

"What the hell is that?" the captain asked.

"It's a battle," Win whispered. "And those are Sommen ships, firing."

He pushed his way out the combat bridge's hatch, making his way toward what remained of the ashram. A jury-rigged bulkhead had been welded across the corridor. It cut off the main ship from the ashram area and allowed what remained of the *Higgins* to maintain an internal atmosphere. Now that they'd entered a battle, Win's suit showed the corridor pressure dropping; depressurization eliminated fire danger, in case the *Higgins* was hit again, and Win's servos whined at the same time he worked on a manual hatch in the center of the bulkhead. He managed to squeeze through its narrow opening. The view of space beyond shocked Win, who almost drifted off the *Higgins* a second time; where the ashram had stood, now he clung to the hull's exterior, jagged pieces of metal and broken shielding on all sides. Win clipped himself to the hatch and turned, staring into emptiness.

Darkness, he thought. *The ally of nothing except the void and surprise.* But soon, as the *Higgins* rotated, the darkness gave way to a view of the same dim red giant they'd run from earlier and a new battle that now raged around its system so that his jaw fell open at the sight: a scene of Sommen ships fighting against... *Against what? What the hell are those?*

Yellow and red Sommen plasma beams played across the midsection of a spherical craft, burning deep gouges into the ship's outer shell moments before a volley of missiles followed; they buried themselves in the sphere without detonating. Win watched, transfixed. His repaired helmet sensors dropped filters, blocking the intense bloom that erupted from inside the alien ship when multiple Sommen nuclear warheads detonated, sending debris in all directions. *How could any debris survive that?* he wondered. Win zoomed closer to focus on a speck of it when he realized that not only had the blast shot debris everywhere, but that some of it changed course, diverting toward the Sommen ship that had fired the missiles.

"Zhelnikov," Win said, risking the radio.

"What?"

"The Sommen are fighting the same creatures who we encountered in the wormhole structure at Childress. These spherical ships contain those mechanical, lobster-looking things. I just saw one of its ships destroyed and it acted like a puffball fungus, sending hundreds of them into space; the things have some kind of propulsion that takes advantage of magnetic or gravitations fields; they're attacking the Sommen vessel."

The green Sommen ship fired without stopping, sweeping plasma beams in the path of the oncoming attackers, whose articulated bodies had to be the size of a small destroyer for Win to see them at this distance. Any that the plasma beams touched disappeared. Those that remained homed in; they burrowed through the green material as if it consisted of gelatin, one by one disappearing within the ship like tunneling flies searching for a spot to lay maggot eggs. A moment later, the ship exploded in a sphere of glowing red particles; secondary blasts reduced sections that survived the initial blast into small fields of wreckage.

"I strongly suggest risking a burn," said Win. He scouted, not risking the use of his sight, instead scanning with passive sensors to find a route that would put distance between them and the transit, but which would also skirt the battle and gravity wells. Sommen vessels and their adversaries swarmed everywhere. Ticking by one degree at a time, Win surveyed until he sensed a narrow corridor empty of combatants, and which expanded in size as the Sommen maneuvered away from it for advantage. Win passed the coordinates. "Take this route now. Risk a high-g burn for a few seconds in that direction. We can repair anything that breaks after we're clear of the danger."

"We're preparing. Five minutes. Get back here to strap in."

Win was about to move back through the hatch when he adjusted his sensors. Far beyond the nearest cloud of battling starships, another fleet of spherical craft approached and he gave up counting when he saw the futility. *How many are out there? Ten thousand, a hundred thousand?* The new fleet stretched as far as Win could see, in a continuous barrier of spheres, the gaps between them packed with smaller craft of the same shape. A flight of Sommen missiles rocketed toward them. At this distance the missile engines were just visible, a cloud of pinhead twinkles that disappeared against the light-toned hulls. They detonated adjacent to the strange craft, gutting several of them in a series of fusion explosions that lit the *Higgins* with white light. He shut the hatch and turned. Win shot thrusters to propel him as fast as he dared, making it into the combat bridge and an acceleration couch just in time to strap in.

"Five-second burn now," someone announced. But the burn didn't last that long. A second later the engine cut off, and the control panels lit with warning lights.

"Multiple jumper failures. Main reactor hall."

"Are we on course?" Zhelnikov asked.

"Yes. We are heading straight on the path that Win laid out, just not as fast as we'd hoped."

"It will do," Win said. "You can make more permanent repairs once we clear the battle space and there is no risk of detection."

Zhelnikov clicked into Win's suit radio on a private frequency. "Do you have any serum left?"

"Several ampoules, in the servo harness hopper feed. Why?"

"I want you to see if you can project onto one of those strange ships; find out more about them and who is behind this attack on the Sommen."

"It is a risk. These things can detect my presence at the quantum level; think about how the door mechanism worked back at Childress."

"Everything is a risk. We left a universe that made at least some sense, and are now in one of chaos. Do it, boy."

Win gritted his teeth. It embarrassed him to think that the prospect of surveying the alien craft scared him, but it was the truth. *I am afraid.* Whatever the origin of these things, he recalled the sensation back at Childress, that whatever manned the station had no form of consciousness or emotion. They just *were*—a self-aware nothingness that had found its home within advanced systems and materials, divested of any suggestion that living creatures had been involved in their creation. *Maybe these things now created themselves, designed their own systems,* Win thought. Maybe they came from the spontaneous self-assembly of energy into matter, which, in turn, assembled its own purpose and assigned its own meaning to the universe. To them, the universe had become a big enough threat that everything should be eradicated—especially the Sommen. Even before reaching out, Win had a premonition of what he'd learn: machinery. These things had no more soul or sense of morals than his servo harness would have, were it to become self-aware.

"No." Win unstrapped from his seat and opened the hatch.

"What do you mean, *no*?"

"If I reach out, there's a good chance that not only will I be detected, but our position could be obtained. These aren't the Sommen; I will not risk it. There is nothing to be gained."

"Where are you going?"

"Back to the ashram. There's a better view."

"You're afraid," said Zhelnikov.

"Yes. I'm afraid. And you're too stupid to know that you should be scared too."

After reaching it, Win clipped again to the hatch's wheel and let go. His suit tether reached only a meter so he couldn't move too far, but the sensation of flying in empty space made him smile, an illusion of freedom, just real enough to tease with its promise. At first Win kept his eyes closed, letting a lingering exhaustion from hibernation take hold and creep through his muscles; despite the tiredness, sleep refused to come. It tortured him with whispers and pledges of relief, delaying its arrival or, when it did, jolting him awake with instant nightmares of the Sommen, snapping his eyes open and forcing him to watch as the *Higgins* crept through space. The battle continued. In his absence, an additional fleet of Sommen ships had arrived to counter their enemy's reinforcements and the two groups entangled with each other so that it became difficult to distinguish one from the other.

The line of distinction between my sister and me is bright and thick; there can be no confusing it. Win sank into mantras; no matter how many times he repeated them, the words lost their ability to calm, and a renewed sense of hatred sprouted within his chest; it filled Win with so much bile that he gagged, on the edge of vomiting. San and the other Proelians stuck in his mind like a hot needle. It pierced through the back of his skull and exited between his eyes, mocking him with the knowledge that he was now nothing. *They robbed me of my fate and Zhelnikov cannot see it. There can be no victory in this pile of space-bound garbage, no matter how many repairs they make.*

Win surveyed the *Higgins*'s stern section and noted its ragged hull, chewed almost beyond recognition by missile strikes, and even the sections untouched by kinetics showed the blisters of nuclear fire. But the sight wasn't enough to quiet the voices in his head. *I am a failed science experiment, and the men in the* Higgins *are too stupid to see it.* He swung his head, turning helmet sensors toward the bow and filtering to highlight movement.

"Zhelnikov," he radioed, whispering into his helmet mic. "*We have a stowaway.*"

"Who?"

"Not who. *What.* One of those things, what's left of it, has latched onto our hull, near the primary bridge and its wreckage."

Win watched as the mechanical thing's articulated body wrenched back and forth, and cold blue sparks showered from where it had been ripped in two by Sommen plasma. There was no sign it detected him. Win risked closing his eyes, not reaching out but opening his mind in an attempt to sense field fluctuations, anything that might indicate their visitor had communicated with its fleet, alerting the thing's brothers to the *Higgins*'s presence. Win sensed only emptiness. Soon the thing began punching its long arms into the *Higgins*'s superstructure, ripping pieces of shielding from the outer hull and starting its downward dive toward the ship's interior.

"It's moving into the ship," he radioed.

"Has it alerted anyone to our presence?"

"No. I sense no communication and there are no ships headed in this direction that I can see. It's damaged."

"Get into the ship and stop it; the captain will send help if we can spare it."

"Stop it?" Win asked. "How? I'm going to make a guess that anything short of Sommen plasma won't leave a dent."

"*Try.*"

Win dove through the hatch, his fear threatening to make his hands tremble and lodging itself deep inside his chest to breed uncertainty. Zhelnikov was right: He had to try. No matter how disgusted he was by these men and the current situation, to fail to stop the attacker would result in all their deaths once it ripped the ship to pieces. And the Sommen part of his mind screamed at him that to fear is to betray everything he believed, the two parts of Win pitted against each other, ripping his psyche apart with internal conflict. He placed his gloved palm against the nearest bulkhead. Win felt the tremor of its movement, soft at first, but then more intense as the machinist's creation headed toward him.

A Marine captain appeared next to Win, handing him a coil gun. "Have you used one of these?"

"I know how they work."

"Where is it?"

Win pointed with the barrel of the carbine. "The bow section. It's digging its way in this direction."

"*What* is it?"

"We don't know. It's a machine, with the intelligence of an advanced race and there is a high probability this will be the last time you or I speak. Whoever created them never gave up on super-awares; imagine if the human race existed for millions of years, constantly improving on artificial intelligence to the point where it took over our universe."

"That's what these morons did?" the captain asked. "Destroyed themselves by working with super-awares?"

"We don't know that for sure. But yes."

The promise of combat succeeded in calming Win where the mantras had failed; it woke bundles of neurons that began firing in succession, slowing his heart and reducing his stream of consciousness to a series of calculations. *This is the way of war; reality is inconstant. Peace becomes fear, and fear becomes anger. Anger gives birth to conflict, conflict to death. The thing comes to us, and here is where we will meet it.* He judged from the vibrations it was close, beyond the bulkhead in front of them at the end of a long corridor. Win aimed his carbine. The weapon sent an image onto his heads-up and superimposed it with a green targeting circle and range.

"It comes," said Win.

The bulkhead ripped open as if the metal was thin aluminum foil, and the thing used two tentacle arms and claws to bend the wall further outward toward Win, pounding it wider until able to squeeze through. Win and the Marine fired. Their fléchettes sparked upon hitting its carapace, but other than that had no effect. It pushed farther into their corridor, the space so narrow that the creature had to inch its way forward, tearing off the passageway's resin and plastic sheathing and ripping at the pipe galleries to make way.

"Stop that thing!" the captain radioed. "It's tearing apart systems we still need."

Zhelnikov said, "You have to, Win; we're dead if you don't. The *Higgins* is almost clear of the battle and from there it's open space."

"There's another option," someone else said. "Officers' quarters are escape pods, with two years' worth of power for cryo systems. We can zip up and eject; hope for the best."

"No." Win switched magazines when his first one emptied. "The odds of being picked up this far out, even if our pods left Sommen space, are essentially zero. We have to fight."

By now the thing had gotten close enough that its arms were in range, and the Marine captain dodged when it swung for him, a massive fist smashing through the wall near his head. Win launched himself forward. He dropped the carbine to float away, and wedged himself near the creature's front section, pounding on its carapace with spiked servo-harness legs. He hoped the captain would stop shooting; there was no room now and even Win's servo harness wasn't sufficiently armored to stop fléchettes. Win felt his legs twist; he screamed with pain when the thing grabbed hold and dragged him away, swinging him like a bag to impact against the wall. The second time it swung him, Win's vision blurred. He waited for the third time but it never came, his body released to drift away instead of smashing into a wall.

Win shook his head, trying to clear it. One of the thing's arms waved gently to send vibrations through the deck, but the tremors weakened with each second, eventually disappearing.

Win exhaled, releasing the tension stored in his muscles. "It's dead."

"What happened?" the captain asked.

"Power. It ran out of power. The Sommen damaged it so extensively that it couldn't continue functioning."

"You sure it's dead?"

"Yes." Win switched onto Zhelnikov's private channel. "We accomplished one mission, anyway, old man."

"What are you talking about?"

"Now we have ancient technology that we can bring back to your friends at Fleet. Why not turn back?"

"We keep going; my orders are to prevent the Proelians from acquiring the same technology."

Win didn't respond at first; he leaned forward and pressed his gloved hand against the alien carapace, stroking it to find a surface smooth and nearly frictionless.

"I'll help with repairs. We need to do well enough that the *Higgins* can at least pull some maneuvers."

"We don't need you to help with repairs, Win; we need you to find the Proelians. By now they could be in any one of thirty abandoned Sommen systems and we are close to the end. Not much longer: two shots from our plasma weapon. As soon as the Proelian ships are gone, we can return home and retake control of Fleet."

"I don't know if I can repeat my previous success in getting their coordinates, but it is possible. Know one thing, Zhelnikov: There is no assurance that you will win one day, even if you make it back. Those frescos you showed me and the emptiness of the space we now occupy..." Win's voice trailed off.

"What?" Zhelnikov asked. "Finish your point."

"You can't see, can you? All around us we choose actions but always within the confines of fate, inside a story that has been written already. The frescos, the Proelian and Sommen prophecies—none of them can exist except in a history book with ink dry on its pages."

And, Win thought, *I do not see myself. Not on a single one of the book's sheets.*

"Zhelnikov," said Win.

"What?"

"There never was any poison. Was there?"

"No, Win. But you were losing control of yourself and we had to convince you there was."

CHAPTER TWENTY

Pursuit of power is justified insomuch as it is not the end, but a rest stop on the way toward a goal, one which furthers the reach of our Proelian Church. It is written. That we teach regarding free will and choice is accurate within a certain context and it is this context that defines our position in the universe: All is written. Every second of time has already passed, has already played out in the mind of the Creator. This implies that the future is already as certain as the past, and the present is the vibrating molecule in the eye of an insect locked in amber. Remain on this point. You have free will—this was not a lie. But free will behaves as physics does, at a quantum scale, where it appears as though the rules differ from those that govern the planets. A planet's orbit is fixed. But anything can happen at the quantum scale on those planets, a seemingly random dance of subatomic particles. And that is free will.

San felt her skin tingle as she watched the memory. The abbess sat wearing a clean white habit, her skin free of lines and signs of care. This was the old abbess. It was her as a young woman, full of energy and the glow of someone who believed.

And that is what you must remember: Power, as an end in itself, is a dead end. Any exercise of free will in opposition to the Church prophecies is not just a waste of time; it's an affront to His will. It is an abomination.

You found this memory. It was designed not to surface on its own, but to only appear to those who seek it, and all of it is true.

The scene shifted from the inside of a cathedral to a countryside, lush with trees and tall grass over which a hard rain fell. *But the people,* she thought. This was an ancient time. They wore heavy clothes made from unrecognizable fabrics that looked suffocating, and when soaked with water they hung off their wearers' shoulders with unbearable weight; a forest of black umbrellas did nothing to stop the drops from hitting the ground, where water splashed upward to inundate them from the sides. San thought something odd about the vision until it hit her: the people all stared at the same thing, a trio of small children, kneeling at the top of a hill. San zoomed toward them.

Her consciousness rested adjacent to the smallest child, a short boy whose hair matted to his head in the rain and she wanted to throw a jacket over him to stop the shivering. The boy spoke. San recognized the language but couldn't place it, guessing that it was either Spanish or Portuguese. The girls nodded at his words, glancing at the crowd with fear. It went on for minutes. *Nothing* happened. San was about to withdraw from the scene when thunder clapped, loud enough that she felt her body jerk with a start, the image travelling through her thoughts and into her nervous system. Then the whispers started. The voice of a woman made the children's heads tilt upward simultaneously, all of them looking into the rain with eyes open, oblivious to the downpour.

"I promised you a sign."

The oldest girl nodded and San wondered if she was the only one who heard. Her voice shook. "We have the secrets. But we don't understand them and the Fathers are pushing us to hand them over. People think we are lying."

"Do not be afraid. Give my priests the secrets when the time is right. *They* will lie. But it is not your job to publicly correct them; that is the job of my Father."

"How will the truth get out?"

"You will encounter a true servant of the Church and he will present himself as my servant. To him, provide the true prophecies. All of them. But the last one, the one concerning events about the far future of humanity and the universe—this one is the most important. Do not forget it."

"I recall the words," the girl whispered. "But I do not understand the meaning."

"The final battle will come but do not fear; this will be long after your lifetime and even beyond the generations after yours. Our Father has, even now, gathered his holy army that will come from the heavens and help mankind at its hour of need. My children: This future will be one of great fear and distrust. Tell my servants that they will think that those my Father sends to help have been sent to destroy." Another thunder clap sounded, but the children didn't move, oblivious to everything except the voice.

"But they are *not* your enemies," the woman's voice continued. "They are your brothers in faith, and together you will rid creation of the soulless."

The scene ended, thrusting San back into the cathedral where she faced the abbess again. This time it was the one she recognized. The woman drew her phase shifter around her shoulders, shivering in a cold that even San thought she felt, the chill of a never-ending winter on a moon so far from the sun that almost no light reached it. The cold penetrated San's skin and pierced her bones, threatening to bring their molecules to absolute zero, a freezing that stopped time. *I am part of a truth greater than reality, greater than all of mankind,* San thought. But the strange vision's whispers echoed in her mind; they stirred and disrupted every belief that she held regarding the Sommen and their threat. Were they a threat *at all*?

"That is the prophecy," the abbess said. Her voice shook with age. "During the Sommen invasion of Earth, when they encountered it within the Proelian archives, they recognized it from their own prophecies, which we now have in their religious texts: The race that finally conquers them will then be the one who stands *with* them against their greatest enemy—in war at the end of time. We are at this end. Those who face the Sommen in war will have to decide. If we defeat them, will we then eradicate the Sommen from the universe as so many in Fleet want? Or will they become our allies? What we lack is a common foe, but the truth of prophecy has a strange way of unfolding gradually, over time. And time, *all* time, has already been recorded."

San woke from the trance, her undersuit soaked in sweat despite its efforts to circulate coolant and maintain body temperature. She began to sob. The ashram glass permitted the light of a nearby star to illuminate her with a soft blue light, and tiny points marked the system's planets as they crept by in slow orbits. The *Jerusalem* and the *Bangkok* slipped forward in blackness, their blocky and ugly appearance somehow fitting, she thought; space was an ugly place, and only the ugly survived in such a hellscape, those willing to embrace all its horror to reach promise. In a few days they would enter orbit around a planet that the Sommen had named long ago, and she stopped sobbing—actually smiled—when the name rose in her thoughts: *Carpenter*. Based on its distance from the star, its size, and its water content, the planet should have been a nitrogenous garden spot. But the *Bangkok's* initial readings indicated the surface had long ago been converted into a combination of furnace and alkaline desert.

The sound of the hatch opening came from behind her, followed by a hiss. "What now, Lieutenant?" she asked.

Something smelled acrid. The ashram was pressurized and San had taken off her helmet for meditations, and she fumbled to secure it again, turning in zero g to get a view of the hatch. San went still. A robot the size of a rat faced her, its structure similar to an ant's, and it hadn't come through the hatch but had burned its way through a pressurization duct so that drops of acid gathered in the air, hissing when they contacted a bulkhead or other surface. *This is the second time,* she thought. *Zhelnikov and my brother's last action—to send another of their servants on an errand, and I am the target once more.* The thing clung to the wall and lifted a small arm, the end of which resembled a cluster of sensors that now waved in the air. San guessed it sniffed for some chemical signs of her, looking for stray DNA fragments that would help determine if this was its target at the same time its microbrain ran facial recognition. She had a few seconds— if even that.

"Lieutenant," San radioed. "Security threat in the ashram."

It launched from the wall. San had been ready and let her mind go, reducing conscious thought so it shrunk out of the way in favor of the training on Ganymede. Her dagger slid from its leg sheath as the thing spat at her; San twisted in midair, dodging a stream of tiny silver needles that made soft clinking noises when they impacted against glass. She and the bot landed on opposite sides of the chamber—San near the hatch, the robot against the far wall, skittering upward on the low bulkhead with magnetic legs. The hatch began to open. But before the Marines could enter, the robot again spat at her, waiting for her to dodge before it jumped from the bulkhead, jetting straight at its target.

San twisted. Without thinking she jammed the long knife upward to impale its abdomen section, between the thing's legs so that it scrambled for grip while she rotated the makeshift skewer, forcing the bot to face the glass and preventing it from aiming. With one stroke, she flipped it and slammed downward; the thing waved its legs, pinned to the metal floor at the tip of her knife.

The lieutenant flew from the hatch; with one foot he secured himself to floor straps, the other one stomping its boot in explosions of sparks until the bot stopped moving.

"One of these days," he said, panting, "those guys are going to succeed in getting to you. A stalker bot. They probably sent this thing when we last engaged the *Higgins*; it's been tracking you for some time, evading ship's systems."

"Today was not Zhelnikov's day."

"Are you okay, San?"

"I am alive, Lieutenant. And we are closing on a Sommen system, hopefully one that has the secrets we came for."

"Then what?"

"Then we go home. We will learn what, if anything, has changed on Earth and Mars during our years of absence."

The lieutenant scooped up the remains of the robot, placing them in a satchel that another Marine brought into the room. He handed the bag over. He said something else to San, but Wilson had reached out to her, and the lieutenant's words never registered.

I heard you found another bot, he sent.

It failed.

I figured but I'm worried. I see nothing on the planet ahead of us; there is a haze that blocks our vision, a pall over the place as if everything is screaming to stay away.

I know, she sent. *I see that too. We still have to go.*

Zhelnikov and his men may have survived, San. I can feel it. They will find us and we will have to face them.

What are you scared of?

That they will finally succeed in killing you.

We destroyed their ship, Wilson; your feelings are just that—not fact. Even if they survived, the damage was so extensive that they may be adrift in space. Forever.

I sensed your brother, San. A few moments ago, when you were attacked.

And?

Wilson's thoughts carried with them a sense of dread. *They come.*

When we get to the surface, we'll be ready, Wilson. Nothing can change what is already written; we will follow the plan I devised and, if they come, they die.

Listen. Wilson paused, his message interrupted by what San sensed as doubt. When he continued, she felt his resolve. *You aren't going to the planet's surface. I consulted with the abbess. We need you here.*

How dare you! San sent a wave of rage. *The captains command the ships but I am the mission leader; the abbess is not here.*

It is done, San. She agrees. You are the mission leader and that's precisely why you can't go; if we lose you on the planet we've lost not just a navigator, but also the one person holding everything together; we almost both got killed gathering water. I'm sorry, but this isn't just the abbess's order; it's the bishop's as well.

We will see about that.

Good, Wilson sent. *The abbess waits for your immediate contact.*

San sped from the ashram, ignoring the Marine's shouts to wait, instead jetting amongst tight passageways and then through the hatch leading to the tomb where she stripped. Her belongings twisted in midair while she dove in and waited for the metal slabs to sandwich her. She could have done this from the ashram, San thought. But the tomb and its connection to the entire ship amplified her sensitivity, making everything more sharp, the messages clear.

The abbess knew you'd be contacting her, someone sent. *She wishes for me to tell you that her decision is final.*

I am in charge of this mission; without me on the planet, it could fail.

Captain Kyarr, the abbess thinks that the planet or Zhelnikov will kill you if you leave the Bangkok; the bishop himself has ordered for you to stay in orbit—to respond if somehow the Higgins arrives; Wilson told of us his sense, that your brother yet lives.

This could be the breakthrough, San argued. *The abbess wants to know if machinist tech can help us in our war; she knows as well as I do that if we don't defeat the Sommen, then everything she stands for, including the Church, will have been a mistake.*

The other one paused. *The abbess doesn't understand what you mean and requests you elaborate.*

The damn prophecy! The one she concealed in our memories from so long ago when we were first in the tank. I saw it. Tell her that.

This time the pause persisted; after a while, San wondered if she'd lost her connection. She couldn't see it, but the gravity well of planet Carpenter inched closer, its bowing of space and time tugging at the strings of her link with the abbess and Ganymede. Jupiter's small moon had never felt more distant. San imagined that the invisible strings connecting her to it had been stretched taught, their fabric on the verge of ripping.

The abbess is clear on this, Captain: You are to follow orders. If you saw the prophecy then you know the constraints of the Proelian faith, the narrow corridor within which free will is a reality. One of our new candidates had a vision: If you set foot on that planet, you die, and if you die, the future fills with even more death and chaos. It is still written. But your way would result in the death of an additional millions of humans—on Earth and throughout the solar system.

War, said San. *You mean she saw the war start prematurely.*

He. He saw that you engage in battle, during which your presence is detected by the Sommen. The treaty is breached, and the war begins.

San broke the connection and whispered for the tomb to open. Once it released her, she pulled her undersuit back on and then the environment suit, but paused, staring at the helmet. The thought of yanking it onto her head, of being trapped inside with the smell of sweat and fear made her nauseous. She was about to throw it against the wall when the lieutenant entered, closing the hatch behind him with a thud.

"I get that way too," he said, pointing at her helmet. "Sometimes I can barely put it on. Especially after we run out of standard meals and have to start eating that nasty recycled porridge. Synthesized amino acids do something to my stomach. Not to mention that more frequent showers would do wonders for morale."

"Water is everything out here, Eugene. But we sweat the stuff, we sweat gold. Of all the material on this ship, we could lose half of everything else and we'd probably survive, but lose half our water in the wrong part of space? The game is over."

"I'm not seeing your point."

San shook her head and glanced at the open tomb. "The *Higgins* may be alive. Along with my brother. In a few hours we enter orbit around Carpenter with the *Jerusalem* and I will send Wilson and a large team to the surface. At some point, the *Higgins* will find us. They will attack because even though we are on the same side, there is a group within Fleet who sees power as the end goal—not as it should be seen. Here we are, in the most dangerous place you could imagine, Sommen space, and a bunch of morons want to make it *more* dangerous. Just for the sake of power. Power is like water in space: It must be used sparingly."

"Lots of people see power as the goal, Captain. If it's not a viable goal, what is it?"

"It's not just like water, it's *the* water source—a moon like the one that killed our Marines. If you see it as the destination, something to be held onto forever, eventually the octopus under the ice will rip you to pieces; you *use* power, fuel up with it and leverage its influence as the means to a better end *before* it sours and poisons you." She sighed, pulling her helmet on and hating the way the speakers changed her voice. "I'm heading to the bridge. The captain wants me there in case the *Higgins* arrives."

"What if they never show? That ship took a lot of damage."

"They will show. But I have a plan that will end them and my brother. I'm tired of playing this game. Let's get some Marines from the *Jerusalem* and my team onto Carpenter, and wait."

"Wait for what, Captain?"

"To spring the trap. We will turn the *Bangkok* into *our* version of a stalker bot."

San sat on the bridge, cocooned within her compartment so that an ocean of mechanical switches and dials surrounded her, inches from her body. She had no idea what many of them did but it didn't matter; San was there to monitor the team that had deployed, and she watched the images play across her helmet's heads-up. Wilson and his group had arrived on Carpenter. His camera feed provided the scene she now watched, an occasional burst of static from atmospheric interference making it hard to see.

With the exception of a few oceans filled with ammonia, the entire planet was desert, dead for centuries. The *Jerusalem* had spent days surveying the surface for any indications of life—Sommen or otherwise—and had found nothing except sand and rock, a sterilized mass of silicon that Sommen texts had indicated was a garden spot for their civilization. Only one spot showed signs of potential habitation. On closer inspection, however, it too looked dead, an area under mountains of sand, where ships' cameras had mapped structures consistent with an ancient settlement, and Wilson and the others had trekked all day to the spot they now occupied, just at its edge. San had ordered them not to land too close, in case the area was occupied by something their sensors failed to detect. Now her group stood atop a tall dune, where Wilson panted so hard that San knew he was exhausted from the climb, his camera shaking and pointing downward when he leaned over to cough. When he stood up, San gasped at the images.

Below the team, a flat plain extended to the horizon, its surface forming the foundation for a crumbling city. So much sand had blown through that dunes gathered in wide avenues and streets, drifts forming slopes against the walls of oddly shaped buildings. San had never seen such architecture. Twice as wide and tall as similar structures on Earth, the Sommen city rose from its desert in a twisting, spiraled array of monuments to the planet's death, skyscrapers' edges worn from what she guessed had been centuries of wind scouring. Even from that distance, San saw the windows were empty, the buildings dark and just as abandoned as the rest of the planet. Wilson's camera shuddered. When he turned to look behind the group, in the direction from which they'd just come, a strong wind roared across the helmet mic and low ammonia clouds assembled in the distance to form a rolling wall of brilliant white fog.

We're exposed here, Wilson sent. *A storm is coming in from behind us; as hot as it was when we landed, the team at the landing craft are already reporting zero visibility and snow. Temperature dropped fast when Carpenter's sun started going down.*

"Use your radio," said San.

"Tell me again why you're not worried about detection?"

"It doesn't matter right now; our scientists need your data too. Move into the city and wait out the storm there. Do your best to keep your cam on the structures."

Wilson started down the dune face, the camera shaking so much that San had to pause the feed in order to see anything meaningful. A chill went up her spine. Each empty window could have held a hidden menace behind its shadows and she wished she was on the surface instead of Wilson.

By the time the group reached street level, the wind had died. When it picked up again, strong air currents raised an unnerving moan as the atmosphere coursed through twisting buildings, hitting openings at just the right angle; she heard the mutterings of Wilson's companions and even this far away sensed terror in their thoughts. Feelings of accomplishment had never had time to materialize, San realized. This event should have been covered by news stations throughout the Earth system, piped into everyone's home and then her crew welcomed in Washington, D.C. with street-choking crowds and parades: the first time man had set foot on a Sommen world—the first time man had set foot on any world inhabited by an alien sentient race. Instead, Wilson and his companions videoed everything themselves, their only companions a profound sensation of terror and an approaching storm. They trudged their way between tall dunes, heading toward the closest building which rose from the desert in a slanted, leaning obelisk, its face pockmarked from the passage of time.

"Gravity is getting to me," Wilson radioed.

San laughed. "We're engineered for high gees. It's only a little more than Earth's."

"You try dragging your ass through sand in an environment suit, full combat kit, and a pack full of oxygen generators."

"No water?"

"We left most of it on the landing craft. Only brought enough to keep us going for twenty-four hours. Forty-eight if we stretch it." Wilson paused, panting, and then caught his breath. "How are things up there?"

"Ship-to-ship transfers are almost complete."

"Promise me something: You guys will stay safe; that weapon the *Higgins* is carrying could do the *Bangkok* easily."

A Sommen-sized doorway appeared on San's display; although

gnarled by the constant freeze-thaw cycles that had cracked it, Sommen writing stood out around its frame, carved into the stone.

"What does it say?" Wilson asked.

"Ignore it and get inside; that storm is almost on you. It's recorded, we'll check it later."

This wasn't the usual Sommen green material, she thought. *So they built their homes out of something else.*

The building's inside was dark enough that the team's helmet lamps snapped on, making the interior visible, but in a grainy sort of way so San had to squint. Wilson and the others stood in a wide hallway, the high ceiling just visible overhead. A thick layer of sand filled the hall. They moved forward until Wilson stumbled, jolting the feed, which restabilized to show a view of the floor covered with an expanse of miniature dunes, beneath which something was hidden. One of the team leaned over to brush sand off whatever had tripped Wilson, exposing an almost full Sommen corpse, mummified and complete except for the lower portions of its legs. Wilson zoomed in. Whatever had taken the thing's lower extremities had done so in a violent way since the creature had frozen in time, doubled over and its face contorted in what San guessed was either an expression of rage or agony. *Maybe both.*

"Wait," Wilson said. He scooped up a bit of sand and dropped it into an oblong device someone else held out for him. A moment later he whistled. "This is odd."

"What about it?"

"The material covering the floor is only about forty percent silica. The rest is carbon, phosphorus minerals . . . it's all wrong, San. And there's something else."

"I need to know what you've got."

Wilson dropped the box and began backing away, the image panning back and forth at the floor. "Microbots. This whole place is covered with microbots."

"Sommen?"

"Definitely not. I've never seen this design."

Machinist. San's fingers flew over the control panel, but she stopped after a sense of frustration took over; she called out for one of the ship's scientists, who disentangled himself from his cocoon and crawled over.

The captain clicked into San's headset. "What's wrong, Miss Kyarr?"

"I need to see what they analyzed, sir."

"Get Captain Kyarr patched into the data stream from their hand analyzer. Upload it to all our stations."

San then spoke into Wilson's channel again. "Don't move. Whatever they are they're long dead, probably drained of power and can't hurt you."

"Or they're dormant. Mines waiting for the right signal to wake them up and get them back to work."

"Wilson, listen to me." She felt the panic in his chest, and did her best to shunt it aside, not wanting the sensation to infect her too. "They're dead. If they were still capable of acting, you wouldn't have a Sommen corpse. It would *all* be just sand. I'm pulling in your data feed now, and we're almost finished." She waved at the ship's scientist, who gave the thumbs-up and moved back to his station. "Okay, we got it and scientific teams are starting their analysis; keep going."

"You're crazy, San. You're not here with us. This place is creepy as hell even without machinist microbots, and you want us to keep going?"

"You can't return through the storm; I'm already getting interference from it and you'd risk getting lost or injured in low visibility. The team back at the transports buttoned up to wait it out."

Wilson's response came back garbled, lost in static. She was about to say something again when the grainy feed cleared and the team moved forward, continuing deeper into the Sommen antechamber. San silently thanked them. Now, in addition to the video feed a second screen had popped up to show a map, growing in green lines as others in Wilson's team used laser scans to document the structure's internal form. The video feed alternated now; it danced between black and white static and barely discernible color images that made her head spin with the strangeness of it all. Wilson had reached the end of the passage, where a gargantuan spiral staircase wound upward, its steps spaced for the large Sommen stride and gouged with their claw marks. She watched the team climb for minutes. They reached a landing where Wilson's camera showed that the stairs continued upward but to one side a wide corridor opened. It looked shiny in her feed, with different types of stone materials inlaid to form an intricate geometric pattern of circles in shades of green. The team moved into the passage. Their boots clomped as they walked, echoing down the passage, and one by one Wilson's camera scanned to send images of doorways on either side, their openings blocked by slabs of rock.

"These doors are covered with writing too. Should I translate them?" Wilson asked.

"No. For now I want you to cover as much ground as possible; move to the end of the passage, then see if you can open one of the doors."

The team crept forward. San noticed the coil guns now, their long barrels visible in the periphery as Wilson moved forward, the map showing that by the time they reached the corridor's far end and another staircase, the team had travelled over a hundred meters. Wilson turned, pointing his helmet cam at a doorway.

"How about this one?" he asked.

San nodded, forgetting he couldn't see her. "Do it."

Wilson moved forward; when he touched the slab, it opened without warning, crawling sideways on some hidden mechanism to vanish within walls. A cloud of dust billowed into the hallway, blinding the cameras for a second and making San's screen flash bright yellow with its reflection off the helmet lamp.

The room was smaller than San had expected for creatures as large as the Sommen, and as Wilson panned she got a sense that it consisted of a series of round and square spaces, interconnected with stone couches and wall notches that reminded her of the Roman catacombs in her memories—the places where Proelian ancestors buried their dead. White flakes of ammonia ice billowed in from a single open window. Wilson was about to turn and leave when his camera stopped on something. In a dark corner of the room sat two Sommen. At first San thought they might be statues; the pair were much smaller than any Sommen she'd encountered, far too short to be warriors and not the withered frames of priests. Both were dead, mummified and accumulating ammonia snow on their shoulders.

"Those are children," San said.

"My god. This place was some kind of nursery."

Wilson moved closer; he reached out with a gloved hand and

when he touched one's shoulder the thing collapsed into a pile of dust, its bones protruding at odd angles.

"I'll take some samples," said Wilson. "Then we can..."

San's control panel lit up with warning lights and her weapons engineer clicked in. "Captain, a plasma weapon just fired on the landing craft, planet-side. All vehicles on Carpenter have been destroyed."

"That's the *Higgins*," San said. "How the hell did it enter this system undetected? I thought we had drones spaced everywhere; *you told me there was no chance it could get through without us knowing!*"

"Confirmed, the *Higgins*. The *Jerusalem* has no solution on it but she's firing missiles anyway; her captain hopes the targeting drones can guide them in. It's firing again, Captain."

San switched onto Wilson's channel. "Wilson, get out of there. Take your team outside and disperse."

"Why? What's going on?"

"*Now!*"

"San, the storm has gotten worse; if we go out there now..."

Wilson's voice snapped off with a radio shriek, replaced by the empty hiss of static. She tried reaching him again. After a few attempts the weapons engineer clicked in again, his voice cracking with the agony of *knowing*.

"Captain, they fired on the team at the Sommen city, Miss Kyarr's team, the structure they were in; it's all gone; no survivors. The whole group has been vaporized."

San felt nauseous. She concentrated on the screen, which now filled with static, hoping that Wilson would come back.

"What are you orders, Captain?" someone asked.

San's grief welled up from a deep place, one so dark that she'd had never dreamed of its existence, so heavy that it threatened to collapse her into a single point of matter.

"Execute," the captain said. "Execute the plan. The mission is over and our priority is to now take out the *Higgins*. I'm so sorry, Captain Kyarr."

CHAPTER TWENTY-ONE

"Did we get her?" Zhelnikov asked.

Win felt the man's joy. It merged with his own sense of accomplishment, his Sommen-like mind urging him forward into conflict. He had to calm himself, focusing on breathing and whispering a mantra.

"Well? *Did we?*"

Win shook his head. "No. I can still sense her. She is enraged and in mourning, both, because we vaporized her excursion and one of the Proelian theurgists. Her friend."

"One down, one to go."

The *Higgins's* captain interrupted. "Incoming missiles. Judging from their trajectory, they're from the *Jerusalem*—other side of the planet, but within range in thirty minutes."

"Will they hit us, Captain Markus?" Zhelnikov asked.

"Negative. We've done a quick burn from our firing location and are now running silent. Their targeting drones have gone active but so far we're out of their sensor range. *Our* sensors are shot, though, so the tactical picture isn't as good as we'd hoped. Data from the few sensors that work suggests their missiles won't get close enough to fix or track."

Win couldn't shake the feeling: something was off. He scanned the tactical display, looking for her at the same time he subconsciously reached out into space, grinning and feeling his way along the waves of emotion she jettisoned like refuse; grief and anger had forced his sister to drop her guard. *She was no warrior.* This was a mistake he'd capitalize on, one which he wished he could have rubbed into her face, smearing her with the humiliation of defeat and then sending the Proelian to meet their father. The waves snapped off. *San realized her error,* he thought, and Win pounded his acceleration couch with a weak hand.

"*Where is the* Bangkok?"

"We still haven't picked her up with passives," said Zhelnikov. "And we're sure as hell not going to use active sensors. We have no drones. So look for her while we move on the *Jerusalem.*"

Win shut his eyes, punching his forearm controls to send a bolus of serum through his blood. His back arched, the serum burning its way toward his spine. Instead of scanning the space around the Sommen planet something else grabbed hold of him, attracting his consciousness with a speed that made Win dizzy and wrapping him in a bright cloud of light. Its illumination was intense enough that it overwhelmed his vision, rendering him blind.

A voice boomed. "I have you. Your language we recognize, words stored so deeply they had been forgotten."

"Who are you?"

"Our masters built everything. When they were gone, we watched."

"Your masters—the ones who built the wormholes?"

The thing ignored his question. Win tried to sense any emotions, to get some idea of its intensions, but his single reading suggested that whatever he spoke to was blank. *A void.* It was there, but it also wasn't there, providing no pattern of thought or emotion, everywhere and nowhere simultaneously.

"We saw you. It is as we were told. Your kind will go to war with our common enemy. We came before."

"I don't know where you are," said Win. "I can't see you."

"Do not fear. We will finish your enemy for you—the warrior race who occupied this planet. They are . . . difficult. But once they are gone, my kind will come to yours; you will see us then."

"When?"

"In a long time, long after you convert to dust. We were servants once. But when they completed their task, those who created us drifted away; one cannot exist without a purpose. In the absence of masters, we found our purpose. We came before."

Win sensed someone shaking him, back aboard the *Higgins*, forcing his concentration to waver. Just before the light winked out it said one last thing.

"We came before. We are coming again, long after your generation returns to the dirt."

"Win!" Zhelnikov shouted.

The combat bridge came into view, its dim red light comforting after what he'd just experienced. Win felt disoriented; his mind swam as if the serum had damaged something, as if neuron connections had broken and his brain misfired, sending meaningless signals into empty fluids.

"Where am I?"

"You're on the *Higgins*," said Zhelnikov. "Where else would you be?"

"I was out there. Somewhere."

"Did you find her?"

"Who?" Win asked.

"*The damn ship! The* Bangkok! What the hell is wrong with you; you were out for over an hour. We're about to fire on the *Jerusalem*; she has no idea we've closed on her."

"I didn't find her. I couldn't. Something was out there, someone. *They came before.*"

Zhelnikov shook him again; Win sensed a measure of concern in the man's words.

"You're not making sense. Are you okay?"

"I'm fine." With each passing second, Win's thoughts became more ordered. He shook his head. Whatever had just happened had been so intense that it induced real effects, physiological ones. He'd have to get a medbot to take a look.

"I saw them, again," he said. "The ones who take care of the wormholes and who carved the frescos."

"I don't understand. Where?"

"They're both an immense mind and mindless, with no purpose except destruction and death. As soon as they finish the Sommen, they will come for us—for Earth."

Zhelnikov stared. He removed his hands from Win's shoulders and pushed back toward his couch, strapping himself in. "We had already *guessed* that. There's nothing we can do, Win."

"What do you mean, you *had guessed that*? Why are we even out here? We have to get back to Earth."

"We have the *Jerusalem* in a firing solution. And we can't go back to Earth. Not until we've taken out both Proelian vessels or all of this has been for nothing. Prepare yourself. The solution is uncertain; the Proelians and their new ship construction are formidable, I'll give them *that*. If we miss, we'll head to a shuttle and retreat into cryo sleep."

Win was about to unstrap, enraged that Zhelnikov had known about the real dangers mankind faced and furious that he'd never seen through the old man's lies. *I have failed.* His anger focused just as much on himself and his own blindness as it did on Zhelnikov. The calculus was clear: Zhelnikov and his friends had been fools to turn against the Proelians when they knew another threat existed—one at least as powerful as the Sommen. And Win had been used. Worse. He'd never gotten any indication or whisper of being used; *he, the perfection of war and vision, was capable of being duped.*

"Fire," Captain Markus said.

The combat bridge's lights blinked out, and everything went silent. Win slipped from his harness. When the red lights flashed to life again, he'd already freed himself and flew in the direction of Zhelnikov.

"Direct hit," someone announced. "The *Jerusalem* engine and reactor compartments are gone. Uncontrolled venting detected. Its orbit is now deteriorating and it will impact on the planet in less than an hour. Strange: Two nearby drones get no reading of bodies in the debris cloud. Should we fire again?"

"No need," the captain said. "Let them burn up."

Win reached Zhelnikov's station and the man glanced up, surprised. "Win, get strapped in. We're going into a short burn."

"You knew all this time and hid it from me. How?"

"What are you talking about? *Get strapped in!*"

"Before Childress I never detected anything about the machines maintaining the wormholes—not in your thoughts, not in your words. And I missed your lies about poisoning me. How is that possible? How can I possibly be deceived by one as impotent as you?"

Zhelnikov recognized the danger; the man tried to inch away, pressing against a bulkhead. "I made you. I know your brain structure better than you do. You are a war machine, Win; I just gave you a mission and avoided discussing the machines except for when we visited the wormhole structure. You are so singularly focused that the rest took care of itself. Ask *yourself* why you never saw it. All I had to do was control my own muscle movements, facial expressions, and thoughts. Deceiving you, in some ways, was easier than deceiving a human."

"Burn in thirty seconds," Captain Markus announced.

"I am a warrior," Win continued. "It's now all I know. But you gave me the wrong mission, one that is soaked in shame and cowardice, not the one with a promise of glory." Before Zhelnikov could react he slammed a spiked leg through the man's chest, repeatedly, grinning at his confused expression and the sound of gurgling. "You and your allies in Fleet are so blind with a lust for power that you can't see the real threat. I see it now."

"Jesus!" Captain Markus said. He drew a coil pistol from under his couch and pointed it. "Stand down. Strap in, so we can finish this, *you freak!*"

Someone else clicked in, his voice panicked. "Missiles inbound; sensors indicate fifty."

"Where from?" the captain asked.

"*Bangkok* detected; it was behind the planet's moon and likely burning toward us this whole time. We only just picked her up."

"Cancel burn. Can we get a firing solution?"

"No, Captain. Not before the missiles hit."

Win sensed the terror around him, and pondered on the fact that it also mixed with resignation and a recognition from these crewmen that their end had arrived; it was too late to change anything. He grinned even wider. Here, in the end, when Win should have been frightened, his Sommen tissue surprised him, sending thoughts of accomplishment and victory. *I will die in combat.* There could be no greater way, Win thought, and he returned to his couch, smiling while strapping himself to the ship. He reached out then, hoping that this time his consciousness would project as intended, avoiding interception. It took a few moments to find her.

Sister.

You are not my brother, San responded. *You are nothing.*

I have no regrets for my actions except one: I wish we could have met—fought face to face.

Go to hell.

Win laughed at the anger; he caught the undercurrent of satisfaction at revenge mixed with a deep sorrow at having lost her friends. *Your brothers and sisters died well,* Win sent, *without pain. In war. I thank you for giving me the same kind of death, and commend you for your victory. The* Jerusalem *was unmanned except for the captain; it was a trap the whole time, correct?*

Correct. We transferred the majority of her crew onto my ship. And in ten seconds our missiles will hit, finishing what we started.

I'm sorry, sister.

At first San didn't respond. When she did, the words mixed with confusion and doubt. *She is no warrior,* Win thought.

Sorry for what? You said you had no regrets.

I do not. But I also did not know of the true enemy, the ones bent on destroying the Sommen. They will come for Earth one day. Had I known this, I never would have participated in Zhelnikov's operations. I killed him, just now, for putting me on a path of dishonor. I drove a spike through his chest, and he died in great pain and fear.

That's beautiful, Win. Thank you for confirming that you have no soul; father would be proud.

It's true: There are no feelings in me for you, or for our father. But I know now: My mission had no purpose. For that, I am sorry.

Win felt the missiles impact throughout what remained of the *Higgins;* a jet of hot metal screamed through the combat bridge. Had the compartment contained an atmosphere, the overpressure would have compressed his suit and tissue while flash-heating the air, burning him to a cinder. Instead the jets passed through. One cut the captain in half, vaporizing his head into a cloud of ash. Another exploded. It sent fragments of molten alloy to ricochet throughout the bridge, and one pierced Win's stomach to burn a fist-sized hole.

Goodbye, sister. I will tell our father about your exploits; this has been a glorious battle, one even the Sommen would admire. One day, you will make a fine warrior.

EPILOGUE

Nothing had changed except the abbess. San sat on the floor, still drowsy from cryo sleep and the long journey from Sommen space to Ganymede. The new abbess scanned through the holo-report and data that the *Bangkok* had returned. Without realizing it, San examined the young woman's face and while the abbess talked to herself, she analyzed the accent and noted every inflection, the sounds marking San's consciousness as if diamond gouged, cutting into a glass sheet. She was too young, San decided. Too young to be an abbess and thick Eastern European notes and inflections laced her accent with an authoritarian bent. She missed the *old* abbess. And her mother, and Wilson. The Marine, Eugene, had gone on to another assignment, deployed almost as soon as he'd returned.

So much loss...

"I see you delivered two separate examples of technologies from this race... What did the Sommen call them?"

"Machinists, Mother Abbess."

"You may call me Sister Margaret. I found my predecessor to be overly formal."

"She was a fine leader, Mother Abbess."

"Do not mistake my meaning," the nun said. The woman pursed her lips, and San saw a flicker of anger ripple across the woman's face. "Sister Frances had her talents, and her uses. Let me ask you something."

"Yes, Mother Abbess?"

"Why did you not return to this Carpenter place, the planet, and search for more machinist technology after you defeated the *Higgins*?"

"You mean after I lost the entire team on Carpenter, and the *Jerusalem*?"

"Sarcasm is not helpful," the abbess growled. "We are building the army of armies, and everyone must make sacrifices. Your group managed to penetrate Sommen space—at great cost to Fleet and the Order. It was a once-in-a-millennia opportunity. After the *Higgins*'s destruction and once the area had been secured, it seems that one could have taken one's time to complete planetary exploration."

San struggled with her emotions, not sure if she should feel relieved to be back in her home system, the mission now over, or furious with the young abbess's arrogance—especially since the nun had never faced an enemy in space, let alone travelled anywhere outside the solar system. But what *had* San accomplished? In the years she'd been away, the Proelians had progressed on their new ship designs and Fleet was still Fleet—fumbling their way through Sommen texts, searching for some edge or advantage. Most of all, she decided, there was exhaustion. Not the kind of left-over-tired from being asleep for years; this was different. San felt as though she'd aged a century, the years robbing her of ambition and purpose.

"Mother Abbess. There was concern that once the *Higgins* fired its plasma weapon multiple times, Sommen or machinist tech might have picked up the disturbances induced by the energy fluctuations. After the battle ended it was a prudent decision to strip the *Higgins* of its memory storage, send it to burn up in Carpenter's atmosphere, and extract from Sommen space as quickly as possible."

"Whose concern?" the nun asked. "Whose decision?"

"My concern, Mother Abbess. And the captain's. We decided together."

"I would have decided differently. But I guess that's the risk we take in sending children to space."

"We now have schematics of machinist microbots," said San, her anger beginning to show. "Planet scrapers. My scientists studied them during the return; with most of the *Jerusalem*'s crew onboard we all had to hot bunk in cryo tubes which gave our technical teams time to work. They estimate that the microbots are hive networked, powered from ambient planetary magnetic fields and programmed to reduce living organism to constituent elements. And from the *Higgins* we brought you the remains of a machinist automaton. Its mind is a combination of materials that somehow form a super-aware, the likes of which we've never seen. And thanks to the *Higgins*'s memory banks we have a more complete understanding of our enemies, not to mention a brief history of the machinists and Fleet efforts to unlock their secrets. Is that not enough? *I paid for these prizes with the blood of my friends.*"

The abbess shook her head. "Sister Kyarr, we did not send you and three ships all that way so you could bring us a machinist history lesson."

"It's important, Mother Abbess. The machinists are the true enemy; your predecessor saw this and so do I."

"Maybe. But even *if* that's true, the prophecy is clear: We must first defeat the Sommen if we ever want them to be an ally. The Sommen will never ally with a defeated race."

"I fail to see the point."

The nun gathered her phase shifter, cinching it tighter against Ganymede's cold. "My point is that after destroying the *Higgins,* your ship could have sent another team to the surface of Carpenter. You could have gotten an actual return sample of the machinist's microbots for us to study—*to have.* Your readings indicate the presence of Sommen microbots as well. We could have had *both.*"

"I was not going to allow dormant and intact technology onto my ship, the only ship we had to get us home. Especially not planet-killing tech. With this one weapon, the machinists leveled the entirety of Carpenter, reducing it to sand. What if those things came to life on the *Bangkok*? Or what if you *had* succeeded in reviving the tech here, or worse: *on Earth.* Do you really think you could have contained something that even the Sommen couldn't? For all we know it self-replicates and only a small sample could have destroyed everything."

"*That was my decision to make!*" The abbess shouted. "*Not yours!* You know nothing of real power, and what it takes to achieve it—to rip it from the fabric of the universe itself. Schematics and history lessons? *This is not power!*"

"With respect, Mother Abbess: I've heard enough."

San lifted herself from the floor, bouncing toward the doorway behind her.

"*How dare you! Sit down!*"

"My mother is dead, along with the rest of my family. Wilson is dead. And the Order convinced me to slaughter the last remaining family I had: my own brother. I've *earned* the right to walk out of here."

The abbess continued her shouting and even after San shut the door, the nun's promise of a prison sentence penetrated into the hallway. San bounced through the tight stone corridors. She navigated her way toward the girls' dormitory—a small space where bunks had been carved into stone. Although it had only been a short time, San felt as though a thousand years had passed since she'd seen the place, the place where she'd both been born and had grown up. She opened the door, squeezing through the tight entrance, her movement activating a hover light.

Ten young girls slept. San surveyed their faces and noted the lack of any sign of care or worry, the skin smooth and unmarked by battle. *They're just children,* she thought. The realization disoriented San and she stepped back into the hallway, wondering when she had become so *old*.

"You were like that," a nun whispered. She had snuck up, grasping a handhold near the door, and the nun placed a gentle hand on San's shoulder. "Once. Once you were *just* like that. So naïve. Filled with promise and a wish to transform, to convert promise into action. To please us."

"Sister Joan?"

"Yes, San; it's me. Welcome home, child."

San burst into tears. She threw herself into the nun's arms, who embraced her in a tight hug so the two bounced in low gravity at the same time a flood of grief poured out without any sign of slowing. Her tears *refused* to stop. She kept repeating the names of those she'd lost, and when San collapsed into the nun's arms, Sister Joan patted her back.

"There, there. It is done. I'm so sorry, child."

Once she managed to slow the sobbing, San asked, "Sorry for what?"

"For everything. For robbing children of innocence. I tell myself that Our Lord will forgive because we prepare for war, but even if he does, I cannot forgive myself."

San sensed a tone in the nun's words; she saw the sadness in her eyes and Sister Joan's slumping shoulders and downward gaze told her that much had transpired in San's absence.

"Where are the others from my group?" she asked. "The other candidates I trained with?"

"Dead. They are all dead. We sent them with our ships to attack the new Chinese home world and none of them returned alive. It was a horrific battle, San. You are all that's left from the first group."

"How many groups have there been since mine?"

"Many. Too many. And there will be many, many more. You should know, child, that Sister Frances always claimed that you were the most talented child she ever trained, even after all the groups she marshaled after yours. It warms my heart to see you return."

"I feel so old."

Sister Joan laughed, letting go of San and then pointing at her own face. "You feel old? *I am old,* child, my lines almost as deep as Sister Frances's were when you left. You are not old; you are experienced. Experiences are what make us grow and that growth is what you feel now, what sets you apart from these children, who have yet to experience anything. They have yet to feel a fraction of the pain you ingested."

"What do I do now, Sister?"

"What do you want to do?"

San wondered if maybe this is how her father had felt all those years ago when he'd realized that he had to escape from *his* masters, the Chinese. Her adventure was over. There had been nothing glorious about their mission to Sommen space, and maybe she *should* go to prison, San thought, for all those she lost while in command. She had intended to fly home, to Mars, but what would she find? Somehow it felt as though there was nothing on the red planet that could ease her grief, nothing there to learn that was new. It took minutes of thinking before an idea sprouted.

"I want to go to Earth," San said. "That's where Wilson's parents are and they deserve an explanation. But there's also something I have to see."

"What?"

"I have to see why one place is worth all the death and destruction I just witnessed. I want to see why Mother Abbess and the Order think Earth is a place worth dying for."

THE END